Vladimir Nabokov as an Author-Translator

Bloomsbury Advances in Translation

Series Editor: Jeremy Munday

Bloomsbury Advances in Translation publishes cutting-edge research in the fields of translation studies. This field has grown in importance in the modern, globalized world, with international translation between languages a daily occurrence. Research into the practices, processes and theory of translation is essential and this series aims to showcase the best in international academic and professional output.

Vladimir Nabokov as an Author-Translator

Writing and Translating between Russian, English and French

Julie Loison-Charles

BLOOMSBURY ACADEMIC
LONDON · NEW YORK · OXFORD · NEW DELHI · SYDNEY

BLOOMSBURY ACADEMIC
Bloomsbury Publishing Plc
50 Bedford Square, London, WC1B 3DP, UK
1385 Broadway, New York, NY 10018, USA
29 Earlsfort Terrace, Dublin 2, Ireland

BLOOMSBURY, BLOOMSBURY ACADEMIC and the Diana logo are
trademarks of Bloomsbury Publishing Plc

First published in Great Britain 2023
This Paperback edition published 2024

A catalogue record for this book is available from the British Library.

A catalog record for this book is available from the Library of Congress.

ISBN: HB: 978-1-3502-4328-6
        PB: 978-1-3502-4336-1
        ePDF: 978-1-3502-4329-3
        eBook: 978-1-3502-4330-9

Series: Bloomsbury Advances in Translation

Typeset by Integra Software Services Pvt. Ltd.

To find out more about our authors and books visit www.bloomsbury.com
and sign up for our newsletters.

This book is dedicated to my parents, who always insisted on the importance of education and hard work, wishing to see me go further than they ever could.

Contents

Acknowledgements

I want to thank my university, Lille University, which granted me a sabbatical semester, my colleagues who took up the extra hours in my absence, and my research team for financing my two trips to the United States. I am also thankful to the devoted staff who helped me in the Nabokov archives, be it in the Berg collection or in Cornell University, but also the staff from the IMEC in Caen, France, or the Gallimard Archives in Paris, France. I want to thank Patricia Lachelier for her friendship and her thorough work on the archives and bibliography.

Thanks are also due to many Nabokov scholars and friends: Stanislav Shvabrin, for his erudition in everything to do with Nabokov and translation, and his heart-warming kindness; Brian Boyd, not only for the ground-breaking research he produced on Nabokov, but also for his precious help with archives; Christine Raguet, for her advice on my project in the very early days; Isabelle Poulin, who was a precursor in studies on Nabokov and translation; Priscilla Meyer, for sending me her book; Lyudmila Razumova, for reading one of the chapters with her keen eye; Dana Dragunoiu, for her kind words and support; and Michael Rodgers, for recommending such a great publisher. My warmest thanks go to the wonderful Agnès Edel-Roy, Marie Bouchet, Yannicke Chupin and Sophie Bernard-Léger, who are colleagues from the French Vladimir Nabokov Society, and friends, "and much, much more".

My colleagues in Translation Studies from Lille have also played a major role. Thank you, Fabrice Antoine, for giving the push I needed to start this new project; Sam Trainor, for your insight on Venuti and post-colonial studies; Claire Hélie, for reading so many pages and giving me useful advice; Corinne Oster, for our discussions on our respective monographs: only you could understand what I was going through in respect to writing.

Thanks are also due to my colleagues from my alma mater, Nanterre University: Emily Eells, for being the best PhD supervisor one could hope to have and for continuing to provide astute advice; Mylène Lacroix, for her insight on multilingualism and translation, and for her friendship.

I also want to thank colleagues for their research and for welcoming me so warmly in their field of expertise: Ronald Jenn for pseudotranslation, Patrick Hersant and Chiara Montini for genetic translation studies, and Rainier Grutman for self-translation.

Last but not least, I want to thank my husband, Patrick Charles, and my three children, Aimie, Dorian and Vivien: thank you for your patience with all the hours away from you, in my study or in the archives, or when I was with you but my mind was still with Nabokov.

Introduction

Nabokov's multilingualism was a constant source of interrogation for his interviewers; for example, they repeatedly asked him how his trilingualism impacted him:

> *Do you think that your knowing three languages, Russian, French and English, has made a difference?*
>
> I like words. Yes, I know these three languages well, this troika, these three horses I have always hooked up to my carriage.
>
> (interview with Anne Guérin for *L'Express* (1959), in Nabokov 2019: 284)

His work is filled with foreign words, but in academia, this variegated prose often seems to be taken for granted, even though Nabokov's use of foreign languages is far from being merely ornamental.[1]

Nabokov's multilingualism causes several dichotomies in his oeuvre, including the distinction between Sirin and Nabokov. Yannicke Chupin is one of the latest critiques to have commented on this difficulty to place the author:

> Vladimir Nabokov has embarrassed many a librarian seeking just the right place for his novels on the bookshelves. The author of *Ada, or Ardor* is not exactly an emigre Russian writer, nor the Great American Novelist, in spite of *Lolita*'s top-rated place in anthologies of American literature. His position in the literary landscape has been the source of many debates: is Vladimir Nabokov the last of the European modernists or the first American postmodern writer?
>
> (Chupin 2017: 740)

A typical example of this librarian's dilemma is Nabokov's complete works: in Russian, only his novels written originally in that language are included (Nabokov 1990), and in English, the same goes in the Library of America collection (Nabokov 1996a, 1996b, 1996c); in French, however, all his novels are gathered in the Pléiade collection (Nabokov 1999, 2010, 2020).

Another crucial dichotomy is the one between Nabokov the author and Nabokov the translator. This clear-cut division is reminiscent of how Nabokov described the separate places that writing and translation occupied in his brain:

> The enervating part is that the translations of Gogol I have to make require another section of the brain than the text of my book, and switching from the one to the other by means of spasmodic jumps causes a kind of mental asthma.
>
> (letter from Nabokov to James Laughlin, 16 July 1942,
> in Nabokov [1989] 1991: 42)

Clearly, Nabokov's relation to translation has always been studied less than his work as an author, and when it *is* studied, the same recurring topics emerge: his practice of self-translation, the scandal surrounding his translation of Pushkin's masterpiece *Evgenij Onegin* ([1833] 2003), *Eugene Onegin* (Pushkin 1964, [1975] 1991), and, to a lesser extent, that of *Alice's Adventures in Wonderland* into Russian. Those topics are indeed fascinating and they are almost a rite of passage for any researcher who wants to tackle the question of translation; I have myself started my research on Nabokov by writing my Master thesis on Nabokov's self-translation of 'Mademoiselle O' and 'Colette' and, in my thesis (Loison-Charles 2014), I dedicated one chapter to his translations of *Onegin* and *Alice*, and another one to the self-translation of his autobiography.

Usually, scholars who dabble in Nabokov's translation practice and theory do it in an article or a paper, but there are not many monographs on the question of translation. For a long time, the only reference monograph was Jane Grayson's *Nabokov Translated: A Comparison of Nabokov's Russian and English Prose* (1977), which dealt mostly with Nabokov's self-translation. Since then, Michaël Oustinoff has published the other reference book on self-translation, though Nabokov represents only one in three authors: *Bilinguisme d'écriture et auto-traduction: Julien Green, Samuel Beckett, Vladimir Nabokov* (2001). And for a long time, not much was published. However, the past few years have seen the publication of several monographs that did not focus on self-translation, but on translation more broadly. In 2015, Julia Trubikhina published *The Translator's Doubts*, and in 2017, two books by French scholars came out: *Le Transport Romanesque. Le roman comme espace de la traduction, de Nabokov à Rabelais*, by Isabelle Poulin, and *Cosmopolitisme et guerre froide. Aragon, Landolfi, Nabokov, traducteurs de Pouchkine*, by Stanislas Gauthier. And in 2021, following two conferences in France and in the United States, a volume entitled *Vladimir Nabokov et la Traduction* came out, with twenty articles in English and in French trying to embrace the great variety of Nabokov's relations to translation.

Unfortunately, just like Nabokov's novels in English and in Russian tend to be shelved in different locations of a library, his activities as a writer and as a translator tend to be analysed separately. However, there are a few articles that do link the two, like Coates's article 'Changing Horses', which starts by stating that 'All translators are writers, but not all writers are translators' (1999: 91). In the 'Translation and Self-Translation' entry in *The Garland Companion to Vladimir Nabokov*, Beaujour (1995) lists several of Nabokov's novels that have been connected with translation:

> Furthermore, many of Nabokov's novels are overtly concerned with problems of translation (e.g., Ember's grappling with Shakespeare in *Bend Sinister,* Conmal's (mis)translation of *Timon of Athens* in *Pale Fire,* or Pnin's classroom exercise in translating Pushkin and his enduring affection for the death of Ophelia in a Russian translation: "*plïla i pela, pela i plïla…* "… she floated and she sang, she sang and floated… ', one of those 'beautiful, noble sonorous lines' which he can never find when he is 'reduced to look up something in the English version'. Critics such as Clarence Brown, Priscilla Meyer and John Lyons have seen translation to be a central metaphor in *Pale Fire* (written in close proximity to the work on *Onegin*), and read Kinbote's demented commentary to Shade's poem as an ironic calque of Nabokov's voluminous notes on *Eugene Onegin* and/ or of Pope's *Dunciad*. Boyd opines that the Russianing of *Lolita* was linguistically generative for the intrinsically polyglot *Ada*.
>
> (Beaujour 1995: 715)

But nothing extensive had been published until 2019, when Stanislav Shvabrin dedicated an illuminating monograph to Nabokov's activities as a translator and the impact of these translations on his creations as a writer. In *Between Rhyme and Reason. Vladimir Nabokov, Translation, and Dialogue,* Shvabrin studies mainly the movement from translation towards creation, but I think many areas lie between the two fields, or rather, the figure of the author and that of the translator have different ways of interacting with one another.

In this monograph, I examine three borderline cases between writing and translating; in that sense, the expression 'author-translator' only has 'author' come first due to the alphabetical order: in no way does it mean that the figure of the writer comes before that of the translation (I could have written 'translator-writer', but did not for obvious idiomatic reasons). My three parts could have come in a different order, but I opted for a chronological organization, hoping it can help the reader perceive Nabokov's evolution within his whole career. The following presentation will be brief because each part starts with an extensive introduction posing the key concepts, and it ends with a conclusion on the whole part.

My first part focuses on pseudotranslation, that is to say texts which are presented as translations when truly, they have no original. In Nabokov's work, pseudotranslations are overwhelmingly present, especially once you know what they are; it is a pattern 'that the finder cannot unsee once it has been seen' (Nabokov [1966b] 1996: 629). As I will show, even if the author *pretends* to be a translator, it does not preclude translation. Chapter 1 concentrates on famous pseudotranslations like *Don Quixote* which impacted Nabokov as a writer and as a translator; in Chapter 2, the pseudotranslations which Nabokov translated are studied, and Pushkin is a recurring figure; finally, Chapter 3 highlights the pseudotranslations which Nabokov wrote himself, for example, the Vivian Calmbrood pieces or short letters inserted in some of his novels.

My second part examines Nabokov's translation of *Evgenij Onegin* by concentrating on the impact which Nabokov's position as an author had on his role of translator. Chapter 4 concentrates on the language used by Nabokov to question whether Nabokov the author appropriated Pushkin's text via translation and thus indulged in *otsebyatina*. Chapter 5 focuses on Nabokov's literalism in comparison with two major figures in translation studies and/or literature: Chateaubriand as an author-translator (he translated Milton's *Paradise Lost*), and Venuti, the translation theorist who fights the invisibility of translators and defends an ethics of translation which bears striking similarities with Nabokov's vision of translation.

My third part concentrates on collaborative translation, namely when Nabokov the author took part in the translation of his novels into French, thus endorsing the role of co-translator. Thanks to various archives, I first examine Nabokov's relationship with his French (co-)translators to underline the tensions between authority and authoriality (Chapter 6) and I then focus on specific elements (like puns) which Nabokov insisted on translating himself (Chapter 7). My contention is that genetic translation studies help prove that these texts need to be re-evaluated as types of self-translation.

In this monograph, I navigate between Nabokov's three languages in order to show how interconnected everything is in his oeuvre. As the quote opening this introduction implies, Nabokov's carriage was pulled by three horses that led it forward. The image of the horse is a recurring one when it comes to Nabokov and translation. Indeed, this is what Nabokov wrote in the foreword to his translation *Eugene Onegin*:

> Pushkin has likened translators to horses changed at the posthouses of civilization. The greatest reward I can think of is that students may use my work as a pony.
>
> (Nabokov [1963a] 1991: x)

Three languages, three parts, three horses: in this monograph, I intend to go beyond the dichotomy between author and translator and to show that the notion of border (borderline cases, but also border as frontier) is fruitful to re-evaluate the totality of Nabokov's creativity.

Part One

Nabokov and Pseudotranslation

1

At the Crossroads of Translation and Literature

Wondering if Nabokov was an author or a translator is very similar to pondering the term one should use to study the texts he wrote while pretending they were translations. The most famous cases are the two pieces he produced under the anagrammatic name 'Vivian Calmbrood', but Nabokov used this strategy repeatedly in several novels. He also had several encounters with this phenomenon when he was a translator. To name but one example, in Pushkin's *Evgenij Onegin*, the narrator explains that Tatyana's letter to Onegin was written in French, which compels the Russian narrator to translate it for his Russian readers. Finally, as a literature professor at Harvard University, Nabokov taught the most famous of all pseudotranslations, Cervantes's *Don Quixote*.

Before looking at the specific cases of pseudotranslation in Nabokov's oeuvre, let's delve into terminology to find out more about 'pseudotranslation', or 'literary hoax', as scholars in literature tend to call this type of text.

What is pseudotranslation?

'Translation with no original': the first part of Emily Apter's chapter on pseudotranslation (2006) sums up the general definition of this phenomenon in Translation Studies. But this definition is obviously problematic: how can a translation have no original? Pseudotranslation is characterized by in-betweenness: it lies in the margins of Translation Studies, or even outside of it for some critics who, understandably, deem it is not a translation since it has no original but is, pretty simply, a literary text, and more specifically a 'literary hoax'. The term 'pseudotranslation' itself is rather recent since it was first used in 1823, in an article dealing with *Walladmor*, which purported to be the German translation of a novel by Sir Walter Scott.[1] But the appropriation of this term by

Translation Studies is even more recent, which is not surprising since this field of research only dates back to the 1950s. At that time, pseudotranslation was a marginal topic, but interest for it grew at the end of the 1970s, first with Popovič: 'An author may publish his original work as a fictitious [or pseudo] translation in order to win a wide public, thus making use of the readers' expectations. The author tries to utilize the translation boom in order to realize his own literary program' (Popovič, qtd in Jenn 2013: 16). In the 1980s, pseudotranslation was put in the spotlight by Gideon Toury, who used the concept (1980, 1981) to show the importance of translations in the target language; thus, he shifted away from the traditional focus of Translation Studies on the fidelity of a translation to the original text which, to him, implied the subservient status of translations (Toury 1981: 9–10). The absence of an original text in pseudotranslations made them the perfect study case to demonstrate the centrality of translations which is at the heart of the polysystem theory. Toury then produced other articles and books in which he defined some criteria which are often quoted in papers dealing with pseudotranslations, and where he also qualified some of their recurring traits. One central element for Toury is that authors use pseudotranslation as a means to introduce innovation in literature, and another one is that there needs to be a certain amount of time between the publication of the text and the revelation of the hoax. However, these criteria are problematic, just like the definition which is found in many translation manuals which state, following Toury, that a pseudotranslation does not have an original:

[*Dictionary of Translation Studies*]

A term used to refer to 'TL [target language] texts which are regarded in the target culture as translations though no genuine STs [source texts] exist for them' (Toury 1980: 31).

(Shuttleworth and Cowie (ed.) 1997: 134)

[*Handbook of Translation Studies*]

Pseudotranslations may generally be defined as 'texts which have been presented as translations with no corresponding source texts in other languages ever having existed – hence no factual 'transfer operations' and translation relationships' (Toury 1995: 40).

(O'Sullivan 2011: 123)

However, those definitions are somewhat truncated. As several critics have shown, including Toury (for example, 1981: 20; 2005: 6–7), pseudotranslations often include some traces of an original. To name but one example for now, Washington Irving insisted that there was some historical truth at the core of his pseudotranslation *A Chronicle of Granada*, published in 1829. This text was presented as Irving's translation of texts written by a monk called Fray Antonio Agapida. The latter was fictitious, but his words came from real historical documents:

> in fact, his exaggerated sallies of loyalty and religion are taken, almost word for word, from the works of some one or other of the monkish historians. Still, though this fictitious personage has enabled the author to indulge his satirical vein at once more freely and more modestly, and has diffused over his page something of the quaintness of the cloister, and the tint of the country and the period, the use of such machinery has thrown a doubt upon the absolute verity of his history; and it will take some time, before the general mass of readers become convinced that the pretended manuscripts of Fray Antoni Agapida is, in truth, a faithful digest of actual documents.
>
> (Anon. [Irving], qtd in Jenn 2013: 74)

This critical article was written anonymously by Irving one year after the publication of his pseudotranslation; in it, he speaks of himself in the third person (which, to a Nabokov scholar, is reminiscent of Chapter 16 in his autobiography *Speak, Memory*). On top of disproving the argument that pseudotranslations do not have originals, *The Chronicle of Granada* also disproves the point on a necessary period of time between the hoax and its revelation, since it was overtly published as a pseudotranslation (Jenn 2013: 71), even if Irving's article was published one year later.

The last problematic criterion is the one stating that a pseudotranslation is used to introduce novelty in a literary system, and this is something Toury insists on, especially in his 2005 article. In fact, it is not always the case, but Toury's premise for this criterion is interesting. Indeed, he underlines the fact that an original work is suspicious and will be questioned for its innovations, whereas a translation will be immune from similar inspection:

> Thus, when a text is offered as a translation, it is quite readily accepted bona fide as one, no further questions asked. By contrast, when a text is presented as having been originally composed in a language, reasons will often manifest themselves – for example, certain features of textual make-up and verbal formulation, which persons-in-the-culture have come to associate with translations and translating – to at least suspect, correctly or not, that the text has in fact been translated into that language.
>
> (Toury 2005: 5)

Even if this is not the aim that Toury had, his argument is very valid and works well for foreign authors such as Nabokov or Andreï Makine.

Just like Nabokov, Makine was born in Russia but was bilingual in French thanks to an old French woman who took care of him, Charlotte Lemonnier. But Makine's French was always subject to scrutiny, so he only managed to publish his first two novels in France by pretending they were translations from his original Russian:[2] *La Fille d'un héros de l'Union soviétique* (1990) was 'translated by Françoise Bour' and *Confessions d'un porte-drapeau* (1992) by 'Albert Lemonnier', a clear wink to the French woman to whom 'he owed the pleasure of hearing/understanding French' (Nabokoff-Sirine 1936: 147; my translation), to use Nabokov's famous description of Mademoiselle O. The hoax turned against Makine when he was asked to produce the Russian original of his second novel so as to facilitate the work of his foreign translators: he struggled to self-translate the book and then confessed. He is now recognized as a true French author and he even entered, in 2016, the prestigious Académie Française, whose mission is precisely to protect the French language.

The irony of pseudotranslation is another dimension that Toury's theory fails to recognize: if literary innovation works for the texts he studies[3] as well as some specific genres like crime,[4] gothic fiction[5] or books pertaining to sex,[6] it leaves out the texts that openly state their fictitious nature and, most importantly, it forgets the ironic dimension of some of these pseudotranslations, like Umberto Eco's *Name of the Rose* (1980)[7] or *On est toujours trop bon avec les femmes* (1947) by Raymond Queneau.[8] As Isabelle Collombat explains (2003: 152), the hoax does not always intend to fool the reader: they can actually be turned into a partner in this game. As we will see, irony was deeply ingrained in Nabokov's use of pseudotranslation, for example, through his use of the anagramme 'Vivian Calmbrood'.

One last point is worth mentioning, especially when it comes to Nabokov: as Jenn demonstrated, pseudotranslations are often highly intertextual.[9] This element is particularly important with Nabokov because, as we will see in the following three chapters, he had many encounters with the most famous cases of pseudotranslation in European literature and they infused his practice as a writer but also as a translator.

Nabokov and pseudotranslation

Nabokov scholars generally focus on his work as a writer and they less often study his translation practice. In Nabokov's practice of translation, interest usually rests on *Eugene Onegin* and self-translation, but when it comes to pseudotranslation, the field is hardly ever explored, which is quite understandable, since the topic itself is rather recent in Translation Studies.

Some critics did approach Nabokov's relation to pseudotranslation, even if they tended to underline the lies and pretence (in what follows, bold type is mine). For example, in the entry 'Nabokov and Pushkin' in *The Garland Companion to Vladimir Nabokov*, Sergey Davydov uses '**pretended** translation' to evoke Calmbrood's poem 'The Night Journey', and he then describes Pushkin's pseudotranslation *The Covetous Knight*[10] in the following terms: 'Pushkin **claimed** that his *Skupoi rytsar* was a translation of Chenston's non-existent tragi-comedy *The Covetous Knight*' (Davydov 1995: 485). Siggy Frank used the term '**mock** translation' for Calmbrood's *The Wanderers*, and uses derogative terms for 'the Night Journey': 'Nabokov returned to this little **hoax** much later in a poem which continues the initial **prank** in another alleged translation' (Frank 2012: 23). As for Brian Boyd, he mentions the two texts in his *Russian Years* and closes his analysis with a very telling use of typography, since the two occurrences of the term 'translation' as well as Nabokov's anagramme are flanked with distanciating inverted commas: 'Sirin read it in the Poets' Club, prefacing the reading of his 'translation' with a few trumped-up biographical details about Calmbrood. Afterward he confessed to the hoax, which had taken everybody in – just as his "translation" from a "Calmbrood" play had foxed his father ten years earlier' (Boyd 1990: 371). This use of inverted commas around 'translation' is recurring when pseudotranslation is studied in literary analyses, and of course the use of literary terminology does not diminish the quality of these scholars' studies. And to be perfectly honest, and a bit tongue-in-cheek, Nabokov himself never used the term 'pseudotranslation' (or 'literary hoax' when it comes to that).

In the present volume, however, I will be using 'pseudotranslation' for several reasons.

First, I wish to avoid the disparaging connotations of words such as 'hoax', 'prank', 'mock' or 'mystification'. I am aware that these connotations exist in the prefix 'pseudo', but they are not as prominent, as is demonstrated by the word 'pseudonym'. Using a word like 'hoax' suggests that the creation is deceitful, but literature itself relies on creation: a novel is a whole invention and the reader is invited not to try and fact-check every aspect of it. The 'willing suspension of disbelief' – a concept coined by British poet Samuel Coleridge in the context of gothic fiction – is now used in relation to literature in general, and even in connection with cinema.[11] The creation of the author is supposed to lie between the pages of the novel itself, but it has gradually come to spread over the limits of the diegesis, straight into the paratext. In Nabokov's work, for example, the preface by John Ray Jr in *Lolita* is fictitious and is already part of the novel, contrary to most forewords that Nabokov wrote to his novels. In the paratext, the name of the author itself can be fictitious: pseudonyms have been used by women writers who were not able to write under feminine names at a time when literature was men's prerogative, for example, in the nineteenth century with authors such as the Brontë sisters, George Eliot or George Sand; for different reasons, men also used pseudonyms and pennames, like Samuel Clemens (Mark Twain) or Vladimir Nabokov (Sirin). But pseudonyms do not turn the books into frauds or hoaxes: the name on the page still refers to the author, even if the real person behind the literary name has another name. But when it comes to books, which are bought in the 'real' world by 'real' people, readers rely on certain pacts between the book and themselves. Thus, one of the elements of the autobiographical pact (Lejeune 1975) is that the person whose name is on the cover of the autobiography is the same one as the person whose life is narrated in the first person. But this pact can also be disrupted by literary creation, as one can see with Gertrude Stein's *The Autobiography of Alice B. Toklas* (1933). Another disruption of the autobiographic pact can be found in Russian-born Nathalie Sarraute's autobiography *Enfance*, which is not only told in the first person, but is also narrated with the pronoun 'you', as Sarraute is split in two: the two instances dialogue as one tells the story and the other is critical of the memories or of the sometimes naïve storytelling of the first figure. In the case of pseudotranslation, another pact is broken: as Collombat (2003) convincingly showed in her article on pseudotranslation, there is a 'reading pact' (149; my translation) between the reader and the translator which derives from the presence of the word 'translation' in the paratext: if a text is presented as a translation, it has to be one for the reader. Therefore, when it comes to pseudotranslation, what is a creation is not so much the fictitious name of the author or translator: it is the relation between the text and its (invented and absent) original which is fictitious. Therefore, a pseudotranslation does have a strong literary dimension because it is a creation, but it should not be viewed negatively as a 'hoax'.

Another reason for not using this expression is that a 'literary hoax' does not always pretend to be a translation and is, sometimes, only based on a fictitious author: a famous example is Washington Irving's book *A History of New-York from the Beginning of the World to the End of the Dutch Dynasty* (1809), which was published as the work of 'Diedrich Knickerbocker', a fictitious Dutch-American historian. A similar hoax can be found in Nabokov's work: he invented Pierre Delalande, who appears repeatedly in his Russian novel *Dar* (Nabokov 1937–1938), but Nabokov only revealed he was invented in the Foreword to the English translation of *Priglashenie na kazn'*, *Invitation to a Beheading* (Nabokov

1960). Pierre Delalande is fictitious and his *Discours sur les ombres* is a literary hoax that we never get to read in full, but it is not a translation and therefore, should not be called a pseudotranslation.[12]

Another reason for my using translation terminology is that I want to insist on the connection between the text and its foreign origins: a pseudotranslation may have no original, but it has roots abroad, especially in Nabokov's practice. As Jenn convincingly showed in his monograph dedicated to pseudotranslation, one should not look back towards the (missing) original, i.e. the prototext; rather, what is essential is the protolanguage and the protoculture that the pseudotranslation is said to derive from (Jenn 2013: 26).

The last reason for my choice of translation terminology to discuss Nabokov's case is that I want to insist on the impact that his translation practice had on his literary creations. It was brilliantly demonstrated by Stanislav Shvabrin's book *Between Rhyme and Reason*, but I want to go further by looking at the motif that pseudotranslation inscribes between Nabokov's literary creations and his translations.

Outline of the first part

In the following three chapters, I will address three dimensions of Nabokov's relationship to pseudotranslation.

I will first show that famous European pseudotranslations left traces on Nabokov's work as a writer, translator and teacher; as we will see, his American novel *Pale Fire* will be particularly central.

I will then study the pseudotranslations that Nabokov translated, not only between English and Russian, but also in relation with French, his third, often overlooked, language.

Finally, I will cover the pseudotranslations that Nabokov wrote himself: this third chapter will lead us to cover different genres like drama and poetry, but also to go from his earlier work as a budding writer in Russian to his later novels as a recognized author in English.

This journey in Translation Studies will take us across a varied literary landscape, usually back and forth between European and Russian literatures, thus showing how transnational and translational Nabokov really was.

Intertextual Links Between Pseudotranslations and Nabokov's Work

Recounting Nabokov's encounters with pseudotranslation actually implies looking at the most famous cases of it in European and Russian literatures. Among them, there are three which he did not translate, namely the Spanish monument that is *Don Quixote* or the infamous *Ossian* from Scotland; a third text is famous as well, but usually not as a pseudotranslation. I will be presenting them chronologically because it places them clearly in the history of literature and because some early cases have an impact on later ones: as mentioned earlier, pseudotranslations are highly intertextual.

As I will show in this chapter, Nabokov used these three pseudotranslations in his work as a writer, critic, translator and teacher, but one novel keeps coming up in relation to those: *Pale Fire* (Nabokov [1962] 1996). In fact, it is hardly surprising since the novel plays with metatextuality as well as questions of authenticity, originality and authorship.

Cervantes's *Don Quixote* (1605): Nabokov and style

Nabokov only taught *Don Quixote* once, when he filled in for Professor Harry Levin on the occasion of 'a visiting appointment at Harvard University in the spring semester of the academic year 1951–1952' (F. Bowers, 'Editor's Preface', in Nabokov 1983: vii). However, his classes on Cervantes are the only ones which are gathered in a volume dedicated to a single author (Nabokov 1983): the two other volumes are *Lectures on Literature* and *Lectures on Russian Literature*.

A few critics have studied the links between Nabokov and *Don Quixote*, but only from a literary perspective: Krabbenhoft (2016) wrote an article on its links with *Lolita*, and Robert Alter presented the Spanish don as an influence for Humbert Humbert and Kinbote as 'literature-ridden madmen' (Alter qtd in Krabbenhoft 2016: 213). However, the most convincing analysis is without a doubt Boyd's work on the relationship between *Don Quixote* and *Pnin* in relation to cruelty: '*Pnin* is Nabokov's reply to Cervantes' (Boyd 1991: 272[1]). Indeed, the eponymous character exclaims that 'The history of man is the history of pain!' and one cannot help but notice the similarity between the word 'pain' and the name 'Pnin', especially after all the comic alterations the Russian surname suffers in the novel, mostly in the first two chapters (Nabokov [1957a] 1996: 315, 319). Another link between Nabokov and *Don Quixote* is not as well-known: as Boyd explains, just after Nabokov arrived in America, he 'proposed an adaptation of *Don Quixote* for the stage, to be carried out in a manner akin to that of his own plays, *The Event* and *The Waltz Invention*' (Boyd 1991: 23). Nothing came of it, but it demonstrates Nabokov's early interest in Cervantes's novel.

Not many scholars have studied *Don Quixote* from the angle of translation[2], let alone pseudotranslation, which could be surprising since most articles on pseudotranslation reference *Don Quixote* as the first pseudotranslation to reach success.[3] The reason why *Don Quixote* has given rise to so few studies might lie in the fact that, when Cervantes wrote his book, pseudotranslations were not so rare in the genre of chivalric novels (Bahous 2010: 240). When Nabokov taught the Spanish epic novel, he did mention translation on a few occasions: first, to specify which English translation he would be using, namely the one published in 1949 by Samuel Putnam (Nabokov 1983: 13), and then, in his chapter-by-chapter 'Narrative and Commentary', when translation was discussed in the novel itself. Thus, in Part I, Chapter 6, two friends of Don Quixote inspect the latter's library and discuss which of his books he can keep or not, based on their merits. Nabokov quotes a long dialogue (about 20 lines) which ends with a discussion on books in translation; his concluding remark is particularly palatable:

> 'however much care they may take, and however much cleverness they may display, they can never equal the original. I say, in short, that this work, and all those on French themes ought to be thrown into, or deposited in, some dry well until we make up our minds just what should be done with them'. These are charming remarks on translation, generally.
>
> (Nabokov 1983: 117)

Later on, in his notes on Part I, chapter 9, Nabokov describes the discovery of the text in Toledo and its subsequent translation from Arabic into Castillan by an anonymous Moorish translator: 'Cervantes finds an Arabic manuscript by Cid Hamete Benengeli, Arabic Historian, which he got translated' (Nabokov

1983: 120). And at the end of the section, Nabokov does not insist on the pseudotranslation itself, but rather on a pleasant ternary repetition: 'as we shall see, Don Quixote does not come out quite as badly in the pretended translation of the pretended Arabian account as the pretended discoverer of this account suggests' (Nabokov 1983: 120). Actually, Nabokov's insistence on pretence is an echo to an earlier part of the class, in which he criticized 'three odd things' (Nabokov 1983: 40) which Cervantes did in his novel; the first one was

> inventing a chronicler, an Arab historian, who supposedly kept track of the life of a historical Don Quixote – which is the kind of device that the authors of the most ridiculous romances employed to bolster their tales with respectable truth, with acceptable pedigrees.
>
> (Nabokov 1983: 40)

Here, it is clearly Nabokov the author who expresses his view on a fellow writer and his poor choices, not Nabokov the translator.

What is surprising is that, later in *Don Quixote* (Part II, chapter 62), there is a whole passage about translation which Nabokov did not even mention in his notes and commentary devoted to this chapter (Nabokov 1983: 203–4). However, the following quote from the Spanish classic is familiar to most translation scholars and should ring a bell to any Nabokov specialist:

> And yet it seems to me that translating from one language into another, except from those queens of languages, Greek and Latin, is like viewing Flemish tapestries from the wrong side, when, although one can make out the figures, they are covered by threads that obscure them, and one cannot appreciate the smooth finish of the right side.
>
> (Cervantes 2000: 915)

By comparing a translation to the 'wrong side' of a tapestry, the lengthy sentence implies that the translation is never as beautiful as the original, but it is also possible to interpret it as a way of saying that a translation is what makes the motifs and patterns in the original more apparent.

The motif of the tapestry has become very common in translation studies, as Kathryn Vomero Santos explains:

> The reverse side of the tapestry has become so prevalent in the titles, epigraphs, introductions, and collections of texts on translation that we might even be inclined to agree with Dale B. J. Randall's claim that 'Cervantes endowed his mad knight with some perfectly sane doubts about the limits of translation'.
>
> (Vomero Santos 2016: 344)

This motif is also fruitful in a literary perspective,[4] and the quote from Cervantes bears striking similarity with a passage from Kinbote's Foreword to *Pale Fire*, in which he defends his work on Shade's poem against academic intrigues by colleagues or attacks by the poet's former 'literary agent':

> Such hearts, such brains, would be unable to comprehend that one's attachment to a masterpiece may be utterly overwhelming, especially when it is the underside of the weave that entrances the beholder and only begetter, whose own past intercoils there with the fate of the innocent author.
>
> (Nabokov 1962: 446)

The 'underside of the weave' is often used to refer to Nabokov's style, as in the title of one of the first theses on the author, 'The Underside of the Weave: Some Stylistic Devices Used by Vladimir Nabokov' by Jessie Lokrantz (1973). The expression is indeed a good illustration of the work that, for an author, goes behind the search for the right word, *le mot juste* as Humbert would say, and in a French interview with Bernard Pivot in 1975, Nabokov used a similar image when he mentioned '*le dessous d'un mot*'. Interestingly enough, it is with the word 'underside' that Boyd translated the French '*dessous*', in the first ever published translation into English of this interview:

> You play a lot with words? You make lots of puns?
>
> One must draw everything one can from words, because it's the one real treasure a true writer has. Big general ideas are in yesterday's newspaper. If I like to take a word and turn it over to see its **underside**, shiny or dull or adorned with motley hues absent on its upperside, it's not at all out of idle curiosity, one finds all sorts of curious things by studying the **underside** of a word – unexpected shadows of other words, harmonies between them, hidden beauties that suddenly reveal something beyond the word. Serious wordplay, as I have in mind, is neither a game of chance nor a mere embellishment of style. It's a new verbal species that the marveling author offers to the poor reader, who doesn't want to look; to the good reader, who suddenly sees a completely new facet of an iridescent sentence.
>
> (Nabokov 2019: 469; bold type mine)

The butterfly image which is conjured up to evoke the 'underside' of words is particularly interesting when one knows that, except for the occurrence in *Pale Fire*, the word is generally used in Nabokov's novels in connection with butterflies (Nabokov [1957a] 1996: 386, 425; [1969] 1996: 350; [1974] 1996: 591); as we will see, the butterfly motif is present in Nabokov's two pseudotranslations written under the name 'Calmbrood'.

It is noteworthy that the connection between the underside of a tapestry (for translation) and the underside of a weave (in a text) should be found in a pseudotranslation, which lies specifically between translation and literature. One cannot help but wonder if Nabokov had the quote from *Don Quixote* in mind when he coined the expression 'the underside of the weave', in which he removed the negative connotation by turning Cervantes's adjective 'wrong' into the more neutral 'under', thus showing translation in a better light.

The second pseudotranslation that has striking connections with Nabokov's creations as a writer and translator does not have the same literary reputation as Cervantes's masterpiece, but it is famous all the same, be it for bad reasons: the *Ossian* is known as a forgery but, as we will see, this status is debatable.

Macpherson's *The Poems of Ossian* (1760–5), *The Song of Igor's Campaign* and *Pale Fire*

Macpherson's *Ossian*[5] is often presented as the most blatant case of pseudotranslation in literature written in English. The most obvious example can be found in *The Routledge Encyclopedia of Translation Studies*; in the entry 'Pseudotranslation', Douglas Robinson retraces the publication history of the various volumes of *Ossian* and makes significant use of inverted commas:

> The textbook case of pseudotranslation is probably James Macpherson's (1736–96) 'translation' of Ossianic poems, *Fragments of ancient poetry translated from the Gaelic or Erse Language* (1760), followed by further 'Ossianic' collections in *Fingal* (1762) and Temora (1763). Ossian was the Anglicized name (popularized by Macpherson) of Oisín, a legendary Irish warrior-poet from the Fenian cycle of hero tales that related the adventures of Finn and his band of warriors, the Fianna Eirann. The young Macpherson had published original poetry that attracted no attention, in his collection *The Highlander* (1758); shortly afterwards he began collecting Gaelic manuscripts and oral poems, and drew on them in writing his Ossian poems, which he called translations from an actual third-century Gaelic poet. It was not known at the time, nor would it be for another century, that no Gaelic manuscripts date back earlier than the tenth century; by the end of the nineteenth century it was finally established that the Gaelic originals from which Macpherson supposedly worked, and which had been published after his death, were actually Macpherson's own translations into bad Gaelic of his original English poems.[6]
>
> (Robinson 2000: 183)

One of the most vocal critics of Macpherson's collection of poetry was writer and lexicographer Samuel Johnson. It is obvious in the following passage from Boswell's prequel to his *Life of Samuel Johnson*, in which the tone of Johnson and Boswell's exchange cannot fail to remind any Nabokov specialist of Shade and Kinbote in *Pale Fire*:

> When Dr. Johnson came down, I told him that I had now obtained some evidence concerning 'Fingal' [...] and reminded him that he himself had once said, he did not require Mr. MacPherson's Ossian to be more like the original than Pope's 'Homer'.–Johnson: 'Well, sir, this is just what I always maintained. He has found names, and stories, and phrases – nay, passages in old songs, and with them has blended his own compositions; and so made what he gives to the world as the translation of an ancient poem'.
>
> (Boswell [1775] 1859: 191–2)

The argument became very heated at the time and it still is now. Indeed, the claim that the originals produced by Macpherson upon request were actually his own fabricated self-translations from English into Gaelic is not at all accepted as a fact: in 1952, Derick Thomson published *The Gaelic Sources of Macpherson's 'Ossian'* to show that a number of Gaelic poems were actually original texts, and since then, the debate has been raging again. Some critics completely dismiss the idea that *Ossian* was a pseudotranslation, as shown by the very beginning of an article published in 1998:

> It is now controversial to call James Macpherson a forger or the poems of Ossian a hoax. Encouraged by Derick Thomson's 1952 demonstration that Macpherson's Ossian indeed echoes authentic Gaelic verse, a group of critics has undertaken to 'rehabilitate' Macpherson, not least through a new critical edition of Ossian's poems and related texts.
>
> (Haugen 1998: 309)

On the other hand, the figurehead of the Johnsonian side is Thomas M. Curley, who published in 2009 *Samuel Johnson, the Ossian Fraud, and the Celtic Revival in Great Britain and Ireland*. In a short text published the same year, he uses very strong language to criticize Macpherson as well as the scholars defending him:

> My interest in Johnson the English truth-teller and in Macpherson the Scottish literary liar began in graduate school at Harvard University and led to some early articles on the phony Ossian poems. When many years later I turned to preparing a book for publication by Cambridge University Press, I was surprised to find that my youthful scholarship on the Ossian fraud had provoked my own

mini-controversy with revisionist academics bent on rehabilitating Macpherson's dubious reputation and regarding him as an important 'creative' author for his powerful impact on the literature of Europe and the United States.

(Curley 2009: 7)

It is interesting to note however that Curley recognizes that there are some original documents, even if, to him, they are a minority:

> Twenty-eight out of Macpherson's thirty-nine titles – 72 per cent of all the individual works comprising Ossian – have no apparent grounding in genuine Gaelic literature and are therefore entirely his handiwork. The remaining 28 per cent of the titles have but generally loose ties to approximately sixteen Gaelic ballads.

(Curley 2009: 8)

Many papers have been written, either to call the Macphersonian scholarship 'revisionist' (Gaskill 2013: 294) or to underline Curley's stubbornness[7] and his devotion to Johnson,[8] but what matters for our present study is Nabokov's perception of Macpherson's *Ossian* and its impact on his work.

The most interesting links are to be found in one translation and one novel by Nabokov: *The Song of Igor's Campaign* (1960) and *Pale Fire* (1962). The most thorough and convincing research on this triangular network is the article by Priscilla Meyer, 'Igor, Ossian and Kinbote: Nabokov's Non-Fiction as Library' (1988b).[9]

As far as *Pale Fire* is concerned, a couple of elements should suffice to show this triangular connection. First, Meyer points the reader towards the fact that 'the novel alludes obliquely to *The Song of Igor's Campaign* when providing the genealogy of Charles the Beloved of Zembla' (69) and quotes the following passage evoking the lover of Charles's great-great granddam, Queen Yaruga:

> Hodinski, her goliart (court jester) and a poet of genius, said to have forged in his spare time a famous old Russian *chanson de geste*, generally attributed to an anonymous bard of the twelfth century.

(Nabokov 1962: 616)

The Russian *chanson de geste* is no other than the *Slovo o polku Igoreve* which Nabokov translated as *The Song of Igor's Campaign* in 1960; Jakobson, on the other hand, translated it into English in the volume entitled *La geste du prince Igor* (1948). The use of French in *Pale Fire* and in Jakobson's edition is one more sign pointing towards the *Slovo*. One can also note the use of the verb 'forge' in the *Pale Fire* quote: as we will see, Nabokov abundantly commented on this issue of authenticity in his commentary to *The Song of Igor's Campaign*, which is one of the reasons why he referred to the *Ossian*.

The relevance of pseudotranslation to *Pale Fire* is striking if one thinks of the two parts of the novel (Shade's poem and Kinbote's foreword, commentary and index) in the perspective of translation studies: indeed, if one uses Jakobson's seminal terminology,[10] Kinbote's texts (especially his commentary) can be seen as an intralingual translation of Shade's poem. The theoretical framework of pseudotranslation is even more interesting if one thinks of the debate that has been going on in Nabokovian studies between Shadeans and Kinbotians,[11] with some claiming that Shade wrote the poem and created Kinbote and his introduction, commentary and index, and others arguing that Kinbote probably wrote the poem from which his three documents stem. Therefore, in the Kinbotian perspective, Kinbote's intralingual translation can be seen as a pseudotranslation, for which he merely invented the original poet (Shade) and his poem.

As for the connections drawn by Meyer between the *Ossian* and *Pale Fire*, one can note her remarks on onomastics:

> MacPherson cooks up some false derivations to footnote his tales. The name Colmal is derived from Caol-mhal, 'a woman with slender eyebrows' [...]. The theme of bad translation in *Pale Fire* is linked to King's Charles Uncle Konmal, the Zemblan translator of Shakespeare. The derivation (as Conmal does a poor job of conning Shakespeare's text) is, on the surface, easily accessible. But as we now see, it also masks an allusion to MacPherson's poorly conned name derivations.
>
> (Meyer 1988b: 71–2)

The presence of the *Ossian* pseudotranslation is even more striking in Nabokov's translation of the *Slovo*.

As Meyer explains, the *Slovo* has long been accused of being a forgery; the fact that the original was impossible to produce did not help of course:

> The slavist is familiar with the famous controversy over the authenticity of the Igor tale, long said to be an eighteenth century forgery. The authorship had been attributed to Count Musin-Pushkin who discovered a sixteenth century copy of the *Song*. He had copies made of it in 1795–1796, which survived when his house was burned down in 1812, but the sixteenth century manuscript was destroyed. He published the *Song* in 1800. Nabokov addresses the question of authenticity at length in his commentary.
>
> (Meyer 1988b: 69–70)

In his foreword to the translation, Nabokov describes the discovery of the manuscript[12] in a similar way and, a few lines after that, he makes a reference to the *Ossian* for the first time by mentioning Macpherson:

> A modicum of internal evidence, which most scholars today believe to be not an injection by a Russian Macpherson, but a natural exhalation of inherent truth, forces one to assume the author of the song composed it in the spring or early summer of 1187.
>
> (*The Song*: 8)

Then, the whole section 3 of the foreword (5–17) is devoted to the authenticity of the *Slovo*, and the first paragraph focuses specifically on the links between the *Ossian* and the *Slovo*. The most interesting passage is at the very beginning:

> Throughout The Song there occur here and there a few poetical formulas strikingly resembling those in Macpherson's *Ossian*. I discuss them in my Commentary. Paradoxically, these coincidences tend to prove not that a Russian of the eighteenth century emulated Macpherson, but that Macpherson's concoction does contain after all scraps derived from authentic ancient poems.
>
> (*The Song*: 15)

What Nabokov implies here is that some elements from the *Slovo* are actually part of the original of the *Ossian*, which goes to ascertain the fact that Macpherson did not merely compose a literary hoax, a pseudotranslation in other words, but did use some original texts, including the *Slovo*. Nabokov then comments on the surprising connection between Scotland and Kiev[13]:

> It is not unreasonable to assume that through the mist of Scandinavian sagas certain bridges or ruins of bridges may be distinguished linking Scottish-Gaelic romances with Kievan ones.
>
> (*The Song*: 15)

The authenticity of the *Ossian* and its role in the *Slovo* is a major difference between Nabokov and Jakobson. The differences between Nabokov and Jakobson were numerous,[14] but when it comes to the *Slovo*, one needs to explain first that Nabokov produced two translations of it, namely *The Discourse of Igor's Campaign* in 1952 version and *The Song of Igor's Campaign* in 1960, and then that Nabokov's opinion on Jakobson's work has not always been negative. Indeed, even if Nabokov claims in the last note to his Foreword that he grew 'dissatisfied' with Jakobson's views when he prepared his own 1960 translation, he explains that he had heavily relied on Jakobson's 1948 recension to prepare his first 1952 version[15] and he does mention Jakobson's translation as one of the 'useful' resources that exist on the *Slovo* (*The Song*: 20). Among the differences that exist between Jakobson and Nabokov about the *Slovo*, one lies in their different approaches: unsurprisingly, the linguist insisted on the non-poetic dimension of the *Slovo*, whereas the writer insisted on its poetry[16]; as Shvabrin writes, 'Nabokov chose to go with the "rhyme" – in the broad sense of poetic artifice – and not the "reason" of Jakobson's cautiously austere "scholarly" conjecture' (2019: 290).

Another difference between Jakobson and Nabokov was their treatment of the *Ossian* in their respective translations. When it comes to Macpherson's text, Jakobson was adamant that the *Ossian* was a hoax and had nothing to do with the *Slovo*. Thus, Goldblatt explains that, according to Jakobson,

> the first editors and commentators had been confronted with the necessity of Ossianizing the text of the *Slovo* in order to make it accessible to the taste of the epoch. The task of Jakobson's scholarly enterprise, therefore, was to restore the medieval text of the *Slovo* and cleanse it of Ossianisms and modernisms superimposed on the work by its editors and commentators.
>
> (Goldblatt 1995: 667)

Contrary to Jakobson who wanted to 'cleanse it of Ossianisms', Nabokov abundantly refers to Macpherson's text, mainly for two reasons.

First, drawing parallels between the *Ossian* and the *Slovo* is a means for Nabokov to insist on what he claimed in his foreword: 'Macpherson's concoction does contain after all scraps derived from authentic ancient poems' (15), namely bits of the *Slovo*. Lexical parallels are found in each of the dozen notes that mention the *Ossian*. For example, the first time the *Ossian* is mentioned is in the note to line 52; after giving his own translation followed by the original transliterated Russian for reference ('Of the times of old: *staravo vremeni*'), Nabokov quotes two passages from Macpherson's text:

> Cf. Macpherson's *Fingal*, Book II: 'To the ages of old, to the days of other years'; and 'Carthon', first line: 'A tale of the times of old! The deeds of days of other years!'
>
> (*The Song*: 87)

The second reason why Nabokov mentions Macpherson's text is to insist on the fact that, even though the latter was very popular in Russia, people used to read it not in English but in the French translation by Letourneur (5). For Nabokov, it is one more proof that the *Slovo* is not a fraud inspired by the *Ossian*:

> in the eighteenth century, and well into the age of Pushkin, English poetry was known to Russians only through French versions, and therefore the Russian

forger would not have rendered, as Letourneur did not render them, the very special details of that curious 'Ossianic' style of which I give examples in my notes.

(The Song: 15)

One cannot fail to see the similarity with Nabokov's insistence on *Onegin's* French intertext. Actually, the aforementioned note continues with Nabokov explaining that the *Ossian* impacted Pushkin's 'Ruslan and Ludmila' (87–8). One also needs to mention that, in his commentary to *Eugene Onegin*, Nabokov mentions the *Ossian* ten times; nine of them are very brief, but the longest one is surprising in the sense that Nabokov uses a terminology which is very different from his earlier comment in the *Slovo*: 'James Macpherson's famous fraud is a mass of more or less rhythmic, primitively worded English prose, which can easily be translated into French, German, or Russian' (Pushkin [1975] 1991: 254–5). One could suggest that, in *Eugene Onegin*, Nabokov was not on a mission to prove the *Slovo's* authenticity as he was in his *Song*, and therefore chose the shortest, easiest way to refer to the *Ossian*, a text which is generally known as a fraud, but it is hardly like Nabokov, especially in *Eugene Onegin*, to favour brevity over exactitude.

If the authenticity of the *Slovo* was at the heart of a debate when Nabokov published his translation, one needs to say that the question has since then been clarified by Zaliznjak (2004) (Sinichkina 2020: 101).[17] However, the relevance of the *Ossian* to the *Slovo* persists, and that of pseudotranslation too. Indeed, in both cases, the presence of an original text is crucial to defining its nature. In a historical perspective, the original proves that the text was indeed created when it was supposed to be – the *Slovo* in the eleventh century, the *Ossian* in the third – and was not a fraud by later authors, editors or annotators of the Romantic period[18]; in a literary perspective, it raises the issue of the appraisal of oral tradition in contrast with written documents: both the *Ossian* and the *Slovo* stem from a national, oral tradition, therefore a written original is debatable in its immutability.[19]

In a translation perspective, the original helps define a text as a translation *per se* when it is present, or as a pseudotranslation when it is lacking. Therefore, depending on how loose the relationship is between an original and its translation, the latter can either be considered a pseudotranslation with only vague sources of inspiration, or a true translation, albeit very free. The difficulty to determine what number of true sources would make the *Ossian* a pseudotranslation or a translation is probably one of the essential reasons why the debate is still raging.

This tension between pseudotranslation and translation is also present in FitzGerald's *Rubáiyát,* which bears striking similarities with the *Ossian,* including Nabokov's encounter with each of them.

FitzGerald's *Rubáiyát of Omar Khayyám* (1859), a pseudotranslation?

FitzGerald's *Rubáiyát* is hardly ever presented as a pseudotranslation, which can seem surprising when one observes the very flimsy link that exists between the so-called original and the 'translation' that FitzGerald published in 1859. After a very tentative start, FitzGerald's book became very popular (John Yohannan even described a 'fin de siècle cult of the *Rubáiyát*' (1977: 202)), and it is still revered as a masterpiece in poetry. Its status as a translation, however, is less than clear.

One of the clearest presentations of FitzGerald's *Rubáiyát* is to be found in the commentary written by George Maine ([1953] 1995). What is striking is the shrinking number of quatrains if one goes from the original text and its translation:

> The original manuscript by Omar Khayyám is thought to have comprised at least seven hundred and fifty and possibly many more quatrains. They were never intended to represent a continuous work or story. [...] the Ouseley manuscript discovered by Cowell among a mass of uncatalogued material in the Bodleian Library, Oxford, in 1856, contains 158 quatrains [...]. From the transcript which he made from Cowell's copy of the original, FitzGerald selected and compounded for his first edition of the *Rubáiyát* seventy-five quatrains, on which he worked for several years.
>
> (Maine [1953] 1995: 14–15)

Maine also underlines the fact that FitzGerald did not merely make a selection from the original manuscript, but actually used other sources:

> About half of the quatrains are faithful paraphrases of the Persian. The remainder are built up of ideas taken from this quatrain and that, of figures which have no prototypes in the original but come from numerous kindred sources such as Háfiz and the *Mantiq al-Tayr* (*The Discourse of the Birds*) of Attár. However the whole underwent so singular a poetic metamorphosis that FitzGerald's rendering is justly considered the apotheosis of craftsmanship – but it is not Omar.
>
> (Maine [1953] 1995: 16)

Of course, the expression 'faithful paraphrases' is particularly intriguing if one thinks of Nabokov, and we will soon see what his position was on the topic.

The free rendering of Omar by FitzGerald makes it difficult to attribute the text to one or the other, which is a recurring problem with pseudotranslation, and one can note that many editions now include the name of the 'author' not in the paratext but in the title: *Rubáiyát of Omar Khayyám*. When it comes to ascribing the text either to FitzGerald or to Omar, it is sometimes difficult to decide, as Erik Gray humorously writes about Borges's short story 'The Enigma of Edward FitzGerald[20]':

> Borges is not alone in refusing to ascribe it either to FitzGerald or to Omar: librarians have had the same dilemma, and anyone looking for editions or references is almost invariably required to look under both names.
>
> (Gray 2001: 771)

This hesitation has even given rise to a portmanteau name, FitzOmar, as one can see in many scholarly publications.[21]

As far as the type of translation is concerned, Maine explains that 'FitzGerald did not so much translate Omar as make a poetic transfusion of the quatrains to suit his own fancy' (Maine [1953] 1995: 15) and he quotes FitzGerald himself to show that the translator never lied about his method. In 1858, FitzGerald sent a letter to Cowell, who had discovered the manuscript and taught FitzGerald Persian:

> My translation will interest you from its form, and also in many respects in its detail, very unliteral as it is. Many quatrains are mashed together, and something is lost, I fear, of Omar's simplicity, which is such a virtue in him. But there it is, such as it is.
>
> (Maine [1953] 1995: 15)

FitzGerald himself underlined that his translation was far from being literal (he even called it a 'transmogrification[22]'), but he did call it a translation; on the other hand, critics have generally agreed on the fact that FitzGerald's text can only very loosely be called a translation, but hardly anyone ever denies that it is a translation[23] or calls it a pseudotranslation. And when they do link it with pseudotranslation, it is usually in order to discredit the theory[24] or to evoke a mere resemblance.[25]

Quite interestingly, Nabokov denied the status of translation in 1928, even if he does not use the term 'pseudotranslation', which is not surprising since the term was only popularized in the 1980s. Nabokov wrote a review in 1928 for Ivan Tkhorzhevsky's Russian translation of the Persian text (Nabokov 2019: 76–9), but he started by evoking FitzGerald's English version, which he highly praises but qualifies as not a translation:

> In 1859, the brilliant English poet FitzGerald published a collection of poems, which he called translations from Omar Khayyám. Undoubtedly, FitzGerald consulted the Persian manuscript, yet it is impossible to consider this book in any way a translation. Despite the abundance of 'Eastern' images, these wonderful poems are suffused with the spirit of English poetry; only an Englishman could have written them. They have about the same relation to Persian Poetry as, say, Pushkin's translations of the poetry of the Western Slavs have to the actual songs of the latter.
>
> (Nabokov 2019: 76)

In his review, Nabokov repeatedly questions the fact that FitzGerald produced a translation. When mentioning that Tkhorzhevsky used FitzGerald's poems as one of his many sources, Nabokov comments: 'he was in reality translating not a Persian poet but a very original English one' (77). Then, he inserts his doubts in a parenthesis when, once again, he devotes his review to FitzGerald rather than Tkhorzhevsky: 'In a footnote to this line, FitzGerald provides (let's hope faithfully) the original line: "O dánad O dánad O dánad O –"'' (78). And finally, the last words of the review repeat Nabokov's doubts on the authenticity of the original: 'I daresay, although Omar Kayyám may never have written such lines, he would nonetheless be flattered and delighted' (79).

It is obvious that Nabokov admired FitzGerald's poems, or at least he did until Anthony Burgess made him change his mind in 1965. In the midst of the controversy on *Eugene Onegin*, the British author wrote a review to defend Nabokov's translation and he happened to mention the Persian poem and its rendition by FitzGerald:

> The trouble begins because of strange alphabets (they take only one hour to learn, but this is too long for many) and because of the apparent lack of familiar linguistic elements (few people are any good at piercing disguises). Here, it seems, arty translations are in order. Literary men who would scorn to read *L'Après-midi d'un Faune* in Aldous Huxley's translation drink up Arthur Waley, FitzGerald, and whoever has rendered (wasted labour) Evtushenko. One of my few endowments is an ability to read Persian, and I grow angry whenever I think of FitzGerald's falsification – a witty metaphysical tent-maker turned into a post-Darwinian romantic stoic. 'Awake! for morning in the bowl of night…' Omar has the muezzin cock-crowing *Ishrabu!* ('Drink!') – frightful blasphemy – and the *bam*, or dome, of the mosque is, in cosmic muscularity,

inverted to become a *jam*, or cup, for the sun's wine to be poured into. And, later, Bahra, who was always catching wild asses (*gur*), has himself now been caught by the *gur* (grave).

If we want to read Omar, we must learn a little Persian and ask for a good, very literal, crib. And if we want to read Pushkin we must learn some Russian and thank God for Nabokov. If it were at all possible to render *Eugene Onegin* into English poetry, Nabokov would be the only man; but Nabokov himself starts off his Preface with this very impossibility.

(Burgess 1965: 74–5)

Nabokov mentioned Burgess's review several times when he addressed the criticism he received for his translation in a piece that was published in the same literary magazine in February 1966 and was entitled 'Nabokov's Reply' (in *Strong Opinions*, it was changed to 'Reply to My Critics'). On two occasions, he uses Burgess's expression 'arty translations' to explain once again his own vision of translation, thus implying that he agrees with Burgess' terminology. And later on, he refers to the author of *A Clockwork Orange* to thank him for his remarks on FitzGerald's *Rubáiyát*:

For obvious reasons I cannot discuss all the sympathetic reviews. I shall only refer to some of them in order to acknowledge certain helpful suggestions and corrections. [...] Anthony Burgess in *Encounter* has suddenly and conclusively abolished my sentimental fondness for FitzGerald by showing how he falsified the 'witty metaphysical tent-maker's' actual metaphor in '*Awake! for morning in the bowl of Night…*'.

(Nabokov [1966a] 1990: 246)

It is interesting to see how FitzGerald's *Rubáiyát* fits in Nabokov's theory of literal translation as a counter example[26], but one can also trace a few links with his novels. The links may be discreet, but they help understand the richness of intertextual references that are weaved in his prose.

First, there is one avian comparison which FitzGerald coined to describe his unliteral translation which is now very well known to evoke free poetic translation.[27] In April 1859, FitzGerald wrote a letter to Cowell in which he explained why his translation is so free: 'But at all cost, a thing must live: with a transfusion of one's own worse life if one can't retain the original's better. Better a live sparrow than a stuffed eagle' (qtd in Taher-Kermani 2020: 151). Now, in the perspective of FitzGerald's *Rubáiyát* as a pseudotranslation, it is interesting to reread the following passage from *Despair*, Chapter 7. Herman has just given in full the letter that he forged and that Felix is supposed to have written to blackmail the narrator:

Signed: 'Sparrow' and underneath the address of a provincial post office.

I was long in relishing that last letter, the Gothic charm of which my rather tame translation is hardly capable of rendering.

(Nabokov 1965a: 91)

The translation refers to the fact that the original letter by Felix was supposed to be in German, even if it is not the language that the reader sees. It should be reminded that, almost from the beginning, Felix and Herman have been conversing in German, even though they met in Prague; Felix asked for a cigarette in the local language, but upon seeing that Herman's cigarettes came from Germany, he switched to German:

'I could do with a smoke', said he in Czech.

[…] 'German yourself?' he inquired in that language, his fingers twirling and pressing the cigarette. I said Yes and clicked my lighter under his nose.

(Nabokov 1965a: 6)

One can note that, on top of the two languages involved in the pseudotranslation (Czech and German), there is a third one, namely that which the book is written in, English in the passage above. *Despair* was originally written in Russian, and the image of the sparrow was also present in the first version (Nabokov [1934] 1990: 405). The novel was published in 1934 but written as early as 1932 (Boyd 1990: 382), so only four years after Nabokov's review on Tkhorzhevsky's translation of the *Rubáiyát of Omar Khayyám*. This letter, allegedly written by Felix, is presented as a translation with no original; as such, it is one of the few pseudotranslations which Nabokov inserted in his novels, as we will see in the chapter devoted to Nabokov's pseudotranslations. The presence of the 'sparrow' and the fact that Nabokov perceived FitzGerald's *Rubáiyát* as a translation with no original is enough to give the reader pause.

One can note another detail which seems to point towards FitzGerald's *Rubáiyát* in no other novel than *Pale Fire*, whose links with pseudotranslations have been underlined on several occasions in this chapter. In my opinion, Kinbote's commentary lacks the poetry that usually infuses Nabokov's prose, but the last paragraph is very poignant, and very poetic. One should pay particular attention to the French words that are used when Kinbote ponders about his own existence:

I shall continue to exist. I may assume other disguises, other forms, but I shall try to exist. I may turn up yet, on another campus, as an old, happy, healthy, heterosexual Russian, a writer in exile, sans fame, sans future, sans audience, sans anything but his art.

(Nabokov [1962] 1996: 657)

The four occurrences of 'sans', written without italics (which is a very rare occurrence for Nabokov's use of foreign words), point in two directions. The most famous one is the end of Jacques's speech on the Seven Ages of Man in Shakespeare's *As You Like It* (Act II, Scene VII), famous for its first line, 'All the world's a stage'. The last age of man is described in the following terms:

[…]. Last scene of all,
That ends this strange eventful history,
Is second childishness and mere oblivion,
Sans teeth, sans eyes, sans taste, sans everything.

(Shakespeare [1623] 1988: 638)

What is crucial here is that these lines describe the end of life in general, which is perfectly fitting for *Pale Fire* since Kinbote is brooding on the end of his own life. Moreover, the Shakespearian monologue is about playing a part: this is what Kinbote evokes, especially with 'disguises', but it is also interesting in the Kinbotians versus Shadeans debate. Lastly, one should note the parallel between Kinbote's final 'sans anything' and Jacques's final 'sans everything', which seems to indicate that Shakespeare was indeed Nabokov's main intertext.[28] However, there is also one stanza in FitzGerald's *Rubáiyát* which uses 'sans' on four occasions (stanza 23 in the first edition, stanza 24 in the fifth edition):

Ah, make the most of what we yet may spend,
Before we too into the Dust Descend;
Dust into Dust, and under Dust, to lie,
Sans Wine, sans Song, sans Singer and – sans End!

Jacques's monologue might be a common source for both FitzGerald's *Rubáiyát* and Nabokov's *Pale Fire*, but the fact that Nabokov had intimate knowledge of FitzGerald's *Rubáiyát* is enough to make one ponder, notwithstanding the fact that two other pseudotranslations, *Don Quixote* and *The Ossian*, left their mark on the novel *Pale Fire*.

Conclusion

Nabokov's novels and translations bear traces of the mere encounters he had with pseudotranslations, be it *Pale Fire* and *Despair* or *The Song of Igor's Campaign* and *Eugene Onegin*. What is even more interesting is to look at the pseudotranslations that Nabokov translated himself into Russian, be it from the French into Russian or from the Russian into English, thus showing once again the multilingual scope of Nabokov's translation practice.

3

Translating Pseudotranslations

In his 2019 book, Stanislav Shvabrin repeatedly shows the impact that the interlingual translations that Nabokov did had on his own creations; his translations of pseudotranslations are no different. They inform some of his major works and, more importantly, his own pseudotranslations (see Chapter 4). They also show the importance of Pushkin in Nabokov's art by shedding light on texts that are hardly ever studied, and this connection between Pushkin and Nabokov *through* pseudotranslation furthers the idea that, as Marijeta Bozovic convincingly showed in her book *Nabokov's Canon* (2016), Nabokov's art was deeply transnational.[1]

Nabokov translated three pseudotranslations, even though the first one was never published. The three texts will be studied in the order of their being translated by Nabokov, since the focus is now on his evolution as a translator; indeed, his approach to each of the three pseudotranslations helps understand how he went from literary translation to literal translation. First, he translated *Les Chansons de Bilitis* in 1918, making it an interesting case of juvenilia; then his translation of one scene from Pushkin's play *The Covetous Knight* was made in 1941 (published in 1944[2]), and it demonstrates an artistic vision of translation which is specifically the one he defended in his 1941 essay 'The Art of Translation'; finally, the last pseudotranslation Nabokov translated is Tatyana's letter, from *Eugene Onegin*, which corresponds to his literalist vision of translation.

Les Chansons de Bilitis (1894), translated by Nabokov in 1918

Les Chansons de Bilitis is one of the most famous cases of pseudotranslation, and it is even presented as a textbook case by Emily Apter or Lawrence Venuti (who gets the publication date wrong):

> There are few more flagrant cases of pseudotranslation than Pierre Louÿs's *Les Chansons de Bilitis*, published in 1894 with the subtitle *traduites du grec pour la*

première fois par P.L. and marketed as the translation of works by a sixth-century half-Greek, half-Turkish poetess.

(Apter 2006: 214)

The literary hoax perpetrated by the French writer Pierre Louÿs, the book-length collection of prose poems he entitled *Les Chansons de Bilitis* (1895), must certainly be classed among the most intriguing of pseudotranslations. Louÿs presented his text as a French translation from the Greek poetry of Bilitis, a woman who was said to be Sappho's contemporary. Yet most of his readers knew that none of Bilitis's poetry survived, and that in fact she seems never to have existed, whether in the sixth century B.C. or in some other period of antiquity.

(Venuti 1998: 34)

To be more specific, *Les Chansons de Bilitis* was presented as an indirect translation: 'When Louÿs delivered the manuscript to his editor Bailly, he maintained that it was a French translation of Heim's German translation from the Greek' (Apter 2006: 215). The German philologist was of course an invention, as suggested by the name ('"G. Heim" puns on the German word for "secret" or "mysterious," *geheim*'. Venuti 1998: 39), but as Apter explains, the fact that Louÿs was a scholar helped the pseudotranslation be accepted as a true translation, at least at first: 'Louÿs's reputation as a classicist passed muster and contributed to the generally favourable reception of *Les Chansons* when it was first published' (Apter 2006: 215).

The demonstration conducted by Venuti in his chapter 'Authorship' is particularly interesting because he shows how pseudotranslation helps reconsider authorship, translation and scholarship:

> By deliberately presenting himself as a translator instead of an author, Louÿs directed his reader's attention to the cultural materials from which he produced his text. This was of course done to give Bilitis an air of authenticity, but it also implied that Louÿs was not an authentic author. [...] And even when reviewers explicit recognized his authorship, they defined it not as self-expression, but as scholarship, although cast in the emotionally evocative language of poetry.

(Venuti 1998: 34)

The links between translation and scholarly research are obviously evocative of both Nabokov's *Pale Fire* and *Eugene Onegin*,[3] but Venuti's repeated argument on authenticity created or validated by scholarship is reminiscent of the debate surrounding the *Slovo* or the *Ossian*:

> Louÿs's hoax blurred the distinctions between translation, authorship, and scholarship. As soon as the reader realized that Bilitis was invented, and that

Louÿs's text derived from numerous literary and scholarly sources, authorship was redefined as historical research that takes the form of a literary imitation which incorporates translation.

(Venuti 1998: 35)

By blurring the distinction between translation and authorship, Louÿs's hoax inevitably questioned scholarship that defined historical truth as a verification of authorial originality.

(Venuti 1998: 39)

Les Chansons de Bilitis impacted Nabokov as a writer, both in Russian and in English: in *Glory*, Martin Edelweiss is given an edition of *Les Chansons de Bilitis* by Alla Chernosvitova (Nabokov [1971] 2006), and in *Ada*, two direct references are to be found, always in connection with lesbianism (Nabokov [1969] 1996: 132, 156).[4]

In August 1918, Nabokov translated three of the 158 poems gathered in *Les Chansons de Bilitis*: 'La Chevelure', 'La Flûte de Pan' and 'Le Tombeau des Naïades' (Shvabrin 2019: 48). According to Shvabrin (49), the explanation for this choice is to be found in a musical adaptation by Claude Debussy, 'Trois Chansons de Bilitis', dating back to 1897–8.[5] At the time, Nabokov's approach to translation was very creative and an analysis of his renditions into Russian confirms this. Shvabrin shows the many liberties that Nabokov took with form: for example 'the unrhymed French poems become rhymed in Russian' or 'On Louÿs's flowing, melodic free verse Nabokov imposes a regular meter and a fairly strict stanzaic structure[6]'.

If one looks at Nabokov's translation of 'Le Tombeau des Naïades', to take but one example, it is clear that his vision of translation at the time was very different from the literal theory he enforced in the 1950s and 1960s, more famously in *Eugene Onegin* (1964, 1975) but also in *A Hero of our Time* (Lermontov 1958). The French version is composed of four paragraphs:

Le Tombeau des naïades:

Le long du bois couvert de givre, je marchais; mes cheveux devant ma bouche se fleurissaient de petits glaçons, et mes sandales étaient lourdes de neige fangeuse et tassée.

Il me dit: 'Que cherches-tu ? – Je suis la trace du satyre. Ses petits pas fourchus alternent comme des trous dans un manteau blanc'. Il me dit: 'Les satyres sont morts.

'Les satyres et les nymphes aussi. Depuis trente ans il n'a pas fait un hiver aussi terrible. La trace que tu vois est celle d'un bouc. Mais restons ici, où est leur tombeau'.

> Et avec le fer de sa houe il cassa la glace de la source où jadis riaient les naïades.
> Il prenait de grands morceaux froids, et, les soulevant vers le ciel pâle, il regardait au travers.

(Louÿs [1894] 1898: 46)

Instead of four paragraphs, Nabokov's translation is presented in the form of a poem made of 18 lines (19 in Debussy's cycle); it starts with three couplets, continues with alternate rhymes, before returning to couplets towards the end. Nabokov adds a few poetical images which are absent from the original. For instance, in the first line of the poem, '*Le long du bois couvert de givre, je marchais*' (along the wood covered in frost I walked[7]), Nabokov translates the adjective '*couvert*' into '*кружевныхъ*' (lace-like). And at the end of the poem, '*ciel*' (sky) is translated by '*небосводъ*' (firmament):

> Il prenait de grands morceaux froids, et, les soulevant vers le ciel pâle, il regardait au travers.
>
> (He picked up some huge cold fragments, and, raising them to the pale sky, gazed through them.)
>
> Nabokov's translation:
>
> Онъ бралъ куски холодные, большіе, (He took big, cold pieces)
>
> и молчаливо сквозь прозрачный ледъ (and silently through the transparent ice)
>
> глядѣлъ на зимній, бѣлый небосводъ. (he looked at the winter, white firmament)

The slight transformation of 'sky' into 'firmament' was probably made to enable the rhyme with '*ледъ*' (ice) in the final couplet (*liod, nebosvod*), which is confirmed by the fact that most liberties with vocabulary taken by Nabokov occur at the end of lines. However, it is not always the case, as one can see with '*молчаливо*' (silently), which is placed towards the beginning of the penultimate line in Nabokov's translation, but has no equivalent in the French original. One could also mention two interesting elements. In the French original, '*il me dit*' (he said to me) is used twice, but Nabokov makes the translation more specific when it comes to the verb, and even to the pronoun on one occasion: '*Мой другъ спросилъ*' (my friend asked); '*онъ воскликнулъ*' (he exclaimed). Therefore, he used two different verbs for one and only verb in French,[8] thus showing that he was not as strictly attached to the respect of repetition as he was going to be years later in *Eugene Onegin*.[9] Another element which Nabokov added repeatedly in his translation is the lyrical 'I' of the female narrator ('*я*' in Russian). Thus, just as he transformed 'said' into 'asked', Nabokov made it explicit that the narrator was answering his friend's question, thus expanding the dash which, in French, can be used to indicate a change of speaker in a dialogue (the French and Russian punctuations are preserved below for the sake of clarity):

> Il me dit: :'Que cherches-tu ?' – Je suis la trace du satyre.
> (He said to me: 'What do you seek?' 'I follow the satyr's track.')
>
> Nabokov's translation:
> Мой другъ спросилъ: 'что ищещь?' И въ ответъ
> сказала я: 'сатира вижу слѣдъ. […]'
> (my friend asked: 'What are you looking for?' And in answer, / I said: 'I see the satyr's track')

Further down, Nabokov adds another 'я', (*ja*) thus replacing the allusion to the laughter of naiads by a reference to the narrator gazing at them; once again the localization at the end of the line can be explained by a need to find a rhyme for the genitive of 'stream' ('*ручья*', *ruch'ja*):

> Et avec le fer de sa houe il cassa la glace de la source où jadis riaient les naïades.
>
> (And with the iron head of his hoe he broke the ice of the spring, where the naiads used to laugh.)
>
> Онъ расщоллъ зеленый ледъ ручья, (He shattered the green ice of the stream)
>
> гдѣ нѣкогда наядъ видала я. (where erstwhile I saw naiads)

One can also notice the addition of the color 'green', which can be linked to Nabokov's interest in colours in translation as well as his multilingualism. Indeed, in French, '*houe*' (hoe) sounds like '*houx*' (holly), which is green, and in English, the translation of '*source*', 'spring', is a season which is associated with the colour green. This interest in colours and associations was expressed years later by Nabokov, thus suggesting that this was a life-long focus for Nabokov, and not one of the aspects that changed over the years in Nabokov's transition from literary to literal translation. It can be found in 1928, for example, in his aforementioned review of Tkhorzhevsky's translation of the *Rubáiyát*:

> Tkhorzhevsky makes a mistake common to all translators from the English. It concerns the color purple. FitzGerald talks of 'flowing purple' seas; Tkhorzhevsky translated 'the sea exhale, burning with a scarlet tremor' (which, besides, recalls Balmont); yet the English 'purple' is not the same as the Russian (or French) *pourpre* (scarlet, vermillion)); but rather, it means 'lilac', 'violet', at times (in poetry) even dark blue.
>
> (Nabokov 2019: 77)

Later, in his seminal essay 'The Art of Translation', Nabokov expressed both his interest in the lexical associations he heard in words and in the presence of colours which tinted his memory of poetry:

> And the central word in Housman's 'What are those blue *remembered* hills?' becomes in Russian *vspom-neev-she-yes-yah*, a horribly straggly thing, all humps and horns, which cannot fuse into any inner connection with 'blue', as it does so smoothly in English, because the Russian sense of blueness belongs to a different series than the Russian 'remember' does.
>
> (Nabokov [1941a] 2008: 10)

Finally, this focus on colours in translation is still present in his later, literal translation *Eugene Onegin*, in which he dedicates more than two pages to the colour of Tatyana's headgear (Pushkin [1975] 1991, II: 181–3).

Nabokov's encounter with *Les Chansons de Bilitis* did not have an impact on his work as tremendous as his engagement with Pushkin, but a close study of this early experimentation with translation is interesting to discriminate between his tendencies, be they those which were prone to change or those which were life-long obsessions.

Pushkin's *Skupoi Rytsar'* (1836), translated by Nabokov in 1941: *The Covetous Knight*

Pushkin wrote four little tragedies and, in 1941, Nabokov translated three of them[10]: *Mozart and Salieri*, *The Feast during the Plague* and *The Covetous Knight*. However, for the latter, he only translated one scene. The play is very short (only one act) and the plot is rather simple. In Scene one, Albert complains of his father's refusal to give him more money, so he tries to get some from Salomon, a Jewish usurer, who suggests he could poison his father to access his money, but is violently rebuked by Albert. In Scene 2, the Baron brings money to one of his many chests of gold, and soliloquizes about the time it took him to get all this money and is angry at the idea that, when he dies, his son will dilapidate what he took so long to acquire. Scene 3 begins with Albert asking the Duke to encourage his father to give him more money, then he hides in another room, and when the Baron enters and hears the Duke's suggestion, he refuses because he argues that his son tried to kill him and to steal his money, which pushes Albert to leave his hiding place and accuse his father of being a liar; the scene ends with the Baron having a heart attack and dying.

Before looking at Nabokov's English translation of *Skupoi Rytsar'* (*The Covetous Knight*), a quick survey of Pushkin's texts is in order to show how pseudotranslation participates in a transnational vision of literature which was common to the two authors.

Pushkin wrote two pseudotranslations which were both published in 1836: a poem, 'Iz Pindemonti' ('From Pindemonte'), and a play, *Skupoi Rytsar'* (*The Covetous Knight*[11]), and Nabokov translated both (however, I will concentrate on the first one, *Skupoi Rytsar'*[12]). The fact that Nabokov's own pseudotranslations as Vivian Calmbrood were also a poem ('The Night Journey') and a play (*The Wanderers*) is one of the many links between Nabokov and Pushkin through pseudotranslation.

Pushkin's pseudotranslations all pointed to real authors; as Pushkin had already acted as a translator of poetry (for example, from French with André Chénier[13] or from English with Robert Southey[14]), readers could willingly trust that they were indeed reading genuine translations. 'Iz Pindemonti'[15] was presented as a translation from a poem by Ippolito Pondemonti (1753–1828), but the supposed author was initially meant to be Alfred de Musset. As for the play *Skupoi Rytsar'* (*The Covetous Knight*), it was presented as a translation from British author William Shenstone (1714–63). Shenstone did exist, even if he is sometimes presented as an invention, 'Chenston' or 'Chenstone', due to Pushkin' erronous spelling ('Ченстон' instead of 'Шенстон').[16] This is what Nabokov explains in his commentary to *Eugene Onegin*:

> *The Covetous Knight*, attributed (perhaps by a French translator) to Shenstone,[17] whose name Pushkin wrote, in Russian transliteration, with a *Ch*, owing to his thinking that *Sh* was the same kind of Gallic mispronunciation as 'Shild-Arold'.
>
> (Pushkin [1975] 1991, III: 180)

In his article 'Pushkin and Shenstone: The Case Reopened', Richard A. Gregg argues that this faulty transliteration was rather widespread among Russians at the time,[18] but more importantly, he shows that Shenstone was widely known and read in Russia and that Pushkin 'almost certainly had some knowledge of the prestigious Shenstone' (1965: 111). For Gregg, the links between Pushkin's pseudotranslation and Shenstone go beyond mere mystification and include intertextuality with one of the texts by the English poet:

> It is only when we compare 'Economy' with *The Covetous Knight* that we find concrete indications that Pushkin had, in fact, read Shenstone, and that this experience left significant traces on a major work of his own.
>
> (Gregg 1965: 113)[19]

Gregg explains that 'Economy' was 'a tripartite 'moral piece' written in blank verse' (111) and shows the many links that exist between Shenstone's text and the second scene of *The Covetous Knight*, namely the soliloquy where the Baron discusses the power bestowed by all his gold:

> as the power of gold forces Pushkin's widow to kneel before the Baron's house, so in Shenstone the poor young poet is obliged 'to bow the knee before his [the miser's] calf of gold, / Implore his envious aid, and meet his frown' (I, 77–8). [...]

> And Shenstone's wrathful words of banishment:
> > Go to thy bags, thou Recreat! hourly go,
> > And, gazing there, bid them be wit, be mirth,
> > Be conversation. (I, 54–6)

> read like a précis of Scene 2, where the Baron, having descended to his *podvaly* (an echo, perhaps, of Shenstone's 'caverned stores'), gazes, gloats, and sololoquizes at length over his coffers. (Gregg 1965: 113)

Gregg underlines here that Shenstone's 'Economy' was a source of inspiration for Pushkin's *Covetous Knight* (albeit minor), thus showing one more time that pseudotranslations are not always total inventions but can include parts and parcels of an existing text. What is even more interesting is that Nabokov chose to translate only Scene 2 of *The Covetous Knight*, which begs the question of this choice: was he interested in differentiating translation from intertextuality in Pushkin's pseudotranslation? This could be another reason to add to the ethical one which was brought forward by Shvabrin, namely that Nabokov disliked the stereotypical treatment of the Jewish character in Scene 1.[20]

Beyond the presence of Shenstone's 'Economy', there are other links with British literature in *The Covetous Knight*: as mentioned earlier, the text was supposed to be a translation from the English, therefore, some motifs are used to reinforce the verisimilitude of the Englishness of the text, like the names of the characters (the Baron is called 'Philip' (Филипп) and his son 'Albert' (Альбер)). Several critics have noted the similarities which *The Covetous Knight* (and, more generally, Pushkin's mini-tragedies) bears with Shakespeare, including Proffer:

> Seen from the literary point of view, the four 'Little tragedies' are examples of Pushkin's interest in Shakespeare's approach to characterization (as well as his verse form and imagery).
>
> (Proffer 1968: 347)

Shvabrin adds another English influence to Shakespeare: 'Infused by his awareness of the Lake Poets, Pushkin's imaginative appropriation of the Shakespearean dramatic idiom in his "little tragedies" is idiosyncratic' (2019: 192).

But the most compelling influence, especially in the framework of pseudotranslation, is Walter Scott. Many scholars have shown the strong ascendancy that the Scottish bard had on Pushkin,[21] more notably Jakubovich. Research usually insists on Scott's influence on *The Captain's Daughter* and *The Tales of Belkin*,[22] but it also exists in Pushkin's pseudotranslation:

> As D. P. Jakubovič has shown, Pushkin's miser-baron could boast a long Western European tradition, ranging from Marlowe's *Jew of Malta* to the medieval usurers in the novels of Sir Walter Scott. [...] Convincing, too, are the parallels drawn by Jakubovič between the soliloquy of the Baron in Scene 2 and certain speeches by Henbane Dwining, the miser-pharmacist in Scott's *The Fair Maid of Perth* (a novel which Pushkin owned).
>
> (Gregg 1965: 109–10)

In Scene 2 (the one which Nabokov translated), only the Baron is present, but in the first one, there is a Jew who is indeed a usurer and whose portrayal is full of clichés. This character is reminiscent of Isaac of York, the Jewish moneylender from Scott's *Ivanhoe*. Other characters and situations ring a bell with Scott's. In Scene 1, Albert mentions the tournament in which he defeated Count Delorge (граф Делорж); this French name echoes another French name in *Ivanhoe*, Brian de Bois-Guilbert, who is defeated too in a tournament by Wilfred of Ivanhoe (under the disguise of a mysterious knight).

Chronologically speaking, the similarities between Pushkin and Scott are far from surprising, and they are rooted in the fashion for literary hoaxes which spread across Europe in the 1820s and 1830s. For example, I mentioned earlier that the supposed author of 'Iz Pindemonti' was initially meant to be Alfred de Musset, and the latter had indulged in pseudotranslation in 1828[23]; moreover, the birth certificate of the term 'pseudotranslation' goes back to 1823, when it was used about *Walladmor*, which was, as indicated earlier, presented as the German translation of a novel by Sir Walter Scott.

The Scottish writer was immensely popular at the time and his inspiration can be noted in some of Pushkin's hoaxes (Pushkin resorted to various types of mystifications in his career, especially in the 1830s). Hoisington (1981) devoted a whole article to the role that Scott played in Pushkin's *The Tales of the Late Ivan Petrovich Belkin* (1831), which were published as a Russian text written by a fictitious author, Belkin, and edited by 'A. P.', which any Russian reader could recognize as Pushkin's initials, thus showing the ironical use that Pushkin was making of his hoax:

> The true author of *The Tales* is clearly presented in the Preface as the editor A. P. Pushkin was not trying to hide behind Belkin. He wanted the public to recognize him – hence the telltale initials.
>
>   (Hoisington 1981: 354)

Both Scott and Pushkin played with the fictitiousness of their editors and authors in their hoaxes, which echoes what pseudotranslation does with the figures of author and translator. Indeed, *The Tales*'s editor has a direct inspiration in Walter Scott:

> The Russian scholar D. P. Yakubovich has demonstrated parallels between the Preface to *The Tales of Belkin* and the mystifications used in Scott's *Tales of my Landlord, Collected and Arranged by Jedediah Cleishbotham* (1816–1819) and *The Monastery* (1820), with its Introductory Epistle to 'the Author of Waverley' from Captain Clutterbuck.
>
>   (Hoisington 1981: 344)

The motif of the hoax in the literature of the early eighteenth century goes even further because it does not stop with Scott but goes as far as America: 'the prefaces to *Tales of my Landlord*, in turn, were undoubtedly inspired by the Introduction to Irving's Knickerbocker's *History of New York*, which Scott had read with great enjoyment in 1813' (Hoisington 1981: 356). It does not seem that Irving influenced Pushkin himself, but this thread shows the transnational connections that united various countries and continents through the device of literary hoaxes.

  Pushkin's mystification *The Tales* and his pseudotranslation *Skupoi Rytsar'* (*The Covetous Knight*) are closely linked chronologically speaking: they were written by Pushkin at the same time, and Nabokov describes these three months in 1830 as 'the most fertile autumn of his [Pushkin's] entire life' (Pushkin [1975] 1991, III: 179). Thematically speaking, Pushkin draws from British intertext and influence, be it Shakespeare or Scott, in his own Russian creations, and by resorting to pseudotranslation, he further interlaces British and Russian literary traditions thanks to a linguistic connection, since he pretends to translate a British author, Shenstone, into Russian. Through intertextuality and various types of hoaxes, Pushkin inscribes a back-and-forth movement between Russian and European literatures, as he did, with different means, in *Eugene Onegin*. Pseudotranslation is a particularly interesting form of hoax in the context of this creation of a transnational literature because translation itself enables a dialogue between Europe and Russia, as Pushkin did when he translated the poetry of Chénier and Southey or pretended to translate Pindemonte in his other pseudotranslation. As we will see, Nabokov resorts to the same type of thematic echoes and linguistic devices in his own Calmbrood pseudotranslations (especially *The Wanderers*).

When it comes to Nabokov's translations of Pushkin, what is noteworthy is that Nabokov particularly insists on their European dimension. Thus, he further tightens in his own English translations the network of connections which are woven by Pushkin in his Russian translations of European texts, and this heightens the relevance of Pushkin (and more generally of Russian literature) for the English-speaking public who can find familiar echoes in a literature that can otherwise be easily deemed too foreign. For *The Covetous Knight* specifically, Shvabrin argues that Nabokov's translations of Pushkin's mini-tragedies are infused with his thorough knowledge of English verse:

> Along with his general knowledge of English poetry, Nabokov's perusal of Shakespeare in general, and his study of the sonnets and Hamlet in particular, makes itself apparent at every step in his renditions of Pushkin's 'little tragedies'.
>
> (Shvabrin 2019: 192)

Here, Shvabrin echoes the fact that Nabokov translated Shakespeare's Sonnets 17 and 27 in 1924 and *Hamlet* in 1930,[24] but one could also evoke the earlier use that Nabokov makes of Shakespeare in his own Russian play *Tragedia gospodina Morna*,[25] written in 1923–4 (but only published in 2008 (Nabokov 2008b)). In the introduction to *The Tragedy of Mister Morn* (the English translation by Anastasia Tolstoy and Thomas Karshan (Nabokov 2012)), Karshan devotes several passages to the role played by Shakespeare in Nabokov's Russian play, calling it 'the shimmering pale fire of Shakespeare's language which is often glimpsed in Nabokov's original Russian' (Nabokov 2012: xxi). In one of these passages, Karshan evokes, though indirectly, the little tragedy *The Covetous Knight* and the links with Shakespeare:

> But in *Morn* Nabokov was trying to emulate Shakespeare not only at the level of image and symbol, but also of character and drama, register and rhythm. The simplest expression of this is that *Morn* is written in the iambic pentameter of Shakespearean tragedy, though Nabokov is more strictly regular in his rhythmic patterns than Shakespeare. Though *Morn*'s prosody alludes to Shakespeare, it does so through the mediation of Pushkin's 'little tragedies' (all written in 1830, the most famous of which is *Mozart and Salieri*). More specifically Shakespearean – and un-Pushkinian – is the language of *Morn*, which, especially

in the philosophic speeches of Tremens, Klian, Morn and Dandilio, is densely metaphorical and highly compressed in the manner of later Shakespeare.

(Nabokov 2012: xv)

The iambic pentameter is probably the most obvious nod towards Shakespeare in Nabokov's translations of Pushkin. For *The Covetous Knight*, both the Russian text by Pushkin and the English translation by Nabokov are written in blank verse, that is, un-rhyming iambic pentameters. Therefore, Nabokov resorted to his English intertext not only thematically, but also formally.

As far as Nabokov's evolution in translation is concerned, it is interesting to note that the iamb was also a central feature of his *Eugene Onegin*:

The work is now finished. In my translation I have sacrificed to total accuracy and completeness of meaning every element of form *save the iambic rhythm*, the retention of which assisted rather than impaired fidelity.

(Nabokov 1959b: 98; italics mine)

Therefore, the iamb remained central, be it in 1941 (*The Covetous Knight*) or in 1964 (*Eugene Onegin*), despite the many changes that occurred between Nabokov's early use of artistic translation and his later policy of literal translation.

As mentioned earlier, Nabokov's translation of Pushkin's little tragedy was launched in 1941, which is the year when he wrote his essay 'The Art of Translation', in which he exposed his vision of artistic translation. And it is true that, in many respects, Nabokov's *Covetous Knight* is an illustration of this vision.

The most striking trait is probably the recurring non-respect of Pushkin's repetitions with the introduction of variation. It is particularly striking when the repetition occurs in close proximity, and a few examples from the first page should suffice. When the Baron brings a few new coins to his vault, he compares the small amount to a story he heard about a Prince who asked his soldiers to bring each a handful of earth, and all of them together amounted to a lot, just like the Baron's treasure. In Russian, Pushkin uses the word '*горсть*' (handful) on three occasions (Pushkin [1994] 2008: 144), but Nabokov uses three different expressions (145):

Горсть золота накопленново всыпать. / some recently collected gold: a **fistful**, (l. 8)

Велел снести земли по **горсти** в кучу, / a **handful** each of earth, which formed a hillock (l. 12)

Так я, по **горсти** бедной принося / So bit by bit I have been bringing here (l. 17)

If we look at the image of the hillock, we can also note the use of variation in Nabokov's translation, with some interesting shifts:

> Велел снести земли по горсти в кучу,
> И гордый **холм** возвысился [...]
> Вознес мой **холм** (l. 12-19)
> a handful each of earth, which formed a hillock
> which swelled into a **mountain** [...]
> and heaped my **hill** (l. 12-19)

In Russian, 'холм' (hill) bears the second stress of its line on both occasions. Nabokov loses this mirroring effect in form and introduces variations in lexicon: the first 'холм' is translated as 'mountain', whereas the second is 'hill', but Nabokov inserts a repetition, an echo so to speak, by translating 'кучу' (pile) by 'hillock'. One can wonder why he did not simply use 'hill' and the answer may lie in his need to have a feminine ending (since the line ends with an unstressed syllable, namely the last syllable of 'hillock'): there are indeed quite a few of those on the page.

Some of the variations introduced by Nabokov are, like 'hill' and 'hillock', very small and negligible, since they are variations of the same basis, but others go beyond a mere alternation between synonyms. In the following passage (in parentheses in the text), the Baron claims he is completely fearless when he goes to open his chests:

> (о, нет! кого бояться мне?
> При мне мой меч: за злато отвечает
> Честной булат) (l. 60-62; Pushkin [1994] 2008: 148)
> (Oh no, whom do I have to fear? On myself I have my sword: to gold answers faithful steel, my literal translation)

Nabokov's translation is much freer than most of his translation:

> (oh, no! whom should I fear? I have
> my gallant sword: one metal guards the other
> and answers for it) (l. 60–2; Pushkin [1994] 2008: 149)

Here, Nabokov's use of the hyperonym 'metal' to subsume both 'gold' and 'steel' is rather surprising, as well as his introduction of the verb 'guard' and the transformation of 'faithful' into 'gallant' (in Russian, it qualifies the steel, in English, the sword).

The last element which is interesting as far as the links between Nabokov's *Covetous Knight* and his 'Art of Translation' are concerned is the occurrence, in very close proximity in the translation, of two words that Nabokov used in his essay to describe the three types of translators. After describing them as 'the scholar', 'the well-meaning hack' (usually a woman) and 'the professional writer', Nabokov explains the centrality of creative genius which the scholar and the hack lack:

> But the point is not that the scholar commits fewer blunders than the drudge; the point is that as a rule both he and she are hopelessly devoid of any semblance of creative genius.

(Nabokov [1941a] 2008: 8)

Strangely enough, the words 'drudge' and 'genius' are used in Nabokov's translation of Pushkin's little tragedy, in close proximity at that:

> unshackled Genius labor as my bondsman,
> and noble merit, and the sleepless drudge
> wait with humility till I reward them.

(l. 27–9; Pushkin [1994] 2008: 145)

The use of the words 'drudge' and 'Genius', which Nabokov capitalizes, is particularly interesting since this passage occurs just after the reference to the Muses (which Nabokov translated as 'the Sacred Nine' in English). The Baron says that he has so much money that he can now build such a wonderful palace that it will attract Nymphs and Muses, originating from mythology. Among the Nine Muses, Nabokov insists specifically on those of arts (since he added in his translation that they 'come with mask or lute') and one cannot fail to see the link with the *art* of translation that he described in his essay.

Finally, one interesting example links Nabokov's artistic shunning of repetition and his fondness for Gallicisms in *Eugene Onegin* (see the second part of this book). Indeed, at the very beginning of the translation, Nabokov introduces two Gallicisms in very close proximity (he then abstains from it in the remainder of the translation). To describe the place where the Baron keeps his gold, Pushkin uses the word 'сундук' (chest) ten times in the whole scene; Nabokov chooses to translate it by the very English 'chest' for five occurrences, but on four occasions (l. 7, 58 twice and 69 in the Russian text), he omits it altogether,[26] and on one occasion (l. 7), he uses the loanword[27] 'coffer', which comes from the Old French *cofre* or *coffer*, as explained in the *Oxford English Dictionary*. The use of the Gallicism is all the more surprising because Nabokov had already avoided the close repetition inscribed by Pushkin by removing one of the two uses of *сундук*:

> В шестой **сундук** (в **сундук** еще неполный) (to the sixth chest (in the chest, it is not yet full); my translation)
>
> to coffer six (which still is not quite sated)

Aside from Nabokov's fondness for French, the justification could lie, once again, in prosody: if Nabokov had used the monosyllabic 'chest', the proximity of 'six' (also a monosyllabic word) would have made the use of iambic pentameters very difficult. On the other hand, the dissyllabic word 'coffer' made it possible to alternate between the stressed first syllable and the unstressed second syllable, thus enabling the next stress to fall onto 'six'. What is interesting is that the variation between 'chest' and 'coffer' comes at the very beginning (respectively l. 5 and l. 7), where one finds another Gallicism. Indeed, Nabokov chose to translate 'свиданья' (date, in the genitive, l. 1) with the very French 'rendez-vous[28]':

> Как молодой повеса ждет **свиданья**
> С какой-нибудь развратницей лукавой (l. 1–2)
> (like a young rake waits for his date with some cunning harlot; my translation)
> Just as a mad young fellow frets awaiting
> his **rendez-vous** with some evasive harlot (l. 1–2)

One could, once again, explain Nabokov's choice of the word 'rendez-vous' with prosody: the three syllables (instead of the very short 'date') made the iambic pentameter much more doable. Another reason could lie in intertextuality: the word 'rendezvous' can be found in several of Shakespeare's plays, more notably *Hamlet* (Act IV, Scene 4, line 4[29]), which Nabokov had previously translated into Russian and knew very well. However, the choice of 'rendez-vous' is somewhat questionable, lexically speaking. Indeed, the Russian word can only apply to an amorous context, whereas 'rendezvous' can be used in more contexts, neutral or military for example. However, the word 'harlot', chosen by Nabokov, indicates that the meeting will be indeed devoted to love, or at least sex; this word has a few added advantages, since it is borrowed from the French (according to the *OED*) and points towards an archaic use of language, as a recent translator of Pushkin's little tragedies suggested when she criticized two previous translators (including Nabokov) for

> the translation of развратницей as 'harlot', a word so totally outdated in English, and so strongly smelling of hellfire preachers quoting the King James Bible, that any attempt actually to use it as a term of contempt is likely to produce a snicker instead.
>
> (Anderson in Pushkin 2000: 19)

One can wonder if Anderson's very modern choice of 'bimbo' (44) is really fitting for Pushkin, but her remark on a brand of English clearly associated with the King James Bible is interesting since it gives an early-modern touch to Nabokov's translation into English, just the way his sometimes Shakespearian English does.

In this translation as in his later *Eugene Onegin*, Nabokov often resorted to some archaic words to keep the texts in their original timeframe. Therefore, there are both differences and common points between Nabokov's early practice of translation and his later position, thus showing the need to approach his evolution regarding translation with care. His treatment of repetition came to vary along the years, but he maintained a strong desire to show the traces of European intertextuality in his translations of Pushkin as well as an enduring faithfulness to iambic pentameters.

Let us now turn to the pseudotranslation by Pushkin which Nabokov translated last: Tatyana's letter, in *Eugene Onegin*. The contrast will be particularly interesting since this translation was a literal one.

Tatyana's letter in *Evgenij Onegin*

Tatyana's letter to Onegin is one of the best known passages of the novel in prose, be it by critics or by Russian people, who often know it by heart. If many scholars have studied the fact that this letter was said to be written originally in French but translated into Russian,[30] not many people refer to it as a pseudotranslation, including Nabokov (it is, to be more specific, an embedded pseudotranslation[31]).

In this letter to Onegin, Tatyana confessed to her love for him, which is at the same time unladylike but also rather bold. Therefore, this letter is full of passion, despite all the reservations that a young lady of Tatyana's stature should have about couching it down in a letter. Her impulse in passion is visible in the fact that only a few lines are needed for Tatyana to make her decision and to write her letter. All this is done in one stanza:[32]

And far away her heart was ranging
as Tatiana looked at the moon...
All at once in her mind a thought was born...
'Go, let me be alone.
Give me, nurse, a pen, paper,
and move up the table; I'll soon go to bed;
good night'. Now she's alone,
all's still. The moon gives light to her.
Tatiana, leaning on her elbow, writes,
and Eugene's ever present in her mind,
and in an unconsidered letter
An innocent maid's love breathes forth.

The letter's ready, folded.
Tatiana! Whom, then, is it for?

(Pushkin [1975] 1991, I: 159)

The narrator is the one who is subjected to self-consciousness because it takes him several stanzas before he allows himself to disclose the letter, right after Stanza XXXI and before Stanza XXXII (the letter is therefore outside of the general structure). The narrator starts by lingering on the fact that other women tend to be indifferent, austere and timid (Stanzas XXII–XXIII), thus suggesting that they play hard to get, as one would say nowadays; he thus suggests that Tatyana is not to be blamed for her 'dear simplicity' or for being 'obedient to the bent of feeling' (Stanza XXIV) and beseeches the reader, 'Can it be that you won't forgive her / the thoughtlessness of passions?' After explaining his reluctance by his fear of exposing Tatyana to ridicule and shame, he underlines another impediment, and this one is linguistic:

> Another hindrance I foresee:
> saving the honor of my native land,
> undoubtedly I'll be obliged
> Tatiana's letter to translate.
> She knew Russian badly,
> did not read our reviews,
> and expressed herself with difficulty
> in her native tongue;
> hence wrote in French.
> What's to be done about it! I repeat again;
> as yet a lady's love
> has not expressed itself in Russian,
> as yet our proud tongue has
> to postal prose not got accustomed.

(Stanza XXVI, Pushkin [1975] 1991: 162)

As the narrator explains, Tatyana's choice of words is not so much unpatriotic as it is the result of a lack of literature in Russian. He goes on, for a couple of stanzas, to encourage poets to write more in Russian and wishes that in the future 'a generation of new belles' will use Russian. After lingering on Tatyana's choice of French, he apologizes for the incorrect translation he is bound to produce, suggesting however that 'to [him] will Gallicisms remain as dear / as the sins of past youth' (Stanza XXIX, lines 6–7). Even though he writes that ''Tis time to occupy myself / with my fair damsel's letter', he drags on for two more stanzas, and finally, in Stanza XXXI, he is finally ready: 'But here's / an incomplete, feeble translation, / the pallid copy of a vivid picture, / or Freischütz executed / by timid female learners's fingers' (Pushkin [1975] 1991, I: 164). As if words were not enough to describe the poor quality of his translation, the narrator resorts to intersemiotic translation[33]: the two nonverbal sign systems he resorts to are painting ('the pallid copy of a vivid picture'), and then music (*Der Freischütz* is 'a romantic opera by Carl Maria von Weber (1786–1826)', as Nabokov explains in the commentary (Pushkin [1975] 1991, II: 384)).

The narrator insists both on his role as a translator and on the reality of the French letter, even if the reader will never see it in its original language; all of this confirms the letter is a pseudotranslation:

> Tatiana's letter is before me;
> Religiously I keep it;
> I read it with a secret heartache
> And cannot get my fill of reading it.
>
> (Pushkin [1975] 1991, I: 164)

As we will see in the chapters devoted to Nabokov's translation of *Evgenij Onegin*, Nabokov strongly insists on the presence of Gallicisms in Pushkin's Russian. His main reason is that the Russian bard read most European classics in French translations, which left its imprint on his Russian. Consequently, Nabokov reflected this Gallic touch onto his own English by frequently turning to French authors or French translations of classical texts which Pushkin read, and he explained his approach in several of, if not all, his essays on translation, but it is in 'The Servile Path' that Nabokov exploits the French presence in Pushkin the most, and for now, only one quote should suffice:

> In a recent article I mentioned some of the complications attending the turning of *Eugene Onegin* into English, such as the need to cope with a constant intrusion of gallicisms and borrowings from French poets. My main contention was, and is, that the translator, in order to be lucidly faithful to his text, should be aware of this or that authorial reminiscence, imitation, or direct translation from another language into that of the text, and that this awareness may not only save him from committing howlers, or from bungling the rendering of stylistic details, but also guide him in the choice of the best wording where several are possible. The English translator of *Eugene Onegin* would seem to need not only a Russian's knowledge of Russian but also Pushkin's knowledge of French.
>
> (Nabokov 1959b: 97)

This recurring use of French in order to translate Pushkin's Russian into English is to be seen, for example, when Nabokov explains his translation 'Religiously I keep it': 'The French formula "je la conserve religieusement" has helped me to render this in English' (Pushkin [1975] 1991, II: 384).

As Tatyana wrote her letter in French, the French intertext becomes even more crucial in Nabokov's commentary to it, and many intertextual justifications are linked to French literature (mainly from the nineteenth century),[34] be it Mme de Krüdener's 1802 *Valérie* (389), Benjamin Constant's 1816 *Adolphe* (390), Chénier's *Les Amours* (391), an elegy by Marceline Desbordes-Valmore (392), whom Nabokov describes as 'a kind of female Musset minus the color and the wit', Racine's *Phèdre* (392) and Vincent Campenon's 1805 *Almanach des Muses* (393).

The main intertext, however, comes from Rousseau's epistolary novel *Julie ou la Nouvelle Héloïse*, which is an exchange of letters between the eponymous heroin and her teacher, then love interest, Saint-Preux. Nabokov quotes two letters in particular (Letter IV and Letter XXVI); below, I insert in parentheses Nabokov's corresponding lines from his translation of Pushkin:

> (l. 5/7: But you, for my unhappy lot / keeping at least one drop of pity, / you'll not abandon me)
>
> See also in Julie's first long letter to Saint-Preux: '... si quelque étincelle de vertu brilla dans ton âme...' (Rousseau, Julie, pt. 1, Letter IV) (Pushkin [1975] 1991, II: 389);
>
> (l. 34: that is the will of heaven)
>
> Cf. Rousseau's Julie (Saint-Preux to Julie, pt. 1, Letter XXVI): 'Non... un éternel arrêt du ciel nous destina l'un pour l'autre...' (Pushkin [1975] 1991, II: 392);
>
> (l. 78: But to me your honor is a pledge)
>
> Cf. Rousseau, Julie (Julie's first long letter to Saint-Preux, pt. I, Letter IV): 'Toutefois... s'il y reste [in her correspondent's soul] encore quelque trace des sentiments d'honneur...' and '... mon honneur s'ose confier au tien...' (Pushkin [1975] 1991, II: 394)

As we will see, these letters will become crucial when it comes to terms of address in French and how to translate them into English.

Tatyana's letter was initially written in French, even if the original is never displayed, which confirms the status of the letter as a pseudotranslation. By reconstituting various sources for the text, Nabokov confirms that the absence of an original does not mean that nothing is at the origin of the text, and such elements can actually help reinforce the 'reality' of the translation for the reader. As I showed in my introduction to pseudotranslation, this is an argument that Gideon Toury often makes on what he calls here 'fictitious translations':

> By enhancing their resemblance to genuine translations, pseudo-translators simply make it easier for their textual creations to pass as translations without arousing too much suspicion.

> Interestingly enough, due to the practice of embedding features in fictitious translations which have come to be associated with genuine translations, it is sometimes possible to 'reconstruct' from a fictitious translation bits and pieces of a text in another language as a kind of an [*sic*] 'possible source text' – one that never enjoyed any textual reality, to be sure – as is the case with so many genuine translations whose sources have not (or not yet) been identified.
>
> (Toury 2005: 7)[35]

After having shown the French intertext underlying Tatyana's letter, Nabokov proceeds to recreate the missing French letter. To do so, he reverts to the 'original' language thanks to an interesting reversal of languages: he provides a back-translation of the letter (from the Russian to the French) by using four French translations of *Onegin* and he makes a collage of the best solutions ever published to render Tatyana's original. He indicates which translation he used thanks to initials, but he also inserts his own creations:

> In the literal French translation of Tatiana's letter given below, which, I repeat, slips beautifully into flat French, I have initialed the borrowed lines: Dupont [Du], Turgenev-Viardot [TV], Lirondelle [L], and David [Da]. The unitialed lines are my creation.
>
> (Pushkin [1975] 1991, II: 387)

Out of the seventy-nine lines, fourteen are Nabokovian creations, and one in particular shows links with his writing as an author. On line 75, '*Вся обомлела, запылала*', Tatyana describes her own feelings when she saw Onegin the first time thanks to two verbs expressing weakness and stupefaction (*obomlela*) and then passion and flames (*zapylala*). Nabokov comments on the line in the following way (once again, French and intertextuality are foregrounded):

> Tatiana has read the *Phèdre* (1677), I, iii, of Racine (who had read Virgil):
>
> Je le vis, je rougis, je pâlis à sa vue;
>
> Un trouble s'éleva dans mon âme éperdue;
>
> Mes yeux ne voyoient plus, je ne pouvais parler;
>
> Je sentis tout mon corps et transir et brûler

I have translated *obomléla* by 'felt all faint', but the latter lacks the melting and tremulous quality of the Russian term, which is somewhat better, but far from perfectly, rendered by the French *se pâmer* or *défaillir*. (Pushkin [1975] 1991, II: 392–3)

Nabokov navigates between languages and compares his own two translations of Pushkin's Russian, ranking the French one above the English one. However, his English version is highly praiseworthy: 'I felt all faint, I felt aflame' (Pushkin [1975] 1991, I: 166). On top of the euphonic alliteration in /f/, one notes the parallelism between 'all faint' and 'aflame', which are both iambs, thus creating a balanced iambic tetrameter. When comparing the Russian original (*Vsya obomlela, zapylala*) and Nabokov's English, one could even be tempted to deem the translation 'I felt all faint, I felt aflame' better than the original,[36] which is reminiscent of Pnin's preference for the 'sonorous' *plïla i pela, pela i plïla* over the original *Hamlet* (Nabokov [1957a] 1996: 353).

The word 'ablaze' has a particularly Nabokovian feel to it, as the author used it on several occasions in his American novels (in *Lolita*, *Pnin*, *Pale Fire* and *Ada*). Two occurrences in particular use a parallelism similar to that of Tatyana's letter: 'abloom and ablaze' in *Pnin* (Nabokov [1957a] 1996: 428), a novel hardly ever compared to *Onegin*, and in *Ada* (Part I, Chapter 19), 'she was fast ablaze–I mean, asleep' (Nabokov [1969] 1996: 92); this expression is evoked again in the next chapter, with 'asleep' *in absentia*, 'fast ablaze in her room' (102).

Priscilla Meyer was probably the first Nabokov critic who underlined the links between Tatyana's letter to Eugene and Charlotte Haze's letter to Humbert in *Lolita*, and even if she does not use the term 'pseudotranslation', her remarks are completely to the point and suggest that Humbert's letter can also be considered a pseudotranslation, be it intralingual:

The letters are reported to us by the novels' narrators, 'Pushkin' (who has a treasured copy of Tatyana's letter) and Humbert (who only remembers the letter). 'Pushkin' laments the fact that he has had to translate Tatyana's letter from the French due to the inability of young ladies to write in their native Russian; Humbert admits that the phrase 'vortex of the toilet' has crept into his transcription from his own lexicon.

(Meyer 1988a: 22)

Further on, Meyer underlines the presence of French in both letters, for example, Charlotte's '*mon cher, cher monsieur*' and '*Departez!*' (Meyer 1988a: 22) But the strongest argument to show that Tatyana's letter was a direct source of inspiration for Charlotte's letter lies in two words: 'я твоя' (I am yours). This declaration of love is probably the most famous quote in the whole of *Onegin*, and before clarifying the links with *Lolita*, it is essential to go back to its origins.

Being a respectable young lady, Tatyana addresses Onegin with the formal pronoun 'вы' (*vy*), but on l. 34, she suddenly resorts to the more intimate 'ты' (*ty*) to express her love for him. This alternation parallels the presence, in French, of similar pronouns: the formal 'vous', and the more personal 'tu', suggesting Tatyana switched from the former to the latter in the original French letter. She then reverts to the formal 'вы' (*vy*), when she manages to collect herself all over again. As Nabokov shows in his commentary, this alternation of pronouns is directly inspired from Rousseau's *Julie ou La Nouvelle Héloïse*:

> It is at this point that Tatiana switches from the formal second person plural to the passionate second person singular, a device well known in French epistolary novels at the time. Thus in her third short note to Saint-Preux Julie starts to *tutoyer* him, mingling the *tu* with *vous*. In Tatiana's letter the initial *vous* comes back only at the very end (l. 78, *vásha chést'*, 'your sense of honor').
>
> (Pushkin [1975] 1991, II: 392)

In his commentary, Nabokov reproduces all the correct pronouns in his French rendition of Tatyana's letter, thus alternating between '*vous*' and '*tu*'. What is particularly interesting is to see how these pronouns are translated, first in Nabokov's translation into English of Tatyana's letter, and then, how they are rendered in *Lolita*, be it the original version in English (1955), the Russian self-translation (1967) and the French translation that Nabokov contributed to (1959a). In that respect, Per Ambrosiani's article 'Translating forms of address in Nabokov's *Lolita*' is illuminating. However, he incorrectly states that

> Vladimir Nabokov, in his translation of *Evgenij Onegin* into English, does not attempt to recreate the shifts between *vy* and *ty* of the source text, although he is obviously aware of them.
>
> (Ambrosiani 2018: 279)

It is incorrect in so far as Nabokov translates the famous two words as 'I am thine' (Pushkin [1975] 1991, I: 166), thus departing from the use of the pronoun 'you'. If Nabokov does reproduce the Russian shifts (from *vy* to *ty*, and back to *vy*) in English with 'you', 'thine' and 'you', he fails to repeat the pronoun 'thee': 'thine' is used only once in the translation, whereas Tatyana uses *ty* for the last two thirds of her letter, before reverting to *vy* one last time. What Nabokov also fails to do is explain his translation choice; it is very surprising from a commentator who can write pages and pages about the intertextuality and the echoes he noticed (I mentioned earlier the two pages dedicated to the various shades of red of

Tatyana's beret). Here, however, he does not justify his choice to use 'thine' just this one time, and not 'thee', 'thy' or 'thine' afterwards. It is true that repeating 'thee' would probably be heavy in English, but Nabokov has repeated loud and clear that he did not aim at readability, but at literality. If the reader can perceive Tatyana's surge of emotions with 'I am thine', they have no idea what Pushkin's Russian was if they do not turn to the commentary.

As we know, in *Lolita*, only 'you' is used, so no trace of alternation between pronouns can confirm a link with Tatyana's letter. However, in the Russian self-translation of the novel, Charlotte oscillates between *vy* and *ty*, even if her pattern differs from that of Tatyana. Below, the markers like conjugation for *vy* are in bold type, and the ones for *ty* are in both bold type and underlined; the version of the 1955 text is given below for reference with the same typographical pointers:

Позволь**те** мне еще чуточку побредить и побродить мыслю, мой драгоценнейший; ведь я знаю, **вы** уже разорвал**и** это письмо, и его куски (неразборчиво) в водоворот клозета. Мой драгоценнейший, mon très, très cher, какую гору любви я воздвигла для **тебя** в течение этого магического июня месяца! Знаю, как **вы** сдержан**ны**, как много в **вас** « британского ». Возможно, что **вашу** старосветскую замкнутость, **ваше** чувство приличия, покоробит прямота бедной американочки! […] Мой дорогой, **твое** любопытство должно быть полностью удовлетворено, если **ты** пренебрег моею просьбой и дочитал это письмо до горького конца.

(Nabokov [1967] 2004: 72)

Let me rave and ramble on for a teeny while more, my dearest, since I know this letter has been by now torn by **you**, and its pieces (illegible) in the vortex of the toilet. My dearest, *mon très, très cher*, what a world of love I have built up for **<u>you</u>** during this miraculous June! I know how reserved **you** are, how 'British'. **Your** old-world reticence, **your** sense of decorum may be shocked by the boldness of an American girl! […] My dearest, **<u>your</u>** curiosity must be well satisfied if **<u>you</u>** have ignored my request and read this letter to the bitter end.

(Nabokov [1955a] 1996: 63)

Charlotte starts her letter with *vy*, just like Tatyana, but her alternation between the formal and the informal second pronouns is more reminiscent of Julie in Rousseau's epistolary novel ('mingling the *tu* with *vous*', as he explained in the commentary to *Onegin* (Pushkin [1975] 1991, II: 392)). Indeed, she uses the formal '*vy*' for the first half of the letter or so, then she uses the informal possessive adjective ('*tvoja*', the informal 'your') just once when she conjures up the 'world of love' she built for Humbert. She reverts to '*vy*' for the next three sentences, and after two sentences without any reference to her addressee 'you' (Charlotte is writing about her years with Mr Haze) which act as a neutral no-man's land so to speak, Charlotte switches back to '*ty*' and writes the last six sentences with this informal pronoun.

This choice of translation suggests two hypotheses: either it confirms that Charlotte's letter was directly inspired by Tatyana's letter (even if it was not visible in the original English), or it means that Nabokov decided to explore, in the Russian version of his novel, an intertextual reference that is so important for the Russian audience. It is true that this reference to Pushkin cannot be but lost on an American audience in 1955 (especially since Nabokov had not yet brought about his own translation of *Onegin* to his American readers), notwithstanding the fact that pronouns in English do not really allow such echoes. French, however, does. As I will show in the third part of this book, Nabokov took an important part in the French translation of *Lolita* by Eric Kahane, so much so that the French translation he collaborated to can be called a mediated self-translation. In the French *Lolita*, Nabokov also failed to play with '*vous*' and '*tu*', thus sticking to a very classical use of French, which is actually rather recurrent in his writing in French. Thus, Charlotte addresses Humbert as '*vous*' all along the letter, and never switches to '*tu*', even after they are married.[37] Nabokov is much more creative in his Russian translation: not only does he alternate pronouns in Charlotte's letter in an echo to Tatyana's letter, but he makes choices in his translation that are 'marked', to use Ambrosiani's terminology. As the researcher indicates, once they are married, Charlotte and Humbert use the pronoun '*ty*'. However, when Charlotte discovers Humbert's diary in Chapter 22, Nabokov makes an interesting change in pronouns and has Charlotte revert to '*vy*', which Ambrosiani describes as 'not expected in a married couple and [...] therefore [to] be seen as marked' (Ambrosiani 2018: 286).

What is particularly interesting in Nabokov's translation of Tatyana's letter is that it reveals the importance of intertextuality in his practice both as a translator and as an author. Indeed, in his translation of the embedded pseudotranslation that Tatyana's letter is, the crucial quality of French literature is foregrounded as Nabokov recreates the French originals, be it Tatyana's purported letter or its French sources, in order to scrupulously stick to them; however, the commentator's silence on his non-systematic use of 'thee' in his translation confirms that he was not always consistent in his literalist approach and that he sometimes let room to the author in him, not just the 'servile' translator. As an author and self-translator, Nabokov exploited the intertextual echoes that existed inside Russian literature on the one hand – between Pushkin's *Onegin* and his own Russian *Lolita* – and, on the other hand, in transnational literature – between Rousseau's *Julie*, Pushkin's *Onegin* and his own *Lolita*, be it in the American canon or in the Russian one.

Conclusion

All in all, Nabokov's translations of pseudotranslations, be it Pierre Louÿs's *Les Chansons de Bilitis*, Pushkin's *Skupoi rytsar'* or Tatyana's letter in *Onegin*, confirm that Nabokov's practice of translation evolved throughout the years from literary to literal translation, but some elements remained crucial all along. The main one is his respect for literatures of various countries, which he took into account in his own translations and novels. By foregrounding the back-and-forth movement between literary traditions in Pushkin and in his own oeuvre as a writer and translator, Nabokov underlined the importance of a shared international canon, beyond borders.

4

Nabokov's Pseudotranslations

Our exploration of Nabokov's relationship with pseudotranslation ends with the ones he actually wrote. Just like the pseudotranslations he encountered which nourished his fiction and the ones he translated, this device can be found in his work during his whole life: it started even before the beginning of his writing career as a prose writer in Russian with his first creation as Vivian Calmbrood in 1921, and it continued over the years, with the last blatant examples in the late 1950s, when he was already a renowned American writer.

I will be examining Nabokov's pseudotranslations chronologically. The first three are pseudotranslations which stand as individual, whole pieces: those are of course his two pseudotranslations as Vivian Calmbrood, but, wedged between them, one also finds a poem in Nabokov's own name which was supposed to be a translation from Heine. The following pseudotranslations were included by Nabokov in his novels, usually in the form of a letter (they are 'embedded' pseudotranslations, like Tatyana's letter from *Eugene Onegin*).

The issues raised by those particular letters will lead us to a much broader question about the status of Nabokov's novels in English, which will be discussed in the general conclusion to our three chapters on pseudotranslation.

Vivian Calmbrood: *The Wanderers* (Скитальцы)

If one looks at Nabokov's creations under the name of Vivian Calmbrood, it may look as if the main influence were Pushkin. Indeed, Nabokov pretended to have translated two pieces by Calmbrood, namely a passage from a play entitled *The Wanderers*, and a poem, 'The Night Journey', just as Pushkin had pretended to translate Shenstone's play *The Covetous Knight* and a poem by Pindemonte in 'Iz Pindemonti'. Therefore, inside the Russian influence, there is a European legacy, but it is not limited to the English literary tradition found in *The Covetous Knight* or the Italian one in the poem. Indeed, as I will show, German literature plays a significant role too, through Schiller's play *Die Räuber* (*The Robbers*), albeit tainted with French. I hope to show that Nabokov's transnational canon showed as early as his creations under the pseudonym 'Vivian Calmbrood'.

If every Nabokov scholar knows about Vivian Calmbrood as one of Nabokov's many anagrammes – usually overshadowed by the very well-known 'Vivian Darkbloom' – the actual contents of the two pieces written under this name is hardly ever studied, especially in research in English, even more so when it comes to *The Wanderers*; as we will see, 'The Night Journey' is a bit more studied because of the literary figures from the Russian emigration it conjures up.

Skytaltsy (Nabokov [1923] 1999) is presented as the Russian translation by Vladimir Sirin of the first act from *The Wanderers*, a play by English author Vivian Calmbrood. The Russian translation is about thirty-page-long, be it in its original publication,[1] or in its reprint in the Symposium edition; however, only a few lines were written about them, so it is useful to start by those.

As often, one needs only to turn to Brian Boyd's biography of Nabokov to find the crucial elements on its context of creation and on its plot:

> In late October and early November [1921], he wrote a playlet, 'Skital'tsy', and sent it to his parents as a translation of the first act of *The Wanderers*, by the English playwright Vivian Calmbrood, an anagram of his own name. Nabokov chose a safely misty past for his first attempt at drama. At a tavern two brothers meet: one who has roamed the world and longs to see his home again, the other who has remained in his native county but voyaged morally to the opposite pole, to become a brigand and a drunkard. The tavern-keeper's fair daughter, we guess, may save one of them or both, or become the ground for their fatal confrontation. V. D. Nabokov assumed that the translation was genuine and warned his son that his sheer love of literature might make him waste time translating works of no real interest. Had *The Wanderers* been a genuine English play of the late eighteenth or early nineteenth century, it certainly would not have warranted translation, but as the work of a twenty-two-year-old twentieth-century Russian it is an impressive exercise in literary impersonation.
>
> (Boyd 1990: 187)[2]

The main element of diegesis is here, namely two brothers who are opposed morally speaking, but I will further unravel the plot, specifically when it comes to the question of good and evil.

In Siggy Frank's book *Nabokov's Theatrical Imagination* (2012), one could have expected to find a lengthy study of Nabokov's first published play,[3] but there is not much more than the usual references to the anagramme, the pseudotranslation and the fact that Nabokov had considered taking up the play again a few years afterwards.[4] There are, however, some interesting elements which are laid out. The first one is that Frank is one of the few critics who made the connection between Calmbrood and Pushkin's *Covetous Knight* via the motif of pseudotranslation (as usual, the term is not used, but there are many references to it, as the words in bold type below show). The most compelling element, however, is the reference to Robin Hood, which unfortunately is not developed further:

> Nabokov wrote his first play (after 'In Spring'), *The Wanderers*, in 1921 during his time at Cambridge. The play, written under the anagrammatic pseudonym Vivian Calmbrood, **purports to be a translation** of the first act of an eighteenth-century English drama into Russian. Later, while working on his first full-length play, *The Tragedy of Mr Morn*, Nabokov considered taking up *The Wanderers* again: 'After Mr Morn [*sic*] I will write a second – final – act for "The Wanderers". Suddenly felt like it'. But the play remained in its fragmentary form. The reworking of the Robin Hood legend in the figure of the outlaw Robert as well as the choice of iambic pentameter, the staple measure of English verse drama, add authenticity to this **mock translation** of an English play. Neither the critics of the published version nor Nabokov's father doubted that the translation was genuine. Although the meter and the subject matter of Nabokov's *The Wanderers* lean towards English drama, its quality as a **mock translation** from English to Russian links it back to one of Pushkin's 'Little Tragedies', which **purports to be a Russian translation** of 'Scenes from Shenstone's tragicomedy: The Covetous Knight'. Nabokov returned to this little **hoax** much later in a poem which continues the initial **prank** in another **alleged translation** of Vivian Calmbrood.
>
> (Frank 2012: 23; bold type mine)

We will see that Frank's intuition is justified, even if the link with the figure of Robin Hood can seem to be rather flimsy. Frank alludes to the legend of Robin Hood rather than its use in Walter Scott's *Ivanhoe*, but it is interesting to see the Scottish writer return once again, albeit indirectly, in connection with pseudotranslation.

Another critic who has commented on *Skital'tsy* is Andrey Babikov, first in an article on 'Natasha' (Babikov 2006), and then in his notes to the play in a collection of Nabokov's plays, *Трагедия господина Морна. Пьесы. Лекции о драме* (Nabokov 2008b). Babikov has not written extensively on the play, but his findings on intertextuality and the motif of the hereafter are noteworthy. First of all, in both of his texts, the critic presents the Russian intertextuality underlying the text, more specifically references to poems by Pushkin and Blok, but it is only in his notes to the play that he mentions some European links. All of them concentrate on the theme of erring or voyaging conjured up by the title, *The Wanderers,* and show once again the centrality of literature in English for the young Nabokov:

> The date when the tragedy was written as designated by Nabokov sends us to L. Sterne's novel 'A Sentimental Journey Through France and Italy' (1768), the main title carries connotations of emigration crucial for the early work of Nabokov, and these connotations are typical of the English Gothic novel (for example, 'Melmoth the Wanderer' by [Irish playwright and novelist] Charles Maturin, 1820[5]) and of books on the Eternal Jew [in English, the Wandering Jew[6]] (for example, 'the dramatic legend' 'Ahasuerus the Wanderer' by [English writer and poet] Thomas Medwin, 1823).
>
> (Babikov in Nabokov 2008b; my translation, with some comments between square brackets)

When it comes to the hereafter, Babikov mentions in his article on 'Natasha' that *Skital'tsy* might contain the very first allusion to the theme of the hereafter (in Russian, *potustoronnost'*):

> In contrast to his story 'Natasha', the theme of the hereafter in the play is represented cautiously. The appearance of Silvia, held deeply in a somnambular trance, and footpad Robert's love for the lost girl that are revealed by the end of the story, allude to it.
>
> (Babikov 2006: n.p.)

One last element dug up by Babikov will prove very important in our study of the play. When Babikov describes the circumstances of this hoax in his notes to the play, he quotes a few excerpts from letters between Nabokov and his parents.[7] After asking his mother whether she liked 'Skital'tsy', Nabokov confesses:

> 'Скитальцы' is meant to look like a translation, так что я не жалею, мамочка, что вы были обмануты. (Babikov, notes, np.)
>
> 'Skital'tsy' is meant to look like a translation, so I'm not sorry, Mummy, that you were deceived. (my translation)

It is particularly interesting that Nabokov wrote the segment 'is meant to look like a translation' in English, because it thus looks like a *mise-en-abyme* of the whole ploy underlying pseudotranslation: English is thus foregrounded, but it is only 'meant to look like a translation'. In confessing to the intentionality of this text which sounds like a translation, Nabokov may have been willing to protect his ego when presenting one of his first creations in dramatic form, just in case it was judged bad (one remembers Nabokov's father used the expression 'works of no real interest'). It seems useful here to quote again Gideon Toury's argument that pseudotranslations are often used to introduce innovation in a literary system:

> From the evolutionary point of view, the most significant aspect of the production and distribution of TL [Target Language] texts as translations into TL is the fact that this strategy offers a convenient and relatively safe way of breaking with sanctioned patterns and introducing novelties into a culture, and not only in the realm of literature. Indeed, it has often been one of very few roads open to writers to divert from norms and traditions without arousing too much antagonism, especially in cultures which were highly resistant to innovations. Given the fact that translations tend to be assigned secondary functions with a cultural (poly)system, there can be no wonder that deviations occurring in texts assumed to have been translated often meet with greater tolerance, and for this very reason.
>
> (Toury 2012: 48–9)

Here, the argument could be revised to show that, on a personal level, it may have been easier for Nabokov to present his own innovation (writing drama) as a translation, thus hoping for greater tolerance. However, we will see that Nabokov's claim that *Skital'tsy* 'is meant to look like a translation' could have another layer of meaning to it, once again in relation to Schiller.

Now that the few existing critical elements have been gathered, let us delve into the pseudotranslation itself. The text starts with the references to the 'original' text:

Скитальцы
Вивиан Калмбруд
(Vivian Calmbrood)
1768 г. Лондон
Трагедия в четырех действиях

(Nabokov [1923] 1999: 647)

The bibliographical elements seem to be all there: the title (*The Wanderers*), the name of the author (Vivian Calmbrood), the date and place (1768, London) and the structure of the play (Tragedy in four acts). It is unclear for the Russian reader whether the alleged English play has been published or not (no publisher is mentioned), but one could trust that this original piece had only been written, not published, and that Sirin was making an unknown literary piece available to the public thanks to his translation, as Nabokov's father suspected his intention was.

The title itself could probably lend itself to very interesting research in terms of intertextuality; we will leave it to others to go down that path and will just list a few titles. As noted earlier, Babikov mentioned the theme of the Wandering Jew, 'Melmoth the Wanderer' (1820) and 'Ahasuerus the Wanderer' (1823); moreover, in his notes, he alludes to the poem 'Странствия' (*Stranstvija*) which Nabokov wrote in May 1921 (*The Wanderers* was composed in October–November 1921) and where the verb 'to wander' is used ('*Мне горько за тебя. Скитался долго ты*'; I feel sorry for you. You have wandered for a long time, my translation). Then, in his book on Nabokov's translations, Shvabrin mentions several interesting elements: in October 1917, Nabokov translated Emile Verhaeren's poem '*Les Voyageurs*' into Russian, '*Stranniki*', which, just like the word '*skital'tsy*', means 'Wanderers' and is translated as such by Shvabrin (2019: 43). The word '*skitalets*' (wanderer) is introduced by Nabokov into his Russian translation of the following lines taken from a poem by Charles Lamb, 'The Old Familiar Faces':

> Ghost-like, I paced round the haunts of my childhood.
> Earth seemed a desert I was bound to traverse,
> Seeking to find the old familiar faces.

The original poem does not use the word 'wanderer', but Nabokov translates 'I was bound to traverse' by '*я был скитальцем*' ('I was a wanderer') (Shvabrin 2019: 123[8]), which Shvabrin explains by astutely linking the image of the desert to emigration:

> For Nabokov, Lamb's sad hyperbole 'Earth seemed a desert I was bound to traverse' was more than a rhetorical figure – as an émigré, he had first-hand acquaintance with the meaning of the word 'traverse' in the sense that Lamb uses in his poem.
>
> (Shvabrin 2019: 123)

Leaving aside the theme of wandering, I will now concentrate on the elements that have to do with translation and the transnationality of Nabokov's work, especially the links with Schiller's play.[9]

When looking at the plot of *The Wanderers*, one can see that the names of the characters and places all have an English ring to them, thus suggesting that the play was indeed the translation of an English text. The first act starts with 'Stretcher' (*Стретчер*) who enters the inn belonging to 'John Colville' (*Джон Колвил*), which is situated not far from 'Gloomy Glen' or 'Starfield[10]'. Stretcher explains that he was attacked by a robber and escaped death only by chance as the robber was apparently drunk and did not shoot properly. Colville says that he was once attacked by the same man, but he was spared when he mentioned he had a daughter, 'Sylvia' (*Сильвия*). In exchange for his life, he now has an agreement with the robber: he can come to the inn to eat and sleep for free whenever he wants, and he does so about eight times a month. Afterwards, a traveller (*проезжий*) knocks on the door, and his voice makes Colville think it is the robber, even though the way he knocks is different. The traveller has a little friendly chat with the owner and explains that, after years of absence exploring distant countries, he is going back to his house in Starfield. Just as he says that indeed, happiness lies at home, someone knocks at the door three times: this time, it is the robber (*разбойник*). After addressing the innkeeper in a rude, but apparently usual, way, he tells him he is once again escaping the woods and their dark magnificence to have a feast at the inn, and he confesses he is already drunk. He then goes to speak to the traveller, and ends up asking him how long he has been 'wandering' (*давно ли / скитаетесь?*), and when the traveller answers 'seventeen years', the robber asks him if he is married; he is not, but he has parents and two brothers in Starfield. The innkeeper mentions that they have similar voices, and the robber seems to put two and two together since he asks the traveller his name: he is called Eric (*Эрик*) and the robber is called 'Robert' (*Роберт*), and they are long-lost brothers. Their first names are very English, and it is also the case of their family name, *Фаэрнэт* (Fairknight? Firenight?). Eric launches into a recollection of their past that is full of idealized pastoral images: he thinks he sees the reddening roof of their family home and hears the unforgettable, so sweet crackling of the gate as it is pushed open hastily; he evokes the snails after a golden rain and the dancing rabbits on the wet paths. It is only then that he asks Robert about their parents and their brother David, and Robert does not answer but asks Colville to say who he is. Colville tries to soften the blow of the truth, but Robert threatens him and Colville ends up saying that he is a killer. Robert insists: he is a murderer! (*'Убийца я!'*) He repeats it several times but Eric will not believe him: he once again conjures up pastoral memories and explains that once (in a distant land, on the bank of a river with an unknown source, on a blue-and-gold day, my translation) he was surrounded by five highwaymen, but when they saw his locket with the image of his younger brothers in it (Robert, 8, David, 6), they spared him. Robert pretends that Eric's speech moved him, that he is a mix of good and evil, but surely his brother, having seen the wide world, has seen God, and he also wants to see Him! He begs his brother to give him all this knowledge he has acquired abroad, and acclaims this meeting of theirs, good and evil, ugliness with beauty. Eric answers that his brother is clearly agitated, but he conjures up the memory of their past and says they should stop wandering the world and go home together. He then thinks Robert is crying, realizes he is in fact laughing and that he was making fun of him the whole time. Eric says that clearly, Robert's soul is dead and wonders what he will say at home, to which Robert says that maybe Eric will not find anyone, maybe they are all dead, or maybe he is lying. Offended by such an awful attitude, Eric leaves and hastens to go back home, leaving Robert with the innkeeper. Robert enquires about Sylvia and says he likes her. When Colville is sceptical, Robert gets angry: does he think Robert cannot love a woman? Maybe he has some good deep inside? When Colville insists on refusing to give away his daughter, Robert is about to kill him, he is already aiming at him but Sylvia enters the room, sleepwalking. She is muttering endearing terms, apparently about the robber: how cold he must be in the woods, he is knocking and yes she will open the door to him, but alas it is too late, he is gone, or is he really? Colville takes her back to her room, and Robert is now alone. He says that she is pure, but he is a miserable beast, a sinner. His whole life is made of fog, screams and blood, but in his darkness, there shines, similar to moonlight, love. And the first – and only – act finishes there.

Calmbrood's *The Wanderers* was supposed to be a play written in English, and there are indeed many intertextual links with English literature, even though they are not very strong. The theme of two brothers who fail to recognize one another has been exploited in comedies, for example, by Shakespeare (*A Comedy of Errors* and *Twelfth Night*), but the genre is here that of tragedy. When it comes to the question of good and evil, one is tempted to think of Robin Hood, who is supposed to steal from the rich and give to the poor (this theme is exploited in the legend rather than in the original story by Walter Scott), but Robert is nothing like him, even if there seems to be some good left in Robert. After all, he spared Colville when he heard of Sylvia, just as the highwaymen spared Eric when they realized he had two young brothers. However, one does find in *Ivanhoe* (and in the legend of Robin Hood) two estranged brothers who are ethically very different: Richard the Lionheart is the good brother whereas Prince John is portrayed as the evil one. But actually, one has to look at a previous intertext to understand why Scott seems to be prevailing in *The Wanderers*.

Indeed, as far as intertextuality goes, there are more convincing links if one looks at German literature: Schiller's first play, *Die Räuber* (*The Robbers*), was written in 1781 and was immensely successful throughout Europe, so much so that it was translated into many languages and impacted many writers, including Walter Scott,[11] who translated several plays from the German, including one play by Schiller.[12] The intertextual link between Nabokov's Russian pseudotranslation and Schiller's *Die Räuber* seems to be confirmed by the fact that, in Russian, the title of Schiller's play is *Разбойники*; the singular form of this word, '*разбойник*[13]', is precisely what Robert is called before he tells his brother his name.

The play by Schiller tells the story of two very different brothers. The older one, Karl, lives a dissolute life in Leipzig and the younger brother, Franz, has stayed with their father in the family castle. Karl intends to come back to redeem himself (the play was initially meant to be entitled *The Prodigal Son* (Frantz 2008: 226)) but his brother steals Karl's letter and rewrites a new, very negative one, and he criticizes his brother so much that their father rejects Karl, who becomes a highwayman, takes the head of a band of robbers who take revenge for some crimes that justice has left unpunished. Franz takes over the castle and leaves his father to starve in an old tower. When Karl comes back in a disguise, Franz recognizes him and tries to kill him, but Karl manages to free his dad and Franz kills himself. Their father dies and Karl turns himself in.

Thematically speaking, one can notice that the figure of the father has disappeared (but the estranged father and his son is reminiscent of the pseudotranslation that Nabokov translated, *Skupoi Rytsar'*); however, the opposition between the two brothers remain, especially revolving around the tension between good and evil.

Several elements point to an influence by Schiller on Nabokov's play, but I will focus on those related to translation. Leland de la Durantaye has claimed that Schiller was 'a writer Nabokov never showed any special interest in and which we are not even sure he ever read' (2013: 602); this argument was used to disprove Thomas Karshan's claim that the name of Lolita's husband, Richard Schiller, was an allusion to Friedrich Schiller. Nabokov may have had little interest for Schiller's writings, but he mentions him in connection with translation. Indeed, he makes a reference to Schiller in his essay 'The Art of Translation' to praise a translation made by Zhukovski[14]:

> We can deduce now the requirements that a translator must possess in order to be able to give an ideal version of a foreign masterpiece. First of all, he must have as much talent, or at least the same kind of talent, as the author he chooses. In this, though only in this, respect Baudelaire and Poe or Zhukovski and Schiller made ideal playmates.
>
> (Nabokov [1941a] 2008: 8)

Nabokov's interest in translations of Schiller is important because a French adaptation of Schiller's play bears striking resemblances with *The Wanderers*. It is also interesting when we remember that Nabokov wanted his translation to read like a translation. If there is indeed no original by Vivian Calmbrood for the pseudotranslation penned by the young Nabokov, one may look for another original and its translations, namely Schiller's play and its translations or adaptations.

One thing we can notice as far as resemblances and differences go is that the name of the highwayman is not an English version of Karl (Charles for example), but Robert. Here, it could be a phonic echo to the title in German (*Räuber*) or in English (*The Robber(s)*), but it is more compelling to turn our eyes towards French literature.[15] Indeed, 'Robert' is the name of the brother in a French version of Schiller's play which is entitled *Robert Chef de brigands* (La Martelière [1792] 1793). The author was a French writer of German descent who studied in Germany with Schiller and his name was Jean-Henri La Martelière (Bourdin 2011: 53). But as Pierre Frantz explains in his article on Schiller's play in France, this text (whose title Frantz misspells) was not really a translation, but rather an adaptation of Schiller's play:

> A young Alsatian man of letters, Schwingdenhammer, who takes the 'Frenchified' name La Martelière (1761–1830), gives his own translation, which he cuts from a lot and *adapts* to French taste. […] It is performed under the title *Robert Chef des brigands* [*Robert Head of the Robbers*] (sometimes *Robert et Maurice ou Les Brigands* [*Robert and Maurice or The Robbers*]) on March 10, 1792 […]. *Robert* roughly follows Schiller's play scene by scene. The author removes a lot, moves the accents, makes the ideology Republican. However, one finds in it, for the most part, the main features of the personalities and Schiller always remains legible beneath this palimpsest.

(Frantz 2008: 221; my translation)

The French play differs from Schiller's *Die Räuber* in many respects. For example, it focuses more on idealism and bears strong links with the ideals of the French Revolution, and it leaves aside the psychological and poetical considerations one could find in Schiller's play (Bourdin 2011: 63). It also insists on the Robin Hood theme more than Schiller's play did (Bourdin 2011: 64). For example, when a man called Rosinsky wants to join the group of robbers, their rules are stated explicitly:

ROBERT

Et! Quel est ton dessein?

ROSINSKY

D'obéir à tes ordres, de vous suivre, de protéger avec vous le foible contre la tyrannie des grands, si telle est votre institution.

ROBERT

Oui, ce sont nos statuts.

(La Martelière [1792] 1793]: 36)

ROBERT
So! What is your goal?

ROSINSKY
To follow your orders, to follow you all, to protect with you the feeble against the tyranny of the great, if such is your institution.

ROBERT
Yes, those are our statuses. (my translation)

But in the German play, the robbers were not completely good:

> In Schiller's play, they threw into the fire a child who was cold; in La Martelière's, they got their beards burnt to save the child from the flames and give him to a nurse.
>
> (Bourdin 2011: 72; my translation)

The French version of Schiller's play is therefore quite different from the original. Actually, it does not pretend to be a translation as such: indeed, on the front page of the published play, the title *Robert Chef de Brigands* is followed by the indication '*imité de l'allemand*' (imitated from the German) with no indication of Schiller's name; likewise, La Martelière does not mention the German playwright once in his foreword, but everyone knew its origin. This very free adaptation is actually not really an exceptional feature: indeed, it is an overwhelming tendency of the time, since the seventeenth and eighteenth centuries are well-known for '*Belles Infidèles*', that is, translations that are beautiful, but rather unfaithful, adaptations. It is also typical of translations and adaptations of Schiller's *Robbers*, in which changes of names and plots abound.[16] The tendency to translate this text very freely makes it all the more plausible that Nabokov's pseudotranslation could pass for an actual translation of Schiller's play: it was, after all, 'meant to look like a translation'.

Nabokov was going to use the figure of Vivian Calmbrood one more time for another pseudotranslation, his poem 'The Night Journey'. But before that, he wrote another pseudotranslation which took its origin, once again, in German literature.

Heine: 'The Ring'

The various connections existing between Nabokov and Heinrich Heine have been extensively studied by Shvabrin in his 2013 paper 'Nabokov and Heine' and some elements are included in various other works by him. This section will therefore quote from Shvabrin's work abundantly, and I will focus primarily on pseudotranslation and borderline cases between translation and writing.

The pseudotranslation '*Кольцо*' ('The Ring') was written on 12 July 1923, if one is to believe the date indicated at the bottom of this poem found in the Nabokov papers. However, Nabokov worked on Heine earlier than 1923. First, in September 1918, Nabokov translated six *lieder* (songs, in German) by the German poet (even if only five of them survived). As Shvabrin explains when he describes 'Russian Heineana', translating or adapting from Heine was rather common in Russia:

> No other foreign poet inspired a comparable number of Russian adaptations, imitations, and parodies, compelling his countless Russian admirers to creativity, whatever the quality of those productions may have been.
>
> (Shvabrin 2019: 58)

Nabokov translated Heine in September 1918, so exactly a month after he translated Pierre Louÿs's pseudotranslation *Les Chansons de Bilitis*. So his translations of Heine's poetry imply Nabokov knew the German poet's work well, but it also gives credit to the idea that his text 'The Ring' was yet another translation, and not a creation: the strategy was perfect to ensure the success of this pseudotranslation.

Another Nabokov-Heine encounter occurred before the 1923 poem, and this time, it is on the side of creation, not translation: on 24 February 1920, Nabokov wrote a poem entitled '*Подражанье Гейне*' ('Imitation of Heine') (quoted in Shvabrin 2013: 394), and its topic is the moon, which travels in the sky while the poetic persona evokes the singing of his heart. It is important to clarify the date and the topic of this 'Imitation of Heine' because another poem bears this name in English in Nabokov's repertoire. Indeed, in the mid-1940 (1944–6), Nabokov translated a poem by Lermontov into English and entitled it 'Imitation of Heine'. The 'original' poem was written by Lermontov in Russian in 1841 and deals with a pine tree that dreams of a palm tree far away. The inverted commas are necessary around 'original' because Lermontov's poem was actually inspired by Heine: its title is '*Сосна (Из Гейне)*' (The Pine Tree, from Heine),[17] which shows that Lermontov also took part in the Russian Heineana which Shvabrin was describing. As noted by Connolly, Nabokov insisted on the Heine intertextuality, rather than on the pine tree, when he chose the title for its English translation. He slightly adapted the translation of *Из Гейне*, 'from Heine', and rendered it as 'Imitation of Heine'. On the contrary, the English translation that Shvabrin chose for Nabokov's poem '*Подражанье Гейне*' is a more faithful translation, since the noun '*Подражанье*' comes from the verb '*подражать*' which literally means 'to imitate'.

The expression *Из Гейне*, 'from Heine', is the second part in the title of the poem written by Lermontov ('The Pine Tree'), but it is also the second part in the title of Nabokov's poem. Indeed, it is entitled 'Кольцо. *Из Гейне*' ('The Ring. From Heine'). However, if there is a German original for Lermontov's adaptation (*Ein Fichtenbaum steht einsam…* [18]), there is not for Nabokov's text: 'The Ring' is a pseudotranslation.

In this poem, composed of 9 stanzas of 4 lines each, mostly in alternate rhymes, the poetic persona imagines how he will wake up on the day when the woman he loves will be getting married to another man; he imagines he will recall fond memories and then he will whistle, which will cause the ring that is supposed to sanctify the marriage to slip from the woman's finger and roll until it reaches the forsaken man, who will then have the ring in his hand, where it will melt, and the poetic persona will thus say goodbye to his memories of past happiness with this woman.

Aside from the supernatural dimension of the poem, the story is very close to the breakup that Nabokov had to go through a few months before writing this poem. Indeed, on 9 January 1923, his engagement to Svetlana Siewert was broken up by her parents because Nabokov had failed to secure a steady job (Boyd 1990: 202). Here, the pseudotranslation could have been a means for Nabokov to protect his own hurt feelings. This is what Shvabrin writes of the autobiographical dimension of the poem:

> Taking on the role of a vaguely Heinean lyrical persona […], 'Kol'co' employs the generic conventions of Heine's confessional verse as a means of protective mimesis, disguising its sheer topicality and autobiographical relevance.
>
> (Shvabrin 2013: 401)

This is one more example (with *The Wanderers*) that ·the device of pseudotranslation can be used in a more emotional perspective for a budding author.

In his article, Shvabrin explains what traits can seem to confirm that the poem was originally written by Heine:

> Superficially, 'Kol'co' displays a number of features familiar to the reader of Heine's poetry. Apart from the presence of a generic brokenhearted lover reminiscent of the 'lyrical hero' of Heinean – and Blokian – poetry, the poem's ballad-like form can be said to evoke that of the longer narrative pieces opening

Buch der Lieder in the section entitled 'Youthful Sorrows' ('Junge Leiden').
The 'I' of these poems often finds himself dreaming of the beloved, whose
marriage to another is likened to a funeral or even a burial, as the imagery of
a phantasmagoric, infernal carnival rages in the background. 'Kol'co's cyclical
composition is not without parallel in Heine's poetry, although it is safe to say
that with the exception of his early experiments with the sonnet, Heine prefers
not to be bound by such rigid formal or compositional constraints.

(Shvabrin 2013: 400)

Shvabrin also underlines the features which, on the contrary, are quite unlike
Heine; thus, he suggests other influences among Russian poetry, like Fet, or
some prosodic elements which are distinctively Nabokovian (Shvabrin 2013:
400). Therefore, this poem has a literary heritage which is both Russian and
German, and in the Nabokov realm, it shows some definite ties with translation
(Heine and Lermontov, who are also German and Russian) and with literary
creation (his piece from 1920 as well as 'The Ring').

Nabokov produced another poem which was in fact a pseudotranslation.
Once again, he pretended to have translated a piece by Vivian Calmbrood, 'The
Night Journey', but here, his use of pseudotranslation has more layers to it than
his *Wanderers*.

Vivian Calmbrood: 'The Night Journey' (Из Калмбрудовой поэмы 'Ночное путешествие')

Despite being much shorter than the first Calmbrood piece, this poem has given
rise to a much more extensive number of commentaries, especially because of
the role it played in the émigré literary scene. But first, let us quickly explain
the plot. The occasional quotes indicate English-sounding words that can point
to an English source-text in the Cyrillic text, thus confirming (deceptively) the
status of translation.

The poetic persona explains that the journey he often makes from Merryfield
to Oldtrove ('*От Меррифильда до Ольдтрова*', in which 'Merryfield' is
reminiscent of 'Starfield' in *The Wanderers*) is rather dull, but on that autumn
night, instead of the dozen fellow travellers who usually snooze and snore next
to him in the diligence (*дилижанс*), there is only one man who is apparently
bent on having a chat. He is a bit plump, wears glasses, a coat and a plaid (*в
[…] пледе*) and starts to tell his story. One day, his publisher asked him to
come meet him, and thus he had to leave the place where he had been staying

since Whitsun and asks his fellow traveller to picture to himself the mirror-like river, the birches and the slope covered in heather where he was writing a little play taking place in the days of knights. He went fishing with his neighbour Wordsworth ('*с соседом, с молодым Вордсвортом*') and he was happy there, so he reluctantly dragged himself to London with his manuscript. He says that he manages to be precise in the service of his lyrical muse, but in the London filth, rhymes escape him, everything is heavy and trembles. He opposes his joyful, lyrical writing in the country to the darkness one finds in the city; he explains that the days of Juvenal are gone and that in an article, they have beaten up Johnson with a candlestick ('*побили Джонсона шандалом*'). He says that he has fallen out of grace in the eyes of another critic when he said that he thought his melancholy was funny, he found his nepotism sentimental, etc., but this poor fellow's bones are screeching and he is bending his Adam's head over the abyss of the tomb. More importantly, nowadays, poets speak of death a lot, their attire is made of a crown and a robe. Petronius is half-smiling, and the time of death is nigh, but wait! Before cutting one's wrists, why not turn towards the soap and clean up just this once?

The fellow traveller stops talking, and the poetic persona reflects that he did not understand everything in this literary discussion. He writes not badly himself, so why would he care about another's poem? But this profile reminds him of someone, and as the sun rises and the obscurity starts to fade away, he thinks he recognizes some features in the man sharing the carriage with him. He asks him his name, and the fellow poet answers 'I'm Chenston', after which there is a line break and the two poets embrace.

The poem starts and ends with the poetic persona, but most of the text is actually Chenston talking, with inverted commas that clearly distinguish his share of the text from the embedding discourse of the poetic persona. Nabokov used the spelling 'Chenston', thus clearly reproducing Pushkin's spelling mistake in his pseudotranslation *Skupoi Rytsar*'; as Nabokov was actually speaking in Pushkin's stead, it seems normal that he should spell, like Pushkin, 'Chenston' and not the name 'Shenstone' that Nabokov knew to be the correct one. In 'The Night Journey', Pushkin's *Covetous Knight* (or rather his Chenston's *Skupoi rytsar*') is evoked rather directly: '*драму небольшую / писал из рыцарских времен*'; a little play / I was writing from the times of knights, my translation). The reference to Pushkin's famous pseudotranslation is particularly ironic and seems to be pointing to the fact that the poem 'The Night Journey' is yet another pseudotranslation. Irony seems to be a prevailing trait in this second Calmbrood piece, but I first need to explain the literary feud hiding behind it.

By referring to 'Johnson', Nabokov is not referring to a British man with that name (like Samuel Johnson, whom I evoked in connection with Macpherson in Chapter 1, or one of the characters in Nabokov's Russian play *The Pole*, written in 1923); rather, as many critics have already underlined, it is a faintly disguised attack against critic and prominent poet Ivanov:

> The poem has already taken a swipe at Ivanov in the person of 'Johnson' (the English equivalent of 'Ivanov'), a critic trounced with a candlestick for a 'marked [as in cards] article': none other than Ivanov's much-deplored *Chisla* attack on Sirin.
>
> (Boyd 1990: 370)

In his text, Nabokov is also critical of Georgy Adamovich who, like Ivanov, is present in a disguised way. In Nabokov's biography, Boyd translates '*он клонится к могильной яме / адамовою головой*' as 'he inclines over the grave pit / his Adamic head' and explains in a note: 'A pun on Adamovich and "Adamova-golova," idiomatically "skull," literally "Adamic head"' (Boyd 1990: 370). The reason why Adamovich and Ivanov were targeted is that they were opposed to Nabokov and Khodasevich in a debate

> over Pushkin's legacy, which developed in the late 1920s and early 1930s in the émigré press. The polemic put into focus the fate of Russian poetry in exile and questioned the vitality of Pushkin's model for Russian literature in the future. G. Adamovich and V. Khodasevich, the two deans of Russian letters in the diaspora, found themselves on opposite sides of the conflict. Adamovich, the leader of the Paris group, called for a turn away from Pushkin. He accused Pushkin of lapidary simplicity, formal perfection, and a lack of concern for content, and, furthermore, declared Pushkin's poetic model inadequate to express the complexity of the modern world and to capture the increasingly introspective human soul. Adamovich questioned Nabokov's mission of keeping Pushkin's tradition alive [...]. Much to Khodasevich's and Nabokov's dismay, the Paris group found Pushkin's verbal perfection 'suspicious', 'empty', and urged young poets to embrace Lermontov's soul-searching rhetoric and the 'inelegant' manner of Pasternak. The Parisian almanac *Chisla (Numbers)*, which boycotted Khodasevich and regularly assaulted Nabokov, became the main tribune for the anti-Pushkin campaign. Nabokov did not participate directly in this critical polemic, yet he missed no opportunity to cross swords with Pushkin's calumniators in his fictional works.
>
> (Davydov 1995: 484–5)

In his pseudotranslation 'The Night Journey', Nabokov (under the mask of Vivian Calmbrood) clearly sides with Pushkin (under the mask of Chenston), and he shows them embracing; as Boyd has written, 'Sirin allies himself with Pushkin' (Boyd 1990: 370). So through the fiction of pseudotranslation, Nabokov and Pushkin are united through their literary doubles.

It is well-known that Nabokov played tricks to Ivanov and Adamovich in several texts, in a way which is reminiscent of Pushkin, thus adding irony to injury:

> Nabokov's hoaxes in which he mocked, under various pseudonyms, Georgy Adamovich and his Paris followers ('From a Poem by Calmbrood', 'The Poets', 'Vasiliy Shishkov') call to mind Pushkin's delightful invention of Feofilakt Kosichkin under whose name in 1831 Pushkin fooled his arch-enemy Faddei Bulgarin.
>
> (Davydov 1995: 483)

Boyd has already underlined that humour was present in the hoax of 'The Night Journey':

> But there was also a much more playful side to the poem. Sirin read it in the Poets's Club, prefacing the reading of his 'translation' with a few trumped-up biographical details about Calmbrood. Afterward he confessed to the hoax, which had taken everybody in – just as his 'translation' from a 'Calmbrood' play had foxed his father ten years earlier.
>
> (Boyd 1990: 371)

The fact that Nabokov quickly confessed underlines that he did not do much to hide that his text was a hoax; this is the first element that shows the deeply ironic dimension of the poem. The irony found in some pseudotranslations tends to be disregarded, but the truth is that some authors were rather vocal on the fact that they had produced a pseudotranslation. Other borderline cases include texts in which the disguise was easily recognizable, like Pushkin's *The Tales of the Late Ivan Petrovich Belkin*: as I mentioned in the previous chapter, the editor's initials, 'A. P.', easily pointed to Pushkin, who was the real author and was not trying very hard to hide his identity and probably did so in a tongue-in-cheek manner. In the second Calmbrood pseudotranslation, Nabokov seems to be hiding in plain sight in the same way. The most compelling detail is probably the fact that Nabokov resorts to the fictitious figure of Chenston, from a text which is famous for being a pseudotranslation. And then there are a few subtle hints, but they can add up pretty quickly for the reader who suspects something is amiss: first, Nabokov had already used the device previously and he had revealed its true nature afterwards (even if we can suspect that it was not an anecdote that was shared widely among the émigré community); then, the name 'Vivian

Calmbrood' is an anagramme that is not that hard to decipher, and 'Calmbrood' could suggest a pun, a joke, since it is similar to the French word 'calembour'. One last element seems to be pointing towards a link between *The Wanderers* and 'The Night Journey': they both make a veiled reference to a specific type of lepidoptera. Indeed, in the play, Stretcher explains that the robber missed when he shot him, so he must have been drunk because he was tottering like a roisterer ('*как **бражник** он качался!*'), but the word '*бражник*' means both a roisterer and a hawkmoth (*Sphingidae* in Latin). In the poem, similar polysemy can be found in the following lines: '*он клонится к могильной яме / **адамовою головой***'. As mentioned earlier, Boyd translated *Адамова голова* (literally death's head or skull) as 'Adamic head' to show the pun behind which Adamovich was hiding, but this expression also designates a genus inside the Sphingidae family, that is to say the death's head hawkmoth (*Acherontia* in Latin).[19] Thus, this discreet sign can confirm a link between the two Calmbrood pieces and point to Nabokov with the reference to moths. This lepidoptera can be understood as a metaphor for the instability of identity that one can find in pseudotranslation, between author and translator.[20]

As far as pseudotranslation is concerned, there are two levels at which this device can be interpreted. Inside Nabokov's work, the two Calmbrood texts used different strategies. For the play, it was probably a way for Nabokov to test the reception of his dramatic work at the beginning of his attempts in this genre; on the other hand, the poem was written when Nabokov did not need to find confirmation of his poetic talent by anyone since he already had quite a literary reputation in the émigré community: it was rather the ironic dimension of pseudotranslation which Nabokov conjured up in his run-on hoax against Ivanov and Adamovich. More broadly, the Calmbrood pseudotranslations can play another role inside Russian literature. Indeed, not only was Russian literature divided in two branches after the Russian Revolution, with Soviet literature on one side and émigré literature on the other, but émigré literature was also at a risk to be divided between those who wanted to follow in the footsteps of Pushkin and those who felt this writer was outdated. In this perspective, it is interesting to see that, for Ronald Jenn, pseudotranslation was a means for American writers to take their distance with English literature:

> If imitating the transfer from one language into another (interlingual translation) is perceived as a means to take a shortcut towards literary consecration on the international scale, it needs to be said that, in the specific case of American authors, pseudo-translation could also be a convenient way to create another divide, but this time within the language.

Indeed, it is possible to hypothesize that, if 19th-century American literature is indeed in the process of taking shape, it is met with a particular difficulty: if it wants to distinguish itself from English literature, with which it shares the same language, and if it wants to be more assertive, it needs to cross the barrier of the common language. […] In fact, American authors find themselves faced with the impossibility to produce a pseudotranslation in British English. This impossibility to get rid of the English language and literature may have turned pseudotranslation into a symbolic means for American writers to take their distance with it. Pseudotranslations from Spanish with Irving or from French with Hawthorne and Clemens are not so much a kind of homage or reaction towards some heritage or a threat coming from Spain or France (even if this dimension cannot be completely excluded), they are the second-best solution in which English is inscribed in a disguised way.

(Jenn 2013: 121; my translation)

If American authors used pseudotranslation to take some distance with the literature of their past (English literature), I argue that Nabokov used it on the contrary to reaffirm his attachment to the Russian literature of his own past and its main figure, Pushkin. Indeed, he reproduced Pushkin's practice of pseudotranslation (a poem and a play) with his own Calmbrood pieces, showing himself to be Pushkin's heir within Russian literature. Moreover, in those texts which were supposed to be English in origin, he reinscribed Pushkin, be it through the figure of Chenston in the poem 'The Night Journey', but also in *The Wanderers*, in which Sylvia paraphrases Pushkin ('*нет счастия на свете*', Nabokov [1923] 1999: 650), thus making the Russian bard all pervasive. And by insisting on the links between Pushkin and European literature in his own pseudotranslations or in the translations he made of Pushkin's pseudotranslations, Nabokov showed that Pushkin was far from being restricted to a Russia of the past, but he proved that it was actually a lively legacy that one could reactivate in new texts and translations.

Let us now look at much later pseudotranslations, namely those which Nabokov included inside his novels in the form of letters.

Nabokov's embedded pseudotranslations: Letters in his novels

Several of Nabokov's novels include embedded pseudotranslations. Among his Russian novels, I have already mentioned the letter that Herman writes in chapter 7 of *Despair*[21] as well as the theory, which Barabtarlo put forward in his 1993 book, arguing that *Invitation to a Beheading* (as a whole, not as a letter) is a pseudotranslation.[22] Let us look at the most glaring examples of pseudotranslations as letters in Nabokov's novels in English, more specifically in *The Real Life of Sebastian Knight* and *Pnin*. Those two novels are particularly interesting in connection with Nabokov himself and how he could play with his representation as a Russian and/or American writer. After a whole career as a Russian writer, Nabokov wrote his first novel in English with *The Real Life of Sebastian Knight* (1941), where the plot revolves around a Russian narrator, V., who investigates the life of his half-brother with a specific agenda: showing Sebastian was not the English author everyone took him for but was or could have been a Russian writer. As for *Pnin*, it contrasts two Russian teachers living in the United States: the main character, Pnin, is shown to have a shaky mastery of English and to be somewhat ridiculous, especially at the beginning of the novel; the other character, who gradually turns out to be the narrator, is represented as extremely gifted and ends up taking Pnin's teaching position on campus. These two novels play with the theme of doubles as well as with the unreliability of the narrator. In this context, the device of pseudotranslation is particularly interesting.

In *Pnin*, the narrator discloses the letter that the eponymous character wrote to Liza in order to confess to his love (she gave it to the narrator, thus hoping to push him into marrying her):

The letter has by chance remained among my papers. Here it is:

'I am afraid you will be pained by my confession, my dear Lise' (the writer, though using Russian, called her throughout by this French form of her name, in order, I presume, to avoid both the too familiar 'Liza' and the too formal 'Elizaveta Innokentievna'). *'It is always painful for a sensitive* (chutkiy) *person to see another in an awkward position. And I am definitely in an awkward position.*

'You, Lise, are surrounded by poets, scientists, artists, dandies. The celebrated painter who made your portrait last year is now, it is said, drinking himself to death (govoryat, spilsya) *in the wilds of Massachusetts. Rumour proclaims many other things. And here I am, daring to write to you.*

'I am not handsome, I am not interesting, I am not talented. I am not even rich. But Lise, I offer you everything I have, to the last blood corpuscle, to the last tear, everything. And, believe me, this is more than any genius can offer you because a genius needs to keep so much in store, and thus cannot offer you the whole of himself as I do. I may not achieve happiness, but I know I shall do everything to make you happy. I want you to write poems. I want you to go on with your psychotherapeutic research – in which I do not understand much, while questioning the validity of

what I can understand. Incidentally, I am sending you under separate cover a pamphlet published in Prague by my friend Professor Chateau, which brilliantly refutes your Dr Halp's theory of birth being an act of suicide on the part of the infant. I have permitted myself to correct an obvious misprint on page 48 of Château's excellent paper. I await your' (probably *'decision'*, the bottom of the page with the signature had been cut off by Liza).

(Nabokov [1957a] 1996: 429)

First of all, the introduction by the narrator ('The letter has by chance remained among my papers. Here it is') can remind the reader of the introduction to another pseudotranslation, namely Tatyana's letter in *Eugene Onegin*:

> Tatiana's letter is before me;
> Religiously I keep it

(Pushkin [1975] 1991, I: 164)

But actually, the introduction to Pnin's letter resembles more closely another passage from Nabokov's translation *Eugene Onegin*:

> The verses chanced to be preserved;
> I have them; here they are[23]

(Pushkin [1975] 1991: 236)

In the letter itself, several things are to be noted. First of all, the comments which are given in parentheses play an interesting role in connection with the pseudotranslation. Indeed, it is in the very first one that we are told that the original letter was in Russian, and then, the parentheses are used to give Russian words: '*a sensitive* (chutkiy) *person*' and '*is now, it is said, drinking himself to death* (govoryat, spilsya)'. These Russian words are not so much the translation of the English words used in the novel, but, rather, the *English* is the translation that the reader is given and the Russian is the original, missing source-text. These Russian words are crucial in this alleged translation as they serve what Roland Barthes called '*effet de réel*' (Barthes 1968: 87): they are here to ascertain the reality of the original and to insist on the existence of an original Russian text.

But one can have serious doubts about the existence of this Russian letter by Pnin. Just as the reader can have doubts about Charlotte's letter in *Lolita* and assume it is rather a free recreation by Humbert at the expense of Charlotte, we can wonder if the narrator, who seems to enjoy ridiculing Timofey Pnin, is not the real author of the letter,[24] or if he has not in fact rewritten the letter partly. Indeed, the first aside in parentheses is very long and seems to overwhelmingly impose the narrator in this love letter from Pnin to Liza. And then, two other elements seem suspicious: on the one hand, the description that Pnin gives of himself is characterized by a very negative, quadruple anaphora (*'I am not handsome, I am not interesting, I am not talented. I am not even rich'*.); on the other hand, Pnin calls the narrator a genius twice (*'this is more than any genius can offer you because a genius needs to keep so much in store, and thus cannot offer you the whole of himself as I do'*). The final doubts come from the end of the letter: *'I await your'* (probably *'decision'*, the bottom of the page with the signature had been cut off by Liza)'. Once again, the commentary by the narrator is rather long, especially in comparison with the one word which, he says, is missing. And the absence of a signature can cast doubt on the fact that Pnin really was the author of the love letter. Indeed, the more we read the novel, the more we realize how unreliable the narrator is; consequently, the pseudotranslation which he provides and supposedly translates needs to be taken cautiously.

In *The Real Life of Sebastian Knight*, two letters can be described as pseudotranslations. The first one is rather discreet, since the original is being burned when the narrator, V., translates into English the few words he manages to glimpse among the flames:

> I sank down in an armchair and mused for some moments. The words I had seen were Russian words, part of a Russian sentence – quite insignificant in themselves, really (not that I might have expected from the flame of chance the slick intent of a novelist's plot). The literal English translation would be 'thy manner always to find…' – and it was not the sense that struck me, but the mere fact of its being in my language. I had not the vaguest inkling as to who she might be, that Russian woman whose letters Sebastian had kept in close proximity to those of Clare Bishop – and somehow it perplexed and bothered me.
>
> (Nabokov [1941b] 1996: 29)

The two bundles of letters seem to represent how torn Sebastian felt between his Russian identity and his English one: he loved an English woman, Clare Bishop, but also a Russian woman whose identity V. will spend most of the book trying to find.

In the second pseudotranslation, this unknown Russian woman is no longer the author, but she is the recipient of the letter, at least initially. The fact that Sebastian did write in Russian is very telling for V., but again, the Russian original remains absent. However, some traces are scattered in the translation into English that V. provides[25]:

> I had spent most of the winter of 1935 in Marseilles, attending to some of my firm's business. In the middle of January 1936, I got a letter from Sebastian. Strangely enough, it was written in Russian.

'I am, as you see, in Paris, and presumably shall be stuck [*zasstrianoo*] here for some time. If you can come, come; if you can't, I shall not be offended; but it might be perhaps better if you came. I am fed up [*osskomina*] with a number of tortuous things and especially with the patterns of my shed snake-skins [*vypolziny*] so that now I find a poetic solace in the obvious and the ordinary which for some reason or other I had overlooked in the course of my life. I should like for example to ask you what you have been doing during all these years, and to tell you about myself: I hope you have done better than I. Lately I have been seeing a good deal of old Dr Starov, who treated *maman* [so Sebastian called my mother]. I met him by chance one night in the street, when I was taking a forced rest on the running-board of somebody's parked car. He seemed to think that I had been vegetating in Paris since *maman's* death, and I have agreed to his version of my émigré existence, because [*eeboh*] any explanation seemed to me far too complicated. Some day you may come upon certain papers; you will burn them at once; true, they have heard voices in [one or two indecipherable words: *Dot chetu?*], but now they must suffer the stake. I kept them, and gave them night-lodgings [*notchleg*], because it is safer to let such things sleep, lest, when killed, they haunt us as ghosts. One night, when I felt particularly mortal, I signed their death warrant, and by it you will know them. I had been staying at the same hotel as usual, but now I have moved to a kind of sanatorium out of town, note the address. This letter was begun almost a week ago, and up to the word 'life' it had been destined [*prednaznachalos*] to quite a different person. Then somehow or other it turned towards you, as a shy guest in a strange house will talk at unusual length to the near relative with whom he came to the party. So forgive me if I bore you [*dokoochayou*], but somehow I don't much like those bare branches and twigs which I see from my window'.

(Nabokov [1941b] 1996: 144–5)

The Russian words which are given here and there between square brackets can be understood in different ways. I see them as serving Barthes's '*effet de réel*', but for Michael Wood, they are key words:

[W]hat seems to V most important about Sebastian's last letter to him is its language. As we have just seen, and he now repeats, he regards Sebastian's Russian, as 'purer and richer than his English ever was', and he patiently transliterates what he regards as all the key words.

(Wood 1994: 40)

Michael Wood uses the verb 'transliterate', thus insisting on the act of writing rather than that of translation, which the verb 'translate' would foreground (Wood does not mention 'pseudotranslation' either). The comments in brackets can also be explanatory: '*maman* [so Sebastian called my mother]' gives the context around this use of French by Sebastian and '[one or two indecipherable words: *Dot chetu?*]' indicates that the passage contained some illegible passages, thus suggesting the letter was handwritten.

A similar strategy is used and developed further in Nabokov's next book, *Bend Sinister* (1947), more specifically in the encounter between Krug and a soldier just after Krug found out about his son's murder. In the following passage, it is clear that the narrator-translator struggles in his task, thus suggesting he is not very reliable in his position of translator:

> Krug was caught by a friendly soldier.
>
> '*Yablochko, kuda-zh ty tak kotishsa* [little apple, whither are you rolling]?' asked the soldier and added:
>
> *A po zhabram, milaĭ, khochesh* [want me to hit you, friend]?
>
> *Tut pocherk zhizni stanovitsa kraĭne nerazborchivym* [here the long hand of life becomes extremely illegible]. *Ochevidtzy, sredi kotorykh byl i evo vnutrenniĭ sogliadataĭ* [witnesses among whom was his own something or other ('inner spy'? 'private detective'? The sense is not at all clear)] *potom govorili* [afterwards said] *shto evo prishlos' sviazat'* [that he had to be tied]. *Mezhdu tem* [among the themes? (Perhaps: among the subjects of his dreamlike state)] *Kristalsen, nevozmutimo dymia sigaroĭ* [Crystalsen calmly smoking his cigar], *sobral ves' shtat v aktovom zale* [called a meeting of the whole staff in the assembly hall] and informed them *[i soobshchil im]* that he had just received a telephone message according to which they would all be court martialled for doing to death the only son of Professor Krug, celebrated philosopher, President of the University, Vice-President of the Academy of Medicine.
>
> (Nabokov [1947] 1996: 345–6)

The imbrication of round and square brackets is particularly telling of the different statuses, between translator and commentator, and the hesitation between the two is put in place in the very first translation after the dialogue: '*Tut pocherk zhizni stanovitsa kraĭne nerazborchivym*' really means what the reader can find in the square brackets, '[here the long hand of life becomes extremely illegible]', but they can be taken as a commentary on the difficulty to decipher a type of handwriting, and this is confirmed by the second comment in square brackets, '[witnesses among whom was his own something or other ("inner spy"? "private detective"? The sense is not at all clear)]'. The hesitation expressed in round brackets is about the word '*sogliadataĭ*', which is the title of one of Nabokov's Russian novels (in English, *The Eye*), thus pointing ironically to Nabokov the author, hidden behind the mask of the narrator-translator. This passage is supposed to be part of the narration, but it is not presented as a written text, for example, as a letter, so it does not seem to be a pseudotranslation at first. However, the presence of a reference to handwriting ('the long hand of life becomes extremely illegible') could make the analogy plausible, especially when one knows that Krug's story is revealed to be just a written text in the end, in order to save him thanks to a compassionate narrator who reveals himself too (Nabokov [1947] 1996: 357).

If we go back to Sebastian's letter, it should be added that, on top of hovering between English and Russian, the letter shows that Sebastian was in a state of mental agitation when he wrote this letter. It is clear especially towards the end of the letter, for example, when he mentions a sanatorium or when he evokes without real cause the branches outside his window which disturb him. A possible cause for this agitation could be the Russian language itself, since this letter in which Sebastian evokes his distress is the only one he wrote in this language; Russian is also the language of the letters which he asked V. to burn (including the Russian one given in translation), lest they would haunt him. Therefore, Sebastian's bilingualism could be a cause of mental unrest for him,[26] and one can interrogate it in relation with pseudotranslation: is Russian the only language in which Sebastian can express his true hardships? Or is it English, since it is the language that the reader is effectively given to read?

Quite conveniently, English makes it possible to hide another sign of Sebastian's distress. As he explains in his letter, he changed addressees in the middle of it. But as Frank argues, the Russian would make it very hard to disguise that the addressee was first a woman, then a man (Sebastian's brother):

> V's English translation of a key passage in Sebastian's last letter, written in Russian, therefore disguises what a retranslation into Russian would reveal. In the letter which Sebastian addresses initially to his Russian lover he asks her to come and see him: 'If you can come, come; if you can't, I shall not be offended, but it might be perhaps better if you came'. In Russian (as in English) the conditional form here would be identical with the past tense form and thus require the speaker to specify the (in this case female) gender of the addressee. [...] The switch from a female to a male addressee, which is unproblematic in English, would not be possible in Russian unless both addressees are of the same gender. It is only in V's translation that this switch can happen smoothly with the different (grammatical) genders securely disguised.
>
> (Frank 2012: 168–9)

It is therefore possible to have doubts on the fact that Sebastian did write in Russian, especially when one sees how devoted V. is to proving the mastery of his brother in this language. In that respect, pseudotranslation becomes a good representation of Sebastian's relationship to his languages: when it comes to the letter, was there indeed a Russian original? And when it comes to Sebastian's books, were they really written in English or were they just translated Russian? There are no original Russian books, so if there is no original Russian except in the writer's mind, why talk of translation? And when it comes to the writers and to doubles, should V. be considered Sebastian's Russian original? The book raises the question at its very end:

> Thus – I am Sebastian Knight. I feel as if I were impersonating him on a lighted stage, with the people he knew coming and going – the dim figures of the few friends he had, the scholar, and the poet, and the painter [...]. The end, the end. They all go back to their everyday life (and Clare goes back to her grave) – but the hero remains, for, try as I may, I cannot get out of my part: Sebastian's mask clings to my face, the likeness will not be washed off. I am Sebastian, or Sebastian is I, or perhaps we both are someone whom neither of us knows.
>
> (Nabokov [1941b] 1996: 159–60)

'I am Sebastian' is repeated twice, so the answer seems to be that V. does not really exist, but of course the end instils doubt: 'or Sebastian is I, or perhaps we both are someone whom neither of us knows'.

Of course, these questions of language and identity are particularly interesting as *The Real Life of Sebastian Knight* was the first book Nabokov wrote in English: was he going to be accused of writing in translated Russian? Would Nabokov's critics always underline his Russianisms, as Wilson and other did for his translation of *Onegin*[27]? Is *The Real Life of Sebastian Knight* to be considered a pseudotranslation? Are all of Nabokov's books in English pseudotranslations?

5

Are Nabokov's Novels in English 'Pseudotranslations'?

That a bilingual author 'writes in translation' or 'lives in a permanent state of translation' is an argument one often hears about multilingual writers in general, and about Nabokov in particular. However, this conception teems with clichés and is wrong in many respects if one takes the care to actually check what linguists, or bilingual people themselves,[1] have to say on that matter. These ideas actually tend to be a sort of metaphor, especially in Comparative Literature where scholars often work on translated texts, but not on the original texts in comparison with their translations, as Translation Studies scholars tend to do. One typical example of that can be found in Pascale Casanova's *The World Republic of Letters* (2004). In a chapter entitled 'The Tragedy of Translated Men' after Salman Rushdie's expression,[2] she explains that her use of the word 'translation' is a generic one when she describes what literary strategies are used by these 'translated' writers:

> The attempts by writers on the periphery to deal with distance and decentering – notions that are subsumed here under the generic term 'translation', which includes adoption of a dominant language, self-translation, construction of a dual body of work by means of translation back and forth between two languages, development of a new writing, and symbiotic merger of two languages [...] – should not be thought of as a set of cut-and-dried solutions separate from one another, but rather as a sort of continuum of uncertain and difficult, sometimes tragic, responses to their predicament.
>
> (Casanova 2004: 257–8)

Therefore, Casanova uses 'translation' even when a writer is not resorting to self-translation but when they resort to their second language directly. The idea that a bilingual person needs to first resort to their mother tongue and then translate from it in order to express themselves is clearly dismissive of the high level of mastery that bilingual people can actually achieve.

And with a writer like Vladimir Nabokov, the question is of course to determine what language was his first and what language was second, and even third, between Russian, English and French. As we know, in his childhood, Nabokov at times mastered English before Russian, be it in speaking or in reading (Boyd 1990: 47, 57). The fact that Nabokov's English was sometimes better than his Russian thus jeopardizes the notion that the language of one's mother (Russian, but this assertion could be questioned as well) is necessarily one's *first* language (in chronological order and in terms of hierarchy). And even when Nabokov became a mature writer, there were (and are) still questions on whether his Russian was tainted by European languages or whether his English was Russianized.[3]

Asking if a bilingual author such as Nabokov wrote directly in English or in Russian or if he resorted to translation does not have a simple answer, but the most compelling summary on how bilingualism acts on the brain and its impact on bilingual writers can be found in Elizabeth Klosty Beaujour's chapter 'The Neurolinguistic Substrate of Bilingual Writing' in her famous book *Alien Tongues*. (1989: 7–27) When it comes to Nabokov, he expressed himself on that issue when he famously said that he thought 'in images', but actually it is what comes after this passage which is particularly interesting:

> I don't think in any language, I think in images. I don't believe that people think in languages. They don't move their lips when they think. It is only a certain type of illiterate person who moves his lips as he reads or ruminates. No, I think in images, and now and then a Russian phrase or an English phrase will form with the foam of the brainwave, but that's about all.
>
> (Nabokov [1973] 1990: 14)

What Nabokov calls 'images' and 'the foam of the brainwave' can otherwise be called 'mentalese', and when Nabokov explains that one or the other language emerges out of this foam, it corresponds to the findings of psycholinguistics:

> The 'language learning' narratives also testify that languages are indeed separate worlds, which cannot be reduced to a simple mentalese expressed in various codes.
>
> (Pavlenko 1998: 17)

The last rebuttal to the idea that bilingual authors write in translation, thus making their books 'pseudotranslations' (with an original being absent on a page and only present abstractly in the mind of its author), is the fact that self-translation is much more complicated than writing directly in a second language. Many quotes by Nabokov testify to that, and Beaujour shows that the torture of self-translation was not experienced by Nabokov alone:

> Many fluent bilinguals have trouble translating, and it is usual for them to express themselves more easily – on almost any subject, in any context – in either of their two languages than it is for them to translate from one to the other. Michel Paradis argues persuasively that the processes underlying translation are very different from those which underlie speaking, understanding, reading, or writing different languages.
>
> (Beaujour 1989: 18)

It is therefore better not to apply the notion of translation to all types of bilingual writing. As for pseudotranslation, it should be restricted to the mystification in which an author pretends that there is a written original to a text that is presented as a translation; it should not be used to describe writings by bilingual authors, lest it should diminish their achievements in any of their languages.

Comparative Literature has been using the concept of 'pseudotranslation' in a way that exceeds that of Translation Studies. For example, this is what Brigitte Rath, a scholar in Comparative Literature, writes about 'World Literature':[4]

> The idea of pseudotranslation sharpens some central concepts of Comparative Literature. 'World Literature', according to David Damrosch, is 'always as much about the host culture's values and needs as it is about a work's source culture'. Foregrounding a text's imaginary origin in a different culture reads this 'double refraction' as already built into a text. It thus stresses the conjecture and transnational imagination that is always involved in reading a text as world literature.
>
> (Rath 2014: n. p.)

This extensive use of the notion of 'pseudotranslation' is not a path I am willing to follow, even if the idea of a 'transnational imagination', or more specifically a transnational canon, is relevant in the case of Nabokov. Indeed, we have seen that his encounters with pseudotranslation show the importance of literature from different countries in his vision of writing and translating: the interactions between European literature on the one hand (mainly English, Scottish, French and German) and Russian on the other are crucial to understanding his canon.

In the next part of this book, I will concentrate on Nabokov's translation *Eugene Onegin* by examining the tension between his role of translator and his status as a writer: did he manage to stick to his position of translator or did he appropriate Pushkin's text? Did he impose his own brand of English onto his translation? The notion of transnationality in translation will be crucial to determine whether a translated book in general, and *Onegin* in particular, needs to be placed in relation to other literary traditions, be it by tracing its origins artistically or by inscribing it in a hierarchical network of existing literatures thanks to an ethical, or even political, approach.

Part Two

Nabokov and the Author Behind the Translator

6

Vladimir Nabokov's Translation Theory for *Eugene Onegin*

When translators are credited for their work, their names usually appear inside the volume, but not on the cover. However, on that of the 1975 revised edition of *Eugene Onegin*,[1] the names of Vladimir Nabokov and Pushkin are both present, and they are written in the same size, except for Pushkin's initials which are slightly bigger than the rest; however, on the tail, their names are exactly the same size. Only the fact that Pushkin's name is above Nabokov's indicates the prevailing hierarchy which usually exists between an author and their translator. Clearly, when the translator happens to be a recognized author, the paratext recognizes the translator, probably because the author-translator wants to be acknowledged, but also because the publisher can expect larger sales. Many authors have dabbled in translation: for example, among writers in English, Mary Wollstonecraft, Thomas Holcroft, Mary Shelley, Jean Rhys,[2] Lydia Davis[3]; for writers in French, Charles Baudelaire, Marcel Proust, François-René de Chateaubriand, Marguerite Yourcenar, etc. But one can wonder if any author translated as much as Nabokov, especially from so many languages.

When Nabokov published his translation of Pushkin's *Onegin* (1964), he was already extremely famous in the English-speaking world: *Lolita* had brought him celebrity in 1955, and later works like *Pale Fire* (1962) confirmed his status of renowned author in his new country, the United States. With this translation of Pushkin, Nabokov also became famous in his role of translator due to the infamous scandal that followed. It does not seem necessary to go into detail on the arguments that critics and Nabokov exchanged at the time or on the feud with Edmund Wilson,[4] but I will be mentioning excerpts of such exchanges when specific examples are under scrutiny.

The fact that Nabokov was a recognized author when he translated Pushkin means that he had a certain style that could possibly invade his translation, but also that he had a certain weight to push forward any agenda he had regarding his vision of translation. One of the main questions that I will look at in this second part is how Nabokov balanced his role of translator with that of author. But before studying Nabokov's practice of translation, it is necessary to look into his theory.

Vladimir Nabokov's strong opinions on translations: A diachronic perspective

Nabokov's position on translation evolved greatly along his life, from free translation bordering on adaptation to strict literalism. A very detailed analysis of Nabokov's evolution throughout the years can be found in Shvabrin's 2019 monograph, but a short way to illustrate it is to contrast Nabokov's 1923 translation of *Alice's Adventures in Wonderland* with his translation *Eugene Onegin*, published for the first time in 1964. In his translation into Russian of Lewis Carroll's book, entitled *Anja v strane chudes*, Nabokov took great liberties with the English text and adapted the cultural references (to take but one example) for the Russian public, thus Russifying it: Anja was target-oriented. On the other hand, in his source-oriented translation of Pushkin's *Evgenij Onegin*, Nabokov was very faithful to the source text, so much so that the English he resorted to was deemed illegible by many critics, as I will explain in the first chapter of this part when I explain his literalist theory in detail.

To be more specific about those two approaches, it is relevant to use what is probably the most widespread terminology in the English-speaking world when it comes to Translation Studies, namely that of Lawrence Venuti. In his 1995 book *The Translator's Invisibility*, Venuti resorts to Friedrich Schleiermacher's 1823 seminal text 'On the different methods of translating', in which the German thinker clearly explained the two positions a translator can have vis-à-vis their author and their reader:

> Now as for the translator proper who truly wishes to bring together these two quite separate persons, his writer and his reader, and to help the reader, though without forcing him to leave the bounds of his own native tongue behind him, to acquire as correct and complete an understanding of and take as much pleasure in the writer as possible – what sorts of paths might he set off upon to this end? In my opinion, there are only two possibilities. Either the translator leaves the writer in peace as much as possible and moves the reader towards him; or he leaves the reader in peace as much as possible and moves the writer toward him.
>
> (Schleiermacher 2000: 49)

Though the dichotomy is clearly explained, there is no clear terminology to designate the two paths; Venuti provides a very useful one:

> Schleiermacher allowed the translator to choose between a domesticating method, an ethnocentric reduction of the foreign text to target-language cultural values, bringing the author back home, and a foreignizing method, an ethnodeviant pressure on those values to register the linguistic and cultural difference of the foreign text, sending the reader abroad.
>
> (Venuti 1995: 20)

So Nabokov's *Anja* was domesticating while his *Onegin* was clearly foreignizing, if we follow Venuti's distinction, for now at least.

Nabokov's evolution within translation theory is also obvious if one looks at the few theoretical texts he produced. The first one, 'The Art of Translation', was published in 1941, and in it, Nabokov clearly defended an artistic vision of translation. Indeed, he argued that there were three types of translators:

> [T]he scholar who is eager to make the world appreciate the works of an obscure genius as much as he does himself; the well-meaning hack; and the professional writer relaxing in the company of a foreign confrère.
>
> (Nabokov [1941a] 2008: 8)

Nabokov explained that nothing can replace 'imagination and style' (8) before detailing the qualities a translator needs to have:

> First of all, he must have as much talent, or at least the same kind of talent, as the author he chooses. In this, though only in this, respect Baudelaire and Poe or Zhukovski and Schiller made ideal playmates. Second, he must know thoroughly the two nations and the two languages involved and be perfectly acquainted with all details relating to his author's manner and methods; also, with the social background of words, their fashions, history and period of associations. This leads to the third point: while having genius and knowledge, he must possess the gift of mimicry and be able to act, as it were, the real author's part by impersonating his tricks of demeanor and speech, his ways and his mind, with the utmost degree of verisimilitude.
>
> (Nabokov [1941a] 2008: 8–9)

This period of relatively free translations was not going to last and, as Shvabrin writes, its end can be dated very precisely thanks to the poem 'Pity the elderly translator':

> His dissatisfaction with the artistic mode of translation, however, reached a high point, prompting him to verbalise it in a poem composed on 17 March 1952.
>
> (Shvabrin 2019: 274).

This poem marked the beginning of Nabokov's literalist of translation, and there are several theoretical texts in which he clarifies his position. Chronologically speaking, one can find the following five texts in English: 'Problems of Translation: "Onegin" in English' ([1955b] 2000); 'The Servile Path' (1959b); his 'Foreword' to *Eugene Onegin* (1963a); 'Pounding the Clavichord' ([1964a] 1990); and 'Reply to my Critics' ([1966a] 1990). And in Russian, there are two sets of 'Notes of a translator' published in 1957 (1957b, 1957c).

One should note however that some premises of his literalist theory are present in this text 'The Art of Translation'. Indeed, even though he thought that the scholar lacked 'creative genius' (like the hack), he wrote:

> The scholar will be, I hope, exact and pedantic: footnotes – on the *same* page as the text and not tucked away at the end of the volume – can never be too copious and detailed.
>
> (Nabokov [1941a] 2008: 8)

Nabokov was also aware of one possible flaw that one could find in an artist:

> Now comes the authentic poet who has the two last assets and who finds relaxation in translating a bit of Lermontov or Verlaine between writing poems of his own. Either he does not know the original language and calmly relies upon the so-called 'literal' translation made for him by a far less brilliant but a little more learned person, or else, knowing the language, he lacks the scholar's precision and the professional translator's experience. The main drawback in this case, however, is the fact that the greater his individual talent, the more apt he will be to drown the foreign masterpiece under the sparkling ripples of his own personal style. Instead of dressing up like the real author, he dresses up the author as himself.
>
> (Nabokov [1941a] 2008: 8)

These last lines seem to foreshadow '*otsebyatina*', which was a fault that Nabokov was going to describe in his literalist theory.

Nabokov's theory of literalism

Nabokov often resorted to classifications when it came to explaining what translation should be, and they were often made of three categories, as we see yet again in his explanation of the different types of translation that exist for poetry:

Attempts to render a poem in another language fall into three categories:

(1) Paraphrastic: offering a free version of the original, with omissions and additions prompted by the exigencies of form, the conventions attributed to the consumer, and the translator's ignorance. Some paraphrases may possess the charm of stylish diction and idiomatic conciseness, but no scholar should succumb to stylishness and no reader be fooled by it.

(2) Lexical (or constructional): rendering the basic meaning of words (and their order). This a machine can do under the direction of an intelligent bilinguist.

(3) Literal: rendering, as closely as the associative and syntactical capacities of another language allow, the exact contextual meaning of the original. Only this is true translation. (Nabokov [1963a] 1991: vii–viii)

For Nabokov, meaning is therefore crucial, not form. This is why he explains that it is impossible to have a rhymed translation:

> Can a rhymed poem like *Eugene Onegin* be truly translated with the retention of its rhymes? The answer, of course, is no. To reproduce the rhymes and yet translate the entire poem literally is mathematically impossible.
>
> (Nabokov [1963a] 1991: ix)

However, there is one element of form which, surprisingly enough, he decides to keep, as he explains in his article 'The Servile Path'[5]:

> The work is now finished. In my translation I have sacrificed to total accuracy and completeness of meaning every element of form *save the iambic rhythm*, the retention of which assisted rather than impaired fidelity.
>
> (Nabokov 1959b: 98; italics mine)

Nabokov must have been aware of the somewhat contradictory dimension of this choice to keep the iambic rhythm[6] because, in the foreword to his translation (1963), he sidesteps the question he formulated himself:

> Should one then content oneself with an exact rendering of the subject matter and forget all about form? Or should one still excuse an imitation of the poem's structure to which only twisted bits of sense stick here and there, by convincing oneself and one's public that in mutilating its meaning for the sake of a pleasure-measure rhyme one has the opportunity of prettifying or skipping the dry and difficult passages? I have always been amused by the stereotyped compliment that a reviewer pays the author of a 'new translation'. He says: 'It reads smoothly.'
>
> (Nabokov [1963a] 1991: ix)

As we will see, the use of iambs sometimes compelled Nabokov to slightly move away from the literalism he advocated for.

For Nabokov, on top of being extremely literal, a translation had to be accompanied by a great number of notes:

> I want translations with copious footnotes, footnotes reaching up like skyscrapers to the top of this or that page so as to leave only the gleam of one textual line between commentary and eternity.
>
> (Nabokov [1955b] 2000: 83)

As is well-known, in the original edition of Nabokov's *Eugene Onegin*, only one volume was dedicated to Pushkin's text (with the translator's introduction), whereas three volumes were filled with scholarly notes. In these, Nabokov justifies his choices of translation by abundantly explaining elements such as intertextuality or the Russian fauna and flora.[7]

Now that the general outline of Nabokov's translation theory is in place, it is possible to go into further detail, all while intertwining two perspectives: the balance between the figure of the author and that of the translator, and the transnational dimension of Nabokov's translation.

Outline of the second part

My analysis of Nabokov's translation will consist of two chapters. First, I will look into detail at its foreignizing traits and their causes as explained by Nabokov the translator-annotator. The main focus will be language: was Nabokov's *Onegin* really written in 'Nabokovese', as the accusation was often made? Arguing that Nabokov's language in the translation was typically the one he used in his own novels in English begs the question of appropriation, and it will lead us to wonder if Nabokov really indulged in what he called '*otsebyatina*'. The next chapter will revolve around the question of transparency and literalism in translation, through a comparison with two leading figures in translation studies. Thanks to a contrasting analysis of Nabokov's translation theory and practice with those of Chateaubriand in his French translation of Milton's *Paradise Lost*, I will show that their vision of translation purported to be a pure homage to the source text. Then, by moving on to Venuti's position on translation, I will question the term of 'ethics', to contrast Nabokov's use of this term with Venuti's more political stance, which will enable us to open the scope to a more polemical vision of Nabokov's translation.

Eugene Onegin, a Translation into Nabokovese?

When Nabokov's translation *Eugene Onegin* was published, several critics complained about the language he used, even arguing that it was hardly English at all. Many even coined the term 'Nabokovese', as a specific variation of 'translatese':[1]

> The *Onegin* translation (4 vols, with commentaries) is vintage Nabokov: expressive, wondrously inventive Nabokovese, with inordinately detailed commentary without proper footnotes (the great anti-scholarly scholar's reputation must be maintained).
>
> (Simmons 1966: 212)

> There is a more essential blemish yet – **an unsuitable vocabulary**. [...] Worse still, this tendency leads to a liberal scattering of **inappropriately stilted or antiquated words** [...].

> It is sad to knock any attempt to bring Pushkin before us. There are long passages without these faults. Nevertheless, on the whole this is too much a transposition into **Nabokovese, rather than a translation into English.** It gives the impression of a foreigner who has not quite learnt the language with the extreme perfection required, perhaps, only at this extravagant periphery of idiom.
>
> (Conquest 1965: 238; bold type mine)

J. Thomas Shaw also used the term when he contrasted Arndt's 1972 translation[2] with that of Nabokov (Pushkin 1964):

> As I have suggested elsewhere ('Translations of Onegin', *Russian Review*, 24 [1965], 119) **Nabokov's translation is written in a language of his own based on English**; furthermore, the English of his usual narrator is acquired, and he rightly emphasizes the narrative and descriptive rather than the conversational. Arndt, in contrast, is often strikingly successful in catching the familiar, idiomatic, and even slangy English of today. His breezy introductions to the book and to the longer poems are poles away from **Nabokovese**.
>
> (Shaw 1974: 314; bold type mine)

In his 1965 review, Shaw had not used the term 'Nabokovese' but he had described in detail what he thought of Nabokov's brand of English in the translation:

> However, as Nabokov himself must be aware, the result is that his translation is in **a language which has never before been written**. It is a *sui generis* mixture of modern English (British and American), of Gallicisms, and of word equivalents taken from or coined on the basis of literary works from the time of Shakespeare to that of Byron. [...] Nabokov has long been conducting **assaults upon the English language**, and they have been largely successful. Perhaps there is no writer who is more a magician with the use of English today than he. But **his English is an invented language, one that could not possibly be written by a native**, and he is obviously entirely correct to have his usual fictional persona-narrator one whose English is acquired, and to emphasize the narrative and descriptive rather than the conversational. Nabokov is a writer of such power and ability that one hesitates to predict that **his own version of English**, even in this translation, will not prove to be not only acceptable but accepted, with the exception of his occasional solecisms in tense constructions with 'since' and 'already'. In the meantime, one may say that Nabokov in this translation, as T. S. Eliot said of the authors of *Paradise Lost* and *Finnegans' Wake*, wrote in **a language of his own based on English**. Nabokov's own prose, in his creative works and in the commentaries of this edition, is often pure poetry, but the poetry of his translation of *Onegin* is determinedly and defiantly – one is tempted to say gloriously – not even prose.
>
> (Shaw 1965: 117–19; bold type mine)

However, it is worth noting that Pushkin's own brand of Russian relied on similar traits:

> Pushkin was writing in a language based primarily on Russian, but with a considerable admixture of foreign words and phrases, either borrowed or simply translated; he utilized interchangeably new and old forms of words, native and foreign.
>
> (Shaw 1965: 118)

> One of the secrets of the novel's irresistible charm lies in Pushkin's ability to mix with magic facility some Church-Slavonic and Russian archaisms with Gallicisms and grass-root colloquialisms.
>
> (Gerschenkron 1966: 337)

In this chapter, I will try to determine where Nabokov's faithful translation of Pushkin's idiosyncratic language stops and where his own brand of English, as an author,[3] starts.

I will start by detailing the specificities of Nabokov's foreignizing translation, and I will then show how Nabokov translated Pushkin's use of foreign words or even added his own. Finally, I will underline some cases of inconsistency in Nabokov's method of translation to establish if Nabokov was indulging in '*otsebyatina*', which is a notion that Nabokov coined to describe the temptation of appropriation that a translator must resist.[4]

A foreignizing translation

In his translation, Nabokov often resorted to a foreignized form of English which appears mainly in two ways: his English syntax is Russified while his vocabulary teems with Gallic words.[5] One could even draw a parallel with Nabokov's description of Eugene: just like the young man is 'a Frenchified Russian dressed like an English fop' (Nabokov [1964b] 1991: 22), Nabokov's *Eugene Onegin* is a Frenchified version of the Russian text, even if it is dressed up to look like an English text.

The marginalization of English syntax through Russian

In comparison with the many pages which Nabokov devoted to the importance of the French language in the original text and in his translation, he did not often comment on the impact that his literalism had on his syntax. In the foreword to his translation, he insisted that he respected the syntax of the target text, at least as much as possible:

> (3) Literal: rendering, **as closely as the associative and syntactical capacities of another language allow,** the exact contextual meaning of the original. Only this is true translation. [...]
>
> Now comes the literalist. He [...] will [...] **rearrange the order of words to achieve some semblance of English construction** and retain some vestige of Russian rhythm.
>
> (Nabokov [1963a] 1991: viii; bold type mine)

However, later in the same text, he hinted at the fact that sometimes, grammar may have suffered from his literalist approach:

> To my ideal of literalism I sacrificed everything (elegance, euphony, clarity, good taste, modern usage, and **even grammar**) that the dainty mimic prizes higher than truth.
>
> (Nabokov [1963a] 1991: x; bold type mine)

Nabokov's literalism means that he respected the localization of words in their original line: if, in Russian, a word was on line 5, it had to be on line 5 in the English translation. When Nabokov revised his translation, he wrote that he strove to 'achieve a closer line-by-line fit (entailing a rigorous coincidence of enjambments and the elimination of verse transposal)' (Nabokov [1972] 1991]: xiii). Nabokov's strict respect of the original place of words in their respective line did not mean that he was reproducing Russian word order, thus making his English syntax a *calque* of the Russian one. However, it meant that the word order in English was sometimes awkward, especially in the case of long sentences running on several lines. Indeed, in Russian, word order is rather free thanks to declensions: they indicate the grammatical function of words, regardless of their position. And as Gerschenkron wrote about Russian, 'Such a language offers greatest freedom for the order of words, and all kinds of inverted constructions can be ventured upon without any loss in terms of lucidity and elegance' (1966: 340). On the contrary, languages like English very much depend on word order to clarify the meaning. Some critics have blamed Nabokov for making his text illegible[6] due to his word order. For instance, Alexander Dolinin wrote:

> He adhered to the principles of interlinearity even in those cases when it resulted in wrenching and twisting the English order of words. Due to the composite inversions imitating Russian syntax some phrases become almost unreadable, like these, taken at random: [...] 'In his backwoods an eremitic sage, / the ancient *corvée*'s yoke / by the light quitrent he replaced' (I, 127; ch. 2, st. 4); 'without an imperceptible trace, / to leave the word I would be sad' (I, 144; ch. 2, st. 39).
>
> (Dolinin 1995: 121)

In the first sentence quoted by Dolinin (to take only one example), one can notice that, on top of peculiar choices in vocabulary (loanwords from the French like 'sage' and '*corvée*', or rare words such as 'quitrent'[7]), Nabokov's sentence is rather bumpy. Instead of 'In his backwoods an eremitic sage, / the ancient *corvée*'s yoke / by the light quitrent he replaced', it would have been clearer to write 'In his backwoods an eremitic sage replaced the ancient corvée's yoke by the light quitrent'. One could even say that Nabokov's sentence looks like the lexical type of translation which he criticized in his foreword:

> (2) Lexical (or constructional): rendering the basic meaning of words (and their order). This a machine can do under the direction of an intelligent bilinguist.
>
> (Nabokov [1963a] 1991: viii)

Sentences like this one probably enticed Edmund Wilson to verbalize the following attack: 'Such passages sound like the products of those computers which are supposed to translate Russian into English[8]' (Wilson 1965).

However, Nabokov repeatedly explained that he deliberately resorted to a bumpy kind of English so that his translation could be close enough to the original:

> EO falls short of the ideal crib. It is still not close enough and not ugly enough. In future editions I plan to defowlerize it more drastically. I think I shall turn it entirely into utilitarian prose, with a still bumpier brand of English.
>
> (Nabokov [1966a] 1990: 243)

Nabokov insists on his choice to not use a normative kind of English through his pun 'defowlerize', which is of course a dig at Henri Watson Fowler's style guide, *Modern English Usage.*

Another example of what native speakers of English could perceive as an attack against their syntax is quoted in 'Reply to My Critics'. After Wilson accused Nabokov of committing a blunder in his use of prepositions due to his native Russian, the translator explained his choice in a typically derisive manner:

> In translating *slushat' shum morskoy* (Eight: iv: 11) I chose the archaic and poetic transitive turn 'to listen the sound of the sea' because the relevant passage has in Pushkin a stylized archaic tone. Mr. Wilson may not care for this turn – I do not much care for it either – but it is silly of him to assume that I lapsed into a naive Russianism not being really aware that, as he tells me, 'in English you have to listen *to* something'. First, it is Mr. Wilson who is not aware of the fact that there exists an analogous construction in Russian *prislushivat'sya k zvuku*, 'to listen closely to the sound' – which, of course, makes nonsense of the exclusive Russianism imagined by him, and secondly, had he happened to leaf through a certain canto of *Don Juan*, written in the year Pushkin was beginning his poem, or a certain *Ode to Memory*, written when Pushkin's poem was being finished, my learned friend would have concluded that Byron ('Listening debates not very wise or witty') and Tennyson ('Listening the lordly music') must have had quite as much Russian blood as Pushkin and I.
>
> (Nabokov [1966a] 1990: 257)

Referring his critics to the great works of literature in English is a way for Nabokov to prove that his being born in Russia does not mean his knowledge of English literature is deficient. As we will see, literary justifications are one of the reasons why Nabokov made abundant use of French in his vocabulary.

The use of Gallic vocabulary

The importance of French language and literature is extensively treated by Nabokov in his articles on translation; in 'The Servile Path' (1959b), he refers to 'Problems of Translation: "Onegin" in English' (1955) by saying:

> In a recent article I mentioned some of the complications attending the turning of *Eugene Onegin* into English, such as the need to cope with the constant intrusion of gallicisms and of borrowings from French poets.
>
> (Nabokov 1959b: 97)

Nabokov goes on and announces what he will be presenting in the rest of his article:

> My contention was, and is, that the translator, in order to be lucidly faithful to his text, should be aware of this or that authorial reminiscence, imitation, or direct translation from another language into that of the text [...]. The English translator of *Eugene Onegin* would seem to need not only a Russian's knowledge of Russian but also Pushkin's knowledge of French.
>
> (Nabokov 1959b: 97)

As French was one of the main targets for Nabokov's critics, and as the translator tackled those attacks in his article 'Reply to my Critics', it means that French is very much present in this text too. Consequently, out of his five articles in English on his translation of *Onegin*, only 'Pounding the Clavichord' did not insist loudly on the topic (which makes sense when one knows that this article was actually a review of, or rather an attack on, Arndt's translation).

Several critics attacked Nabokov for his tendency to Frenchify Pushkin's text. Edward J. Brown summed up most of these criticisms, especially regarding the translator's annotations:

> Pushkin's poem emerges in the Commentary not as a narrative concerned with Russian realities, characters, or problems but as the work of an imagination steeped in French culture and French literature working upon characters and themes either provided by French literature or refracted through the prism of French translations.
>
> (Brown 1965: 697)

Let us examine the many reasons why Nabokov so abundantly resorted to French: they mainly have to do with intertextuality and linguistics.

Nabokov's justifications

In his essays and in the preliminary pages to his translation, Nabokov insisted on the importance of French in Pushkin's Russia: in the eighteenth century, Russian aristocrats and poets spoke French almost fluently, and they read French books in the original language: 'Pushkin's French was as fluent as that of any highly cultured gentleman of his day' (Nabokov [1955b] 2000: 75). They also read English and German literature in French translation:

> As a rule, the St. Petersburg fashionable, the ennuied Hussar, the civilized squire, the provincial miss in her linden-shaded chateau of painted wood – all read Shakespeare and Sterne, Richardson and Scott, Moore and Byron, as well as the German novelists (Goethe, August Lafontaine), in French versions, and French versions only.
>
> In consequence, Shakespeare is really Letourneur, Byron and Moore are Pichot, Scott is Frenais, and so on.
>
> (Nabokov 1959b: 97–8)

As a result, Pushkin was very much influenced by French poetry, in particular when it comes to form. For example, Nabokov argues that the type of sonnet that Pushkin used in Russian finds its model in the sonnet used by Malherbe, Scévole de Sainte-Marthe (Nabokov [1955b] 2000: 72–3) or La Fontaine (Nabokov [1964b] 1991: 10), among others.

Nabokov also explains that Pushkin's brand of French was not very creative and was actually a collage of ready-made sentences (Nabokov 1959b: 98). In Russian, Pushkin's choice of words was directly inspired from the French:

> The *douces chimères* of French elegies are as close to the *sladkie mechtï* and *sladostnïe mechtaniya* of Pushkin as they are to the 'delicious reverie' and 'sweet delusions' of eighteenth-century English poets. [...] Pushkin was acquainted with English poets only through their French models or French versions; the English translator of *Onegin*, while seeking an idiom in the Gallic diction of Pope and Byron, or in the romantic vocabulary of Keats, must constantly refer to the French poets.
>
> (Nabokov [1955b] 2000: 75–6)

Therefore, according to Nabokov, the Russian language incorporated images directly taken from French poetry, and these *calques* need to be rendered by Gallicisms. For example, if we take the two Russian words that Nabokov quoted in the passage above, *мечта* and *мечтание* (dream) are most of the time translated into English as 'reverie' or 'chimera', not 'dream'.

French poetry is not the only source of Gallicisms in Russian. Another reason for their use is a widespread Francophilia among the educated classes, which left an imprint on the Russian language. For example, here is the stanza in which Onegin learns that his uncle is about to die:

> All of a sudden he received indeed
> from a steward a report
> that uncle was nigh death in bed
> and would be glad to bid farewell to him.
>
> (Pushkin [1975] 1991, I: 121)

According to Nabokov, his strange formulation 'uncle was nigh death in bed' is justified by the fact that Pushkin's formulation itself, 'дядя при смерти в постеле' (Pushkin [1833] 2003: 42; the uncle [was] by his death, in bed, my literal translation), is a *calque* from the French:

> The wording from this stanza is awkward in the original. [...] In l. 3 the *pri smerti v postéle* (from *postelya*, not *postel'*) is the dissolution of a Gallicism, *sur son lit de mort*, 'on his deathbed' (which had long ago entered Russian as *na smertnom odre*).
>
> (Pushkin [1975] 1991, II: 194)

Since Pushkin was not using the expression that had entered Russian, but another, stranger expression, Nabokov could not resort to 'on his deathbed' in his translation.

Though many critics praised Nabokov's exposition of the underlying presence of French in Pushkin's text, they also reproached him for not paying similar attention to the Russian intertext.[9] And when it comes to Nabokov's Frenchified vocabulary in English, it was severely attacked. Indeed, critics felt that this French dimension was inelegantly exaggerated by Nabokov in his translation:

> Though in each case Nabokov's choice was caused by his desire to render Gallic or Old Russian overtones of *Eugene Onegin*'s diction with absolute accuracy, he often heavily overplayed the strangeness of the original word and, as a result, turned a stylistic nuance into a loud splash. As Alexander Gerschenkron pointed out in his persuasive, though not wholly impartial review of *Eugene Onegin*, Nabokov tended to ignore the process of Russification, started long before Pushkin, 'in the course of which the values and connotations of [Gallic] words and phrases were subtly, and sometimes not so subtly, changed, and the feeling for the foreign origin was lost'.
>
> (Dolinin 1995: 120–1)

To be more specific, Gerschenkron recognized that French had an impact on the Russian language as well as Russian literature, but he disagreed on its lasting effect:

Modern Russian – like other Slavic and Germanic languages – was formed under strong French influence. Russian poetry of the eighteenth and early nineteenth century bears all the marks of that highly beneficial influence. But two things must be remembered: (1) the penetration into Russian of *calques* (or *Lehnuebersetzungen*) from the French started before Pushkin, and (2) most of such permanently retained Gallicisms were subject to a process of Russification in the course of which the values and connotations of words and phrases were subtly, and sometimes not so subtly, changed, and the feeling for their foreign origin was lost. What on the face of it might look like a direct *calque* very often contained strong elements of creative adaptation. Such a change occurred almost inevitably and instantaneously when the *calque* merely added a new usage to a well-established Russian word. Then, also, the foreign meaning was automatically Russified. Therefore, in retranslating a Russian Gallicism into French the original French term will not necessarily yield the semantically correct translation.

(Gerschenkron 1966: 338)

One of the things that the critic underlines is the difference that exists between words which were, in Pushkin's days, perceived as foreign (*calques* for example), and those that are no longer perceived as such nowadays, having acquired the status of loanwords. This is very clear in the following example. When Onegin is seducing the woman whom his friend Lenskij loves, the young man is shocked: '*Ленский сам / не верит собственным глазам*' (Pushkin [1833] 2003: 172; Lenskij himself does not believe his own eyes, my literal translation). According to Nabokov, Pushkin was using 'A common Gallicism (*ses propres yeux*) instead of the correct *svoim glazam*, "his own eyes"' (Pushkin [1975] 1991, III: 544). Consequently, he translated the sentence into English as 'Lensky himself / does not believe his proper eyes' (Pushkin [1975] 1991, I: 222). However, one needs to note that nowadays this 'Gallicism' is completely normal for Russian speakers, and in the *Oxford Russian English Dictionary*, it is translated merely by 'one's own eyes' (Wheeler 1972: 752). Therefore, Nabokov reinjected a foreign dimension into the text.

The difference here seems to lie in the perspective undertaken by the translator in respect to diachrony or synchrony. Indeed, Nabokov was translating for his contemporary reader with the intention of reproducing the feelings of the Russian reader of the past reacting to Pushkin's text.[10] However, with his extensive knowledge of literature and his keen sense of nuances, Nabokov seems to have been influenced by the perceptions of Pushkin's contemporaries and he may have overplayed them, as Dolinin suggested with 'loud splash'.

As it appeared with 'proper eyes', the degree of foreignness can vary from one period to another and from one reader to the next. Among linguists, the difference between borrowed words (or loanwords) and foreign words (or xenisms) is often debated, but one of the easiest ways to distinguish them is to consider their assimilation into the language:

> One can distinguish two categories: peregrinisms, or xenisms, that is to say words which are felt as foreign and are in a way quoted [...] and loanwords as such, which are words that are completely naturalized.
>
> (Deroy 1956: 224; my translation)[11]

In written language, one criterion that is rather common in typography is the use of italics for foreign words. As for loanwords, their presence in the dictionary is a rather reliable clue; for English in particular, a useful resource is the *OED* because it clearly indicates the foreign origins of loanwords. Another useful term is 'code-switching', which designates the phenomenon consisting in switching languages in one's discourse:

> Most scholars consider that code-switching occurs when bilingual or multilingual speakers mix elements from more than one language within a single act of communication, whether within a sentence or in successive sentences.
>
> (Durkin 2014: 10)

If we go back to Pushkin, it is true that his Russian was strongly influenced by French, especially in terms of etymology.

Etymological links between French and Russian

In his dictionary of comparative etymology, linguist Serguei Sakhno shows there are three causes that explain the proximity between certain French and Russian words. First, some borrowings result from intense contacts between the two languages over many centuries, and these borrowings can be direct or indirect (2001: 334). Secondly, French and Russian have a common origin, namely the (Proto-)Indo-European language (2001: 10). The third category is that of *calques*: their forms are different, but there exists an analogy in the way that the words are constructed (335). Therefore, some Russian words were created to resemble French models, be it on purpose or unconsciously.

Let us look at two concrete examples from *Eugene Onegin*. When the narrator describes how he met with his main character, he writes: '*Мне нравились его черты*' (Pushkin [1833] 2003: 37; I liked his features, my literal translation). Here, Nabokov argued that the Russian word '*черты*' (*čerty*) comes from the French: 'Traits / *chertï*: A Gallicism, *ses traits*, his features, his "lines"' (Pushkin [1975] 1991, II: 168). He, therefore, chose to translate it not as 'features' but as 'traits': 'I liked his traits' (Pushkin [1975] 1991, I: 114). However, etymologically, the word '*черты*' does not have a French origin, which can suggest that Nabokov thought it was a *calque*. As for the English word 'trait', it does have a French etymology; here is what the OED indicates:

> Etymology: < French *trait*, in obsolete French *traict*, *tret*, draught, stroke, touch, line = Provencal *trait* feature < Latin *tractus* drawing, draught: see tract n.3. The pronunciation /treɪ/, after modern French, in the 19th cent. considered in England the correct one, is becoming less general; in U.S. /treɪt/ is the established one.

The two pronunciations (the British one, *à la française*, and the American one, where the 't' can be heard) confirm how subtle the limit can be between a loanword and a xenism. So, Nabokov translated what was a *calque* in the Russian into a loanword in English.

But it is not always easy to distinguish between the different parts that can be played by borrowing, a common origin or a *calque* in construction. Indeed, in the next example, several causes seem to be acceptable. In the last chapter, Onegin finally decides to go back to high society after months of self-inflicted isolation: '*где зимовал он, как сурок*' (Pushkin [1833] 2003: 274; where he had hibernated like a marmot, my literal translation). In his commentary, Nabokov underlined a link with a French expression: 'A locution adapted from the French (*hiverner comme une marmotte*)' (Pushkin [1975] 1991, III: 231). He translated the Russian segment by the following: 'where he had hibernated like a marmot' (Pushkin [1975] 1991, I: 303). Therefore, the whole Russian expression seems to be a *calque* from the French. But more precisely, if one looks at the verb '*зимовать*' (to hibernate), two other causes are to be found. First of all, in his translation, Nabokov does not use the verb 'to winter' or 'to spend the winter', which are the first two translations which are given by the *Oxford Russian-English Dictionary*. Instead, he uses 'to hibernate', which is a borrowing from the Latin 'hibernare', just like the French verb 'hiverner'. And on top of the *calque* and the borrowing, it appears that the common origin of languages can explain Nabokov's choice: indeed, the Latin word '*hiems*' (winter) and the Russian word '*zima*' have a common origin (Sakhno 2001: 108).

To sum up, the proximity between a French word and a Russian one can have many linguistic causes, and it is not always easy to distinguish between them. Nabokov also suggested a few other links. Some of them, as I will show, are debatable, specifically when it comes to his translation choices.

Let us now look more specifically at the foreign words which can be found in Pushkin's text and in Nabokov's translation. I will demonstrate whether there is a correlation between them or if the translator overplayed the French presence.

Translating foreign words

Nabokov's translation gives a major role to the French language, sometimes excessively so. In his 1985 article 'La traduction comme épreuve de l'étranger', translation theorist Antoine Berman underlined that the variety of languages had to be taken into account by the translator, and that it was one of the biggest challenges of translation:

> [T]he superimposition of languages is threatened by translation. The relation of tension and integration that exists in the original between the vernacular language and the koine, between the underlying language and the surface language, etc. tends to be effaced. [...] This is the central problem posed by translating novels – a problem that demands maximum reflection from the translator.
>
> (Berman 2000: 295–6)

In this article, Berman explained what deforming tendencies altered the original, and two of these seem to be predominant in Nabokov's *Onegin*, namely clarification and exoticization. Indeed, by adding a great number of xenisms and loanwords into his translation, Nabokov made more explicit what was, to him, the Gallic dimension of Pushkin's language. Berman's description of the negative aspect of clarification is evocative of Dolinin's 'loud splash':

> Of course, clarification is inherent in translation, to the extent that every translation comprises some degree of explicitation. But that can signify two very different things:
>
> (1) the explicitation can be the manifestation of something that is not apparent, but concealed or repressed, in the original. Translation, by virtue of its own movement, puts into play this element. [...]

> The power of illumination, of *manifestation*, (1) as I indicated apropos Hölderlin,
> is the supreme power of translation. But in a negative sense, (2) explicitation
> aims to render 'clear' what does not wish to be clear in the original.
>
> (Berman 2000: 289)

Loanwords and xenisms underline the Gallic dimension of the text in Nabokov's translation. More specifically, by adding xenisms (which are in italics), Nabokov also indulged in another deforming tendency, namely exoticization:

> Exoticization can take two forms. First, a typographical procedure (italics) is
> used to isolate what does not exist in the original. Then, more insidiously, it is
> 'added' to be 'more authentic', emphasizing the vernacular according to a certain
> stereotype of it (as in the popular woodcut illustrations published by Épinal).
>
> (Berman 2000: 294)

As I will show, adding some French elements is not limited to xenisms: loanwords are also inserted into the text.

In order to study concrete examples of clarification and exoticization, I will first focus on xenisms present in the Russian text and how Nabokov added some in his translation. And then I will analyse the presence of loanwords from the French in the translation to see whether they are justified or not. This will lead us to bring into question the heterogeneity of Nabokov's translation.

Translating Pushkin's xenisms

There are quite a few xenisms in Pushkin's text, and they are twice signalled as foreign through typography: not only are they in italics,[12] but they are also in Latin letters, while the rest of the text is in the Cyrillic alphabet. Nabokov tackled xenisms in two different ways depending on their language in Pushkin's text.

Nabokov usually keeps the italics that were used by Pushkin, but since there is no longer any Cyrillic character, the double signalling disappears: only the difference between italic and Roman remains. In the following examples, I intentionally leave the quotes in Cyrillic and do not transliterate them; that way, the foreign dimension of the xenism in Latin characters appears more clearly:

> В конце письма поставить *vale* / put at the bottom of a letter *vale*
>
> (Pushkin [1833] 2003: 14; Pushkin [1975] 1991, I: 98)

> Готов охлопать *entrechat* / is ready to applaud an *entrechat*
>
> (Pushkin [1833] 2003: 20; Pushkin [1975] 1991, I: 102)

Уж отворял свой *vasisdas* / already opened his *vasisdas*

> (Pushkin [1833] 2003: 33; Pushkin [1975] 1991, I: 111)

Therefore, italics signal the presence of the foreign language, be it foreign to the Russian or to the English.

However, for the following xenism coming from the English, Nabokov signalled it differently. Indeed, he used inverted commas:

Того, что модой самовластной

В высоком лондонском кругу

Зовется *vulgar*. (Не могу…

Люблю я очень это слово,

Но не могу перевести […]) (Pushkin [1833] 2003: 255)

what by the autocratic fashion

in the high London circle

is called 'vulgar' (I can't –

– much do I like that word,

but can't translate it […])

> (Pushkin [1975] 1991, I: 288–9)

It is interesting to note that the narrator specifically insists on untranslatability: it is because 'vulgar' cannot translate properly into Russian that he uses the English word. On the other hand, in the translation into English, the inverted commas around 'vulgar' underline the word not as foreign but as a mere signifier: they put it at a distance.

Unfortunately, this is one of the few cases in which the English language is shown in its foreignness in the translation. In fact, Pushkin's French and English xenisms are usually erased or toned down by the translator: italics disappear, whether the words are English or French. In the following example from Pushkin's text, the foreignness of the words in English and in French stands out thanks to typography:

Monsieur прогнали со двора.

Вот мой Онегин на свободе;

Острижен по последней моде,

Как *dandy* лондонский одет –

И наконец увидел свет.

> (Pushkin [1833] 2003: 13)

But in Nabokov's text, there is no longer any visual difference, except for the capital letter added to 'dandy':

Monsieur was ousted from the place.
Now my Onegin is at large:
hair cut after the latest fashion,
dressed like a London Dandy –
and finally he saw the World.

(Pushkin [1975] 1991, I: 97)

For the English word 'dandy', one can regret that Nabokov did not signal its presence in his translation, but this is something that happens often in translation: when the language which was foreign in the original text becomes the target text, it usually disappears.[13] However, in a novel like *Lolita* in which there are many French words in the English text, one could find in the translation a typographical signalling of code-switching. Interestingly enough, Nabokov collaborated to this translation so he knew of this strategy. Thus, this is how the first French expression is written: 'Et lui, *mon cher petit papa**'; and at the bottom of the page, a footnote explains that 'words in italics and followed by an asterisk (*) are in French in the text' (Nabokov 1959a: 15; my literal translation). In Nabokov's *Onegin*, asterisks could have allowed for the English from the original to be visible; alternatively, Nabokov could have included an indication on the page about the original language of the word 'dandy'.

When it comes to 'Monsieur', the foreign dimension linked to French is toned down: what was a xenism in Pushkin's text becomes a loanword in the translation. Of course, the word 'Monsieur' exists in English (the *OED* states clearly that it is 'a borrowing from the French'), so it can seem excessive to suggest that it should be written in italics. However, as I will show, Nabokov did not hesitate to italicize words that are naturalized as English words, and he even added xenisms in places where the Russian text had none.

Xenisms added by Nabokov in the translation

Sometimes, Nabokov included xenisms without any clear justification. For example, he argued that, in the following quote, 'Кувшины с яблочной водой' (Pushkin [1833] 2003: 53; pitchers with apple water, my literal translation), the Russian expression for a drink made with apples was a translation from the French (Pushkin [1975] 1991, II: 223); he, therefore, translated the passage with the French expression itself, and not its translation into English: 'pitchers of *eau-de-pomme*' (Pushkin [1975] 1991, I: 130). In some other cases, Nabokov resorted to loanwords that used to be French, but he insisted on their foreignness by adding italics, thus exoticizing them. This is the case in one of the examples quoted above by Dolinin: 'In his backwoods an eremitic sage, / the ancient *corvée*'s yoke / by the light quitrent he replaced' (Pushkin [1975] 1991, I: 127). The *OED* explains that 'corvée' comes from the French and has been used with this spelling in English since the end of the eighteenth century. However, since Nabokov added italics, it made it look even more French than the accent could and turned it into a xenism.

Sometimes, Nabokov clearly justified the foreign origin of some words that Pushkin had not signalled as foreign. The justification can rely either on semantics or on literature.

To translate a Russian word, Nabokov sometimes used a French word when he contended that the usually accepted English translation did not correspond to the original Russian. One should remember that Nabokov often seemed to treat monolingual dictionaries like bibles (the *OED* and *Webster* for English, *Dal'* for Russian), but he harshly criticized bilingual ones because they were not precise enough or they lacked nuance. This is what he wrote following Wilson's review of his translation:

> I shall stop only a moment to consider Mr. Wilson's pathetic assumption that [...] a reliable and complete *Russko-angliyskiy slovar'* [Russian-English dictionary] not only exists (it does not) but is more easily available to the student than, say, the second unabridged edition (1960) of Webster's, which I really must urge Mr. Wilson to acquire. Even if that miraculous *slovar'* did exist, there would still be the difficulty of choosing, without my help, the right shade between two near synonyms and avoiding, without my guidance, the trap-falls of idiomatic phrases no longer in use.
>
> (Nabokov [1966a] 1990: 251)

Therefore, in his own translation, he often favoured his own vocabulary over the recommendation of published dictionaries.[14] In the first chapter of Nabokov's translation, one can find the following sentence: 'the upper *ton* is rather tedious' (Pushkin [1975] 1991, I: 113). In the original,[15] the word that '*ton*' is supposed to translate is 'тон' (*ton*). Therefore, this word is not written in French (in Latin characters) in Pushkin's text, so it is not a xenism in Russian (even if its proximity with French suggests it must be a loanword). And if one looks up this word in the *Oxford Russian Dictionary*, it is translated as 'tone'. In his commentary, Nabokov explains what looks like a contradiction or a mistranslation:

> Pushkin was fond of this French word, which the English sometimes did not italicize in those days. It was used in the sense of social style in Russian drawing rooms as well as in the English ones. A Russian of today would be

apt to confuse with *ton* its homonym meaning 'tone', individual manner of speaking, assumed attitude and so on. *Ton*, in the early nineteenth century sense, was the 'bon ton[16]'.

(Pushkin [1975] 1991, III: 189)

Therefore, Nabokov explains that, in this context, the word has nothing to do with intonation or voice, which justifies his use of the French word '*ton*'. Semantic precision is also the argument that Nabokov uses to justify why he resorts to a French xenism in his translation, even though the Russian original included no word in French (in italics and Latin characters). In his translation of the following passage, taken from the last chapter, Onegin describes an elegant lady he sees in the *ton*; she reminds him of Tatyana, his neighbour in the countryside who had sent him a love letter several years ago but was rejected by him. Not only is he about to discover it is indeed Tatyana, but she is also out of reach now (and of course he will now fall madly in love with her):

> 'Tell me, Prince, you don't know
> who is it there in the *framboise* beret talking with the Spanish ambassador?'
> The prince looks at Onegin:
> 'Aha! Indeed, long have you not been in the *monde*.
> Wait, I'll present you'.
> 'But *who* is she?' 'My wife'. (Pushkin [1975] 1991, I: 289)

Here, French is closely associated with elegance and fashion,[17] for example, with the loanword 'beret', which translates the Russian word '*берет*' (*beret*), which is itself a loanword from the French. Here, there is a perfect symmetry between the two words in Russian and in English. But the French dimension of the description is reinforced by the xenism *framboise* which does not have an equivalent in the Russian text; indeed, '*малиновый*[18]' is the adjective coming from '*малина*' (raspberry), but there is nothing French in it. Once again, Nabokov uses semantics to justify his translation, but there is also a more aesthetic dimension:

> A soft, brimless headgear; of crimson velvet, in this case. I have used *framboise* because 'raspberry' as a color, both in Russian and in French, seems to convey a richer, more vivid sense of red than does English 'raspberry'. I see the latter tint as associated rather with the purplish bloom of the Russian jam, or the French jelly, made of it.
>
> An elegant lady in 1824 would use a flat beret of claret-colored or violet velvet for day wear [...]. Other fashionable colors were *ponceau* (poppy red) and *rouge grenat* (garnet red).

(Pushkin [1975] 1991, III: 181)

For Nabokov, 'raspberry' does not mean '*малина*': the colour is not the same.[19] It is interesting to note that he associates Russian and French not only through their similarities in colours, but also through food ('the Russian jam, or the French jelly'): Nabokov's synesthesia seems to be at play here. In his commentary, Nabokov displays a whole array of reds, but for him, only one of them corresponds to the headgear that Tatyana is wearing.

When Onegin asked the prince who this elegant lady in a beret was, he exclaimed: 'Aha! Indeed, long have you not been in the *monde*'. This French xenism was also added in the translation by Nabokov, but this time, the justification is more literary. The corresponding Russian word, 'свет', *svet*, means both 'light' and 'world'. But when it is the second meaning that is necessary, Nabokov often resorted to the French xenism '*monde*', and not 'world' or 'society', as is recommended by the *Oxford Russian-English Dictionary*. Here is how he justifies his translation choice in the commentary:

> *Svet*, in this sense, is *le monde, le beau monde, le grand monde* (*bol'shoy svet*), 'the world of Fashion', 'the Gay World', 'the Great World', 'High Life', 'High Society' – a bouquet of synonyms.
>
> Cf. Pope: 'My only Son, I'd have him see the World: | His French is pure…'
>   (*Imitation of Horace*, bk. II, ep. II).
>
> Cf. Byron: 'Don Juan saw that Microcosm on stilts, | Yclept the Great World…'
> (*Don Juan*, XII, LVI, 1–2).
>   (Pushkin [1975] 1991, II: 44)

The Russian word does not have a French etymology that could justify Nabokov's use of the French xenism, but he argues that English writers used to refer to the notion of 'world'. One thing that Nabokov does not explain is why he favours the French '*monde*' instead of the English word that these authors were using. However, when he was attacked for this use of the word '*monde*' by Wilson (1965), he repeated his literary justification, but this time he argued that English authors used '*monde*'. Quite conveniently, for once, he did not have his *OED* at hand:

> According to Mr. Wilson it should always appear with its '*le*' in the translation of the poem. This is an inept practice, of course (advocated mainly by those who, like Mr. Wilson, are insecure and self-conscious in their use of *le* and *la*), and would have resulted in saying '*le* noisy *monde*' instead of 'the noisy *monde*' (Eight: xxxiv: 12). English writers of the eighteenth and nineteenth centuries wrote 'the *monde*', not 'le monde'. I am sure that if Mr. Wilson consults the OED, which I do not have here, he will find examples from Walpole, Byron,

Thackeray, and others. What was good enough for them is good enough for Pushkin and me.

(Nabokov [1966a] 1990: 258)

Another inconsistency is that Nabokov did not always use '*monde*' to translate '*свет*', *svet*. Sometimes, he used English words, namely the noun 'world', with or without a capital (Pushkin [1975] 1991, I: 97; 296) or the adjective 'social' ('Tedious to him became the social hum' (Pushkin [1975] 1991, I: 112)). For this expression, Nabokov did indicate in his commentary that it was a Gallicism ('*svéta shum*: An old French cliché, *le bruit, le tumulte, le fracas du monde*' (Pushkin [1975] 1991, II: 148)) but he still used English words in his translation. What is surprising is that, for one and only term used by Pushkin, Nabokov decided to use a variety of terms; it is all the more surprising because, in his texts defending his translation theory, Nabokov clearly advocated for the strictest respect of authorial repetition. This is how he responded to one of Wilson's criticisms:

> If in translating *toska lyubvi Tat'yanu-gonit* (Three: xvi: 1), 'the ache of love chases Tatjana' [...], I put 'chases' instead of the 'pursues' that Mr. Wilson has the temerity to propose, I do so not only because 'pursues' is in Russian not *gonit* but *presleduet*, but also because, as Mr. Wilson has not noticed, it would be a misleading repetition of the 'pursue' used in the preceding stanza (*tebya presleduyut mechty*, 'daydreams pursue you'), and my method is to repeat a term at close range only when Pushkin repeats it.

(Nabokov [1966a] 1990: 259)

Nabokov argued that not respecting authorial repetition could be allowed in only one situation:

> A point has been made of preserving the recurrence of epithets (so characteristic of a Russian romanticist's meager and overworked vocabulary), unless a contextual shade of meaning demanded the use of a synonym.

(Nabokov [1963a] 1991: x–xi)

Here, Nabokov seemed to argue that he could distinguish between the shades of meanings when Pushkin himself used the same term again and again, which seems to suggest that he knew better than his author what meaning was the good one. It boils down to modifying the artistic creation of the author by clarifying what could have been his intentions. In that case, Nabokov seems to be assuming the privileges of an author more than the duties of a translator to his text. I will go back to the question of a potential appropriation of the author's text by the translator in the last section of this chapter.

With xenisms, the degree of Gallicization is extremely high, but in terms of quantity, the most widespread phenomenon which makes the translation more French is the use of loanwords.

Using loanwords in the translation

Different causes can explain why loanwords are justified in Nabokov's translation; however, a great number of these loanwords seem unjustified or exaggerated.

As with xenisms, etymology can give sufficient cause to use loanwords. Thus, in several cases, the use of a loanword from the French in Nabokov's translation is justified by the fact that the corresponding Russian word in Pushkin's text is also borrowed from the French. And actually, etymology merely confirms what pronunciation could suggest to the reader who is not versed in linguistics. A case in point would be the word '*берет*' (*beret*), studied above.

If some loanwords could be justified by etymology, this is not the case for a great number of them in Nabokov's translation. These come from the French, whereas some English equivalents could have been chosen, as I suggest in square brackets:

детский праздник / Children's fete [not 'party, celebration, holiday']
(Pushkin [1833] 2003: 19; Pushkin [1975] 1991, I: 102)

Свидание / rendezvous [not 'meeting, date, appointment']
(Pushkin [1833] 2003: 42; Pushkin [1975] 1991, I: 118)

в чистом поле / in open champaign [not 'in open country']
(Pushkin [1833] 2003: 201; Pushkin [1975] 1991, I: 246)

Nabokov insisted even more on this Gallic touch when he revised the translation in 1975, and thus fulfilled the wish he had expressed in his text 'Reply to My Critics' in 1966: 'It is still not close enough and not ugly enough. In future editions I plan to defowlerize it more drastically' (Nabokov [1966a] 1990: 243). Thus, between the 1964 translation and the 1975 revision, the following changes occurred: 'hall porter' became 'concierge',[20] 'new' was replaced by 'novel',[21] and the very English 'lady of the house' was changed into the Frenchified 'chatelaine'.[22]

If etymology is a linguistic justification for the use of a loanword, Nabokov more often resorted to literary reasons to explain why he used Gallicisms, and there are mainly three of them.

First of all, it can be justified by rhythm. As explained previously, Nabokov made the debatable decision to write his literal translation in iambs, in particular because Pushkin's verse was in iambic tetrameter (Nabokov [1964b] 1991: 3). When Nabokov translated the following sentence, 'На шубах у подъезда спят' (Pushkin [1833] 2003: 24), he decided to translate the word '*шубах*' ('fur coats' in the locative case) as 'pelisses', with the following result: 'Sleep on the pelisses at the carriage porch' (Pushkin [1975] 1991, I: 104). According to Gerschenkron, the French loanword was chosen because of Nabokov's self-imposed rhythmic constraint: 'Only because of the meter the very Russian fur coats have been converted into French "pelisses"' (1966: 339).

Another reason is Nabokov's wish to convey part of the Russian euphony to his reader. Already in his 'Art of Translation' (1941), the translator insisted that sounds had to be taken into account when choosing a translation, and also what associations those sounds conjured up; this is how he explained his choice not to translate the verb '*помнить*' (to remember) by the verb 'to remember':

> *Yah pom-new* is a deeper and smoother plunge into the past than 'I remember', which falls flat on its belly like an inexperienced diver; *chewed-no-yay* has a lovely Russian 'monster' (*chúdo*) in it; and a whispered 'listen' (*chu!*); and the dative ending of a sunbeam (*luchú*), and many other fair relations among Russian words. It belongs phonetically and mentally to a certain series of words, and this Russian series does not correspond to the English series in which 'I remember' is found. And inversely, 'remember' though it clashes with the corresponding 'pom-new' series, is connected with an English series of its own whenever real poets do use it.
>
> (Nabokov [1941a] 2008: 10)

When it comes to French, one should remember that Nabokov used to say that it was the language whose sonority was, to him, the most enchanting.[23] And in the following passage from Nabokov's *Onegin* which deals with the burial of Eugene's uncle, the phonic justification seems to explain why Nabokov translated '*похоронили*', *pohoronili* by 'interred',[24] which is a French loanword,[25] and not by 'buried'. And in his commentary, Nabokov insisted on the musicality of the words surrounding the verb:

> The Russian-speaking reader will enjoy the amusing sets of alliterations in ll. 4 and 5 – a rare rhythm, and exceptionally rare in consecutive lines [...]. The components of *pohoronili* seem to have gone on a spree.
>
> (Pushkin [1975] 1991, II: 196–7)

More specifically, Nabokov underlined the alliterations that existed between the verb *pohoronili* and the words from the previous line, *Ohotniki do poxoron*. It seems that the choice of 'interred' made it possible to retrieve the 'r' as well as the 'n' from the Russian verb *pohoronili*.

The third literary cause stems from Nabokov's knowledge of Pushkin's biography. This biographical justification explains the translator's use of the word 'sapajou', which provoked the ire of many critics who could not understand why Nabokov used it to translate the word '*обезьяна*' (monkey). This is how Nabokov justified his choice:

> True, *obez'yana* means any kind of monkey but it so happens that neither 'monkey' nor 'ape' is good enough in the context.
>
> 'Sapajou' (which technically is applied to two genera of neotropical monkeys) has in French a colloquial sense of 'ruffian', 'lecher', 'ridiculous chap'. Now, in lines 1-2 and 9-11 of Four: vii ('the less we love a woman, the easier 'tis to be liked by her … but that grand game is worthy of old sapajous of our forefathers' vaunted times') Pushkin echoes a moralistic passage in his own letter written in French from Kishinev to his young brother in Moscow in the autumn of 1822, that is seven months before beginning *Eugene Onegin* and two years before reaching Canto Four. The passage, well known to readers of Pushkin, goes: '*Moins on aime une femme et plus on est sur [sic] de l'avoir… mais cette jouissance est digne d'un vieux sapajou du dix-huitième siècle*'.
>
> Not only could I not resist the temptation of retranslating the *obez'yan* of the canto into the Anglo-French 'sapajous' of the letter, but I was also looking forward to somebody's pouncing on that word and allowing me to retaliate with that wonderfully satisfying reference. Mr. Wilson obliged – and here it is.
>
> (Nabokov [1966a] 1990: 255–6)

As we have seen, Nabokov's use of a Frenchified vocabulary can usually be justified by etymology or by literary reasons, but in some cases, his explanations are a bit more personal and one could almost call them 'Nabokovian' reasons (especially his synesthetic reasons). But a few years after his translation was published, Nabokov used another justification to explain some of his debatable choices.

Nabokov's 'signal words'

This method is almost philological: with some specific words in his translation, which he called 'signal words', Nabokov intended to attract the reader's attention to some specificities of Pushkin's language. He explained this translation method of his own in the text 'Reply to My Critics' (1966) and in a short text added in the 1975 revised translation ('"EO" Revisited'). The fact that signal words were not evoked anywhere before Nabokov's translation was published (and attacked) suggests that he came to realize that his very own vision of translation had to be more strongly justified. For Nabokov, his signal words are meant to attract the reader's attention to some specificities such as repetitions (Nabokov [1966a] 1990: 259), rare words (252), archaisms and particular sounds (253). Here is a more general explanation he gives, in which he happens to mention his Gallic choices:

> The phrases I decide upon aspire towards literality, not readability. They are steps in the ice, pitons in the sheer rock of fidelity. Some are mere signal words whose only purpose is to suggest or indicate that a certain pet term of Pushkin's has recurred at that point. Others have been chosen for their Gallic touch implicit in this or that Russian attempt to imitate a French turn of phrase. All have pedigrees of agony and rejection and reinstatement, and should be treated as convalescents and ancient orphans, and not hooted at as impostors by a critic who says he admires some of my books. I do not care if a word is 'archaic' or 'dialect' or 'slang'; I am an eclectic democrat in this matter, and whatever suits me, goes. My method may be wrong but it is a method, and a genuine critic's job should have been to examine the method itself instead of crossly fishing out of my pond some of the oddities with which I had deliberately stocked it.
>
> (Nabokov [1966a] 1990: 252)

When it comes to Gallicisms, signal words can include xenisms as well as loanwords, as the following examples will show.

The word 'sauvage' was used without italics in the 1964 translation but with italics in the revised edition: the *OED* does not reference this word, so Nabokov was right to amend it. Nabokov was criticized for using this term as a translation for '*дика*', *dika* (Pushkin [1833] 2003: 67), and yet again, he explained his choice with a literary justification. He started, however, by indicating its status of signal word:

> [A]part from the fact that it has no exact English equivalent, I chose this signal word to warn readers that Pushkin was using *dika* not simply in the sense of 'wild' or 'unsociable' but in a Gallic sense as a translation of '*sauvage*'. Incidentally, it often occurs in English novels of the time along with *monde* and *ennui*.
>
> (Nabokov [1966a] 1990: 258)

Nabokov also explained that the word 'mollitude' was another signal word (259), which was justified by its being used in French poetry:

> In using *nega*, Pushkin and his constellation were trying to render the French poetical formulas *paresse voluptueuse, mollesse, molles délices*, etc., which the English Arcadians had already turned into 'soft delights'. Elsewhere I have rendered *nega* by the archaic but very exact 'mollitude'.
>
> (Pushkin [1975] 1991, II: 186)

This commentary is given to explain the word 'voluptuousness' in the first translation (Pushkin 1964: 119), revised as 'sensuousness' in 1975 (Pushkin [1975] 1991, I: 116); indeed, in this passage, the Russian word '*nega*' was not translated by 'mollitude', which was used 'elsewhere', as Nabokov writes himself. This inconsistency is similar to that observed for '*monde*' and it is now time to explore the limit between the author and the translator in Nabokov's case.

Appropriating Pushkin? From inconsistency to *otsebyatina*

Inconsistency

Semantic justification versus the artist leaving his mark

As mentioned before, Nabokov sometimes translated one word in the original text by various terms in his *Onegin*. For the word 'nega[26]', here are the different nuances that Nabokov explained he could perceive:

> *Nega* ranges from 'mollitude' (Fr. *mollesse*), i.e., soft luxuriousness, 'dulcitude', through various shades of amorous pensiveness, *douce paresse*, and sensual tenderness to outright voluptuousness (Fr. *volupté*). The translator has to be careful here not to overdo in English what Pushkin is on the point of overdoing in Russian when he makes his maiden burn with all the French languors of flesh and fancy.
>
> (Pushkin [1975] 1991, II: 337)

Therefore, for Nabokov, it is because of a great variety of meanings that the word '*nega*' can be translated by several Gallicisms (like the loanword 'mollitude' or the xenism '*douce paresse*') or by words which are strictly English: for example, according to the *OED*, 'sensuousness' was invented by English poet Milton and then adopted by Coleridge.

But inserting variation in places where the source text was repeating itself almost suggests that the translator knew better than the author what nuance the author had in mind. Of course, there are some words in every language which have various meanings, like *svet* which can mean 'world' or 'light' depending on context, and of course a translator will know the difference; and in translation, it is also a common place to say that things depend on context. But here, Nabokov is presenting such subtle variations of nuances that it seems to go beyond a mere question of context and polysemy. It looks as if these different terms for one and only word are rather a means to leave one's mark on the translation, thereby appropriating it slightly. And when Nabokov wrote that 'The translator has to be careful here not to overdo in English what Pushkin is on the point of overdoing in Russian', one feels that he was aware of the slippery slope he was on.

These variations are all the more surprising because Nabokov insisted on the importance of strictly respecting authorial repetition.[27] But there are many examples that show that, as a translator, he did not always repeat what the author had repeated. For example, in Pushkin's text, the expression 'острые слова' (Pushkin [1833] 2003: 34; sharp words, my translation) is used twice, but they are translated in two different ways by Nabokov. The first time, he used a loanword from the French for the adjective, and an English word for the noun: 'piquant sayings' (Pushkin [1975] 1991, I: 112). And for the second occurrence (Pushkin [1833] 2003: 281), Nabokov used the English word 'witticism' in the 1964 edition (Pushkin 1964: 318), but in the 1975 revision, however, he chose the loanword 'bons mots' (Pushkin [1975] 1991, I, p. 308). In both occurrences, Nabokov resorted to French, but he did insert some variation in his translation whereas Pushkin used the same word.

This variation adds a creative dimension to Nabokov's supposedly literal translation: behind the translator, the author seems to lurk.

Nabokovian vocabulary

It so happens that some of the words mentioned previously are to be found in some of Nabokov's own writings, more specifically his novels and his interviews (for which, as is well known, he would always write his answers in advance, thus inscribing these interviews in the realm of the written word).

For example, the *OED* indicates that 'mollitude' was used in *Ada* in 1969, which makes it the only occurrence since 1767. This word is even used twice in the novel (Nabokov [1969] 1996: 281, 378). As for the word 'monde', Nabokov used a variation of it, 'beau monde', on several occasions (he had used it with a hyphen, 'beau-monde', in his translation (Pushkin [1975] 1991, I: 240)). For example, in an interview in 1969, Nabokov resorted to the expression to describe Pushkin:

> Pushkin, professional poet and Russian nobleman, used to shock the *beau monde* by declaring that he wrote for his own pleasure but published for the sake of money. I do likewise, but have never shocked anybody – except, perhaps, a former publisher of mine who used to counter my indignant requests by saying that I'm much too good a writer to need extravagant advances.
>
> (Nabokov [1973] 1990: 144)

Of course, it is particularly interesting to note that Nabokov is here comparing himself directly to the Russian bard. The expression also appears in several of Nabokov's novels published after his translation of Pushkin: twice in *Ada* (Nabokov [1969] 1996: 202, 296) and once in *Look at the Harlequins!* In that particular case, the reference to *Onegin* is even explicit: 'In a word, her appearance in the *beau monde* of *émigré* literature echoed amusingly Chapter Eight of *Eugene Onegin*' (Nabokov [1974] 1996: 652).

These similarities in vocabulary between Nabokov the translator and Nabokov the author can only give the observer pause: either he incorporated these words into his prose after having used them in his translation of *Onegin*, or these words were already part of his vocabulary when he decided to use them in his translation, meaning he left his lexical mark on Pushkin's text.

This Nabokovian dimension of the language used in the translation and some of his unjustified choices suggest that Nabokov was now and then indulging in *otsebyatina*, which is a term that he used to describe what he deemed one of the worst faults in a translator.

Nabokov's *otsebyatina*

This term is a neologism in English which Nabokov coined with Russian words to describe a translator's tendency to appropriate the text they are supposed to translate:

> *Otsebyatina.* This convenient cant word consists of the words *ot*, meaning 'from', and *sebya*, meaning 'oneself', with a pejorative suffix, *yatina*, tagged on (its *ya* takes improper advantage of the genitive ending of the pronoun, coinciding with it and producing a strongly stressed *bya* sound which to a Russian's ear connotes juvenile disgust). Lexically translated, it can be rendered as 'come-from-oneselfer' or 'from-oneselfity'. It is employed to describe the personal contributions of self-sufficient or desperate translators (or actors who have forgotten their speeches).
>
> (Nabokov [1964a] 1990: 238–9)

Decades before his publication of *Eugene Onegin* and before his theory of literal translation, Nabokov had a different vision of translation: in his essay 'The Art of Translation', he defended artistic translations and claimed that ideally, the translator should be an artist. He seemed to think that the best translator possible should be an author-translator:

> [H]e must have as much talent, or at least the same kind of talent, as the author he chooses. [...] while having genius and knowledge, he must possess the gift of

mimicry and be able to act, as it were, the real author's part by impersonating his tricks of demeanor and speech, his ways and his mind, with the utmost degree of verisimilitude.

(Nabokov [1941a] 2008: 8–9)

But at the time, he was also aware of the risk that such a translator could represent for the text:

[T]he greater his individual talent, the more apt he will be to drown the foreign masterpiece under the sparkling ripples of his own personal style. Instead of dressing up like the real author, he dresses up the author as himself.

(8)

Therefore, while Nabokov recommended that the author-translator should be able to imitate the real author, he knew that the risk was that he could transform the text into one of his own creations: 'he dresses up the author as himself'.

When defending his translation of *Eugene Onegin*, Nabokov made a clear distinction between his two identities (author and translator):

Unlike my novels, *EO* possesses an ethical side, moral and human elements. It reflects the compiler's honesty or dishonesty, skill or sloppiness. If told I am a bad poet, I smile; but if I'm told I am a poor scholar, I reach for my heaviest dictionary.

(Nabokov [1964a] 1990: 241)

Therefore, Nabokov did his best to translate this text as a scholar, not as a poet, but it seems that he did indulge in *otsebyatina* occasionally and that the author he was sometimes struggled to disappear behind his role of translator. What probably made the task even harder was the fact that Nabokov was translating Pushkin, the author he revered the most; worse: he was tackling his masterpiece *Onegin* after having tried his hand on so many of his texts (poems, plays, pseudotranslations, etc.). But if the author in Nabokov sometimes seemed to lurk behind the translator, the main author he was serving remains Pushkin: it is for him that he was willing to defend his translation with his 'heaviest dictionary'.

Conclusion

Despite the faults that one can find in Nabokov's translation, one has to recognize that they are limited to isolated words and to the exaggerated importance that is given to some of their characteristics. Moreover, the foreignizing dimension of Nabokov's *Onegin* probably makes it hard to read indeed, but one should not forget why Nabokov started the translation in the first place:

> This opus owes its birth to a casual remark my wife made in 1950 – in response to my disgust with rhymed paraphrases of *Eugene Onegin*, every line of which I had to revise for my students – 'Why don't you translate it yourself?' This is the result. It has taken some ten years of labor. [...] My translation is, of course, a literal one, a crib, a pony.
>
> (Nabokov [1973] 1990: 38)

But Nabokov denied having had his students in mind when preparing this translation: in 1963 he mocked this ambition that Arndt claimed to have[28] and then in 1966 he said that this ambition was falsely ascribed to him when really, it was only Arndt's.[29] But it is surprising that he could so bluntly pretend to have forgotten what he wrote in the foreword to his own translation:

> Pushkin has likened translators to horses changed at the posthouses of civilization. The greatest reward I can think of is that students may use my work as a pony.
>
> (Nabokov [1963a] 1991: x)

It is noteworthy to see how often he used terms such as 'pony' and 'crib', as he did in yet another interview:

> My only ambition has been to provide a crib, a pony, an absolutely literal translation of the thing, with copious and pedantic notes whose bulk far exceeds the text of the poem. Only a paraphrase 'reads well'; my translation does not; it is honest and clumsy, ponderous and slavishly faithful.
>
> (Nabokov [1973] 1990: 7)

What is interesting is that, in American slang, a 'pony' means 'A literal translation or summary of a text used as a short cut or study aid; a crib' (*OED*). Therefore, it is closely associated with the idea of studying. Likewise, a crib is defined by the same dictionary as 'A translation of a classic or other work in a foreign language, for the illegitimate use of students. (*colloquial*)' His translation was therefore made to assist anyone who was willing to read Pushkin's text in the original, and it was not meant to read well, as Nabokov wrote on several occasions. Consequently, the following remark by Gershchenkron is not the criticism it initially looks like, at least from the perspective of Nabokov's literalist stance: 'Nabokov's translation can and indeed should be studied, but despite all the cleverness and occasional brilliance it cannot be read' (1966: 340). As I will show in my next chapter, this facilitated access to the original text is a legacy from another great author-translator.

In the translation, the exaggeration of certain terms was intended to attract the eye of the reader, or rather of the student, to peculiarities in Pushkin's text, as Nabokov explained with his 'signal words'. Moreover, Nabokov was accused of insisting too much on French intertext. I will also show in my next chapter that these two types of exaggeration in translation can have qualities which go beyond ethics: they border politics.

8

Investigating Nabokov's Literalism, from Chateaubriand to Venuti

When Nabokov's translation of *Onegin* was published, it provoked shockwaves because it did not correspond to the standards of translated literature at the time; however, it would be wrong to think that his vision of translation was unheard of: Nabokov's literalism has predecessors, and some translators still advocate similar principles today. In this chapter, I shed further light on the precepts of Nabokov the author-translator by comparing them to the translation method of two eminent figures.

The first one is François-René de Chateaubriand, who like Nabokov was not only an author but also a translator: in 1836 he produced a literal translation of Milton's *Paradise Lost* into French.[1] Many Nabokov scholars have studied the role and influence that Chateaubriand the author had on Nabokov,[2] but his major role as a translator is hardly ever mentioned,[3] even though Nabokov opened his 'Translator's Introduction' with an epigraph by Pushkin praising Chateaubriand's endeavour, which was a clear sign of how inspirational this translation could have been in his own translation of Pushkin.

I will then contrast Nabokov's position regarding translation to that of Lawrence Venuti, one of the leading translation theorists nowadays. He advocates for a type of foreignizing translation, but not for literalism necessarily. I mentioned Nabokov's foreignizing translation in the previous chapter, but as we will see, Nabokov's practice and that of Venuti have differences; more importantly, their motivations are different: Nabokov seems to be motivated by the sheer love of art and poetics, the desire to respect the many nuances of Pushkin's text as he sees them, whereas Venuti has a political agenda. I will show, however, that Nabokov's translation can also be analysed through the prism of politics, through Venuti but also through Pascale Casanova's *The World Republic of Letters*; in that respect, Marijeta Bozovic's book *Nabokov's Canon: From Onegin to Ada* will be particularly helpful.

But before analysing each figure in comparison with Nabokov, it is necessary to dwell on the notion of 'transparency' in translation[4] because it is used by Chateaubriand and Venuti, but in opposite ways.

Transparency in translation: A few contradictory terminologies

Nabokov opened the introduction to his translation with a quote from Pushkin referring to the French romantic writer:

> Nowadays – an unheard of case! – the foremost French writer is translating Milton word for word and proclaiming that an interlinear translation would be the summit of his art, had such been possible.
>
> Pushkin, from an article (late 1836 or early 1837) on Chateaubriand's *Le Paradis perdu*, 1836
>
> (Nabokov [1964b] 1991: 1)

In this article, Pushkin tends to assimilate word-for-word translation, interlinear translation and literal translation in spite of their differences,[5] but he praises Chateaubriand for sticking to the text very closely, thus going against the tendency of 'corrective translation' (26); he is referring here to the well-known '*Belles infidèles*', which are beautiful renderings of the original but are unfaithful: they adapt and rewrite it. This is how Pushkin ends his essay:

> [T]he two volumes of this translation are as brilliant as all his previous work, whatever harsh critics choose to say about its imperfections. The undeniable beauty of its pages are worthy of the highest achievements of the great writer, and this will save his book from the condescending reader despite any flaws.
>
> (Pushkin 2013: 26)

To explain his vision of literal translation, Chateaubriand used the metaphor of transparency: 'I traced Milton's paper through glass' (Chateaubriand [1836a] 1861: iii; my translation[6]). Just like a child would use tracing paper (*papier calque*) to copy a drawing, Chateaubriand refers to the translation process as a piece of glass which enabled him to make a French copy of Milton's *Paradise Lost*, even if this version could be considered a *calque*. Therefore, for Chateaubriand, the transparent glass means that the reader has direct access to the original text, which is given in a source-oriented translation.

However, for most translation scholars, the image of glass is used in the opposite way. Thus, translation theorist Georges Mounin opposed two visions of translation, transparent-glass translation or coloured-glass translation:

> Either you translate in such a way that the text, literally made French, with a language which is not strange in the least, always looks as if it had been thought and then written in French, that is to say, in a way, fulfilling the ambition of 'belles infidèles', but without the unfaithfulness: this is the first type of translation.
>
> Or else you translate word by word in such a way that the reader, line after line, has the exhilarating impression that they are reading the text in the original forms of the foreign language (semantic, morphological, stylistic), so that the reader can never forget for a second that they are reading in French a text which was first thought and then written in such or such foreign language: this is the second type of translation.
>
> (Mounin [1955] 1994: 74)

For Mounin, 'transparency' refers to unhindered access to a text, so much so that you cannot guess that the text is foreign. The quote he uses as a starting point for transparent-glass translations is an image formulated by Russian writer Gogol: 'To become a glass so transparent that one believes there is no glass' (Gogol qtd in Mounin [1955] 1994: 75; my translation from the French). In Russian, Gogol used the metaphor of transparency on two occasions when he was commenting on Zhukovski's translation of *The Odyssey*; first of all, in an essay he wrote:

> Invisibly, the translator became a kind of interpreter of Homer, he became a kind of clarifying looking glass for the reader, through which all the innumerable treasures of this work appear even more clearly defined and vivid.
>
> (Gogol 2013: 30)

And then, in a letter to the translator, he repeated the image in a different formulation, which is the one used by Mounin:

> The translator behaved in such a way that you do not see him: he turned into a glass so transparent that it seems like there's no glass at all. In the second volume of 'The Odyssey', it is even more striking than in the first. (my translation from the Russian)[7]

To the best of my knowledge, Nabokov did not mention this vision of translation in his book on Gogol, but the fact that he thought of calling it *Gogol through the Looking Glass* (Boyd 1991: 54) can make us wonder if there was more to it than a reference to the second volume of *Alice*.

Lawrence Venuti also uses the notion of transparency in a similar sense. His most thorough description is to be found in *The Translator's Invisibility* (1995). In this title, the idea of transparency is pushed further than with Mounin since the translator is so transparent that he is invisible, so he cannot be seen or perceived (hence his difficulty to be recognized and paid enough, especially in contemporary Anglo-American culture). Venuti starts his book with the following epigraph:

> I see translation as the attempt to produce a text so transparent that it does not seem to be translated. A good translation is like a pane of glass. You only notice that it's there when there are little imperfections – scratches, bubbles. Ideally, there shouldn't be any. It should never call attention to itself.
>
> (Shapiro qtd in Venuti 1995: 1)

The similarity with Gogol's image in Shapiro's quote is striking, but Venuti never mentions the Russian writer. The translation theorist seems to be forging his terminology against Shapiro, and on the very first page of his book, he explains what a transparent translation is for him:

> A translated text, whether prose or poetry, fiction or nonfiction, is judged acceptable by most publishers, reviewers, and readers when it reads fluently, when the absence of any linguistic or stylistic peculiarities makes it seem transparent, giving the appearance that it reflects the foreign writer's personality or intention or the essential meaning of the foreign text – the appearance, in other words, that the translation is not in fact a translation, but the 'original'. The illusion of transparency is an effect of fluent discourse, of the translator's effort to insure easy readability by adhering to current usage, maintaining continuous syntax, fixing a precise meaning.
>
> (Venuti 1995: 1)

The idea of 'fluency' is closely linked to that of transparency: the translation process should be transparent so that the resulting translation should read fluently. Transparent translation is ethnocentric and domesticating, and this is a type of translation that Venuti rejects; instead, he recommends foreignizing translation, which is directly inspired from Schleiermacher:

> Foreignizing translation signifies the difference of the foreign text, yet only by disrupting the cultural codes that prevail in the target language. In its effort to do right abroad, this translation method must do wrong at home, deviating enough from native norms to stage an alien reading experience – choosing to translate a foreign text excluded by domestic literary canons, for instance, or using a marginal discourse to translate it.
>
> (Venuti 1995: 1)

Therefore, the notion of transparency has two very different meanings for Chateaubriand and for Venuti: for Chateaubriand, the focus is on the source text, and for Venuti, it is on the target reader.

Now that the contradictory terminology has been clarified, let us look at Chateaubriand's vision of translation, in particular to underline its many similarities with Nabokov's.

A literalist translation *à la Chateaubriand*

When Chateaubriand publishes his translation, *Le Paradis Perdu*,[8] he is in stark contradiction with the tendency of his time in terms of translation, namely '*Les Belles infidèles*', and he hopes that, one day, people will start to find that 'faithfulness, even when it lacks beauty, has some worth to it' (Chateaubriand [1836a] 1861: xiii)). On the very first page of his 'Remarks' to the translation (which Nabokov had read (Pushkin [1975] 1991, III: 31)), the French translator explains his method in a slightly ironical tone:

> If I had only wanted to make an elegant translation of *Paradise Lost*, it will maybe be granted that I know the art well enough so that it would not have been impossible for me to reach the height of a translation of that nature; but it is a literal translation, with all the strength of the term, that I undertook, a translation that a child or a poet will be able to follow on the text, line by line, like a dictionary open before their eyes.
>
> (Chateaubriand [1836a] 1861: i)

The links with Nabokov can already be underlined. Not only did Nabokov pride himself on the fact that his translation was not elegant, but, with the mention of the crib, he also argued that his text could help students access the original text (Nabokov [1973] 1990: 7). Both translators are willing to write an inelegant translation if it means that it gives the best access to the source text for anyone willing to read it.[9] To provide such an access to the original language implied for Chateaubriand that he sometimes had to go against the rules of French grammar:

> I was not afraid to change the regime of verbs when staying more French would have meant that I made the original lose something of its precision, originality or energy: it will be clearer with examples.
>
> The poet describes the palace of hell; he says:
>
> Many a row
>
> Of starry lamps…

… Yielded light

As from a sky.

I translated it as: Plusieurs rangs de lampes étoilées… émanent la lumière comme un firmament. However, I do know that in French, *émaner* is not an active verb; a sky *does not emanate light*, light *emanates from a sky*: but translate it like that, and what does the image become? At least the reader accesses here the genius of the English language; he learns the difference there is between the regime of verbs in that language and in ours.

(Chateaubriand [1836a] 1861: iii–iv)

Among the examples studied in the previous chapter, this reference that Chateaubriand makes to the agrammaticality of his verbs recalls the example of 'listen to', where the absence of 'to' prompted Wilson to think that Nabokov had committed a Russianism (see Nabokov [1966a] 1990: 257). Chateaubriand also writes that he may have gone against French syntax on a few occasions (Chateaubriand [1836a] 1861: v), for example, when he translated the famous passage '*Rocks, caves, lakes, fens, bogs, dens, and shades of death*' without articles.

Another similarity with Nabokov is Chateaubriand's attention to sonority and archaisms:

Here the repeated word *many* is translated by our old word *maintes*, which gives both a literal translation and almost the same consonance.

(Chateaubriand [1836a] 1861: v)

In order to indicate the archaic note in *vospomnya* (used by Pushkin in One: XLVII: 67 instead of *vspomnya*, or *vspomniv*, or *vspominaya*), as well as to suggest the deep sonorous diction of both lines (*vospomnya prezhnih let romany*; *vospomnya*, etc.), I had to find something more reverberating and evocative than 'recalling intrigues of past years', etc., and whether Mr. Wilson (or Mr. N. for that matter) likes it or not, nothing more suitable than 'rememorating' for *vospomnya* can be turned up.

(Nabokov [1966a] 1990: 253)

Such use of archaisms was meant to reproduce those of the original, and Nabokov often insisted on that point:

In several instances, English archaisms have been used in my EO not merely to match Russian antiquated words but to revive a nuance of meaning present in the ordinary Russian term but lost in the English one. Such terms are not meant to be idiomatic. The phrases I decide upon aspire towards literality, not readability.

(Nabokov [1966a] 1990: 252)

Chateaubriand also laid stress on the necessity to take into account the old words used by Milton thanks to old words in his translation: thus, in the 'Warning' to his *Sketches of English Literature with considerations on the spirit of the times, men and revolutions*, he explains that 'the poet uses old English words, often of a French or Latin origin; I translated them with the old French word, while respecting the rhythmic language and its obsolescent quality' (Chateaubriand 1836b: 13).

Another similarity between Nabokov and Chateaubriand as translators is that they pay a great deal of attention to foreign intertextuality and make sure they render it in their translations. As I showed in the previous chapter, Nabokov abundantly used French literature to produce the best translation possible, for example, by providing literal translations of the original French, not of Pushkin's Russian imitation of the French. As for Chateaubriand, he explained that Milton 'has a multitude of words which cannot be found in dictionaries: he is full of hebraisms, hellenisms, latinisms' (Chateaubriand 1836b: 12) and that he 'is ceaselessly imitating the ancients' (Chateaubriand [1836a] 1861: x). In order to reproduce these imitations and sources, Chateaubriand 'surrounded himself with all the disquisitions of scoliasts': 'I read all the French, Italian and Latin translations I could find. The Latin translations, with the easiness they have in rendering literally words and in following inversions, have been very useful to me' (Chateaubriand [1836a] 1861: xiv). Therefore, he often translated into English from these foreign texts in order to translate Milton's foreignisms as well as possible.[10] As a consequence, it is clear that Nabokov and Chateaubriand were not afraid to foreignize the language they were translating into, even if it implied "mak[ing] violence" to it.[11]

One difference we can note, however, between the two author-translators is that Chateaubriand is not as self-righteous as Nabokov is. Indeed, Nabokov was very protective of his translation and commentary, which he was willing to defend with his 'heaviest dictionary' (Nabokov [1966a] 1990: 241). He argued that he had provided only facts, and that Pushkin's text was not open to interpretations:

> My 'most serious failure', according to Mr. Wilson, 'is one of interpretation'. Had he read my commentary with more attention he would have seen that I do not believe in *any* kind of 'interpretation' so that his or my 'interpretation' can be neither a failure nor a success'.
>
> (Nabokov [1966a] 1990: 263)

And when Nabokov writes about Pushkin's knowledge of English (to take but one example), he uses expressions like 'I supply the evidence', 'I prove with absolute certainty that... ' or 'My demonstration remains unassailable' (265). Nabokov's hubris has often been commented upon,[12] and one can suppose that, had he been less arrogant about his translation of Pushkin, the feud around it would have been less spectacular. On the other hand, Chateaubriand is much more modest: in the first pages of his 'Remarks', he explains that there may be a few 'misinterpretations' (Chateaubriand [1836a] 1861: ii), though he asks the reader to see the difference between a wrong interpretation and a passage open to several interpretations (Chateaubriand [1836a] 1861: ii). He later adds: 'in everything I have just said, I am not justifying myself, I am merely looking for an excuse for my mistakes. A translator is not allowed any glory: he must only show that he has been patient, docile and hard-working' (Chateaubriand [1836a] 1861: xiv).[13] One cannot help but remember that Nabokov claimed he had the same intention when he used the expression 'servile path' in the title of one of his essays on translation. Another example of Chateaubriand's modesty is that he was happy to hear that new translations of Milton would soon be published, adding that the more the better, and he even hoped that his translation would help other translators (Chateaubriand [1836a] 1861: xiii); he does criticize, however, the translation by 'abbé Leroy' who 'adapted' Milton, for example, by removing a long passage about Orpheus (vi). Nabokov, on the contrary, was very critical of his predecessors, and he devoted a whole essay to his harsh attacks against Arndt (his 'Pounding the Clavichord').

By contrast, Nabokov praised Chateaubriand's translation of Milton into French. He mentioned it only twice, but when he did, it was with very positive epithets: 'a marvelous prose translation of Milton's poem' (Pushkin [1975] 1991, III: 31), 'his excellent translation of *Paradise Lost*' (87). However, the best evidence of Nabokov's deference to Chateaubriand remains the epigraph he chose for his 'Translator's Introduction', thus closely associating his author, Pushkin, and the only author-translator who had defended a translation theory similar to his own, Chateaubriand.

After this analysis of Chateaubriand's literalism to understand how close it is to Nabokov's, let us turn to the question of foreignizing translation as it is presented by translation theorist Lawrence Venuti.

Eugene Onegin as a 'scandalous' translation: Reading Nabokov with Venuti?

In his career, Nabokov stirred up scandal twice: as an author with his novel *Lolita* and as a translator with *Eugene Onegin*. In this section, the idea is not to dwell on this scandal, but rather to shed light on the echoes that can be found with Venuti's translation theory, especially in his book *Scandals of Translation* (1998).

The fact that Nabokov rejected readability in translation somehow prefigures Venuti's criticism of 'fluent' translations. In the following excerpt from *The Translator's Invisibility*, Venuti quotes reviewers of translations who all praise fluency:

> A fluent translation is written in English that is current ('modern') instead of archaic, that is widely used instead of specialized ('jargonisation'), and that is standard instead of colloquial ('slangy'). Foreign words ('pidgin') are avoided, as are Britishisms in American translations and Americanisms in British translations. [...] A fluent translation is immediately recognizable and intelligible, 'familiarised', domesticated, not 'disconcerting[ly]' foreign, capable of giving the reader unobstructed 'access to great thoughts', to what is 'present in the original'. Under the regime of fluent translating, the translator works to make his or her work 'invisible', producing the illusory effect of transparency that simultaneously masks its status as an illusion: the translated text seems 'natural', i.e., not translated.
>
> (Venuti 1995: 4–5)

Therefore, 'under the regime of fluent translating', a translator is supposed to shun archaisms, specialized language and foreign words, but this is everything Nabokov loves and does in his *Eugene Onegin*. In my previous chapter, I have called his translation 'foreignizing', which is the opposite of a transparent (or fluent) translation in Venuti's terminology. Therefore, it seems that Nabokov's translation corresponded to what Venuti was going to theorize decades later. However, it is not the case.

Actually, Venuti used the term 'foreignizing' to describe the vision of translation that Schleiermacher favoured, but the American scholar did not subscribe to foreignizing translation which, to him, was an elitist form of translation:

> And since Schleiermacher's advocacy of the foreignizing method was also an advocacy of discourses specific to an educated elite, he was investing this limited social group with considerable cultural authority, going so far as to assign it a precise social function – to 'generate a certain characteristic mode of expression', developing a national language, 'influencing the whole evolution of a culture' [...]. Here it becomes clear that Schleiermacher was enlisting his privileged translation method in a cultural political agenda: an educated elite controls the formation of a national culture by refining its language through foreignizing translations.
>
> (Venuti 1995: 102)

Instead, Venuti advocated for 'minoritizing translation'. Venuti forged this concept by building on two theories of language: Deleuze and Guattari's work on minor literature (after Kafka) and Jean-Jacques Lecercle's work on 'the remainder'. I will briefly explain those to shed light on Venuti's theory and how it relates to Nabokov's style in his *Eugene Onegin*. It will lead me to a comparison of Venuti and Nabokov as translators and translation theorists.

Venuti's concept of minoritizing translation

For Venuti, heterogeneity is a central concept in his vision of minoritizing translation. He does not define heterogeneity when he uses it at first, but one can easily gather while reading him that it is a mixture of old and new, foreign and native, jargon and normal language, etc.: it seems to be the opposite of 'fluency' or smoothness. It is only towards the end of *The Translator's Invisibility* that one finds a condensed definition of heterogeneity, that is, when Venuti describes the language used in the translations of two authors:

> The discursive heterogeneity of the Zukofskys' Catullus mixes the archaic and the current, the literary and the technical, the elite and the popular, the professional and the working-class, the school and the street.
>
> (Venuti 1995: 219)

> Blackburn followed the modernist innovations that were developed by Pound but marginalized by the regime of fluency in English-language translation. This meant cultivating an extremely heterogeneous discourse (a rich mixture of archaism, colloquialism, quotation, nonstandard punctuation and orthography, and prosodic experiment) that prevented the translation from being taken as the 'original' and instead asserted its independence as a literary text in a different language and culture.
>
> (Venuti 1995: 270–1)

With the notion of heterogeneity in translation, the premises of 'minoritizing' translation were present in Venuti's book *The Translator's Invisibility*, but it is in his next book, *The Scandals of Translation*, that he developed this theory.

His book has a crucial subtitle: *The Scandals of Translation: Towards an Ethics of Difference*. For Venuti, the translator can make the deliberate choice to use a heterogeneous language that will go against the hegemony of the major language that English is:

> To shake the regime of English, a translator must be strategic both in selecting foreign texts and in developing discourses to translate them. Foreign texts can be chosen to redress patterns of unequal cultural exchange and to restore foreign literatures excluded by the standard dialect, by literary canons, or by ethnic

stereotypes in the United States (or in the other major English-speaking country, the United Kingdom).

(Venuti 1998: 10–11)

If we concentrate more specifically on the 'discourses' which are developed by the translator, we see that they stem from the qualities of the foreign texts that the translator has chosen strategically:

> Foreign texts that are stylistically innovative invite the English-language translator to create sociolects striated with various dialects, registers and styles, inventing a collective assemblage that questions the seeming unity of standard English. The aim of minoritizing translation is 'never to acquire the majority', never to erect a new standard or to establish a new canon, but rather to promote cultural innovation as well as the understanding of cultural difference by proliferating the variables within English: 'the minority is the becoming of everybody'.

(Venuti 1998: 11)

In the wake of Berman's work, Venuti argues that translation should focus on the foreign and he uses Deleuze and Guattari's concept of minor literature (1975) as well as Lecercle's theory of the remainder to argue that a translation can and should be minoritizing:

> Good translation is demystifying: it manifests in its own language the foreignness of the foreign text.
>
> This manifestation can occur through the selection of a text whose form and theme deviate from domestic literary canons. But its most decisive occurrence depends on introducing variations that alienate the domestic language and, since they are domestic, reveal the translation to be in fact a translation, distinct from the text it replaces. Good translation is minoritizing: it releases the remainder by cultivating a heterogeneous discourse, opening up the standard dialect and literary canons to what is foreign to themselves, to the substandard and the marginal.

(Venuti 1998: 11)

Of course, 'reveal[ing] the translation to be in fact a translation' is evocative of Nabokov's ironic position towards translations that read smoothly (Nabokov [1963a] 1991: ix), but before putting Nabokov and Venuti in parallel, I need to explain the two concepts at the core of the sentence 'Good translation is minoritizing: it releases the remainder by cultivating a heterogeneous discourse', namely 'minoritizing', or rather 'minorising',[14] and 'the remainder'.

Deleuze (and Guattari): Minorizing literature

The starting point of Gilles Deleuze's philosophy of style is this famous sentence by Proust: 'Les beaux livres sont écrits dans une sorte de langue étrangère' (Great books are written in a kind of foreign language). In the following quote, Deleuze explains what great writers do to language:

> What they do, rather, is invent a *minor use* of the major language within which they express themselves entirely: they *minorize* this language, much as in music, where the minor mode refers to dynamic combinations in perpetual desequilibrium. They are great writers by virtue of this minorization [...]. He is a foreigner in his own language, he carves out a nonpreexistent foreign language *within* his own language. He makes the language itself scream, stutter, stammer, or murmur.
>
> (Deleuze 1997: 109–10)

Then, in the book on Kafka which Deleuze wrote with Guattari, *Kafka: Pour une littérature mineure* (1975), the two French thinkers used again this idea taken from Proust. Here is the only passage in which Venuti quotes (and translates) from their book on Kafka:

> Certain literary texts increase this radical heterogeneity by submitting the major language to constant variation, forcing it to become minor, delegitimizing, deterritorializing, alienating it. For Deleuze and Guattari such texts compose a minor literature, whose 'authors are foreigners in their own tongue'. In releasing the remainder, a minor literature indicates where the major language is foreign to itself.
>
> (Venuti 1998: 10)

If one goes back to Deleuze and Guattari's book, it is clear that this quote by Proust is only a tiny element of their philosophy, but here is the passage where they develop the elements quoted by Venuti:

> Only the minor is great and revolutionary. To hate all literature of masters. Kafka's fascination with servants and employees (the same fascination in Proust, with servants, their language). What remains interesting is the possibility of making one's own tongue, supposing it unique, or, if a major tongue now or in the past, then supposing the possibility of a minor use. To be as a stranger in one's own language. [...] Even if it is major, a tongue is capable of intensive use which spins it out along creative lines of escape, a use which now forms and constitutes an absolute deterritorialization.
>
> (Deleuze and Guattari 1983: 26–7)

Actually, both Proust and Kafka have their words used and stretched in a political way by the two thinkers.[15] According to Pascale Casanova, they misread the German-language writer:

> Deleuze and Guattari, in rereading Kafka's text, diminish the specifically literary character of literature by applying to it – particularly in connection with the highly ambiguous notion of 'minor literature' – a crude and anachronistic interpretation that deforms his meaning. [...] While it is true that Kafka had political interests, as his biographer Klaus Wagenbach has demonstrated, they could not have been the ones ascribed to him by Deleuze and Guattari, whose anachronistic conception of politics leads them into historical errors. They project upon Kafka their view of politics as subversion, or 'subversive struggle', whereas for him, in the Prague of the early twentieth century, it was identified solely with the national question. 'It is the glory of such a literature to be minor', they write, 'which is to say revolutionary for all literature' – noting that 'minor' no longer characterizes certain literatures; instead [it refers to] the revolutionary conditions of all literature called great (or established).
>
> (Casanova 2004: 203–4)

It is this revolutionary dimension of Deleuze and Guattari's work that Venuti uses when he argues in favour of 'minoritizing translation', and he combines it with Jean-Jacques Lecercle's work on the 'remainder'.

Lecercle and the remainder

In his book *The Violence of Language* (1990), Lecercle explains that 'The speaker is the locus of two contradictory tendencies. He speaks language, i.e. he is the master of an instrument, and he is spoken by language, in other words it is language that speaks' (Lecercle 1990: 58). A simple way of reformulating this would be to take the example of Nabokov's puns: either one argues that Nabokov was so creative that his puns were his unique inventions, or one admits that, with his keen eye for language (and probably thanks to his multilingualism, which enabled him to see language afresh), Nabokov created puns with what language presented him with. Lecercle explains that the truth is certainly in the middle ground:

> Such is the language game that the remainder induces us to play – not only being naughty with language, but doing violence to it, which begins when we become aware of its violence.
>
> (Lecercle 1990: 60–1)

To be more specific, the remainder is what lies beyond rules. A very clear definition of the concept can be found on the back cover of Lecercle's book:

> Any theory of language constructs its 'object' by separating 'relevant' from 'irrelevant' phenomena, and excluding the latter. As a result, all theories of language leave out a 'remainder'. This remainder is the odd, untidy, awkward, creative part of how all of us use language all the time. It is the essence of poetry, and of metaphor.
>
> (Lecercle 1990: n. p.)

Lecercle's theory of the remainder, like Deleuze and Guattari's theory of minor literature, has a stylistic dimension as well as a political dimension. It is my impression that Venuti takes the theory of the remainder mainly in its political dimension, especially when he refers to 'collective forms' in the following passage, thus evoking Deleuze and Guattari's work on the collective (1983: 18):

> A literary text, then, can never simply express the author's intended meaning in a personal style. It rather puts to work collective forms in which the author may indeed have a psychological investment, but which by their very nature depersonalize and destabilize meaning. Although literature can be defined as writing created especially to release the remainder, it is the stylistically innovative text that makes the most striking intervention into a linguistic conjuncture by exposing the contradictory conditions of the standard dialect, the literary canon, the dominant culture, the major language.
>
> (Venuti 1998: 10)

With all these clarifications on Deleuze and Guattari's theory of minorizing language and on Lecercle's notion of the remainder, we can understand better Venuti's defense of minoritizing translation:

> Good translation is minoritizing: it releases the remainder by cultivating a heterogeneous discourse, opening up the standard dialect and literary canons to what is foreign to themselves, to the substandard and the marginal.
>
> (Venuti 1998: 11)

Even if Venuti's theory sometimes seems to stretch the concepts forged by others, the result is very interesting: a translator needs to translate with heterogeneity in order to let the foreign shine through, be it in terms of language ('standard dialect') or in terms of literature ('literary canons').

Venuti advocates for a heterogeneous discourse in translation, which is evocative of Nabokov's heterogeneous translation, *Eugene Onegin*, be it in its specific use of language or in its exaggerated dimension; as Dolinin wrote, 'he often heavily overplayed the strangeness of the original word and, as a result, turned a stylistic nuance into a loud splash' (Dolinin 1995: 120).

The parallels between Venuti and Nabokov

As translators and translation theorists, Nabokov and Venuti often advocate for similar choices regarding vocabulary.

The first parallel is their use of archaisms. In his book *Scandals of Translation*, Venuti illustrates his theory of minoritizing translation by the strategy he used when he translated an Italian text called 'Fosca' by Tarchetti:

> What especially attracted me to Tarchetti's writing was its impact on the very act of translating: it invited the development of a translation discourse that submitted the standard dialect of English to continual variation. From the beginning I determined that archaisms would be useful in indicating the temporal remoteness of the Italian texts, their emergence in a different cultural situation at a different historical moment.
>
> (Venuti 1998: 14)

Nabokov also used archaisms, but he did so not because they lent themselves to a specific translation discourse, but because they signalled the exact meaning of the Russian words (Nabokov [1966a] 1990: 252, 256).

Then, both Venuti and Nabokov resorted to words that were foreign and foreignizing, but they did so for different reasons. For example, Venuti used Britishisms to further foreignize his translation: 'I imagined my readership as primarily American, so the effect of strangeness could also be obtained through Britishisms' (Venuti 1998: 16). Venuti also played with different registers to underline the genre he perceived in the text:

> Yet to indicate the element of near-parody in Tarchetti's romanticism, I increased the heterogeneity of the translation discourse by mixing more recent usages, both standard and colloquial, some distinctly American. [...] At a few points, I made the combination of various lexicons more jarring to remind the reader that he or she is reading a translation in the present.
>
> (Venuti 1998: 17)

As for Nabokov, he resorted to calques and French words, but he did so with a reason, for example, when he wanted to insist on Pushkin's mastery of French.

Therefore, Nabokov always strove to defend the original text and the original author, even if it resulted in a foreign and clumsy translation; on the other hand, Venuti uses minoritizing translation to defend an ethics of translation first and foremost. And this is the major difference between Nabokov and Venuti: Venuti's heterogeneity is a strategy, whereas Nabokov's translation *happens* to be heterogeneous.

But a few years after his translation was published, Nabokov put forward a method that implied that his heterogeneous translation was also part of a strategy, namely his method of 'signal words'.[16] He explained that these were meant for the reader to notice specificities in the original Russian text:

> They are steps in the ice, pitons in the sheer rock of fidelity. Some [phrases] are mere signal words whose only purpose is to suggest or indicate that a certain pet term of Pushkin's has recurred at that point.
>
> (Nabokov [1966a] 1990: 252)

With the images of steps in the ice and pitons in the rock, Nabokov suggests that Pushkin's text is like a mountain that the reader has to climb, but the words he foregrounded (like archaisms and Gallic words) are meant to help them in their endeavour. Pushkin's text is meant to be difficult, and Nabokov did not aspire to readability; however, he did have his students in mind when he prepared his translation of *Eugene Onegin*, and he wanted to draw their attention to Pushkin's idiosyncrasies. Venuti, on the other hand, uses heterogeneity because he wants to draw the reader's attention not so much on the original text, but on the fact that there is an original text and that the reader is actually dealing with a translation.[17] Contrary to Nabokov, Venuti aspires towards readability, at least to a certain extent:

> The heterogeneity needn't be so alienating as to frustrate a popular approach completely; if the remainder is released at significant points in a translation that is generally readable, the reader's participation will be disrupted only momentarily.
>
> (Venuti 1998: 12)

For Venuti, a translation which alienates the reader too much (for example, a foreignizing translation in Schleiermacher's terminology) is useless because the reader will stop reading and they will not even discover the foreign works of literature out there. Therefore, the translator has to accept the ethnocentric dimension of translation, but with an ethics of difference:

> Institutions, whether academic or religious, commercial or political, show a preference for a translation ethics of sameness, translating that enables and ratifies existing discourses and canons, interpretations and pedagogies, advertising campaigns and liturgies – if only to ensure the continued and unruffled reproduction of the institution. Yet translation is scandalous because

it can create different values and practices, whatever the domestic setting. This is not to say that translation can ever rid itself of its fundamental domestication, its basic task of rewriting the foreign text in domestic cultural terms. The point is rather that a translator can choose to redirect the ethnocentric movement of translation so as to decenter the domestic terms that a translation project must inescapably utilize. This is an ethics of difference that can change the domestic culture.

(Venuti 1998: 82)

From ethics to politics: A political reading of Nabokov's translation?

The term 'ethics' is used in different ways by Venuti and Nabokov. For Venuti, ethics is a moral positioning: 'My preference for minoritizing translation also issues from an ethical stance that recognizes the asymmetrical relations in any translation project' (Venuti 1998: 11). More importantly, it is closely linked with politics; actually, Venuti often associates the adjectives 'ethical and political' when he describes minoritizing translation, as we can see in the following examples:

> Linguistics-oriented approaches, then, would seem to block the ethical and political agenda I envisaged for minoritizing translation.
>
> (Venuti 1998: 22)

> And clearly the translators' violations will carry ethical and political implications, not only in their usefulness to the field that the translating is designed to serve, but also in their concern with the larger issues of peaceful international relations and the fair administration of justice.
>
> (25)

> This necessitated an adherence to the popular aesthetic, explaining the work of author and publisher alike by reference to their lives and editing the book to emphasize its ethical and political content.
>
> (140)

For Nabokov, the adjective 'ethical' is closer to the idea of morality, more specifically the respect he has, as a scholar, for Pushkin and his text:

> Unlike my novels, *EO* possesses an ethical side, moral and human elements. It reflects the compiler's honesty or dishonesty, skill or sloppiness. If told I am a bad poet, I smile; but if I'm told I am a poor scholar, I reach for my heaviest dictionary.
>
> (Nabokov [1966a] 1990: 241)

Now, even if Nabokov did not claim to have a political agenda for his translation of Pushkin, it is possible to see some elements that suggest otherwise.[18]

For Venuti, Nabokov's theory of translation is that of an elitist, which corresponds to his vision of Schleiermacher's foreignizing translation.[19] In the volume he edited, *The Translation Studies Reader*, Venuti included Nabokov's article 'Problems of Translation: "Onegin in English"', and this is what he wrote about him in his presentation:

> In the essay that appears here (1955), Nabokov describes the complicated resonances and allusions of Alexsandr Pushkin's poem *Eugene Onegin* so as to rationalize his own scholarly version of it: close to the Russian, devoid of Anglo-American poetic diction, and heavily annotated. For Nabokov, paraphrastic versions that 'conform to the notions and prejudices of a given public' constitute the worst 'evil' of translation. Yet **he too privileges the values of a given public, even if an elite minority: an academic readership who might want a literal translation that combines native proficiency in the foreign language, historical scholarship in the foreign literature, and detailed commentary on the formal features of the foreign text.**
>
> Nabokov's views on translation are very much those of **a Russian émigré writer living the United States after 1940. He nurtures a deep, nostalgic investment in the Russian language and in canonical works of Russian literature and disdains the homogenizing tendencies of American consumer culture.** Few English-language literary translators at the time follow Nabokov's uncompromising example. The dominant trend favors just the sort of 'poetical' language he detests, free versions that seek to produce poetic effects in the translating language, usually deploying standard usage and canonical styles.
>
> (Venuti 2000: 68; bold type mine)

But it is my impression that Venuti, blinded by Nabokov's aristocratic origins, quickly dismisses the possibility that Nabokov's translation could serve one of the political goals that Venuti underlines in his *Scandals of Translation*, specifically in relation to the formation of literary canons:

> Translation wields enormous power in constructing representations of foreign cultures. **The selection of foreign texts and the development of translation strategies can establish peculiarly domestic canons for foreign literatures, canons that conform to domestic aesthetic values and therefore reveal exclusions and admissions, centers and peripheries that deviate from those current in the foreign language.** Foreign literatures tend to be dehistoricized by the selection of texts for translation, removed from the foreign literary traditions

where they draw their significance. And foreign texts are often rewritten to conform to styles and themes that *currently* prevail in domestic literatures, much to the disadvantage of more historicizing translation discourses that recover styles and themes from earlier moments in domestic traditions.

(Venuti 1998: 67; bold type mine)

Venuti fails to consider the hypothesis that Nabokov was trying to change the literary representations that Americans had and maintained about Russia in general, and Russian literature in particular. Was Nabokov not trying to change the perception of Russia every time he insisted on the dangers of communism, starting with Lenin who tended to be idealized by some American literary figures?[20] The same argument holds about pre-revolutionary Russia: Nabokov repeatedly insisted that the Revolution did not free the masses from oppressive tsarism, but he explained, time and again, that a process of democratization had been started, for example, with his father, and that Bolshevism merely thwarted these efforts.[21]

In his book, Venuti underlines that the Japanese literary canon which was projected in the United States evolved when political circumstances changed; in the following passage, he is quoting from an article partly entitled 'On the Art and Politics of Translating Modern Japanese Fiction':

> The various interests of these academic translators and their editors – literary, ethnographic, economic – were decisively shaped by an encounter with Japan around World War II, and the canon they established constituted a nostalgic image of a lost past. Not only did the translated fiction often refer to traditional Japanese culture, but some novels lamented the disruptive social changes wrought by military conflict and Western influence [...]

> Thus, the nostalgic image projected by the canon could carry larger, geopolitical implications: 'the aestheticized realms [in the novels selected for translation] provided exactly the right image of Japan at a time when that country was being transformed, almost overnight in historical terms, from a mortal enemy during the Pacific War to an indispensable ally during the Cold War era'. The English-language canon of Japanese fiction functioned as a domestic cultural support for American diplomatic relations with Japan, which were also designed to contain Soviet expansionism in the East.

(Venuti 1998: 72–3)

It seems ironic that Venuti managed to see that the context of the Cold War played a role in the choices of translation for Japan, but failed to consider a similar hypothesis for Russian literature.[22] When Nabokov, a revered American by then, chose to translate Pushkin's masterpiece, he could help reshape the

English-language vision of the Russian canon and show that it went beyond Soviet literature for the twentieth century or Dostoyevsky for the nineteenth, or at least the end of it (this reshaping of the Russian canon can shed a new light on Nabokov's constant attacks against the author of *Crime and Punishment*).

Reshaping Russia's literary canon was probably a goal, albeit unconscious, for Nabokov. In that respect, Casanova's *World Republic of Letters* is illuminating, more specifically through the analytical lens provided by Marijeta Bozovic in her book *Nabokov's Canon: From Onegin to Ada*.

Nabokov's *Eugene Onegin*, or the Reshaping of the Russian Canon in the World Republic of Letters

In her book *Nabokov's Canon: From Onegin to Ada*, Marijeta Bozovic convincingly defends the following argument:

> Nabokov attempted to reimagine a nineteenth-and-twentieth-century canon of interpenetrating European traditions – with the Russian novel as a central, rather than marginal, strain. Nabokov's canon is pointedly transnational and translinguistic, continental but also specifically Russo-Franco-American-centric, and serves to legitimize his own literary practice.
>
> (Bozovic 2016: 4)

Bozovic underlines the importance of Nabokov's three literary traditions thanks to her study of three generations of writers:

> The canon traced in Nabokov's immense *Commentary* to *Onegin* and then animated in *Ada* rests on 'great triads' of French, English, and Russian novelists: Chateaubriand, Byron, and Pushkin in the first generation; Flaubert, Dickens, and Tolstoy in the next; and finally Proust, Joyce, and Nabokov himself.
>
> (Bozovic 2016: 5)

For Nabokov's translation of *Eugene Onegin*, she even wrote that 'Nabokov insisted that the Russian canon was always richly interwoven with English and French literary sources, as well as the other way around (and especially in the generations subsequent to Pushkin)' (Bozovic 2016: 84). My contention is that the French language and literary tradition are particularly important in the reshaping of the Russian canon, especially in the English-language world. Indeed, Pascale Casanova has insisted on the prestige that Paris (and indirectly the French language) provides in the literary world:

> And so it was that Paris became the capital of the literary world, the city endowed with the greatest literary prestige on earth. [...] Paris was therefore at

once the intellectual capital of the world, the arbiter of good taste, and (at least in the mythological account that later circulated throughout the entire world) the source of political democracy: an idealized city where artistic freedom could be proclaimed and lived.

(Casanova 2004: 24)

Bozovic strongly relies on Casanova's book in her first chapters, and in her introduction, she sums up Casanova's thesis very accurately while underlying the faults one can find in *The World Republic of Letters*, especially if the Russian canon is concerned:

> She thus imagines a highly combative world republic of letters, where national canons compete for prestige and cultural capital. [...]
>
> Casanova's account of world literature is not without problematic oversights and assumptions: David Damrosch notes the 'implicit triumphalism' in *The World Republic of Letters*, 'which might be better titled *La République parisienne des lettres*'. And yet, with due correctives (for instance, Casanova takes little account of Russia and eastern Europe), the republic of letters proves a provocative and useful model for the cultural positioning of the Francophilic Pushkin and doubly Francophilic émigré Nabokov.

(Bozovic 2016: 9–10)

Indeed, upon reading Casanova's book, it is very hard to know where Russia is to be placed in the opposition she draws:

> The world of letters is a relatively unified space characterized by the opposition between the great national literary spaces, which are also the oldest – and, accordingly, the best endowed – and those literary spaces that have more recently appeared and that are poor by comparison.

(Casanova 2004: 83)

Russian literature is probably somewhere in-between: not exactly with the many new literatures coming from emerging countries, in which Casanova is impressively well-versed, but rather on the heels of Western literatures like the French or the British ones.

In this opposition between 'great national literary spaces' and those which are 'poor in comparison', Casanova underlines on several occasions the role of translators who can effectively make a literary space move up in the world republic of letters:

> The great, often polyglot, cosmopolitan figures of the word of letters act in effect as foreign exchange brokers, responsible for exporting from one territory to another texts whose literary value they determine by virtue of this very activity.

(Casanova 2004: 21)

Critics, like translators, thus contribute to the growth of the literary heritage of nations that enjoy the power of consecration: critical recognition and translation are weapons in the struggle by and for literary capital.

(Casanova 2004: 23)

The next quote is particularly relevant if we go back to Nabokov's translation of the Russian bard's masterpiece:

Translation is the major prize and weapon in international literary competition, an instrument whose use and purpose differ depending on the position of the translator with respect to the text translated – that is, on the relation between what are commonly called 'source' and 'target' languages.

(Casanova 2004: 133)

It is indeed interesting to question the position of our translator. Nabokov is already a *major* author in the United States and worldwide when he very visibly steps into the role of translator in 1964 in order to provide his own literal translation of Pushkin, with all the foreignizing elements I have mentioned previously. Therefore, saying that his translation was minoritizing can seem paradoxical.[1] But actually, it is probably because he was a recognized author that he could have his way in translation, thus sidestepping the invisibilization of translators and the overwhelming domination of transparent translations that Venuti has described so well. Likewise, it is probably thanks to his being a leading figure in translation that Venuti can pursue his very own method of minoritizing translation and claim for idealistic changes in terms of copyrights for translators.[2] Therefore, being an author-translator of international stature was a crucial element in Nabokov's contribution to the promotion of the Russian canon in the world republic of letters, especially in the English-speaking world.

If we go back to the image of transparency in relation to Nabokov as an author-translator, it is interesting to see that, for his translation of *Onegin*, Nabokov was far from transparent and invisible, so much so that he could be accused of appropriating Pushkin's text, but at the same time, he used his fame and power to defend the text. But as I will show in my next part, Nabokov acted in a very different way in his role of author when he co-translated his novels into French: while refusing to step aside and be transparent as an author being translated by others, his role of co-translator has been almost completely erased in the paratexts of the French renderings of his novels. It is all the more surprising because, as I hope to show, these can actually be considered a type of self-translation.

Part Three

Nabokov as a French Self-translator

10

Collaborative Translation as Mediated Self-translation

In Nabokov's multilingual practice, French is clearly the most underestimated language. With the aid of unpublished documents found in France and the United States, I intend to show that his creative involvement with French goes beyond his writing of short pieces like 'Mademoiselle O' and 'Pouchkine, le vrai et le vraisemblable' and should be re-evaluated. When the relationship between writing and translating is explored, it is usually through the question of self-translation, which is probably the topic in Nabokov's involvement with translation that has been the most extensively studied.[1] But it is usually the self-translations between Russian and English that are analysed, which is quite understandable since there are more of them and Nabokov was an established writer in both languages. However, it is clear to me that his practice of self-translation with French needs to be acknowledged more. To this day, his only known self-translation into French was that of the short story 'Muzyka'[2]:

> Nabokov has made little active use of French. In the 1920s he translated some French poetry and prose into Russian. [...] When Nabokov left Europe for America in 1940 he abandoned writing in French. As far as can be ascertained, his only work in French since that date has been a translation of one of his Russian stories: *Muzyka* (*Musiques*). This appeared in *Les Nouvelles littéraires* in 1959, the year of Nabokov's return to Europe.
>
> (Grayson 1977: 11–12)

Jane Grayson was right in using the expression 'as far as can be ascertained'. Indeed, there exists another self-translation which has never been published: that of the Russian short story 'Bakhman' (1924), entitled 'Bachmann' in French and in English. In the Berg Collection (New York Public Library), there are two French translations of the short story and an English translation by 'Dmitri Nabokov in collaboration with the author'.[3] One French version is by Nabokov, and for the other one, the reference merely indicates 'translator unknown', but a quick inspection suffices to see that the 'unknown' translation is that of Gérard-Henri Durand, which was published in 1977. Indeed, if one looks at the first paragraph, only two differences stand out (in bold type below), and they are mere nuances in vocabulary or spelling:

> Récemment, un bref entrefilet dans la presse annonçait la disparition de Bachmann, un pianiste et compositeur qui avait eu son heure de gloire, mais qui était mort oublié du monde dans le hameau suisse de Marival, au foyer **Ste.** Angélique. **Cette annonce** me rappela soudain l'histoire d'une femme qui l'avait aimé. La voici, telle qu'elle me fut contée par l'impresario Sack.[4]

> Récemment, un bref entrefilet dans la presse annonçait la disparition de Bachmann, un pianiste et compositeur qui avait eu son heure de gloire, mais qui était mort oublié du monde dans le hameau suisse de Marival, au foyer Sainte-Angélique. Ce faire-part me rappela soudain l'histoire d'une femme qui l'avait aimé. La voici, telle qu'elle me fut contée par l'imprésario Sack.[5]
>
> (Nabokov [1977] 2000: 217)

By contrast, the differences between Nabokov's version and the published text are much more extensive (underlined below):

> Il n'y a pas longtemps, un entrefilet dans les journaux a annoncé que le pianiste et compositeur Bachmann, naguère célèbre, était mort oublié du monde dans le hameau suisse de Marival, à l'asile Ste Angelica. Cela m'a rappelé l'histoire d'une femme qui l'a aimé. Je la tiens de l'impresario Sack. La voici.[6]

The fact that Nabokov's two self-translations into French deal with music recalls the following quote, in which Nabokov underlined his preference for French when sound was concerned:

> *Which of the languages you speak do you consider the most beautiful?*
>
> My head says English, my heart, Russian, my ear, French.
>
> (Nabokov [1973] 1990: 49)

But there is one notable difference between the two French translations: 'Musique' was translated from the original Russian, but 'Bachmann' seems to be translated from the English translation made by 'Dmitri Nabokov in collaboration with the author' (one could wonder if the presence of his son trumps the appellation 'self-translation').

As I will show, the blurred lines between self-translation and collaborative translation with the author (be it acknowledged or not) are frequent in the paratext surrounding Nabokov's translations.

Nabokov and collaborative translation

Let us start by explaining briefly what collaborative translation means in general, before zooming in on Nabokov's case.

Collaborative translation obviously stems from 'collaboration'. As Cordingley and Frigau Manning (2016) indicate, scholars have often been quick to insist on the negative connotations which the noun still holds in connection with Nazi occupation and, more generally now, political collaboration, even if recently, the term has been associated with more positive ideas like cooperation and transparency (17). The adjective 'collaborative' has therefore been favoured in Translation Studies to describe the activity consisting in having more than one person involved in a translation, be it the author and the translator, or more than one translator working on one text without the author. Drawing from the debates around 'sharing authority' (4) and 'collaborative authorship' (5) since the Renaissance, Cordingley and Frigau Manning underline a useful terminological nuance:

> Following the distinction made by certain Shakespeareans, it is possible to speak of the difference between co-translation and collaborative translation. Co-translation already has the specificity of designating the act whereby self-identifying translators work together on the creation of a translation, simultaneously or otherwise.
>
> (24)

For example, it is the terminology which Claire Davison uses in one of the only monographs dealing with collaborative translation, *Translation as Collaboration: Virginia Woolf, Katherine Mansfield and S. S. Koteliansky* (2014): Davison calls 'co-translators' the two British female novelists as well as the Russian-born British translator who translated together Russian novels of the nineteenth century. Personally, I will be using the term 'co-translator' broadly, so it can refer to Nabokov and his collaborators alike.

In his article 'Author-Translator Collaborations: A Typological Survey', Patrick Hersant explains that collaborative translation includes 'more or less extensive degrees of collaboration' (2016: 91). The less intrusive category, 'carte blanche and recommendation', certainly does not correspond to what Nabokov indulged in when his texts were translated into languages he mastered. The second category, 'revision, questions-and-answers, back-and-forths', though it represents a 'much higher degree of involvement', is also different from what Nabokov was doing[7]; Hersant defines revision as follows: 'the author inspects a translation submitted for his or her judgement. Provided that he sufficiently masters the target-language, such an author thus becomes his translator's corrector' (93). In fact, Nabokov's practice of collaborative translation seems to hover between the two higher degrees of involvement: 'closelaboration' (a neologism coined by Guillermo Cabrera Infante for 'close collaboration') and 'authorial appropriation'; however, revision cannot be omitted altogether, especially early in his career.[8]

The difficulty in pinpointing what type of collaboration Nabokov induced with his translators seems to depend on two factors: the target-language and the type of elements that need translating.

In his article, Hersant shows that Nabokov was a typical case of 'authorial appropriation'[9] when it came to the English translation of his Russian novels (101). There is no argument about the validity of this argument, and as Brian Boyd states in his biography of Nabokov,

> Once he had polished the English translation to his satisfaction, he would then arrange for subsequent translations into other languages to be made from the English rather than the Russian text, not only because there were far more translators available from English than from Russian, but also because Nabokov regarded the English-language versions with the minor glosses as textually definitive for non-Russian readers.
>
> (Boyd 1991: 484)

For the translations from Russian into English, things are clear: Nabokov's collaborative translations become new originals and are recognized as self-translations through the process of 'authorial appropriation'.

However, when the target language is French, hardly anyone would use the term 'self-translation', at least not outside some French scholars[10]; at best, specialists think that Nabokov revised the French translations, but they are usually unaware of Nabokov's role in the translating process, which is not surprising if one looks at the paratexts: in the French *Lolita* (Nabokov 1959a), Nabokov is not mentioned at all; in *Feu pâle* (Nabokov [1965b] 2020), a note by the translators explains that the modifications to the original were made following requests of the author, but it does not use the word 'collaboration' at any time; as for *Ada ou L'Ardeur* (Nabokov 1975), one can only see that Nabokov revised the translation (*'traduction revue par l'auteur'*). If Nabokov did not defend his role in the translations into French as much as in the translations into English, I think it is because he had different agendas: in English, he wanted to be recognized as an (American) author; however, he had no intention of becoming a French author in the 1950s and after (he had tried, and failed, to become a writer in France before he moved to the United States).

For French translations, it is my contention that several of them should be considered 'mediated self-translations'. Hersant describes 'closelaborations' as consisting 'in adapting the original with the author's active collaboration'. He further adds:

> We can glimpse in this practice a particular form of mediated self-translation, or of four-handed translation, in which the final text sometimes appears as the joint work of the author and his or her translator.
>
> (Hersant 2016: 95)

In Nabokov's collaborative translations into French, it is not easy to know where one category stops and where the next starts, be it 'revision', 'close collaboration' or 'authorial appropriation'. First of all, it is hard to determine from one novel to the next, and then, it is also difficult to pinpoint the difference inside one text itself. However, a very useful help can be found in genetic criticism, more precisely genetic translation studies.

The usefulness of genetic translation studies

Anthony Cordingley and Chiara Montini provide a very clear definition of this field in their article 'Genetic translation studies: an emerging discipline':

> Over the past decade a new field of research has emerged that may be termed 'genetic translation studies'. It analyses the practices of the working translator and the evolution, or genesis, of the translated text by studying translators' manuscripts, drafts and other working documents. Genetic translation studies focuses therefore on the transformations of the translated text during the process of its composition.
>
> (Cordingley and Montini 2015: 1)

As they explain, this emerging field stems from 'the application of the methodology of *critique génétique*' (2; genetic criticism in English), and then they explain the goal of this mother field:

> Genetic criticism offers a methodology with which to gain a window upon the writer's workshop. It maintains that the published text is but one phase in the text's evolution, and that this process of textual transformation continues well *after* the work's publication through its reeditions, its retranslations and its different reception by heterogeneous communities of readers.
>
> (2)

They add that:

> *Critique génétique* was born in France in the mid-1960s, on the cusp of the shift from structuralist to post-structuralist conceptions of text and in an intellectual climate where the authority of the author as well as the stability of both the published *oeuvre* and the written word were brought into question.
>
> (2)

To put it in a nutshell, genetic criticism questions the authority of the writer, while genetic translation studies, when applied to collaborative translation, help distinguish the role of the translator and that of the writer.

It can seem daunting to launch into an extensive study of Nabokov's manuscripts, especially when one remembers the following pronouncement by Nabokov:

> Rough drafts, false scents, half-explored trails, dead ends of inspiration, are of little intrinsic importance. An artist should ruthlessly destroy his manuscripts after publication, lest they mislead academic mediocrities into thinking that it is possible to unravel the mysteries of genius by studying canceled readings. In art, purpose and plan are nothing; only the result counts.
>
> (Nabokov [1964b] 1991: 15)

Hoping to fare better than 'academic mediocrities' and to confirm Shrayer's statement about 'the future of Nabokov studies' being 'in archival and manuscript research' (Shrayer 1999: 564), I intend to delve into the archives found in the United States (in the Berg Collection and in Cornell University) and in France (the publishing company Gallimard as well as IMEC[11]) in order to help re-evaluate Nabokov's creative involvement in the French translations of his novels. To be more specific, not all his novels will be represented in the same way because my work is the reflection of existing material, so the content of the following pages is strongly dependent on the content of archives. As Hersant explains, most translators do not keep their working documents, and several parameters can explain the presence or absence of some documents:

> A collaboration which has been followed and documented, either in the form of archives or in a posthumous publication, is close to a miracle. Indeed it requires conditions as strict as they are numerous: the author and translator must be contemporaries, must accept to work together, must master the other's language and, above all, leave written traces of their exchanges.
>
> (Hersant 2016: 98)

One example of this conundrum is *Ada*. First of all, some correspondence with the publishing company Fayard and pertaining to its translation used to be in Montreux, but since the Nabokov archives were moved, mainly to the New York Public Library, these documents are nowhere to be found, so it is only thanks to the notes of Brian Boyd that I could know of some letters, or thanks to letters which were published in 1989 in *Selected Letters*, before their original was lost. A few letters were quoted by Erik Orsenna, from The Académie Française, in his 1997 novel *Deux étés*, so it seems that he had privileged access to some archival fund. If the correspondence around *Ada* is very limited, however, there are many versions of the draft, some including no revisions, others with the revisions by the author, or by translator Gilles Chahine, or by both, so that one has to try and decipher handwriting and clues in order to deduce who did what.

As a reflection of what actually exists in the archives in terms of translation, the novels *Lolita*, *Pale Fire* and *Ada* will be much more represented than the other novels written originally in English.[12] However, when dealing with the relationship between Nabokov and his translators through their correspondence, I will sometimes talk about some translators from Russian.

Outline of the third part

To highlight the different aspects of Nabokov's practice of collaborative translation into French, I will first insist on the relationships that Nabokov had with his collaborators. Therefore, the first chapter of this part will focus on the interpersonal dimension of their collaborations, with a particular interest in their correspondence and, sometimes, their personalities. The second chapter will shed light on some linguistic categories that Nabokov insisted on translating himself; thus, within the French mediated self-translations, there are some elements of unmediated, pure self-translation: one could even go as far as using the image of nestling dolls to represent the self-translated elements embedded in the wider (mediated) self-translations.

11

Nabokov and his Collaborators

In the context of collaborative translation, the bond between an author and their translator depends on several criteria:

> Seen from the point of view of the translator, the issue becomes autonomy. For trust to be possible, there must be some risk that the trusted person will disappoint us. For trust to be warranted, there must be reason to be believe [*sic*] that this will not happen. Arguably, many instances of author involvement in the translation of their work stem from uncertainty that the translator will produce a translation that aligns with the author's own aims. Conversely, the translator must also trust that the author (or editor or publisher) will respect the translator's autonomy and not intervene or worse yet 'dragonise' the draft prior to publication without the consent of the translator.
>
> (Trzeciak Huss 2018: 394)

Interestingly enough, Trzeciak Huss is here quoting Nabokov when she mentions that the author can 'dragonize' a translation, thus not respecting the translator's autonomy by meddling with the draft.[1] It is one of the recurring problems in Nabokov's dealing with his translators: Anokhina (2016) underlined that Nabokov wanted absolute control on the translations from the Russian, and this observation also holds for his translation into English.

In this chapter, I will start by general features on Nabokov's collaborative translations: I will explain recurring patterns in Nabokov's correspondence, some working habits as well as the particular traits that Nabokov generally looked for in a translator. Then, I will focus on some of his translators, and I will do so by looking at one after the other, chronologically, which will be helpful to understand a possible evolution in Nabokov's vision of translation.

The archives I quote from are sometimes in English, sometimes in French, sometimes in both; I try and indicate those linguistic details as much as possible. Since most of them have never been published before, I give my translation from the French (in that case, the English is in italics), but if they are included in

Selected Letters, I indicate the page but not details pertaining to the original language or a possible translation. In the following pages, I will first use a name in full, and then I will only give the family name, but if several people are concerned, I will use their initial, except for the Nabokovs: the writer will be called by his family name and his wife 'Véra Nabokov'. Lastly, some archives are sometimes to be found in several locations, but I merely indicate where *I* found the archives I am quoting from; if no location is indicated, it means that I am referring to lost documents which are nowhere to be found now.

General parameters in Nabokov's collaboration with translators

For Nabokov, the translation of his novels was of paramount importance, even if it meant not being published:

> *I am convinced that the importance of a faithful translation (and at the same time literary) cannot be exaggerated. It is obvious to me that a mediocre translation is not worth being done nor published, for it is not the same book anymore.*
>
> (letter from Nabokov to Doussia Ergaz, 1 June 1957, Cornell)

The writer was often distressed by the time and energy it took him to revise and rewrite the translations of his novels, as he wrote about *Pnine*: '*the thought that each of my French translations demands so much toil from me is rather nightmarish*' (letter from Nabokov to Ergaz, 16 January 1962, Cornell). Véra wrote similar comments: '*nothing afflicts my husband more than those translations that are only half good*' (letter from Véra Nabokov to Ergaz, 10 June 1960, Cornell).

But these translations were crucial all the same because they were part of Nabokov's creative process.

Translation as improvement

For Nabokov, self-translation was a means to provide a new, better version of his novels. This is what he explained in his Foreword to *Invitation to a Beheading*:

> If some day I make a dictionary of definitions wanting single words to head them, a cherished entry will be 'To abridge, expand, or otherwise alter or cause to be altered, for the sake of belated improvement, one's own writings in translation'.
>
> (Nabokov [1960] 2010: ix)

But Nabokov could not provide self-translations for all of his novels; he even once described the process of self-translation in the following terms: 'translating oneself, sorting through one's own innards, and then trying them on for size like a pair of gloves' (letter from Nabokov to Zinaïda Schakovskoy, qtd in Beaujour 1989: 51). An ideal solution was for someone else to provide a faithful translation, so that Nabokov could then amend it to his taste, but without being tempted to revise the text too much. Grayson gives a very clear description of why Nabokov favoured this type of collaboration, as he explained to one of his co-translators:

> He [Nabokov] has admitted on occasion that he finds it difficult to resist the temptation to emend his early work when translating, and Scammell recalls a discussion in which Nabokov explained that this was one reason why he commissioned others to do the work.
>
> (Grayson 1977: 8)

Nabokov found an ideal translator in his son, as he describes in the Foreword mentioned above:

> [...] when my son gave me to check the translation of this book and when I, after many years, had to reread the Russian original, I found with relief that there was no devil of creative emendation for me to fight. [...] My son proved to be a marvellous congenial translator, and it was settled between us that fidelity to one's author comes first, no matter how bizarre the result.
>
> (Nabokov [1960] 2010: ix)

Nabokov's expression to describe his urge to revise the text, 'devil of creative emendation', is particularly interesting, and it is somewhat echoed in Beaujour's description of self-translation for authors like Nabokov as 'the hell of self-translation' (Beaujour 1989: 37).

When it comes to French, the fact that collaborative translations into English replaced the Russian originals (Boyd 1991: 484) is confirmed by a letter about the translation of the short story 'Spring in Fialta': Nabokov was very annoyed that the French translator took the liberty to mix passages from the original Russian and from the English; he could have tolerated a good, faithful translation from the Russian, but he would have preferred the English version to be used because, as Véra wrote, '*my husband is himself responsible for the translation and, **taking advantage of his right as the author**, he made many changes when translating*' (letter from Véra Nabokov to Ergaz, 10 June 1960, Cornell; bold type mine).

The French translations which Nabokov collaborated to were never presented as new originals; however, they were also the occasion for Nabokov to constantly revise his earlier work. As I will show in the section devoted to his translators, Nabokov insisted he wanted *Invitation to a Beheading* to be published in the French translation made by Jarl Priel because he had closely collaborated to it in the 1930s (letter from Nabokov to Denise Clairouin, 27 November 1945, Berg Collection); however, when it was finally published in 1960, Nabokov expressed his disappointment because he had not been given a chance to revise it once again, which led Michel Mohrt, his main interlocutor in Gallimard, to express his surprise to Véra: 'I thought that he already knew the translation made by Jarl Priel of *Invitation to a Beheading*, that he agreed with this translation, and that he had no intention of correcting it again' (letter from Mohrt to Véra Nabokov, 24 March 1960, Berg collection).

When Nabokov found translators whose work he enjoyed, he repeatedly asked to work with them again, especially because he found it really hard to get the qualities he enjoyed in one and the same person.

Portrait of the ideal translator

From the letters exchanged between Nabokov and his agents (Doussia Ergaz and then Marie Schébéko) or his publishers, several features stand out. First of all, Nabokov clearly preferred to be translated by men, as he stated again and again to his publishers:

> I need a man who knows English better than Russian – and a man, not a woman. I am frankly homosexual on the subject of translators.
>
> (16 July 1942, letter from Nabokov to James Laughlin,
> in Nabokov [1989] 1991: 41)

> *My books can only exist as far as their style is respected. You'll forgive me if I allow myself to state that the virility of this style means that it works better with the art of a male translator than with that of a female translator who cannot help bring a certain 'feminine touch' to the way she expresses herself. [...]* BEND SINISTER *(like* INVITATION, *actually) will need, I believe, a male translator.*
>
> (IMEC, letter from Nabokov to Colette Duhamel, beginning of 1953)

One should note, however, that Nabokov appreciated one female translator in particular: Doussia Ergaz (his agent). She had translated *Kamera Obscura* from the Russian in 1934 and, three decades later, Nabokov asked her to translate *The Gift* into French, and he was sorry to hear that she was not going to do so due to medical reasons (letter from Nabokov to Ergaz, 29 January 1965, Cornell) (she was to die in 1967).

Next to the sexist remarks above,[2] other qualities are mentioned. First of all, Nabokov wanted a translator who had a good mastery of the source language in general, but for translations into French, he never seemed to find someone that suited him: on 2 December 1968, Véra wrote to Schébéko that 'not one of his translators into French really knew English' (Cornell) and in his remarks to translators, he repeatedly underlined their blunders or imprecise knowledge of the original language. He was ready, however, to help with the English, but what he would not deal with was poor style. This is what he wrote about the translation of one of his short stories:

> *It is true that it reads easily and that there are few blatant mistakes. However, it is no less true that when it comes to finding an equivalent for an image or an expression which is a little bit original, the translator sees himself compelled to substitute it with a cliché. There's nothing worse for the author!*
>
> (letter from Nabokov to Ergaz, 18 January 1948, Cornell)

For Nabokov, the worst translator he ever had in respect with style was Michelle Sibon. She had translated his *Gogol*,[3] but when it was suggested that she could translate his autobiography, he was adamant:

> *The matter of style being* extremely *important to me when it comes to this book, there is no way it can be given to anyone who does not possess a deep knowledge of English, a noble style in French.*
>
> (letter from Nabokov to Ergaz, 30 September 1952, Cornell)

Nabokov had similar concerns with Yvonne Davet, who translated *The Real Life of Sebastian Knight*; it was her vocabulary which was particularly problematic:

> *When I write, in English or in Russian, I always look for the new word, the expression that has not lost its value with repeated use. On the contrary, Mme Davet, when she chooses her words, looks for the support of a mass of writers, be they good or bad, who came before us.*
>
> (15 August 1950, Cornell)

He was, however, much more pleased with her translation of *Conclusive Evidence* (*Autres Rivages*, 1961).

In order to check the quality of potential translators, Nabokov always insisted on having sample translations. This condition was offensive for many major translators: Nabokov's agent or publisher sometimes could not imagine asking for a sample translation, and some translators were offended by the request: for example, the female translator of Henry James and Thomas Mann was '*deeply hurt*' when asked to provide a sample for 'That in Aleppo once' (letter 27 May

1960, Cornell). Only for one translator did Nabokov make an exception: Blaise Briod, whom he repeatedly asked for in his career but never managed to get. Nabokov was willing to forswear a sample for once because of his style ('*his style made a great impression on my husband*', letter from Véra Nabokov to C. Duhamel, 6 June 1954, IMEC).

Nabokov wanted all of his suggestions and corrections to be taken into account, and he repeatedly made sure that the final version included all of them, even the latest; for example, this is what he wrote to Henri Hell at Fayard:

> What you call *manuscript définitif* will only exist when the entire monster is neatly retyped. My French may not be always impeccable; yet I know exactly what nuance I want in my French and would not care to have my corrections recorrected unless I am consulted in every case, and this also takes time.
>
> (letter from Nabokov to Hell, 30 November 1974,
> in Nabokov [1989] 1991: 539)

It seems that one anecdote in particular made him inflexible: he was deeply upset when Denis Roche (the first translator of *The Defense*) quietly gave the publisher uncorrected proofs, which was all the more shocking because Nabokov had closely revised the text with the translator.[4] He was also angered when the translation of 'The Vane Sisters' was published without his approval, especially because it did not contain the crucial acrostic that ends the short story (letter from Nabokov to Maurice Nadeau, 11 July 1959, Cornell).

Nabokov was 'touchy' on another matter, as Véra wrote to Schébéko on 3 October 1967 (Cornell) about translator Raymond Girard and publisher Gaston Gallimard: '*he believes that all his letters should be answered, especially when they are sent to his publisher and his translator*'. As we will see, it was one of the reasons why his relationship with Eric Kahane, his co-translator for *Lolita*, strongly deteriorated at one point.

One final element can sum up the qualities which Nabokov was looking for in a translator: docility. In a letter dated 3 March 1976 (Cornell), Véra wrote that Nabokov suggested as a possible translator Georges Magnane, who had translated *The Eye*, because 'he, at least, was a "docile" translator'.

Nabokov sometimes asked to work again with some translators he was happy with: Priel, Kahane, Coindreau and Girard, as we will see in my next section, or Magnane and Marcel Stora (he had translated *Despair* (*La Méprise*) and Véra wrote that Nabokov praised his work in a letter on 28 January 1953, Cornell). However, in some respects, Nabokov's ideal translator seems to have been perfect *before* he worked with them, especially if this collaboration did not come to fruition. Thus, Nabokov repeatedly asked to work with two translators in particular: Blaise Briod and a Greek man called Léon G. Marcantonatos. He was the Consul for Greece in Tunis and, on 23 April 1954 (Cornell), Véra wrote that, one year before, he had sent two chapters of *Invitation to a Beheading*, and that Nabokov thought this translation was beautiful. He repeatedly asked for this translator, but nothing came of it. On the other hand, Nabokov changed his mind about another translator he had praised before working with him: he was enthusiastic about the style of Michel Chrestien (the *nom de plume* of Jacques Silberfeld) after he read his book *Cher Monsieur Moi, ou le premier mouvement* and he wanted him to translate *Lolita* (letter from Nabokov to Gaston Gallimard, 7 May 1957, Gallimard Archives), but since it was taken by Kahane, it had to be *Pnin*. But when he collaborated with Chrestien, Nabokov spent hours correcting his mistakes; he was faced with his lack of competence, his poor style with no rhythm and what particularly angered him was the translator's carelessness. Aside from Sibon's work, Nabokov deemed Chrestien's translation of *Pnin* the worst he ever had for any of his books (letter to Ergaz, 28 July 1962, Cornell).

One last thing to be said is that, even when Nabokov did not appreciate a translation greatly, he defended his translators' rights so that they would get fair payment. Thus, he pledged for Denis Roche on 16 February 1955, or for Jarl Priel many times, for example on 24 April 1957 (Cornell).

Let us see now how the correspondence between Nabokov and his translators usually unravelled.

Structures and patterns in Nabokov's letters

Nabokov's letters to his translators usually have a recurring pattern which shows the ambivalent relationship he had with them: Nabokov starts by praising the quality of the translation, and then he gives a long list of the various blunders committed by the translator. This is the case in the following letter to Raymond Girard, one of the translators working on *Feu Pâle*:

> *I have read with a lot of attention and pleasure your translation of the foreword to* Pale Fire. *Its style is admirable, the sentences are perfectly cut and it is full of brilliant finds. However, I have found more than one small inaccuracy in the understanding of the English text. I am sending you in attachment the list of my corrections.*
>
> (letter from Nabokov to Girard, 4 October 1963, Cornell)

Usually, those lists come with precise references to the pages and they are presented in two columns: 'instead of' and 'should be'. But sometimes, the mistakes are explained in a letter, and Nabokov goes into detail to clarify why the translator's suggestion does not work.

Nabokov also likes to classify his translators' mistakes. Thus, in the letters accompanying the list of corrections, he usually explains his typology, as in this letter sent to Gallimard about *Feu Pâle*:

> The corrections may be divided into three main groups: 1. Obvious mistranslations owing to insufficient knowledge. 2. Translations not sufficiently clear or complete. And 3. Mere slips, awkward repetitions etc.
>
> (letter from Nabokov to Mohrt, 19 January 1965, Cornell)

Those typologies are actually reminiscent of the lists he drew in his essays on translation, be it on the three types of translation that exist (Nabokov [1963a] 1991: vii–viii) or on the different kinds of translators (Nabokov [1941a] 2008: 8).

As for the tone of the letters, Nabokov is always very polite, even if his annoyance is sometimes visible through his use of irony or humour (he can, however, be more straightforward and critical of the translator when he writes to his agent or his publishers). Nabokov is polite, but he never seems to make an effort to soften the blow of his criticisms: he attributes a mistake to a translator's bad knowledge of English, for example, but does not present it as a jarring vision of his style between the author and his translator. Only once does he suggest such a thing to Michel Mohrt:

> I do not want to be told again by Coindreau that I am guilty of barbarisms when he is guilty of not being specific. The only important point is that I have sufficient French to know more exactly than he when his French does not correspond to my English.
>
> (letter from Nabokov to Mohrt, 19 January 1965, Cornell)

The use of the possessive ('*my* English') is revealing of the personal dimension of Nabokov's style, and it seems to me that he was often flabbergasted not to find in his collaborators' translations the French formulation that he would have picked, had he written directly in French. I suspect that, if Nabokov had hidden his criticism under a more polite guise, for example, by stating that he wanted a literal translation that he could then rewrite to make it correspond to his vision of his oeuvre in French, his collaborations would have gone more smoothly.

Among Nabokov's various collaborations, four are extensively documented in the archives I analysed, and they show the variety of relationships that could exist: some were heated at times, but they could also be more agreeable, even friendly on some occasions.

Close-up on four collaborations

In examining these collaborations in chronological order, Nabokov seems to have grown harsher along the years, and this can probably be connected with Nabokov's growing defence of literalism. He defended literalism more and more when he translated books by others, and it is only fair to suppose he expected the same from translators of his own books.

Invitation au supplice: 'Cher ami'

Nabokov wrote *Priglashenie na kazn'* in 1934 and it was published in Paris in 1938. Apparently, Jarl Priel translated it into French quickly after that date, or even before, if one is to believe the chronology mentioned by Nabokov in 1952:

> *I am very sorry that the wonderful translation of Jarl Priel is not accepted. But even if a new translation of this book was to be made, the new translator would have to base it on that of Jarl Priel which I have spent a lot of time revising and amending about fifteen years ago.*
>
> (letter from Nabokov to Ergaz, 29 December 1952, Cornell)

It is only in 1960 that Priel's translation into French was published, but Nabokov started to ask for this version to be chosen as early as 1945. When the Second World War was finished, Véra asked his literary agent, Denise Clairouin (sometimes spelt 'Denyse'), to find the only copy that had been left with her when the Nabokovs left Paris in May 1940 (letter from Véra Nabokov to Denise Clairouin, 27 November 1945, Berg Collection). In March 1946, Vladimir enquired again about the whereabouts of this translation, and he finished his letter by writing he hoped that she had survived the six years of the war without suffering too much. But Clairouin, who was in the Resistance, died in deportation[5] and in a letter dated 9 April 1947, Nabokov mentions he has just heard of Clairouin's *'tragic destiny'* and he writes that he is happy to know that Doussia Ergaz is taking over the business (her letters have the letterhead 'Bureau

Littéraire Denise Clairouin'); he also informs Ergaz that he has promised Jarl Priel the translation of *The Real Life of Sebastian Knight*.

If Nabokov kept praising Priel's *Invitation au supplice*, it is not only because he had collaborated to it, but because he thought very highly of Priel's work as a translator. Again and again, he asked for him to translate his work not only from the Russian, as with *Priglashenie na kazn'*, but also from the English: he even wrote that 'SEBASTIAN *must be translated by Priel, or not be translated at all into French for the moment*' (letter from Nabokov to Ergaz on 6 May 1949, Berg collection); and in 1958, he suggests Priel's name to finish translating *Lolita* into French because Eric Kahane is taking too long (letter from Nabokov to Mohrt, 16 August 1958, Berg Collection).

I see several reasons for Nabokov liking Priel so much. First, Priel seems to have always been very reverential towards Nabokov, be it as a naturalist or as an author. Thus, in 1943, Priel sends several questions about the fauna and flora of Florida to Nabokov for a book he is translating; he apparently sent the same type of questionnaire to Nabokov when they collaborated on *Invitation au supplice* because, in a letter about the translation of *The Real Life of Sebastian Knight*, Priel writes:

> *I have to warn you, but then you've been asking for trouble: from July on – this is around that time, I am told, that the deal around Sebastian Knight will be sealed – you should expect the insidious questionnaires, the kind of trick questions that I offered you while translating Invitation to a Beheading. But joking aside, is it not better to turn to the author, to reach full agreement with him, instead of betraying his thought, or even to commit abominable mistranslations [?].*
>
> (letter from Priel to Nabokov, 16 June 1947, Berg collection)

Secondly, Nabokov often praised Priel's style and vocabulary (Véra writes in a letter to Ergaz that he 'admires' it, 29 March 1960, Cornell). Indeed, he seemed to find in his translator the taste he had himself for the *mot juste*:

> *What I like in Jarl Priel is precisely that he never spares any effort to find the original, but exact, word.*
>
> (letter from Nabokov to Ergaz, 15 August 1950, Cornell)

Unfortunately, publishers tended to disagree on the quality of Priel's work: at Albin Michel Publishing, they thought his translations were '*burdensome*' (letter from Ergaz to Nabokov, 1 December 1948, Cornell) and Ergaz called them '*probably faithful but awfully heavy*' (letter from Ergaz to Nabokov, 24 December 1952, Cornell); and at Gallimard, the two reviews were very bad (letter from Ergaz to Nabokov, 21 March 1958, Cornell) before Priel's translation was finally accepted.

Nabokov did not have a chance to revise Priel's translation of *Invitation to a Beheading* as he wanted to, but shortly later, he managed to get Priel to revise Denis Roche's translation of *The Defense*, and this was an occasion for disenchantment. On 15 October 1961, Véra wrote to Ergaz that the corrections were '*far from satisfying*' (Cornell), and on 2 March 1962, she wrote that her husband '*recognizes that it is indeed his fault if the correction of Denis Roche's translation was entrusted to M. Priel (he believes, however, that M. Priel could have made a better job if he had not been limited to 300 francs and to correcting mistranslations only)*' and he therefore declared that he would pay for Priel's honorarium and reimburse Gallimard for it.

In the Nabokov-Priel correspondence, which goes from 1938 to 1960, what is particularly striking is the very friendly tone used by both men. Nabokov usually starts his letters by '*Cher ami*' (Dear friend) and he regularly enquires about Priel's career. Priel was not only a translator from Russian (he translated Gogol and Bunin for example); he was also an author (he even wrote a novel entitled *Cincinnatus chez les Soviets*, which was published in June 1927[6]), and his career started taking off only when he started writing plays in Breton (a language spoken in Brittany). Nabokov asks Priel once '*please give me news about the staging of your play, it vividly interests me*' (letter, 3 June 1947, from Nabokov to Priel, Berg collection). He is also very friendly when he finishes his letter dated 4 February 1949 and he mentions the things he regularly sends Priel:

> *I wish you success for your new book. It would truly please me if you had good news to give me about it. No detective stories for the moment, but I will try and find some. Meanwhile, here are some stamps for your grand-daughter.*
>
> (Berg collection)

The two men, especially Priel, write about how sorry they feel they could never meet in real life (they both lived next to Antibes around 1935–7), and unfortunately, the French translator died in 1965 before having a chance to meet the author he admired so much.

In all the archives pertaining to Nabokov and his translators into French, this relationship between the two co-translators is the warmest, and in many respects, it is evocative of Nabokov's collaboration with Peter A. Pertzoff,[7] about which Shrayer wrote that 'Nabokov was very pleased with Pertzoff's work and hoped to continue their collaboration, which was beginning to turn into a friendship after Nabokov had visited Pertzoff in Ithaca in 1944' (Shrayer 1999: 560). The fact that Nabokov was very friendly to Priel and Pertzoff, but also to Ergaz, despite her being a female translator, suggests he was nicer to his translators from the

Russian than from the English (his correspondence with Michael Glenny is also rather friendly). It is interesting to note that, when Russian is concerned, Nabokov is prone to say that dictionaries are not up to the task, which might explain his greater benevolence towards translators: 'If I enclose here a list of your worst errors, it is only because I know that Russian is a language poorly dealt with in lexicons' (letter from Nabokov to Glenny, 20 November 169, Berg collection).[8]

There are some elements of complicity in Nabokov's collaboration with Kahane, even though it was more marked in the translator than in Nabokov, as with Priel. However, the moments of tension were also quite important, be it at the beginning or in the middle of the collaboration, but in the end, Nabokov was satisfied with his co-translator.

Lolita: A collaboration with ups and downs

Finding a translator for Nabokov's novel was a difficult matter. It was initially meant to be Blaise Briod, as evidenced by a letter from Raymond Queneau to the translator in which Queneau writes that '*Nabokov will be happy to hear that you accept to translate* Lolita' (3 August 1956, Gallimard Archives). However, a few months later, Michel Mohrt wrote a letter to Eric Kahane to ask him if he could take care of the translation since the translator who had been initially chosen was '*defaulting*' (letter from Mohrt to Kahane, 3 April 1957, Gallimard Archives). The reason why he asked this translator specifically is that Kahane had penned a translation of some passages of *Lolita* which were published by the journal 'La Revue Nouvelle'; however, since the publication was made without the final consent of Nabokov, Gallimard and others, Ergaz wrote on 5 February 1957 that she was '*outraged*' at this publication (letter from Ergaz to Gaston Gallimard, Gallimard Archives). When Nabokov learnt that Briod would not be the translator, he first had his wife write to Ergaz to give his opinion on Kahane's translation:

> *My husband agrees that if Briod does not take care of LOLITA, another translator must be found. He rather likes the translation sample by Kahane that you sent him. Here is what he asks me to tell you about this matter:*
>
> *'Thank you for sending the translation by Eric Kahane. Nobody had sent it to me (as you guess in your letter). […]*
>
> *Kahane's translation is excellent when it comes to style, but there are mistranslations on each page. I'm sending you the list for the first four small chapters.*

I have nothing against M. Kahane's French, but it is his English that is amiss. I could only consent to have him for my translator if he consents to let me see his text and to take into account the corrections I will bring to it. I must particularly insist on the fact that he should follow my text more faithfully, in particular when it comes to images or precise technical terms.

(letter from Véra Nabokov to Ergaz, 16 April 1957, Cornell)

But the whole passage, except the sentence about finding a new translator, is crossed out, and Nabokov then wrote to Ergaz himself:

My wife had just written the long letter you will find enclosed when I received a letter from M. Girodias which I am sending you a copy of. I also send you a copy of my answer.

Besides, if Eric Kahane happens to be M. Girodias's brother, there can be absolutely no question of entrusting the LOLITA translation to him. Another book, why not (BEND SINISTER for example), but not LOLITA. I find myself already too much 'involved' – so much so that journalists ask me if I am not a partner of Olympia Press.

(letter from Nabokov to Ergaz, 16 April 1957, Cornell)

Maurice Girodias and Eric Kahane were indeed brothers, even if their names were different: the Jewish name 'Kahane' could bring trouble to the publisher as he lived in Paris during the occupation, so he took his mother's maiden name (Edel-Roy 2017). Discovering the connection between Kahane and his French publisher, with whom Nabokov already had lots of issues, made Nabokov reluctant to work with Kahane, but at that point, he did not change his mind about the quality of his work. However, a few days later, Nabokov had a chance to read the passages that Kahane translated for 'L'affaire Lolita' and his opinion of the translator worsened:

I have just read 'L'Affaire Lolita' – and I am torn between two feelings: 1. very vivid gratefulness for Olympia which managed to present things in such a brilliant masterly way; 2. helpless rage when I see the ridiculous blunders and mistakes in the translation which disfigure my article, that of Dupee and the fragments of LOLITA. What I cannot understand is that, despite my repeated cries and supplications, I am not given the chance to see and correct before the publication, and instead of translations, what is quietly published is inept paraphrases which have me say banalities and unbelievable drivel!

I retract all the praise I expressed about M. Kahane.

(letter from Nabokov to Ergaz, 25 April 1957, Cornell)

A few days later, Nabokov wrote to Gaston Gallimard that he was '*worried by the difficulty to find a translator able to make a version of [his] book which would be faithful and artistic at the same time*', and he suggested Michel Chrestien for the translation (letter from Nabokov to Gallimard, 7 May 1957, Cornell). But on 17 May, Nabokov was shocked to discover that Gallimard had signed a contract with Kahane for the *Lolita* translation despite his letters (letter from Nabokov to Ergaz, 17 May 1957, Cornell). Nabokov finally surrendered; on 1 June, Véra wrote:

> *In order not to cause difficulties and delays, my husband, though very reluctantly, has decided to accept M. Kahane as the translator of LOLITA. He has just written so to M. Mohrt while asking him to submit the translation to him as it goes and to insist with M. Kahane that all the revisions made by the author will be respected.*
>
> (letter from Véra Nabokov to Ergaz, 1 June 1957, Cornell)

Once the translator was chosen, the collaboration had a few bumps in the road, as Edel-Roy (2017) has shown extensively.

First, in June, Mohrt informed Kahane of Nabokov's wish to see the translation as it went, bits by bits, but Kahane apparently disapproved of this method, preferring to send the whole thing when it was finished. Nabokov grew more and more exasperated; on 10 September, Nabokov was surprised that he still had not received anything from the translator; on 7 November, he wrote that he was extremely vexed, and on 21 November, he expressed the following feelings: '*I still have not heard from the LOLITA translation. It is disheartening. This is what matters the most to me, and what causes me the greatest worry*' (letter from Nabokov to Ergaz, 21 November 1957, Cornell).

For months, Kahane only writes to Mohrt at Gallimard, but not to Nabokov directly, which causes a great exchange of letters to go through the publisher, who expresses his annoyance at this. But the direct correspondence between Nabokov and Kahane starts on 20 November 1957 (Berg collection), when Kahane, after months of delays and more or less credible excuses, finally finds the courage to write to Nabokov with the translation of the first part of the book. Nabokov's answer shows his relief; this is what he wrote to Mohrt:

> *After his rather disappointing translations in L'AFFAIRE LOLITA, I did not expect so much carefulness, exactitude and faithfulness from Eric Kahane. I congratulate him, as well as myself.*
>
> *However, I ask him to take into account all the changes I enumerated in my list, even if some of them seemed trifles to him.*
>
> (letter from Nabokov to Mohrt, 1 January 1958, Gallimard Archives)

On the same day, he also writes to Kahane. After mentioning a few alterations and substitutions ('but <u>all</u> of them are important to me for reasons of style, precision and association'), he invites Kahane to feel free to offer his own suggestions: 'In several cases I am suggesting several choices and naturally, in these cases, you might be able to find something even better'; 'Any suggestions, or criticisms of my suggestions, on your part are, of course, very welcome'. He ends the letter by paying the translator compliments:

> This said, I would like to tell you how much I admire your translation, and how grateful I am to you for taking such minute care of every detail of wording. I find the quality of your work admirable and am eagerly looking forward to the rest of the translation.
>
> (letter from Nabokov to Kahane, 1 January 1958, Berg collection)

Everything seems to go smoothly for the first months of 1958: on 12 March, Véra writes to Ergaz that Nabokov has just sent back the translation of the first volume of *Lolita*, which he finds excellent. But after that, no one hears from Kahane anymore. At the end of May, Ergaz informs Véra that the translator had been ill for two months, but Véra expresses her husband's exasperation with the whole situation on 8 June. Then, several letters are exchanged between Véra and Ergaz, or Nabokov and Mohrt, in which they evoke a change of translator if the translation is not finished by the end of September, then October. On 1 November, Nabokov revokes his contract, arguing: *'with the publication of LOLITA already 14 months overdue, I see no other recourse than to invoke Clause 4 of our agreement, which I am doing with this letter'* (letter from Nabokov to Mohrt, 1 November 1958, Gallimard Archives). But a few days later, Mohrt explains that there was a mistake: Kahane did send most of his translation before the end of October, and Mohrt had written to Véra about it on 27 October, but Mohrt's secretary sent everything to Nabokov by classical mail, not airmail, which explains the delay. Finally, mid-November, Nabokov had received nineteen chapters out of the remaining thirty-six, and then, on 11 December, Véra wrote he had received eleven more, but still expected the last six; they were due any day since, on the previous day, Kahane wrote a letter to Nabokov saying that 'Messrs. Gallimard have in hand the last pages of <u>Lolita</u> and are sending them to you'; he then apologizes for the delay, explaining that *'this second part was not easy and raised a few issues that did not exist in the first, particularly what one could call the "touristic" aspect of <u>Lolita</u>'* (letter from Kahane to Nabokov, 10 December 1958, Berg collection). Nabokov answers at the beginning of January 1959:

> I am delighted with your magnificent work and wish to thank you for this acrobatic faithfulness to my text. […] I think your omissions are all very sound

and you will see that I have made some additional small deletions myself. [...]
Wishing you a Happy New Year, I remain, Sincerely Yours, Vladimir Nabokov
(letter from Nabokov to Kahane, 6 January 1959, Berg collection).

The last letter from Nabokov to Kahane shows, once again, all the good that the author thought of his co-translator: 'I have reread with great delight your magnificent translation and am returning the page proofs tomorrow. [...] Our collaboration has been a very pleasant one and I have no doubt that your work will receive the high praise it deserves'[9] (letter from Nabokov to Kahane, 15 March 1959, Berg collection).

In their correspondence, the discussion revolves around puns at the very beginning but, towards the end of the collaboration, the focus is rather on poetry and botany (and Nabokov writes that he is taking care of them); I will look into detail at those topics in my next chapter. What is important is that these exchanges show that the *Lolita* translation was truly the result of collaboration, and as a mediated form of self-translation, it entailed a part of recreation: as the archives show, Nabokov agreed to the changes made to the text and very often, he was the one who instigated them. In that respect, it may be true that the 1959 translation does not stick to the original perfectly (and Couturier's 2001 retranslation is indeed closer to the original), but it is due to the fact that it is a partial recreation, filled with originality. Nabokov did not claim to prepare a literal translation, but a translation that would be both faithful and artistic, as he wrote to Gaston Gallimard on 7 May 1957.

What should be kept in mind is that Nabokov approved of the French translation, as evidenced by the fact that, in his 1967 Russian self-translation (in the post-scriptum to the Russian edition), he insisted that 'of all the translations, in terms of precision and completeness, I answer only for the French, which I checked myself until it went into print' (Nabokov 1967 [2006]: 358; my translation from the Russian). Another proof of his approval is that, after the French translation of *Lolita* was published, Nabokov repeatedly asked Gallimard to turn to Kahane again for the translation of his other books; when the revision was finished and the book was ready to be published, Nabokov wrote: 'I wish to state again that Mr. Kahane has proved to be an admirable translator and I would want him to translate my other works when you are ready to prepare them for print' (letter from Nabokov to Mohrt, 11 February 1959, Gallimard Archives). Nabokov repeatedly asked for Kahane again until 1965 (for his novel *The Gift*), when he was told that the French translator was now very expensive[10] (letter from Ergaz to Nabokov, 26 January 1965, Cornell).

Feu Pâle: The confrontation of two hubrises

When *Pale Fire* was published in 1962, Nabokov was at the peak of his glory, and in France, the publication of his most famous novel, *Lolita*, had happened only three years before. Therefore, Gallimard wanted to take good care of their author and they looked for a translator that would honour Nabokov's reputation.

For Nabokov, finding the right translator was always hard, and with *Pale Fire*, the difficulty was heightened by the fact that the book included both poetry (the poem by John Shade, made of 999 lines and divided in four cantos) and prose, written mostly as a commentary to this poem by the mad annotator, Kinbote. The discussion between Nabokov and his agents started in the autumn 1962, and difficulties quickly emerged: first, good translators were hard to find (and sometimes too expensive), and then the demand by Nabokov to always see a sample translation was considered insulting by famous translators.

On 31 October (Cornell Library), Ergaz sent the author a sample translation by Pierre Quillet, which was rejected on 5 November, with Véra explaining in a letter to Schébéko that the translator's English was too poor and suggesting her husband's idea to look among Canadian writers (the fact that the word '*écrivains*' and not '*traducteurs*' is used indicates how important the question of style was for Nabokov). The idea of a Canadian translator is quickly rejected because their French would be too archaic, but it will be raised again. On 29 November 1962, Ergaz explains that Mohrt does not dare to ask a sample translation from such a prestigious poet and author as Jean Dutourd (he wrote around seventy novels and translated Truman Capote and Ernest Hemingway into French); in January 1963, she argues that writer Pierre Leyris would be the best choice in her opinion as he is also a great translator (he translated T. S. Eliot into French), but she is later told by Mohrt that Leyris is expensive and will refuse to have his translations corrected. On 21 March 1963, Doussia Ergaz writes with three very prestigious names to offer. First, she mentions her personal choices: writer Pierre Leyris, once again, and translator Jacques Papy, who translated many classics such as Lewis Carroll's *Alice's Adventures in Wonderland* and several books by Steinbeck or Lovecraft. The third name is Mohrt's suggestion: Raymond Girard is an excellent translator, who happens to be French Canadian, and he works in partnership with a prestigious translator, Maurice-Edgar Coindreau.[11] A few words will suffice to give an idea of how famous Coindreau is in France: he was the translator of Faulkner and boosted the latter to international fame, as well as other American authors: Sartre famously declared in 1948 that '*La littérature américaine, c'est la littérature Coindreau*'. Last but not least, Coindreau has a translation prize named after him.

The duo Girard-Coindreau is quickly selected, as shown by a letter sent by Ergaz on 31 April. The collaboration starts with Girard only, and letters are very cordial: in what seems to be Nabokov's first letter to the translator (previously, Véra wrote to Girard or Nabokov wrote to Ergaz), Nabokov congratulates him on the quality of his translation but, as usual, he sends a very long list of corrections. However, he is now willing to admit that his French is a bit rusty and that the translator can improve on his suggestions about the mistakes he corrected: '*I only give you their literal meaning, and it is up to you to find the right formulation in French, if I make an idiomatic mistake*' (letter from Nabokov to Girard, 19 October 1963, Cornell). Nabokov had made a similar remark to Ergaz a few months before: on 6 May 1963 (Cornell Library), Nabokov wrote that he had placed question marks after his suggestions for Girard, commenting that he made them diffidently due to his 'insufficient command of French'.

On 12 December 1963, Giraud writes to Nabokov to tell him that he should receive the second Canto by Coindreau shortly, and a month later, Coindreau does send the canto, but his letter to Nabokov is rather vehement. As Coindreau explains, he strongly objects to Nabokov's method, which he deems unacceptable: he agrees when Nabokov points out mistakes and misunderstandings, but he refuses suggestions which are, to him, either barbarisms in French or mistranslations of what the author himself writes in English. The climax of the letter comes on the third page. Coindreau wants to clearly distinguish where the limit lies between his role and that of Nabokov:

> I have not published thirty-three translations without having learnt that a translator has certain imperious duties towards the author whom he translated. He must consult him in order to avoid semantic contradictions, misinterpretations, to resolve insoluble problems which may require makeshift stopgaps. [...] But a translator's duties stop there where the author's begin, duties which may be summarized by one rule: let the translator be master of his own syntax and vocabulary.
>
> (letter from Coindreau to Nabokov, 6 January 1964, Berg collection, qtd in
> Nicholas Manning's translation in Anokhina 2017: 117)

To Coindreau, the only insoluble problem for which the translator needs to consult the author is puns, and as he says, in that case only, the author's translations will be more than welcome. He finishes the letter by writing that, for the time being, the translation is at a stop and that Nabokov is free to ask Gallimard for new translators if their conditions are not to his liking.

In the whole letter, Coindreau is vehement about his role as a translator, but he is also very keen on being corrected for his real mistakes and is extremely respectful of the author's work, which is why he refuses to accept Nabokov's suggestions if they do not correspond to the original: in fact, what Coindreau objects to is Nabokov's creative rewriting. The writing of the translation should therefore be left to the translator, not the author. This borderline case between writing and translating can also be seen in the following remark by Coindreau about the translator: *'he has a public who expects from him books in which it will find the qualities it is used to. Therefore, he cannot lower the level of one of his oeuvres by welcoming with closed eyes erroneous mistakes'.*

In his answer, Nabokov is prompt to underline the fact that, in the context of their collaboration, it is not that easy to put a clear limit between writer and translator:

> You mention your rights as a translator. They are undisputable. Nevertheless, there are borderline cases where our rights overlap.
>
> (letter from Nabokov to Coindreau, Berg collection, 14 January 1964, qtd in Nicholas Manning's translation in Anokhina 2017: 118)

Interestingly enough, Nabokov shifts from Coindreau's mention of 'a translator's duties' to 'rights as a translator'.

On the whole, Nabokov's answer is rather similar in tone to that of Coindreau: he politely explains at length why this or that translation of his is the right one, but he also starts and finishes his letter by the expression of his irritation. Thus, he begins in the following manner: 'You tell me, Monsieur, that you have published 33 translations. I myself have had more than sixty translators' (qtd in Nicholas Manning's translation in Anokhina 2017: 118). He then proceeds to list Coindreau's answers to his queries and explains his own choices again on three pages. The end of Nabokov's letter is as strongly worded as Coindreau's, though it remains polite: 'Given that, up until now, I have allowed myself no interference with your style (or M. Girard's), the *violence of your fighting against thin air* does not seem justified to me' (letter from Nabokov to Coindreau, Berg collection, 14 January 1964, quoted in Nicholas Manning's translation in Anokhina 2017, 118). Nabokov continues with a rather ironic tone: '*I indicate, I signal those little careless mistakes and I would not want you to lose your temper against me as if I had damaged your bumper by trying to overtake you on a road covered in ice'.*

Once the storm was over, the collaboration resumed, but it is obvious that efforts were made on both sides and that everyone felt a bit sour. Indeed, one year later (19 January 1965), Nabokov sent the whole translation with his annotations to Mohrt, and he started by writing that he deemed the whole translation superb (he even thought it was the finest he had ever been given). He added that he was happy that the translators took into account most of his corrections, but he still finished the letter by saying that, in his corrections, he only wished to give the literal meaning of the English, so that he would appreciate it if Coindreau could refrain from telling him once again that his French was full of barbarisms.

For the translators, Nabokov's corrections were still a moot point, and Girard and Coindreau asked for a note to be included, which reads as follows in the final version: 'The modifications which were brought to the original text – omissions, additions, insertions of words and sentences in English were made at the request of the author' (Nabokov [1965b] 2020: 1318; my translation). Nabokov was a bit piqued by its formulation:

> *I find the 'translators' note' rather unclear. 'Omissions' and 'additions' are too important terms for those trifles. My omissions almost exclusively have to do with untranslatable puns, and the small additions generally are mere clarifications for allusions which are common in English, but not in French. I don't know if it should not be added to the note that it is I who drew the translators' attention to the* mistranslations*. As an old goalkeeper I am a little surprised that nobody has thanked me for the many saves I have made.*
>
> (letter from Nabokov to Schébéko, 30 September 1965, Cornell)

Nabokov resented not being thanked for his collaboration, and he was probably all the more bitter because he had asked to be paid for all the work he put in for the revisions as early as January 1963; however, it was objected to him in September that Gallimard could not afford it, especially because Coindreau's fees were rather high.

Despite his grudge against the note, Nabokov was very pleased with the translation, as he wrote at the end of his letter:

> I wish to add in a loud and clear voice that the texture of Girard and Coindreau's translation is a marvel, a masterpiece, limpid, stylish and taut. It is a great compliment to my novel, and I am grateful to everybody concerned for devoting so much care to my stuff.
>
> (letter from Nabokov to Schébéko, 30 September 1965, Cornell)

The collaboration with Girard and Coindreau was at times tumultuous, but Nabokov was deeply satisfied with their work. The pair was suggested for the translation of *The Gift* and on 1 April 1965, Véra wrote: '*My husband asks me to tell you that, despite M. Coindreau's nasty temper, he is glad to see that*

MM. Girard and Coindreau will take care of the translation of The Gift' (letter from Véra Nabokov to Ergaz, 1 April 1965, Cornell). However, in the end, only Girard was to take care of it.

In comparison, the relationship with the translator of *Ada* was also difficult, but never once did Nabokov ask to work with him again.

Ada ou l'ardeur: Men on the verge of a nervous breakdown

Ada and Ardor was published in the United States in 1969, but it took six years for it to appear in French. As usual, a translator needed to be found. In 1970, Nabokov was presented with two sample translations: one by Jacques Tournier (with Roland Delouys) and one by Gilles Chahine. Nabokov was very critical of Tournier's work, but he was pleased with Chahine's work. This is what he wrote to Charles Orengo[12] from Fayard, his new publisher (Nabokov had just left Gallimard because he deemed that the publishing house did not put enough effort into the publicity of his works):

> *I am truly very happy with the translation: it is faithful, intelligent, and full of trouvailles – meaning, incomparably more beautiful than the other one. Thank you for finding me such a good translator.*
>
> (letter from Nabokov to Orengo, 29 January 1970)[13]

Unfortunately, Nabokov's enthusiasm was not going to last. Still in January, Orengo received a letter from the translator, Gilles Chahine, who expressed his anguish: he wrote that when he had received the novel, he had read through it and had been charmed by it, but now that he had to translate it, he saw that the number of allusions and puns was properly maddening and he questioned the translatability of the book, thinking he would never be up to the task (letter from Chahine to Orengo, January 1970). Orengo transmitted the letter to Nabokov, and only two days after the letter where he praised Chahine's translation, the author expressed his exasperation and repeatedly quoted from the letter of the translator (whose name he often misspelled):

> *Allow me first to make a few general remarks. The first mistake of M. Chahim is to have thought that it was sufficient to 'read through [my book] for a long time' instead of reading it quietly once, which would have taken him (if he knows English well) only one weekend. His second mistake is to think that the book is 'an uninterrupted game of verbal coquetries'. I cannot understand why translators (for M. Tournier also sees inexistent puns everywhere) take my metaphors for spoonerisms and the right word for a play on words.*
>
> (letter from Nabokov to Orengo, 31 January 1970)

One cannot help but feel that Nabokov's remarks on the absence of puns look like a bout of bad faith.

Despite Nabokov's annoyance at this letter, the relationship between the writer and Chahine was rather good at the beginning of their collaboration. After mentioning Chahine's mistakes, this is what Nabokov wrote in September 1971:

> Although my task was laborious, let me assure you that it was a delightful one owing to the friendly presence of Mr. Chain's [*sic*] talent and to my feeling that whatever changes had to be introduced his and my aim remained always the same.
>
> (letter from Nabokov to Orengo, 24 September 1971, Cornell)

In another letter, Nabokov uses his classical mix of praise and listing of mistakes, as well as other recurring traits:

> I repeat that I am delighted with Mr. Chahine's work, in general structure and in many details. I have eliminated, though, a number of little stylistic props (such as 'l'ami Van' etc.) as well as the translator's ornamental or explanatory additions. Some paragraphs, however, present veritable constellations of indispensable corrections. As I mentioned before, I must beg Mr. Chahine to take into account all my modifications, no matter how trivial (a few are aimed at avoiding a proximate repetition). If he can find a better French term whilst retaining the exact sense I indicate in my correction, so much the better; otherwise, I am afraid good usage must be sacrificed to the barbarism proposed for the sake of absolute fidelity (a course followed, not without storms and explosions, in FEU PALE). Incidentally, I would like the attribution of the translation to Mr. Chahine to be accompanied by the formula 'with the author's collaboration'.
>
> (letter from Nabokov to Orengo, 20 October 1971)

Several things are noteworthy: first, the importance of absolute fidelity is a clear echo to Nabokov's literalism as defended in *Eugene Onegin*, as well as his sacrifice of good usage. And then, Nabokov is now asking to have his collaboration recognized as such, and not merely through payment, as he asked for *Feu Pâle*.[14] As I will show, this mention will not be used as such but will be amended in the final publication.

Nabokov and Chahine's relationship started deteriorating when the translator turned out to be very slow. It is really in May 1972 that the translator's limited pace is frankly discussed, first by Nabokov's agent Marie Schébéko and then by Véra, who writes that her husband is 'worried by the slowness of ADA's translator' and that 'this is a disaster' (letter from Véra Nabokov to Schébéko, 12 May 1972, Cornell). Nabokov complained more and more of how slow the translator was, which meant that his work as an author started to suffer from it, and publishers spent their time asking Chahine to work more, and more quickly, as shown by this letter from a publisher that Orsenna quotes in his book *Deux étés*, which documents the difficulty Chahine had to translate *Ada*: 'Since M. Nabokov does not belong yet to the infinitely patient crowd of deceased people, we allow ourselves to ask for an acceleration of your pace' (Orsenna 1998: 48, my translation).

One of the reasons why Chahine took so long to send his translation is that he feared Nabokov's reaction, and he kept reworking his translation, again and again; it was therefore not laziness, but rather a brand of perfectionism pushed to its utter limit. For example, Schébéko writes to Nabokov that, according to Henri Hell (from Fayard), the situation is actually not as bad as it looks: '*he assured me that Monsieur Chaim [sic] had already made a draft version of the whole book and that mere adjustment are left to be done before the final typing*' (letter from Schébéko to Véra Nabokov, 13 December 1972, Cornell). A few months later, Hell went to see the translator on his island next to Britanny and could see for himself this perfectionism bordering madness:

> *The news from the translation of ADA are not great but they are not desperate either: it is Monsieur Henri Hell who went to Bréhat to see Monsieur Chahine. He saw, he tells me, literally thousands of pages written in the hand of the translator who sometimes made up to 16 (!) versions of some passages.*
> (letter from Schébéko to Véra Nabokov, 31 March 1973, Cornell)

In November, a new visit had to be made to entice the translator to stop revising his work:

> Mr. Orengo is sending his so called literary director, Henri Hell, again to Bréhat to see whether he might induce Chahine to drop the polishing and to part with his draft translation of those pages.
> (letter from Schébéko to Véra Nabokov,
> 29 November 1973, Cornell)

Actually, the whole 'disaster' seems to have had a somewhat comical dimension, at least for the publisher and literary agents involved, as several letters between Véra and Schébéko suggest:

> *After yet another call to Fayard to know what is happening with the batches of translations we were promised, Monsieur Orengo read to me the epic correspondence*

of the last few months with Monsieur Chaïm [sic]. I asked him to send you photocopies of these letters, which are worthy to be included in an anthology – which I would like to see published – on the problems which translations raise. I hope he will do so and will tell you that after many hesitations we agreed that he would not send the threatening telegramme he had prepared (for fear that, upon reception, everything which has already been translated should be thrown to the sea by the instable person that this translator is) and that he would go meet him himself, be it in Paris or Bréhat if the two batches don't get here by the end of next week.

(letter from Schébéko to Véra Nabokov, 14 February 1973, Cornell)

My husband received a charming letter from M. Orengo with photocopies of the very amusing exchange of correspondence between M. Hell and M. Chahine. […] The correspondence stops at a point where M. Chahine declares 'that he will no longer open any telegramme or letter to avoid myself trouble that brings the greatest damage to my work'.

(letter from Véra Nabokov to Schébéko, 19 February 1973, Cornell)

The letters to and from Chahine have been lost apparently, but Orsenna's novel offers an illuminating perspective on what the situation was from the perspective of the translator, especially as it suggests that collaborating with Nabokov was indeed no small feat.

Chahine actually had a nervous breakdown due to the translation and his relationship with the author (Boyd 1991: 644). In a letter written in 1972, Nabokov's agent even described Chahine in the following terms: *'it has taken the translator, who seems to be hypersensitive, several weeks to recover from Monsieur Nabokov's suggestions and observations!!'* (letter from Schébéko to Véra Nabokov, 8 May 1972, Cornell) But Nabokov was far from being indifferent to the translator's situation and offered his help: *'I really am aware of the difficulties that the poor translator of ADA has to overcome, but tell him that I am always at his disposal to assist him'* (letter from Nabokov to Orengo, 28 July 1972, Cornell). He repeated his offer several times, for example, in a letter by Véra in April 1973:

He asks me to add: 'As to Chahine's labors I would like to repeat that the translator would save himself an abyss of time and effort if he finally understood that I shall supply the wordplay and certain exact terms, and that those corrections and changes of mine will be final, no matter how "ternes" he may find them'.

(letter from Véra Nabokov to Schébéko, 4 April 1973, Cornell)

Brian Boyd mentions how much Nabokov took it to heart to help the translator:

> Because of his translator's breakdown, he considered himself obliged to revamp
> the whole text: the translator's life would be ruined, he felt, if he did not bring it
> up to standard.
>
> (Boyd 1991: 646)

For five years, Nabokov complains again and again of the time it takes him to correct Chahine's translation. In July 1974, he wrote he spent a couple of hours every morning revising the translation; in November, it had increased to 3 to 4 hours, and in January 1975, it was up to 6 hours a day. On 23 July 1974, Nabokov finally resolved to ask for help:

> I wonder if something could not be done about it – by an editor's checking in the
> remaining pages of Chahine's text the kind of errors I list above? [...] I am sure
> you will agree with me that this is an impossible demand to place on an author.
>
> (letter from Nabokov to Hell, 23 July 1974, in Nabokov [1989] 1991: 534)

His request was met with the appointment of Jean-Bernard Blandenier, and Nabokov was utterly satisfied by his work, even if Chahine's part of the job was still problematic:

> M. Blandenier's help in deflating the translator's banalities is admirable, but
> I alone can step in when Chahine despairs. [...] I don't want to Chahinate
> [*chahiner* in the original], but today is 15th January and I strongly doubt that I
> shall finish before 15th February.
>
> (letter from Nabokov to Alex Grall, 15 January 1975,
> in Nabokov [1989] 1991: 541–2)

The letters that Nabokov sent to Blandenier show his satisfaction: 'Thank you for your good words. Yes, our collaboration was great fun and I will always remain grateful to you for frenchifying my Ada so stylishly' (7 March 1975). His satisfaction was such that Blandenier was chosen to translate Nabokov's last novel, *Look at the Harlequins!*, into French.[15]

Despite the long hours that Nabokov spent on the *Ada* translation and his request for the mention 'with the author's collaboration' to be included in the paratext, this is not what is written on the book; instead, only his revision was acknowledged in the paratexts: '*traduit de l'anglais par Gilles Chahine avec la collaboration de Jean-Bernard Blandenier, traduction revue par l'auteur*'. In French, the verb '*revoir*' can imply various meanings such as 'see again', 'revise' or 'proofread'; in any case, it implies a rather light contribution and certainly does not do justice to Nabokov's investment in time and energy. It is probably because of the collaboration with Blandenier that the mention of Nabokov's collaboration could not be included and was thus toned down to mere revising.

Conclusion

As I have shown, one of the reasons why there were tensions between Nabokov and his co-translators is that the author insisted on the fact that he should always have the last word in the translation, especially because he mastered French, and those requests were not always received gracefully, according to the Nabokovs:

> *Besides, he would like to be paid for the time it takes him to correct the French translation. This task would be much easier for him if there were not the hostility and the carelessness with which the French translators tend to receive his requests for change in their texts.*

> (letter from Véra Nabokov to D. Develdere, 9 July 1969, Cornell)

But actually, the archives suggest that Nabokov's mastery of French was not as good as he thought, or at least, his written French did not correspond to the standards of his time, as one can infer from his opinion on two translators. For Nabokov, Marcelle Sibon was the worst translator he had ever had (letter from Nabokov to Ergaz, 28 July 1962, Cornell), but in France, she was considered one of the top four or five translators (letter from C. Duhamel to Nabokov, 22 January 1953, IMEC); on the other hand, Nabokov praised Jarl Priel's job for years, but publishers found the translator's style too heavy and rejected his translation on many occasions. One can wonder if these disparities in the perception of French do not reflect, indirectly, what kind of French Nabokov had; as we will see in the next chapter, he often used somewhat old-fashioned French words in the translations he collaborated to.

To be more specific, Nabokov's mastery of French declined over the years, or at least his perception thereof. He does not seem to have doubts about his French until the early 1960s, which suggests that when he left the United States and settled down in French-speaking Switzerland, he was confronted with his actual level of French. As I showed in the *Pale Fire* section, Nabokov mentioned on several occasions, in 1962 and 1963, for example, that he knew his French was far from idiomatic or impeccable, but he insisted he had enough French to discriminate between what corresponded to the nuances in his English and what did not. In 1962, there was another occasion for Nabokov to express how self-conscious he had grown about his French. A movie was to be made of *Camera Obscura* and Nabokov's involvement was going to depend on the language of the film:

> *It would be easier for him to collaborate on the shooting if it was a version in English because he would not like to try creating dialogues in French (he says his French is* 'rusty and unwieldy'*) while in English he could bring all the necessary changes right there.*
>
> (letter from Véra Nabokov to Ergaz, 13 November 1962, Cornell)

Interestingly enough, in this letter written in French, it is in English that Nabokov's insufficient mastery of French is expressed.

Nabokov seemed to realize his French was not as good as his Russian or his English in the early 1960s, but earlier documents indicate that his French was problematic before that. Indeed, when his agent discussed the choice of translator with Jacques Duhamel (from the French publishing house called La Table Ronde), she explained that Nabokov would never agree to have Marcelle Sibon for *Conclusive Evidence* and she added:

> *What can you do, he is one of those unbearable authors who know a language enough to pretend they can rule over their translator without understanding its demands and necessities. The proof is that I have a very beautiful short story by him which he translated himself with such an amount of gross mistakes that 'Les Nouvelles Littéraires' sent it back to me declaring that they would only take it if the translation were revised.*
>
> (letter from Ergaz to J. Duhamel, 22 January 1953, IMEC)

Since 'Musique' was published in 1959 by 'Les Nouvelles Littéraires', it seems plausible that this was the short story in question, though one cannot exclude 'Bachmann' since the manuscript of Nabokov's self-translation is undated. As for this short story, Nabokov's insufficient mastery of French could explain why the version that was published was not Nabokov's, but that of a French translator; however, reading the self-translation did not reveal to my eyes of native speaker anything shocking. Going back to Ergaz's letter, it is interesting to see that Nabokov's agent also had something to say about his corrections to the work of French translators:

> *There is another female translator who is absolutely remarkable: it is Léo Lack, but she would be intransigent where Nabokov's corrections would risk to make the French text banal and I don't know how we'd get out of it.*
>
> (letter from Ergaz to J. Duhamel, 22 January 1953, IMEC)

Translator Yvonne Davet was also critical of Nabokov's corrections: '*Only I would like to see again one last time the modifications inserted by V. Nabokov because the French language does not always allow for his excess of originality*' (letter from Davet to C. Duhamel, 17 April 1957, IMEC).

The fact that Nabokov's French was not impeccable recalls recurring debate about writing in a second language,[16] and more generally revisions: should any work which has been revised and altered be considered not the work of its author? Nabokov had people checking his writing in English at the beginning of his career, and it is only later that he grew confident enough to discard such corrections by insisting on the specificities of his art.[17] The fact that Nabokov was known and perceived as a foreigner probably influenced the way his texts were perceived, which is reminiscent of the case of Andreï Makine.[18] Nabokov's peculiar brand of French might have been so original that it was deemed foreign, which is reminiscent of Sebastian Knight:

> My interlocutor had known him so intimately that I think he was right in suggesting that Sebastian's sense of inferiority was based on his trying to out-England England, and never succeeding, and going on trying, until finally he realized that it was not these outward things that betrayed him, not the mannerisms of fashionable slang, but the very fact of his striving to be and act like other people when he was blissfully condemned to the solitary confinement of his own self.
>
> (Nabokov [1941b] 1996: 35)

In my next chapter, I will look into specific cases of Nabokov's creative involvement in order to further show how much the term 'mediated self-translations' applies to the French translations which Nabokov took part in.

12

Nabokov's Creative Involvement in French

In the translations into French which Nabokov collaborated in, he insisted on translating some elements himself, but it usually did not show in the paratext. More often than not, only an investigation inside unpublished archives helps reveal the true extent of Nabokov's creative involvement in several elements like the fauna and flora, poetry and puns; moreover, Nabokov had strong opinions on the way to deal with foreign languages in the translations of his novels.

Focusing on Nabokov's verbal creativity is all the more important in the context of self-translation, as it is characterized by an association of creation and translation, as Michaël Oustinoff showed in his book on self-translation:

> Self-translation is a field that obeys a specific logic which is due to his authoriality and which is also the privileged place where the problems linked to bilingual writing appear the most clearly. It is eminently *both* translation and writing, so that one should not reduce it to mere writing alone (thus putting it in the field of recreation), as people tend to do too often.
>
> (Oustinoff 2001: 57; my translation)

By exploring the way in which Nabokov translated into French those four elements of Nabokovese, I intend to shed light on those items of *full* self-translation hidden within his *mediated* self-translations into French.

For each linguistic category, I will start by offering a general view by mentioning elements found in the archives pertaining to various novels, and then, I will zoom in on some novels where the linguistic category is more particularly discussed by Nabokov and his co-translators.

Collaborating with a naturalist

Apparently, the fauna and flora are the elements which have the least to do with style. One can note however that Nabokov repeatedly paired poetry and natural sciences when he mentioned the corrections he made for the French translations of his works, more specifically *Lolita*, *The Gift* and his autobiography (*Autres Rivages* in French):

> Here's a curious matter: My Humbert Humbert is not a naturalist (I am). Some of his mistakes are obvious to an American reader but would only mislead a French one. I have corrected his mistakes for the French edition. I have also supplied the correct ornithological and botanical terms wherever you have not understood them. I have also taken care of the poems.
>
> (letter from Nabokov to Kahane, 6 January 1959, Berg collection)

> *If you think it appropriate, you could maybe point out to M. Mohrt that my husband generously gave away his time by checking word by word the translations of LOLITA and AUTRES RIVAGES, and that he translated himself the verse and everything having to do with butterflies in the latter among those two books.*
>
> (letter from Véra Nabokov to Schébéko, 2 March 1962, Cornell)

> *My husband is taking care of the revisions to the French text of THE GIFT. He has discovered blunders, which are important not so much by their number, but rather by the enormity of the error; many mistakes in places having to do with butterflies (which is forgivable); and very mediocre translations of the poems which, in the present case, must be in verse because otherwise the separate lines which are embedded in the text in prose would go unnoticed.*
>
> (letter from Véra Nabokov to Schébéko, 18 October 1966, Berg collection)

Very often, translating fauna and flora implies looking at the Latin names of animals to make sure that the term in the source text does correspond to the right term in the target text. The most famous instance must be Nabokov's coinage 'racemosa' in *Eugene Onegin*[1] because he was unhappy with the existing terminology in English for the Russian 'cheryomuha', so he used a Latin word present in its scientific name.[2]

In the Nabokov papers, the most interesting archives on translating plants and animals have to do with *Pale Fire*, but one short mention should be made to a particularly delightful exchange in the *Lolita* correspondence.

Lolita and gooseberry

In France, gooseberries are not a common type of berry, and their name sounds rather unpleasant: '*groseille à maquereaux*' translates back as 'mackerel redcurrant'. This is probably why Nabokov looked for something else. The author-naturalist was apparently very proud of his translation because he wrote to his co-translator at the very beginning of their correspondence: 'I hope you will like the beautiful word for "gooseberry" that I have discovered. Any suggestions, or criticisms of my suggestions, on your part are, of course, very welcome' (letter from Nabokov to Kahane, 1 January 1958, Berg collection). In *Lolita*, the word 'gooseberry' did not occur in any botanical context; rather, it was used to describe Lolita's skin in Part I, Chapter 11: 'and finally, when I had completely enmeshed my glowing darling in this weave of ethereal caresses, I dared stroke her bare leg along the gooseberry fuzz of her shin' (Nabokov [1955a] 1996: 41).

Nabokov amended Kahane's translation and suggested, for 'the gooseberry fuzz of her shin', 'le duvet d'embresaille qui se hérissait sur le devant de son tibia' (Berg collection). Kahane enjoyed his co-translator's suggestion and indulged in a bit of banter:

> Ah ah! 'Embresaille'. It is a beautiful word. But where in Himmel did you find it? It is unknown in the Grosser Larousse, the Littré, the Robert, &c. I would love to use it, but can you produce its french [*sic*] birth certificate? No proof, no soap, and that would be a shame. Aber, as Humbert's uncle Gustave used to say, sicher ist and must be sicher.
>
> (letter from Kahane to Nabokov, 7 February 1958, Berg collection)

I will have a chance to go back to Kahane's use of German with Nabokov, but what is interesting is that he asks for proof. Nabokov must have provided the birth certificate (the word seems to be used in some part of French Savoie or in Switzerland to describe some types of blueberries or cranberries): indeed, Nabokov's word is in the published version, though the spelling is rectified with an initial 'a' and the rest of the sentence is slightly different, suggesting that Kahane followed Nabokov's suggestion to feel free to amend his translations: 'le duvet d'ambresailles qui striait l'arête de son tibia' (Nabokov 1959a: 55).

The translation of this botanical term was made in a spirit of complicity between Nabokov and Kahane, but for *Feu Pâle*, ornithological and botanical terminology was hotly debated between Coindreau and Nabokov.

Pale Fire: A thorny translation into French

When Coindreau joined the *Feu Pâle* translation team, his first letter to Nabokov was rather vehement, and one major point of disagreement was the translation of fauna and flora. Nabokov used his scientific expertise in different ways. First, he corrected mistakes having to do with species and genus; for example, for '*Waxwings,* birds of the genus *Bombycilla*' (Nabokov [1962] 1996: 667) which had been translated as 'de l'espèce Bombycilla' ('espèce' means 'species'), Nabokov reinstated the italics and translated 'genus' by 'genre' (Nabokov [1965b] 2020: 401; corrections by Nabokov, 29 January 1965, Berg collection). Then, he sometimes made drawings, for example, to explain the difference between 'streaks' and 'stripes'. He finished his comment by insisting on his expertise that exceeded that of dictionaries:

> *if you do not want* pointes, *put* 'traits' *or even* 'stries'; *but* 'rayure' *is not* <u>streak</u> *here – and you can believe me that, in my quality of naturalist, I know this stuff better than Webster.* (letter from Nabokov to Coindreau, 14 January 1964, Berg collection)[3]

Many terms were discussed, like birds ('wood duck', 'waxwing', etc.), flowers ('michaelmas daisies', 'star of trillium', etc.) and trees[4] ('shagbark' for instance), but I will not detail them here because what is particularly interesting is what these discussions reveal of Nabokov's vision of translation, and how problematic it could be for a translator like Coindreau.

On several occasions, Nabokov wanted to add something in the French version in order to clarify the text for the reader. Indeed, the main problem is that trees (for example) that seem to have the same name in different places are actually not the same. In that respect, transparent translation turns out to be deceitful, and this is what Nabokov explained to Coindreau: '<u>cedars</u>. *What is called* <u>cedar</u> *in America is not a* cèdre *but a* genévrier *(which I prefer to* genièvre)' (letter from Nabokov to Coindreau, 14 January 1964, Berg collection). But for Coindreau, most of Nabokov's suggestions were unacceptable because they implied rewriting the text:

> *for* 'the suburban impostor, the gross fowl' *etc. you would like* 'au merle migrateur, à l'imposteur des pelouses' *etc. It is not translation, but commentary. You did not speak of* 'merle migratoire' *[migratory blackbird] but of* 'gross fowl' *so we will not speak of it either.*
> (letter from Coindreau to Nabokov, 6 January 1964, Berg collection)

The explanation that Nabokov sent a week later is interesting because it shows how deceitful translation can be and also that notes were particularly impossible in this specific book:

> Merle migrateur *(p. 2). This is a clarification that I would have liked to insert in the text. It is not a real* <u>red robin</u>, *that's to say* rougegorge, *but really the* merle migrateur, <u>Turdus migratorius</u>, *an American bird that the French reader is not supposed to know. Unfortunately, we cannot explain this* merle *in a note since*

a 'translator's note', here and elsewhere in this book, would risk getting horribly mixed up with the notes by parodic Kinbote.

> (letter from Nabokov to Coindreau, 14 January 1964, Berg collection)

The most interesting, and entertaining, debate between Coindreau and Nabokov associates several of the elements above. For the sentence 'I had a favorite young shagbark tree', Coindreau writes the following rant:

I now come to <u>Hickory</u>, p. 89: M. Girard translated this word by 'noyer', he was right because, contrary to what you write to him, the hickory belongs to the family of noyers [the walnut family]. See Webster, which gives for this tree the following definition: 'Any of a genus (hicoria) of North American trees <u>of the walnut family</u> (I underline)… What's more, you do not know, certainly, that the word <u>hickory</u> has entered the French language, as evidenced by its insertion in such modest dictionaries as the Petit Larousse […]. Therefore, we will keep either noyer, *either* hickory. *Before leaving that tree, allow me to say that, when M. Girard translates <u>his favorite hickory</u> by* son <u>hickory favori</u>, *he translates exactly what you have written. You haven't written his <u>beloved</u> hickory and, consequently, we do not accept* son hickory <u>bien-aimé</u>. *Rest assured that we will make enough mistakes ourselves without you inviting us to add a few ones.*

> (letter from Coindreau to Nabokov, 6 January 1964, Berg collection)

In his answer, it is noteworthy that Nabokov seems to be copying some expressions by Coindreau, and his irritation transpires in those places:

<u>Hickory</u> (p. 18). I now come to a series of mistakes which, coming from you, surprise me. You tell me that, following Webster, the <u>hickory</u> belongs to the <u>walnut family</u>. It is indeed correct, but you are confusing, Monsieur, family and genus! Translating hickory by 'noyer' is just as strange as translating <u>chestnut</u> by 'hêtre' [beech] and <u>oak</u> by 'marronnier' [chestnut] (because all three belong to the family of Fagacese beech!) or translating 'chat' by tiger, and <u>jaguar</u> by 'lynx' because all four belong to the Felicidae family! Therefore, we will put 'hickory', not 'noyer'. To this strange taxonomic excursion, you add the following sentence: What's more, you do not know, certainly, that the word <u>hickory</u> has entered the French language, as evidenced by its insertion in such modest dictionaries as the Petit Larousse'. But it is you, Monsieur, who do not know that, among the <u>queries</u> sent to M. Girard on 19 October 1963, it was precisely me who suggested to him 'hickory', while adding 'hickory which I find even in the execrable Petit Larousse'. And before leaving that tree, please note that if I suggested (in the same list of October 19 which you did see) to replace 'hickory favori' by 'hickory bien-aimé', it was because the rime annoyed me. Keep it if you like.

> (letter from Nabokov to Coindreau, 14 January 1964, Berg collection)

In several places in Nabokov's letter, his tone oscillates between anger and humour, probably to try and defuse the situation. For example, for his answer about 'wood duck', he writes: '*Decidedly, we have no luck with birds*'.

If botanical and ornithological terminologies do not have much to do with style, they do reveal this specific language which Nabokov mastered in his other life as a naturalist. More importantly, he imported it in his art as a writer-translator.

Translating embedded poetry

In his novels in prose, Nabokov often inserted poems, and translating them often proved difficult for the author's French co-translators, so he often took care of them (strangely enough, poetry does not seem to have been an issue for *Pale Fire*, at least not from what exists in the archives). In the context of his collaborations, it is interesting to see that poems are sometimes explicitly presented as Nabokov's self-translations into French thanks to a note, for example, in *Lolita* and in *Le Don* (*The Gift*). In the collaboration with Kahane, things seem to have gone rather smoothly, but it was not the case with Girard for *Le Don*.

Lolita and poetry

It is only towards the end of the Kahane-Nabokov collaboration that the poems are discussed. Nabokov explains to his co-translator what important prosodic rules have to be respected, but he also elaborates on his creative choices which are anchored in French intertextuality:

> The only trouble is the old one: prosody. As I tell Mr Mohrt in my letter to him in order to explain my introduction of new changes, I had to rework the Carmen poem and a few lines of the 'Perdue: Dolores Haze' Poem. In your re-version of my remanipulation of the Carmen piece you had an impossible sequence of rhymes (all feminine in the second quatrain!) and some extra syllables. In the other poem, the first line is all wrong and some of the rhymes are impossible. My Humbert is a prosodist of the old school. You will notice that I have introduced, by a flash of mimetic genius, a parody of Chateaubriand ('et la montagne, et le grand chene') and an entire line from Verlaine ('et tout le reste est litterature'). The versions as I have corrected them now, are definitive and final; if you

disagree with my final versions of the Carmen poem (p. 73) and of the other poem (pp. 296–7), credit them (or it) to me in a footnote.

(letter from Nabokov to Kahane, 15 March 1959, Berg collection)

In the published translation, the two poems are indeed credited to Nabokov with the following note: 'This song has been adapted in French by the author, as well as the poem on pages 296–7. (*Note of the Translator*)' (Nabokov 1959a: 73; my translation). It is indeed an adaptation because the translation is far from being faithful and literal: one can note, for example, the rewriting of the stars-cars-bars alliteration, which in French relies on *départs*, *gares*, *soirs* and *bars*.

Below, I give first Nabokov's poem in English, then Nabokov's self-translation into French, and finally, my literal translation of the French self-translation:

O my Carmen, my little Carmen!
Something, something those something nights,
And the stars, and the cars, and the bars, and the barmen –
And, O my charmin', our dreadful fights.

And the something town where so gaily, arm in
Arm, we went, and our final row,
And the gun I killed you with, O my Carmen,
The gun I am holding now. (Nabokov [1955a] 1996: 57)

Petite Carmen, rappelle-toi
Nos départs et les gares (lesquelles ?)
Et les soirs et les bars et les – quoi ?
Oh ! Carmen, nos affreuses querelles…

Et la montagne et le chêne nain,
Et notre dernière querelle,
Et l'automatique dans ma main,
Et la balle dans ton front ma belle. (Nabokov 1959a: 73)

Little Carmen, remember
Our departures and the train stations (which ones?)
And the evenings and the bars and the – what?
Oh! Carmen, our awful rows…

And the mountain and the dwarf oak,
And our last row,
And the automatic in my hand,
And the bullet in your forehead, my beauty. (my translation)

For anyone familiar with Nabokov's work, the second stanza is reminiscent of *Ada*, which had not been published yet but which contains a poem (Nabokov [1969] 1996: 112) where Nabokov heavily reused Chateaubriand's poem 'Souvenir du Pays de France'. As Morgane Allain-Roussel (2021) underlined, Nabokov used Chateaubriand's poem to enrich the French translation of *Lolita* with an additional referential echo in connection with incest.

On the same day Nabokov wrote the letter to Kahane about the poem, he sent another one to Mohrt, which is very similar for many elements, but which also shows the importance of prosodic rules for the author:

> Mr. Kahane had a bad time with my Humbert's poems, and I notice that despite my explication of French versification and of what old rules were to be followed, he has, in re-working my re-manipulations of his first attempts, re-injected into the little Carmen poem (p. 73 in the proofs) improper sequence of rhymes, extra syllables, hiatus and so forth. I have known many fine prose writers who cannot understand prosody, and so what I am saying here is no reflection on Kahane's abilities.
>
> (letter from Nabokov to Mohrt, 15 March 1959, Berg collection)

It is noteworthy that the prosodic elements Nabokov describes are the ones he will mention in connection with the poems in the French translation of *The Gift*.

Poetry in *Le Don*

In the first letter mentioning the many poems in this novel, Nabokov seems to be very open to the idea of collaborating, but he explains the rules that Girard should respect:

> *You will see that, in some cases, I have found it necessary to make rhymed translations from the Russian verse (though I enjoyed a lot your translation in prose from the English versions). I may have made some mistakes in French, but when correcting them, please be careful not to add or remove syllables or to introduce a hiatus, or to have a singular rhyme with a plural in the verbs. And generally speaking, if the corrections I suggest needed to be corrected themselves, I ask to please make them, I will be thankful for them, but I would like to know your reasons – and see the result – before the proofs / galleys make the page numbers disappear.*
>
> *I am convinced that any amelioration which can be brought to a translation, be it as beautiful as yours, can only serve our common interest. I therefore ask you, Monsieur, not to take offense of my pedantism.*
>
> (letter from Nabokov to Girard, 9 January 1967, Berg collection)

What is particularly interesting is that, within this French mediated self-translation, these poems are actually self-translations from the original Russian, as if poetry were not to be revised, contrary to the prose which had been through the (intermediary) translation into English.

A few months later, Nabokov was surprised to see that some of his corrections on the poems were not taken into account, but he apparently attributed it to some confusion:

I want to thank you for taking into account most of my <u>revisions and corrections</u>. It is probably only due to a misunderstanding that some of my very important corrections were forgotten. [...]

You will remember that I had tried, in the course of our correspondence, to reproduce some puns as well as all the rhymed poems in the text, but unfortunately my desires have not always been respected.

(letter from Nabokov to Girard, 21 August 1967, Berg collection)

However, at the end of the letter, Nabokov hinted at the fact that Girard might have taken issue with his self-translated poems, and he offered to resort to a note, as he had done with Kahane:

The completely useless corrections that were brought to them have demolished in one stroke of a quill rhythm and rhyme. All these things, I have now redone. Since you do not completely agree with the eccentricities of my poetic style in French, I would like to offer you to leave their responsibility to me by including a note which would indicate that the puns and the rhymed poems have been translated by the author.

(letter from Nabokov to Girard, 21 August 1967, Berg collection)

The French translation was published in 1967, but the month is unclear; it was apparently after August since Nabokov was suggesting a note was still possible. In any case, in December, the Nabokovs received copies of the book and the author was very distressed by what he saw in them, or rather did not see:

Thank you for the five justification copies of 'Le Don'. Unfortunately the list of errata is still missing in them. My husband is very bothered by that. He is even more bothered by the absence of a note indicating that it is him who translated the poems.

(letter from Véra Nabokov to Schébéko, 5 December 1967, Berg collection)

This suggests that the published text could not be amended to remove some mistakes but that Nabokov had been offered the consolation that an errata list would be included; unfortunately, it did not happen. At the end of the same month, Véra wrote again to Schébéko to explain Nabokov's anger and the origin of the note:

> This, by the way, was the outcome of previous correspondence in which my husband asked Mr. Girard to preserve the integrity of meter and rhyme in case he found it absolutely indispensable to change anything in the French verse translations, and of M. Girard ignoring these requests.
>
> (letter from Véra Nabokov to Schébéko, 30 December 1967, Cornell)

Nabokov was therefore very upset by Girard's refusal to comply, as Véra described several months later; after mentioning the cost of sending proofs and galleys, she added:

> Not to mention VN's hours of work checking Gallimard's translators, and hours lost to his own work while recovering from the vexations every time he had to deal with M. Girard.
>
> (letter from Véra Nabokov to Schébéko, 15 June 1968, Cornell)

The collaboration thus ended in bad terms, and Nabokov's creative involvement in the translation of the poems was never recognized as such.

Rendering multilingualism

Nabokov's novels in English are filled with foreign words, mainly Russian and French xenisms, and translating multilingualism entails specific issues and strategies.

According to Sternberg (1981), there are two main ways of dealing with foreign words in a translation: either the translator makes an effort to try and convey multilingualism, or they erase it. This is how the scholar describes the first strategy, called 'vehicular matching':

> Vehicular matching [...], far from avoiding linguistic diversity or conflict, accepts them as a matter of course, as a fact of life and a factor of communication, and sometimes even deliberately seeks them out – suiting the variations in the representational medium to the variations in the represented object.
>
> (Sternberg 1981: 223)

The second strategy is called 'homogenizing convention':

> The recourse to the *homogenizing convention*, finally, retains the freedom of reference while dismissing the resultant variations in the language presumably

spoken by the characters as an irrelevant, if not distracting, representational factor.

(224)

In this section, I will be looking at three specific cases: first, when the foreign language is foreign in the original text as well as in the French translation (with Russian for example); then, the translation into French of the French words of the original[5]; and finally, I will look at one creative way that Nabokov resorted to in order to reinject some multilingualism in his French translations.

Translating L3 into French in *Ada ou l'ardeur*

Many scholars in linguistics use the expression 'L3' for a language which is foreign in the original text as well as in the translation; for instance, Zabalbeascoa and Corrius describe the terminology in the following terms: 'L3 is used to refer to any language which is not the main language of a text, as would be the case of L1 for the [source text] and L2 for the [target text]' (Zabalbeascoa and Corrius 2014: 255).

When the language of the xenism is not that of the target text, the translation is quite straightforward, and the xenism is usually kept as such. The following examples from *Ada*[6] include Latin, German and Italian:

> I suspect your uncle has a cache behind the solanders in his study and keeps there a finer whisky than this *usque ad Russkum*. Well, let us have the cognac, as planned, unless you are a *filius aquae?* (Nabokov [1969] 1996: 193)

> Je soupçonne ton oncle d'avoir une cachette derrière les bouquins postiches de son bureau et d'y loger un whisky meilleur que cet *usque ad Russkum*. Hé bien, goûtons au cognac comme prévu, à moins que tu ne sois un *filius aquae?* (Nabokov 1975: 204)

> Dr Stella Ospenko's *ospedale* (Nabokov [1969] 1996: 200)

> l'*ospedale* du Dr Stella Ospenko (Nabokov 1975: 211)

> He's a Baltic Russian' (turning to Van) 'but really *echt deutsch* (Nabokov [1969] 1996: 209)

> (Se tournant vers Van). 'Ce Miller est un Russe balte, mais en réalité *echt deutsch*' (Nabokov 1975: 219)

In the French version, the foreign words follow the same convention as in the English original: they are written in italics.

When it comes to words from the Russian, they are written in the Latin alphabet in the text in English as well as in the French translation, usually without problem in the transliteration.[7] Carrying over the Russian from the English into the French translation is usually very simple, but it sometimes entails a slight change in spelling because the rules of transcription vary between those languages, especially for sounds like 'sh' or 'u'. This is obvious in the following quote describing a Russian meal in Ardis[8]:

> Tonight she contented herself with the automatic ceremony of giving him what she remembered, more or less correctly, when planning the menu, as being his favorite food – *zelyonïya shchi*, a velvety green sorrel-and-spinach soup, containing slippery hard-boiled eggs and served with finger-burning, irresistibly soft, meat-filled or carrot-filled or cabbage-filled *pirozhki* – peer-rush-KEY, thus pronounced, thus celebrated here, for ever and ever. After that, she had decided, there would be bread-crumbed sander *(sudak)* with boiled potatoes, hazel-hen *(ryabchiki)* and that special asparagus *(bezukhanka)* which does not produce Proust's After-effect, as cookbooks say.
>
> (Nabokov [1969] 1996: 202)

> Ce soir, elle se contentait de célébrer automatiquement le rite qui consistait à servir à Démon les mets que sa mémoire lui avait désignés avec plus ou moins d'exactitude, au moment où elle composait son menu, comme étant ceux qu'il préférait: le *Zelionyïa chtchi*, une soupe à l'oseille et aux épinards, verte, veloutée, où roulent des œufs durs glissants, servie avec des *pirojki* chauds à se brûler les doigts, tendres irrésistiblement et fourrés de viande, de carotte, ou de chou (des PIRACHKI, c'est ainsi qu'à Ardis on prononce, on célèbre ce nom, depuis toujours et à tout jamais). Marina avait choisi de faire servir, ensuite, de la sandre *(soudak)* panée accompagnée de pommes de terre bouillies, des gelinottes rôties *(riabtchiki)* et cette variété particulière d'asperge *(bezoukhanka)* qui ne produit point après coup ce que les livres de cuisine appellent 'effet Proust'.
>
> (Nabokov 1975: 213)

Except from this morphological adaptation, it seems rather logical that all L3 terms from the original will remain in the translation. However, on some rare occasions, these xenisms were erased in the process of translation by Nabokov himself. It is clear in the files noted 'typescript [...] with the author's ms. corrections' or on the pages of the draft translation if one can recognize Nabokov's handwriting. The following Russian words were erased by the author himself:

> Marina had spent a *rukuliruyushchiy* month with him (Nabokov [1969] 1996: 26)
>
> [...] un mois roucoulant (Nabokov 1975: 23)

'Reader, ride by' (*'mimo, chitatel'*,' as Turgenev wrote). (Nabokov [1969] 1996: 39)

'Passe, cavalier, passe', comme disaient Tourgueniev et Yeats. (Nabokov 1975: 37)

In the second quote, it is interesting to see that the loss of the Russian is balanced, in the French, by the addition of a reference to literature in English. Sometimes, a whole dialogue loses several occurrences of Russian, as in this passage from Chapter 38:

> 'What was faintly off-key, *ne tak*, about the whole evening?' asked Van softly. 'You noticed?' […] 'But what went wrong tonight? You were tongue-tied, and everything we said was *fal'shivo*.
>
> (Nabokov [1969] 1996: 211)

> 'Il y avait quelque chose qui détonnait légèrement dans toute cette soirée, tu as remarqué?' demanda Van à voix basse. […] Mais, qu'est-ce qui est allé de travers, ce soir? C'est à peine si tu as ouvert la bouche, et tout ce que nous disions sonnait tellement faux.
>
> (Nabokov 1975: 221)

Interestingly enough, the different versions which exist in the archives (three for this passage) show that there was a lot of hesitation about those two cases of code-switching. Thus, '*ne tak*' is absent in the first version, reinstated in the second (apparently by Chahine) and then it disappears again in the third; as for '*fal'shivo*', it is present in the first and the second as '*fal'chivo*', but it disappears in the third version by Nabokov.

Translating French into French: 'En français dans le texte' and *Lolita*

Since the French language is usually abundantly represented in Nabokov's novels, one could expect that the author would want to keep all the multilingual nuances of his text, but as I have shown with the Russian, it is not always the case. When it comes to the French, it is even more pronounced.

First of all, Nabokov refused to have footnotes indicating 'In French in the (original) text'. In the following passages taken from the correspondence of Nabokov and his translators or publishers, I clarify what novel is being discussed in brackets when necessary:

[*King Queen Knave*]

Nowhere should there be any note 'en français dans le texte' – an old battlefield between me and my French publishers. (letter from Nabokov to Georges Magnane, 30 December 1970, Cornell)

[*Mary*]

'<u>En français dans le texte</u>' should be eliminated wherever it occurs. French words which appear in French in the English original must not be italicised. (letter from Nabokov to Orengo, 28 August 1972, Cornell)

Nabokov underlined his reluctance especially in the later part of his career, particularly when he was working with Fayard and no longer Gallimard. Indeed, it should be noted that the treatment of French xenisms varies from *Lolita*, published in 1959 by Gallimard, and *Ada* for example, published in 1975 by Fayard. Thus, in the French *Lolita*, the first occurrence of French is signalled by a note. Therefore, the segment 'Et lui, *mon cher petit papa**' is accompanied by the following footnote: 'The words in italics and followed by an asterisk (*) are in French in the text. (Note of the Translator)' (Nabokov 1959a: 15; my translation) But in *Ada ou l'Ardeur*, there is no trace at all of the original French: no note, no italics, no asterisk. However, Nabokov did think of the impact that the translation into French would have in the notes by Darkbloom, where those French words are explained to foreigners: 'Obviously all the French there must be left out, but possibly other notes might be added' (24 September 1974, letter from Nabokov to Orengo).

Nabokov was against footnotes, but he was willing to accept typographical indication. In a letter to Donald Harper, the main translator of *Transparent Things*, Nabokov wrote 'Please, no "en français dans le texte" footnotes. Just the asterisc' (letter from Nabokov to Harper, 7 January 1974, Cornell). And a few lines down, he expressed his distaste for footnotes in general: 'substitute "ce monde où le passé s'accumule." for "le monde que Jack a construit". (the footnote gives too much importance to "Jack". I always try to avoid footnotes in the translations of my novels)'.

The most extensive justification is to be found in a letter about the translation of *Pale Fire*, where Nabokov explains why he does not like references to the French language in English, but also why this specific novel could not work with footnotes. His touch of humour at the end is rather delightful, though:

Another thing: I strongly object to the customary footnotes 'en français dans le texte'. They are absurd in our cosmopolitan era. Moreover, this particular novel, which is organically based on a system of notes, cannot have other notes attached to it at tort and travers. [...]

Ceci dit (en français dans le texte), I wish to add in a loud and clear voice that the texture of Girard and Coindreau's translation is a marvel, a masterpiece, limpid, stylish and taut.

(letter from Nabokov to Schébéko, 30 September 1965, Cornell)

Let us now zoom in on *Lolita*, where the translation of French words was, once again for this translation, the result of a real collaboration between Nabokov and Kahane. Both brought up the topic at the beginning of 1958:

> You will note that I have eliminated some French formulas which clash with my imagery.
>
> (letter from Nabokov to Kahane, 1 January 1958, Berg collection)

> Moreover, I should like to tone down a bit some of the French words or sentences in the original version. They have a raison d'être in English, but they often clash with a French context (most of them being colloquialisms of sorts inserted in a very academic context); furthermore, if printed in italics (with an asterisk added), those words acquire a visual importance which is often unnecessary and far-fetched. So, if you agree, I'd like to 'incorporate' in the text the most awkward of them (and, here or there, remodel them), so as not to give them undue pre-eminence.
>
> (letter from Kahane to Nabokov, 7 February 1958, Berg collection)

In the published translation, my research shows that only 50 per cent of the French words are indicated as such (with italics and asterisk): the others have been incorporated. A typical example is the treatment of the two occurrences of a French dish:

> Although I told myself I was looking merely for a soothing presence, a glorified *pot-au-feu* (Nabokov [1955a] 1996: 22)
>
> J'avais beau me dire que je ne voulais à mes côtés qu'une présence lénitive, un *pot-au-feu** sublimé (Nabokov 1959a: 32)
>
> we tacitly dismissed the *pot-au-feu* (Nabokov [1955a] 1996: 23)
>
> Nous avions tacitement éliminé le pot-au-feu (Nabokov 1959a: 33)

In their translation, Nabokov and Kahane clearly favoured the 'homogeneizing convention' described by Sternberg: French is usually carried over and it is not replaced by a foreign language, except in one case which I will analyse in my section on puns. However, on a few occasions, compensation is used since some other languages appear in passages where there was no foreign word in the original. In my next section, I will focus on the insertion of English, but the few times where the translation uses Italian are worth mentioning; here are three examples:

> a brightly lit set of rooms (Nabokov [1955a] 1996: 27) / une suite de pièces éclairées *a giorno* (Nabokov 1959a: 38)

in a rising rhythm (Nabokov [1955a] 1996: 38) / qui allait *crescendo* (Nabokov 1959a: 51)

muttered with insane rapidity (Nabokov [1955a] 1996: 122) / débita *prestissimo* je ne sais quelle insanité (Nabokov 1959a: 151)

Despite Nabokov's insistence on removing any French in his translation, he apparently resented the loss of one of his foreign languages. Thus, his novels in English are often trilingual thanks to the presence of code-switching in French and Russian, but the verbal migration to French often meant shrinking to bilingualism. This is probably why Nabokov inserted some English words in several of his French translations.

Adding English into French

In terms of translation strategies, English is inserted into the French mainly in three different ways: an English word from the original is carried over into the French text, so that it stands out as a foreign word (usually with italics); sometimes, an English word is inserted into the French text, even if it was not present in the original; the last strategy is to mention elements from the American or British culture (usually, those are references to food, clothes or the English language).

Lolita

First of all, in a letter at the beginning of 1958, Kahane questioned Nabokov on some terms in English which Nabokov had suggested for the translation: he congratulated him on his use of 'Beefouteurs', but was not convinced by 'swooners' or 'saddle oxfords' in French' (letter from Kahane to Nabokov, 7 February 1958, Berg collection). In the same letter, Kahane asks Nabokov if he is sure they should use the word 'majorette'; once again, his use of humour through a reference to Nabokov's text is rather entertaining:

> 'Majorette'. I do know what they are. In fact, I was once – mais je digresse. I had decided to let it go as 'pin-up de l'équipe de rugby', as the Mashall Aid has introduced the pin-up in Europe but not the drum majorette nor the cheerleader. Here again, the long explanation slows down the action, and the whole idea is not really indispensable. However, if you want to keep it, we'll manage somehow.
>
> (letter from Kahane to Nabokov, 7 February 1958, Berg collection)

In the margin, Nabokov's answer is written in pencil: 'I do'. If one looks at the passage which is discussed, it is interesting to see that 'majorette' is not used in the English, where Charlotte is very critical of her daughter:

> Now, at twelve, she was a regular pest, said Haze. All she wanted from life was to be one day a strutting and prancing baton twirler or a jitterbug.
>
> (Nabokov [1955a] 1996: 42)

In the French translation, 'majorette' has been kept, with 'drum' before it, but a reference to sport has been added:

> Aujourd'hui, à douze ans, poursuivit Haze, c'était une vraie peste. Elle n'avait d'autre ambition dans la vie que de danser le jitterbug et être une des *drum majorettes* de l'équipe locale de rugby.
>
> (Nabokov 1959a: 56)

Another element should be underlined: when reading *Lolita* in French, I was stuck by the use of a few words that looked like anglicisms, for example, '*une terreur insane*' (Nabokov 1959a: 105) or the word 'couple'. This word exists in French in the masculine (to describe the couple formed by two lovers for example), but it was used in the feminine and in the numerical sense: '*cette école de garçons qui m'employa une couple d'hivers*' (Nabokov 1959a: 21; in English, 'a school for boys employed me for a couple of winters' (Nabokov [1955a] 1996: 13)). I initially suspected it was a calque from the English, but the feminine form made me suspicious. And actually, this word does exist in French, just like 'insane', even if they are not frequent. It is interesting to note that this word was used by Chateaubriand (in *Rancé*, 1844[9]), whom Nabokov admired. As I will show for *Ada*, this Chateaubriand-like vocabulary seems to have left quite an impression on Nabokov.

Ada

There are many examples from *Ada*, but I will limit them to the most revealing in terms of strategy. In Chapter 38, the dinner is composed of many dishes from different cultures, and Van has previously complained that the Russian 'sudak' was not really *sudak* (sander in English); the text provides a confirmation of his hunch:

> (Marina, having failed to obtain the European product in time for the dinner, had chosen the nearest thing, wall-eyed pike, or 'dory', with Tartar sauce and boiled young potatoes.)
>
> (Nabokov [1969] 1996: 204)

In the French translation, no less than three references to English are inserted:

> (Marina, n'ayant pu se procurer à temps ce produit de l'Europe, l'avait remplacé par ce qu'elle avait trouvé de plus ressemblant, le *walleyed pike,* sandre américaine, servie avec une sauce tartare et des pommes de terre nouvelles à l'anglaise.)
>
> (Nabokov 1975: 214)

The most striking change is the inclusion of words in English and in italics: 'walleyed pike'. More specifically, the French text does not translate the original 'wall-eyed pike' but carries it over directly into the French, with only slight arrangements in its morphology ('wall-eyed' is written in one word) and typography (italics are used in French). The two other inclusions are more lexical than typographical: what was called 'dory' in the original version is called 'sandre' (sander, as seen previously) but is branded as being American; likewise, 'boiled young potatoes' are qualified as being English or, rather, English-style ('à l'anglaise').

When it comes to the archives, it is interesting to note that it is only in the third version that Nabokov massively inserted English, as one can see in the following example. Here is the original: '"That's very black of you, Dad," said pleased Van' (Nabokov [1969] 1996: 191). In the first two versions, Van's sentence is written entirely in French ('"Quelles noires pensées"'), but in the third version, Nabokov inserted two English words and underlined the first one: '"C'est bien <u>"black"</u> de ta part, Dad"'. And this is the translation that one finds in the published version: ('"C'est bien *"black"* de ta part, Dad"', Nabokov 1969: 203). Here, Nabokov seems to revert to literalism (the original was "That's very black of you, Dad"') with the mere carrying over of English words into the translation.

But sometimes, words that look English to the French eye are used in the translation, but they were not present in the original (in the following quotes, I use bold type to make things clearer):

> Demon shed his monocle and wiped his eyes with the **modish** lace-frilled handkerchief that lodged in the heart pocket of his **dinner jacket**. (Nabokov [1969] 1996: 189)
>
> Démon laissa tomber son monocle et se tamponna les yeux avec le mouchoir **fashionable** ourlé de dentelle qui habitait la poche de poitrine de son **smoking**. (Nabokov 1975: 201)

'Smoking' is a loanword from the English expression 'smoking-jacket', and it is used instead of 'dinner jacket'. Likewise, 'fashionable' is used to translate 'modish', but it looks very much like a calque from the English; however, the *CNRTL* indicates that this word exists in French and, like 'couple', that it was used by Chateaubriand (the website references two occurrences in his memoirs[10]). This presence of English-looking words in Nabokov's prose in French shows that his knowledge of French was deeply impacted by authors of the nineteenth century, which could explain why his brand of French sometimes looks a bit peculiar or old-fashioned to the modern reader.

Let us now look at the last category of Nabokov's self-translation: puns.

Translating puns

The translation of verbal humour tends to confirm that Nabokov's translation with Kahane was the result of true collaboration, while later translations in the sixties and seventies underline that Nabokov tended to favour literalism, even if it meant leaving out some puns.

Lolita: **Puns and banter**

In Kahane's first letter to Nabokov, he mentions that he had some difficulty with the translation of his puns, and he asks for Nabokov's opinion on his translations in the first draft. What is particularly interesting is that Kahane starts teasing Nabokov by using a pun the author had coined in the novel. Thus, explaining that cultural references have to be dealt with cautiously, he mentions '*le poème de Poë-Poë*' (letter from Kahane to Nabokov, 20 November 1957, Berg collection), which is a clear reference to a passage form Part I, Chapter 11: "'Monsieur Poe-poe," as that boy in one of Monsieur Humbert Humbert's classes in Paris called the poet-poet' (Nabokov [1955a] 1996: 39). In Nabokov's answer on 1 January 1958 (Berg collection), the writer explains that he has modified or toned down some of them, thus showing that he agrees with Kahane's suggestion.

The translator continues to combine teasing and compliments in other letters at the beginning of the collaboration, trying probably to make up in flattery the time it took him to get the translation started. For instance, on 7 February 1958 (Berg collection), Kahane congratulates Nabokov on his use of puns, for example, when Nabokov turns Charlotte's affected pronunciation 'called an envelope an ahnvelope' (Nabokov [1955a] 1996: 69) into '*âne-veloppe*' (Nabokov 1959a: 89). Thus, Nabokov inscribes the French word for 'donkey' (*âne*) into the word '*enveloppe*' and creates a pun in his self-translation where the original has no such play-on-word. On the next line, Kahane comments on another great find by Nabokov and teases him again by asking Nabokov if he is trying to make him lose his job. However, this teasing is not as frequent towards the end of the collaboration: Kahane has proved his worth as a translator and is dealing with Nabokov on an equal footing, telling him when he thinks he is wrong or when he agrees with the author's translation.

Three puns in particular are well documented in the archives. The first two are mentioned in Kahane's initial letter and will finally disappear from the French translation, while the third is a bilingual pun on '*souffler*' which is translated by the two men in a true spirit of collaboration.

In Part I, Chapter 11, Humbert is repeatedly invited to go to a lake with Charlotte Haze, his lodger, and her daughter Dolores, better known by her nickname Lolita: 'We (mother Haze, Dolores and I) were to go to Our Glass Lake this afternoon, and bathe, and bask' (Nabokov [1955a] 1996: 39). The same spelling is used on two more occasions (41; 44), and it is only in Chapter 20 that Humbert the narrator realizes that he misunderstood the toponym completely: 'There was a woodlake (Hourglass Lake – not as I had thought it was spelled)' (76). For this pun, the decision is very quick: on 7 February 1958 (Berg collection), Kahane thanks Nabokov for skipping some tricky elements, and he mentions specifically the Hourglass pun. Nabokov's justification is to be found in a batch of typed corrections, in which he explains that Humbert's mistake is not worth translating.

The 'little Carmen' pun took much longer in negotiation before Nabokov agreed to remove it. Carmen is one of the names that Humbert gives to Lolita, and it is associated with many crucial episodes, notably the infamous davenport scene (Part I, Chapter 13): while singing to Lolita 'the words of a foolish song that was then popular – Oh my Carmen, my little Carmen, something, something, those something nights, and the stars, and the cars, and the bars, and the barmen' (Nabokov [1955a] 1996: 54), Humbert manages to masturbate and climax next to the young girl, apparently without her noticing. Two chapters earlier, Humbert had laid the foundations for this song full of variations on the name 'Carmen' by exposing a pun he seemed to be proud of: 'In the house, Lolita had put on her favorite "Little Carmen" record which I used to call "Dwarf Conductors," making her snort with mock derision at my mock wit' (Nabokov [1955a] 1996: 41). This pun is also mentioned by Kahane in his first letter, but in the same undated set of corrections, Nabokov insists on keeping it, with the addition of an explanation (in bold type below), which I translate after the quote:

'Petite Carmen', Little Carmen, que j'avais rebaptisé 'Conducteurs Nains' **(puisque 'car' signifiait 'wagon' et 'men' 'hommes'**: je l'entends encore renâcler avec une dérision feinte devant l'esprit que je feignait [*sic*] à mon tour).

(since 'car' meant 'wagon' and 'men' 'hommes' [...])

Kahane objects that the explanation is lengthy and heavy, but writes 'But if you insist…' (letter from Kahane to Nabokov, 7 February 1958, Berg collection) In the margin, a scribbled inscription reads 'I do'. The question is raised by Kahane again almost one year later, and this time he is more assertive: he decided to remove the pun altogether because the explanation gave too much importance to a pun that, according to the translator, a French reader cannot understand anyway (27 January 1959). None of the following letters mention the pun anymore, but the published translation speaks for itself: the pun is nowhere to be found and the translation stops after the mention of the record (Nabokov 1959a: 54).

The last pun is present in the second part of the novel, so it is dealt with only in later letters. When Humbert manages to find Lolita after she escaped from him, she is older and pregnant, and more importantly, she finally tells him who she ran away with: Clare Quilty. Humbert is particularly hurt to discover that, though Lolita never loved him, she deeply cared for Quilty. However, this man left her because she refused to comply with all his sexual desires:

> 'Crazy things, filthy things. I said no, I'm just not going to [she used, in all insouciance really, a disgusting slang term which, in a literal French translation, would be *souffler*] your beastly boys, because I want only you. Well, he kicked me out'.

(Nabokov [1955a] 1996: 260)

Shocked as he is by Lolita's revelation and immodest language, Humbert hides in French disguise the verb 'blow' referring to oral sex in English, but of course not in French. In the translation, the device of italics with an asterisk which is used for half the French xenisms would not work here because this solution would fail to disguise the sexual meaning behind a foreign language, and Nabokov and Kahane resorted to German to achieve a similar effect, apparently on Kahane's suggestion. Indeed, the translator writes on 27 January 1959 (Berg collection) that he is very proud of his find and adds that Nabokov's modification makes the result perfect. This is how the published translation reads:

> (ici, elle employa, en toute insouciance je vous l'assure, un terme d'argot des plus répugnants qui, traduit mot à mot dans le *Schweizerdeutsch* de l'oncle Trapp, serait *auspumpen*).

(Nabokov 1959a: 320)

In his first suggestion, Kahane had used '*Schweizerdeutsch* de mon enfance' (the Swiss German of my childhood), thus referring to Humbert having a Swiss father (as mentioned in Part I, Chapter II). However, Humbert is always presented as speaking French, not German. Nabokov's correction in order to refer to his Swiss relative ('de l'oncle Trapp') is particularly brilliant because, in the second part of the novel, Humbert repeatedly compares the man following Lolita and him throughout the United States to his uncle Trapp, the first and clearer example being in Chapter 18:

> I saw him scratch his cheek and nod, and turn, and walk back to his convertible, a broad and thickish man of my age, somewhat resembling Gustave Trapp, a cousin of my father's in Switzerland.
>
> (Nabokov [1955a] 1996: 204)

Humbert will then repeatedly call the man 'Trapp', and it is only in Chapter 29, when Humbert discovers that Lolita ran away with Clare Quilty, that Humbert and the reader realize that the man resembling Gustave Trapp was actually Clare Quilty all along. Using Swiss German is all the more fitting because, one page before the '*souffler*' pun, Humbert asked Lolita who she ran away with and, just before she confessed, he used German to describe her smoking: 'She was smoking herself. First time I saw her doing it. *Streng verboten* under Humbert the Terrible' (Nabokov [1955a] 1996: 259).

This translation is therefore the result of Nabokov and Kahane's joint efforts, and what makes it particularly delightful is that, almost a year before the Swiss German pun was found, Kahane was already using German to tease Nabokov, especially in his letter dated 7 February 1958. He starts doing so when he congratulates Nabokov on his find for 'gooseberry', which I mentioned in my naturalist section, and then, at the end of the letter, Kahane informs Nabokov that Maurice Girodias (Kahane's brother and Nabokov's first publisher) won his lawsuit against the censorship of the French government.[11] However, Kahane did not write 'my brother': he used 'mein Bruder', which is reminiscent not only of Trapp directly but also of Humbert's use of 'Reader! *Bruder!*' (Nabokov [1955a] 1996: 246). This pun is particularly interesting because it shows that Nabokov could still use 'artistic translation' in the late fifties, and that he was building up on his translator's suggestions (and maybe banter).

In the *Pale Fire* collaboration, no such discussion seems to have occurred for puns: very quickly, Nabokov knew what had to be omitted, even if he did take care of some puns.

Feu pâle

In *Pale Fire*, Nabokov resorted to several types of verbal humour: word golf and more classical puns. Word golf consists in changing one letter in a word to create another one, and so on, and it was invented by Lewis Carroll, the author of *Alice's Adventures in Wonderland*, which Nabokov had translated into Russian in 1923. When it comes to translating word golf, there is one instance of this verbal game that Nabokov insists on translating himself. In the poem (l. 347–8), Shade reminisces about his dead daughter, Hazel: 'She twisted words: pot, top, / Spider, redips. And "powder" was "red wop"' (Nabokov [1962] 1996: 466). Then, in his commentary to the two lines, Kinbote comments on the word golf specifically:

> One of the examples her father gives is odd. I am quite sure it was I who one day, when we were discussing 'mirror words', observed (and I recall the poet's expression of stupefaction) that 'spider' in reverse is 'redips', and 'T.S. Eliot, 'toilest'. But then it is also true that Hazel Shade resembled me in certain respects.
>
> (Nabokov [1962] 1996: 577)

In the undated typescript (Berg collection), Nabokov crosses out Coindreau's suggested translations for 'pot, top. Spider, redips' and replaces them with '*port, trop, Toile, Eliot*', and he writes in the margin '*Please put* Toile, Eliot. (*We agreed that I am responsible for the play on words in this book*)' (Nabokov's italics). He only uses the last two words in his comment because they are particularly important for the story, especially in connection with Shade's daughter. As he explains in his list of queries, he is rather pleased with his find: '*See how fitting "toile" (spiderweb) and "Eliot" are, since he is indeed the author of the poem* (Four Quartets) *which Shade's daughter reads with so much attention on lines 364–379*' (letter from Nabokov to Coindreau, 14 January 1964, Berg collection).

It appears that, when a pun plays a role in the diegesis, Nabokov insists on translating it himself, but when puns are more ornamental, it is quite different: as the archives show, most of them were simply deleted by Nabokov. Thus, for the pun on 'his porch or perch' (Nabokov [1962] 1996: 647), Nabokov instructed in his corrections to remove the literal translation of 'perch' (*perchoir*) because the pun was not rendered. He made the same recommendation for the pun relying on Americans' mispronunciation of 'Mont-Blanc' as '*Mon Blon*' (Nabokov [1962] 1996: 479) and indicates that the pun does not work in translation (Berg collection).

One pun is the opportunity for longer discussion between Girard and Nabokov, which starts at the very beginning of their collaboration. In his poem (lines 96–8), Shade writes 'from the local *Star* / A curio: *Red Sox Beat Yanks*

5–4 / On Chapman's Homer, thumbtacked to the door' (Nabokov [1962] 1996: 459). In his commentary, Kinbote misses the pun and the allusion to baseball:

> *Line 98:* On Chapman's Homer
>
> A reference to the title of Keats' famous sonnet (often quoted in America) which, owing to a printer's absent-mindedness, has been drolly transposed, from some other article, into the account of a sports event. For other vivid misprints see note to line 802.
>
> (Nabokov [1962] 1996: 519)

The only solution that Girard found was to give an explanation in a footnote, as he wrote to Nabokov on 16 October 1963 (Berg collection). Nabokov crosses the whole thing out and explains in his letter (19 October 1963) that the dictionaries are wrong in translating the American 'homerun' as *'but'*, which is used in European football, and provides an explanation and a translation ('parcours'). More importantly, he insists that no note should be included in the translation because they might be confused with Kinbote's notes to the poem; he concludes that the pun will be lost on the French reader as it is on Kinbote.

As the archives show, Nabokov had to discriminate between the puns that needed to be translated and those which could be omitted. Doing so in the process of the translation confirms that translating into French was closely connected, for Nabokov, with assessing his previous work, revising it and possibly recreating it. It also shows how much Nabokov was often torn between fidelity and creativity. *Ada* was no exception to that tension.

Ada ou L'ardeur

For this translation, the question of puns was raised even before the translator was chosen, since it was discussed in connection with the two sample translations which Nabokov received in 1970. Nabokov accepted Chahine's work, but he was very critical of Tournier's sample translation, and in a letter about it (31 January 1970), he expressed his preference about puns: '*I always prefer to retain the direct meaning if it is necessary to choose between an untranslatable pun and the meaning of the sentence*'. And next to one of the explanations by Tournier about a pun, Nabokov scribbled a huge question mark and wrote 'Give up! Fidelity before everything' (my translation).

Let us look at two puns which show different aspects of Nabokov's translation strategies. Here is the first pun, taken from a long description of Russian dishes:

finger-burning, irresistibly soft, meat-filled or carrot-filled or cabbage-filled *pirozhki* – peer-rush-KEY, thus pronounced, thus celebrated here, for ever and ever.

(Nabokov [1969] 1996: 202)

The pun here relies on three English words that, put together, form the proper pronunciation in Russian. It makes sense especially if you know that Lucette always hides to PEER at Van and Ada when they have sex in a RUSH, and she does so through the KEYhole. Here, Nabokov chooses not to translate the pun: according to him (letter of 31 January 1970), there is no pun, and the only reason he used these English words was to show the right pronunciation of the Russian word, but as the French transliteration is close to the Russian, he suggests 'pirache-qui'. But in the last version of the drafts, Nabokov offers another transcription, which is the one that appears in the definitive version:

> des *pirojki* chauds à se brûler les doigts, tendres irrésistiblement et fourrés de viande, de carotte, ou de chou (des PIRACHKI, c'est ainsi qu'à Ardis on prononce, on célèbre ce nom, depuis toujours et à tout jamais).

(Nabokov 1975: 213)

The second pun is quite complex and relies on etymology and botany:

> 'Let me preface the effort of a cousin – anybody's cousin – by a snatch of Pushkin, for the sake of rhyme –'
>
> 'For the *snake* of rhyme!' cried Ada. 'A paraphrase, even my paraphrase, is like the corruption of "snakeroot" into "snagrel" – all that remains of a delicate little birthwort'.

(Nabokov [1969] 1996: 196)

For the translation of the pun on 'sake' and 'snake', the role of Nabokov is very straightforward: he did everything, as Chahine avoided this section altogether, without even mentioning it. In the draft (Berg collection) as well as in the published version, this is how Nabokov translated the pun: "*rien que pour le plaisir d'une rime'. – Le poison d'une rime!" s'écria Ada*' (Nabokov 1975: 207). Therefore, Nabokov recreated a pun without any input by Chahine.

I will finish with a third pun because of what it reveals of the role of this French translation for researchers. In Part I, Chapter 24, Van coins a pun which evokes his promiscuity and his proximity in his incestuous relationship with Ada:

> Ada said: 'Officially we are maternal cousins, and cousins can marry by special decree, *if* they promise to sterilize their first five children. But, moreover, the father-in-law of my mother was the brother of your grandfather. Right?'

'That's what I'm told', said Van serenely.

'Not sufficiently distant', she mused, 'or is it?'

'Far enough, fair enough'. (Nabokov [1969] 1996: 120)

In the draft, a first version reads 'Suffizamment pour les zamants' (sufficiently for the lovers): there is an internal rhyme between the first word and the last, and a 'z' is inserted inside both words to make the resemblance more striking. But in the 'typescript [...] with the author's ms. corrections', Nabokov superimposes an 's' over the 'z' in 'suffizamment', thus reinstating the correct spelling, and he crosses out 'les zamants' and writes 'être amants' (to be lovers). This shows that he was willing to make an effort to have euphony, but not to do anything excessive that would break the classic writing of French just for the sake of a rhyme.

What is interesting is that the published version, 'Suffisamment pour être amants' (Nabokov 1975: 126), is quoted in *AdaOnline*, the website launched by Brian Boyd to help understand *Ada*. On several occasions, *AdaOnline* uses the French version to shed light on the text, in particular when it comes to puns or verbal ambiguity, thus confirming that Nabokov's mediated self-translations can be considered recreations.

13

Should Nabokov be Retranslated?

Delving into Nabokov's archives shows how important his creative role was. In that respect, it seems important to re-evaluate the translations of his novels into French as partial self-translations, or mediated self-translations.

However, defending these texts could possibly question the value of retranslations or even revisions. One question in point is Couturier's 2001 translation of *Lolita*. Unfortunately, the translation made by Kahane and Nabokov was heavily criticized when *Lolita* was retranslated in 2001, but it seems excessive to attack the lack of fidelity to the original text (Couturier 2000: 521) by arguing that Nabokov probably did not revise this translation as much as he could have if he had had more time (Couturier 2000: 522) and that he was dissatisfied with the translation. Indeed, Couturier quotes letters in which Nabokov criticized Kahane's translation *before* it was amended, but not the ones he wrote when the pages were amended accordingly or when the translation was over. This argument has been made before by Michael Oustinoff regarding *Lolita* when he argued that it was partially a self-translation (Oustinoff 2004: 119) and called it not '*traduction Kahane*', but '*traduction Kahane-Nabokov*' (119).

Couturier was right in arguing that his translation was more faithful to the original, for at least two reasons. First, the Kahane-Nabokov translation implied a high degree of creativity, which is normal if one takes it as a type of self-translation; in that respect, it is creative instead of 'merely' translating. Secondly, translation theory tends to confirm the natural tendency of second translations for more literalism. Berman underlined the importance of the 'temporality of translation' (Berman, qtd in Rigeade 2007; my translation), which explains that 'only a retranslation can literalize' (Rigeade 2007; my translation).

Generally speaking, retranslations are needed to give closer access to the original. As Berman (1990) and Bensimon (1990) argued, new translations are generally more faithful to the source text than the first translations (this is usually called 'the retranslation hypothesis'). Therefore, the reader's access to the original is facilitated by the new translations, and it is even more the case when they are published in annotated editions, as it is now the case for Nabokov's work in the prestigious Pléiade collection, which was edited by Maurice Couturier.

But there are two potentially problematic issues in connection with the Pléiade volumes of Nabokov. First, all translations were revised, but as Bernard Kreise wrote in connection with Jarl's translation, the fact that Nabokov praised it so much tended to preclude revision:

> When reading this praise, it was hard to tamper with a translation which constantly received Nabokov's imprimatur, all the more so because, in spite of some surprising dimensions, it has such coherence that touching a few elements, just to 'cleanse' it, would risk making it lose its unity. We have only corrected a few mistakes in the light of the Russian text and chosen to leave the text in the state approved by the author. (Pléiade I, 1691; my translation)[1]

The fact that Nabokov expressed his opinion on some translations, and was deeply involved in others, can encourage the scholar and the annotator not to change anything. In that respect, one should be careful not to sacralize a translation once Nabokov touched it. This shows a new type of impact for the 'tyranny of the author', which Couturier has described so well. The second issue is that the Pléiade included Couturier's retranslation of *Lolita* and of *Pnin*, but not the ones which Nabokov took part in. Unfortunately, first translations are usually considered obsolete once the retranslations are published, maybe not for the scholar, but in all practical matters: indeed, Couturier's translation has literally replaced the first translation in bookshops, and it is virtually impossible to find the Kahane-Nabokov translation if one does not go looking in some hidden nooks on the internet.

My contention is that there is a case for defending the validity of several translations (especially when one of them is a self-translation) because all of them shed a different light on the text. One can expand on some of the concepts exposed in Benjamin's 'The Task of the Translator' about translation and languages:

> Fragments of a vessel which are to be glued together must match one another in the smallest details, although they need not be like one another. In the same way a translation, instead of resembling the meaning of the original, must lovingly and in detail incorporate the original's mode of signification, thus making both the original and the translation recognizable as fragments of a greater language, just as fragments are part of a vessel.
>
> (Benjamin [1968] 2000: 21)

Thus, various translations can be entries to the original text and can help open it up to have access to the nucleus (19), not necessarily of pure language, but of the pure text. It is particularly relevant in the case of self-translation, be it mediated or not: several originals are deemed to exist and form a palimpsest (Oustinoff 2001: 26). In that respect, having access to several translations is a chance to explore the original text in the best, most complete way. And it is actually something that has been done in the first volume of the Pléiade: indeed, *Kamera Obskura* was first translated from the Russian by Doussia Ergaz as *Chambre Obscure*, and then Nabokov's self-translation from the English, *Laughter in the Dark*, was translated by Christine Raguet-Bouvart as *Rire dans la nuit*. It is probably because the status of self-translation is so clear for the two versions in Russian and in English that such an inclusion was possible; however, as I showed, it is more disputed and debatable for Nabokov's mediated self-translations into French.

But there is now hope for a similar approach even in the prestigious Pléiade collection. Indeed, in 2021, a new translation of *The Divine Comedy* has come out in a bilingual edition, meaning the collected works of Dante now include two different translations.[2] Therefore, this translation is not supposed to replace the previous one, but to add to it. In that respect, one could imagine giving its full scope to Nabokov's masterpiece *Lolita* with a volume in French that would include the Kahane-Nabokov translation, that of Couturier, and even a French translation of Nabokov's self-translation into Russian; of course, something similar could be done in English. And thus, a full kaleidoscopic version of *Lolita* would be accessible with the many layers of its palimpsest.

Conclusion

There are many topics related to translation that still remain to be explored, even from a literary perspective: the most glaring one is related to 'the fictional turn' in translation studies, which is the emerging representation of translation and translators in fiction. The expression was used for the first time by Else Vieira in 1998, but it has been taking place increasingly from the beginning of the twenty-first century, as Delabastita and Grutman describe:

> But there is no denying that there has been a growing number of fictional representations of translation and multilingualism, as well as an upsurge in their study. At the object-level, one cannot help being struck by an increase of fictional materials that have explicitly multilingual and multicultural settings and that involve translation scenes.

> (Delabastita and Grutman 2005: 28)

In Nabokov's fiction, there are different novels which are perfectly suited for such a study.[1] Jenefer Coates listed a few in her 1999 article:

> Translation was itself to become a topos of increasing importance in his writing: woven into the drama of the narratives, it is openly discussed by protagonists in *Bend Sinister* (1947), *Pnin* (1957), *Pale Fire* (1962) and *Ada* (1969), with direct allusions to Shakespeare (for example, *Hamlet*, *The Tempest*, *Timon of Athens*). Translation becomes a central metaphor that is obvious in *Pale Fire* but less obvious in *Lolita*, where the European Humbert 'misreads' the American Lolita.

> (Coates 1999: 100)

One of these topics includes the representation of mistranslation, and one can think of many scenes in *Ada*, including the first line of the novel, or the following passage in *Look at the Harlequins!*:

> To return to the trivia: I recall regaling the company with one of the howlers I had noticed in the 'translation' of *Tamara*. The sentence *vidnelos' neskol'ko barok* ('several barges could be seen') had become *la vue était assez baroque*. The

eminent critic Basilevski, a stocky, fair-haired old fellow in a rumpled brown suit, shook with abdominal mirth – but then his expression changed to one of suspicion and displeasure. After tea he accosted me and insisted gruffly that I had made up that example of mistranslation. I remember answering that, if so, he, too, might well be an invention of mine.

(Nabokov [1974] 1996: 609)

The topic of mistranslation can also be found in Nabokov's articles on translation, for example in 'The Art of Translation':

Insufficient acquaintance with the foreign language involved may transform a commonplace expression into some remarkable statement that the real author never intended to make. '*Bien-être general*' becomes the manly assertion that 'it is good to be a general'; to which gallant general a French translator of 'Hamlet' has been known to pass the caviar.

(Nabokov [1941a] 2008: 4)

Mistranslation is also present in Nabokov's habits as a teacher:

He would usually embark on teaching a new text by drawing attention to mistakes in the translations being used: his lectures, published in book form carry reproductions of the copious changes and comments annotating his teaching copies.

(Coates 1999: 98)

The fact that Nabokov mentioned translation in his classes is relevant to another issue which, in my opinion, needs to garner more attention: the place of translation in literature classes.

In his 1998 book, Venuti underlined the importance of mentioning the translated status of texts which are studied in class:

The marginality of translation reaches even to educational institutions, where it is manifested in a scandalous contradiction: on the one hand, an utter dependence on translated texts in curricula and research; on the other hand, a general tendency, in both teaching and publications, to elide the status of translated texts as translated, to treat them as texts originally written in the translating language.

(Venuti 1998: 89)

Venuti argues for a 'pedagogy of translated literature' which, he states, 'can help students learn to be both self-critical and critical of exclusionary cultural ideologies by drawing attention to the situatedness of texts and interpretations'

(Venuti 1998: 93). Leaving aside the political dimension of ideology in literature, it is crucial to mention when a text is a translation. Of course, with Nabokov, things are at the same time more complicated and easier: if a class studies Nabokov in English, chances are he revised the translation and made it the new original (Boyd 1991: 484). However, it is important to insist on its status as a translation, otherwise, the risk is that Nabokov's novels in Russian will only be perceived by Anglophone readers are pseudotranslations: they will become translations without an original.

Venuti also mentions academia ('research', 'publications'), and it is striking that, in Nabokov studies, some scholars pair the English title of a novel with the publication date of the Russian original; it is particularly confusing when one knows of the differences which usually exist between the Russian original and the English (self-)translation.

It is actually rather ironic that translation should be studied so little in Nabokov studies if one takes into consideration the fact that, as scholars, we need to rely extensively on translation because most of us do not master all of Nabokov's languages and we need to read him in translation. It is also surprising because many Nabokov scholars have to translate Nabokov themselves when they want to quote from sources which have not been published yet. It is especially the case for archives. In that respect, someone like Brian Boyd has done a lot to bring visibility to many texts which did not exist in English: one can think of the many documents which are quoted in English in his biography of Nabokov, or, more glaringly, of the volumes he not only edited, but translated with Russian colleagues, like *Letters to Véra* (with Olga Voronina) or *Think, Write, Speak* (with Anastasia Tolstoy). The latter also contains many items translated from the French by Boyd himself (though he thanks Maurice Couturier and Marie Bouchet for their 'help with occasional turns of French phrase or allusion' (Nabokov 2019: 485)) and some others from the Italian or the German (for which he thanks respectively Chiara Montini and Dieter E. Zimmer). It has been one of my goals in this book: to make scholars know of research that is written in languages other than English, mainly by giving English translations of articles, archives and books written in French, but also, on occasions, written in Russian; I have also given references to articles in Portuguese or Serbian.

There is, however, a subtle line to walk when it comes to scholarship in English: English is the main language of communication, but its hegemony risks erasing other languages, or at least, it risks making research in other languages irrelevant, or less relevant, less visible. Therefore, translating research into

English could confirm that English is the language to favour, thus implying that writing research directly in English is the most sensible path to follow, especially in a world where efficiency and visibility (but also profitability) are encouraged, even in academia.

One possible way to avoid the all-dominant hegemony of English as well as the possible invisibility of scholarship in other languages is to actively include translation in research. For example, the question has often been raised at Nabokov conferences organized by the French Vladimir Nabokov Society: what languages should panels be held in?[2] Panels in English are inclusive of foreign scholars, but they can feel inaccessible for French scholars who are not fluent in English, thus risking alienating colleagues who are not specialists in English studies but who are valuable scholars in comparative literature and Russian studies, for example. On the other hand, panels in French often mean that colleagues who do not master the language can get bored during the presentations (in the best-case scenario), or wander off to visit the neighbourhood (in the worst-case scenario). Some possibilities include conference interpreting (which implies funding or the active involvement of bilingual colleagues), or alternatively organization in advance: one can imagine asking participants to provide their papers several weeks before the conference so that the papers can be translated in advance and then distributed to colleagues; bilingual powerpoints can also be used, with key points written in one language on the slide to accompany a paper given in another language. When it comes to publications, a very interesting course has been taken in Chovich et al. (2014): for example, the article by Stankovic on French in *Pnin* (quoted in my last chapter) is written in Serbian, but on the last page of the article, it is summarized in French (136); besides, the volume has a bilingual conclusion, one in Serbian, one in English and in the conclusion in English, there is an extensive summary (almost 3-page-long) of the 25-page-long article which thoroughly details the author's findings. Thus, I could not read the article in Serbian, but I had access to most of it thanks to its French and English summaries, and it enabled me to discover the work of a scholar which I did not know of because of my not speaking Serbian.

This reflection on translation in academia can mean that each scholarly author can become a translator, a self-translator or a co-translator. Indeed, collaboration between researchers means that colleagues can help one another translate their work, their abstract or even just their title. Of course, those suggestions do not have to remain ideals: funding can and should be asked and made available to make research more visible.

Avoiding the erasure of translation in literature means not turning foreign works into pseudotranslations, and taking part in the translation of research implies becoming a translator, or a co-translator. Those are of course evocative of the three parts of this monograph, and I hope they are one more way to show the relevance of associating literature and translation, of linking the author and the translator by more than just a hyphen.

Notes

Introduction

1   For an analysis of the use and functions of multilingualism in Nabokov's prose in English, see Loison-Charles 2016.

Chapter 1

1   For more on this pseudotranslation, see Jenn 2013: 45–61.

2   As such, he twisted the classical concept of a pseudotranslation, since the author usually pretends to be the translator and invents the original author; for Makine's case, see Lievois 2014 and Bocquet 2019.

3   More specifically, *Papa Hamlet*, *Book of Mormon* and works by the 'Kazakh poet' Dzhambul Dzhabayev.

4   For crime fiction pretending to be Italian, see O'Sullivan 2005 and Maher 2013.

5   For Russian pseudotranslations of the 'English gothic novel', see Toury 2012: 51.

6   For sex manuals, see Koçak 2015; for erotic literature, see Branch 2013; for pornographic novels, see Toury 2012: 51. In France, the collection of romance novels *Harlequins* is famous for using pseudonyms that are meant to sound as English or American as the name of best-selling author Barbara Cartland.

7   See Collombat 2003: 150.

8   On the irony pertaining to this pseudotranslation and to those of Romain Gary, see Martens 2010.

9   See, for example, Jenn 2013: 5, 68.

10   I want to thank Stanislav Shvabrin for bringing this pseudotranslation by Pushkin to my attention.

11   See my book on screen translation (Loison-Charles 2022), where the concept of 'double suspension of disbelief' in dubbing is borrowed from Nolwenn Mingant 2010.

12   About Pierre Delalande as an invention in Nabokov's work, see Wood 2019: 24–8. After mentioning that, at the end of *The Gift*, Fyodor wanted to translate 'an old French sage' (probably Delalande), Wood evokes a case that could be called a pseudotranslation, even if the word is, once again, not used: 'Gennady Barabtarlo ingeniously suggests that Fyodor's translation of Delalande is in fact *Invitation to a Beheading*, the book he wrote between his *Chernyshevski* and *The Gift*' (Wood 2019: 27–8).

Chapter 2

1   Somehow, Krabbenhoft misunderstands, or pretends to misunderstand, Boyd: the latter has drawn his analysis based on the questions of cruelty, ridicule and humour (Boyd 1991: 212–4; 271–2); however, Krabbenhoft argues that a comparison between *Don Quixote* and *Pnin* does not stand as far as the love relationships between the characters are concerned and because Pnin is no madman. At no point did Boyd make those arguments.

2   See, however, the links established between Nabokov and Cervantes through translation in Poulin 2017, especially 44–61, 86–131 and 147–81.

3   On *Don Quixote* as a pseudotranslation, see, in English, Bahous 1990, in French, Bahous 2010 and Coadou 2018, and, in Portuguese, Cobelo 2007.

4   See for example Olson 2013.

5   The spelling of the author's name varies in the documents I quote.

6   Another example makes similar claims and similar use of inverted commas: 'James MacPherson's 1760 "translation" of "Ossianic" poems, *Fragments of Ancient Poetry Translated from the Gaelic or Erse Language*, clearly warrants designation as such' (Apter 2006: 212).

7   'Even though, as Fiona Stafford has pointed out, in 1952 Derick S. Thomson identified the Gaelic poems that Macpherson used, at least one Johnson scholar still believes that Ossian's authenticity remains "a nagging question … that refuses to go away"' (Bristow and Mitchell 2015: 117).

8   See in these reviews of Curley's book, Wickman (2013: 277) and Sandler (2010: 142).

9   See also Meyer 1988a: 53–64.

10 Jakobson distinguished three types of translation: '1. Intralingual translation or *rewording* is an interpretation of verbal signs by means of other signs of the same language. 2. Interlingual translation or *translation proper* is an interpretation of verbal signs by means of some other language. 3. Intersemiotic translation or *transmutation* is an interpretation of verbal signs by means of signs of nonverbal sign systems' (Jakobson [1959] 2000: 114).

11 See Alladaye 2013. Three chapters in particular (from 4 to 6) are devoted to the question of authorship, in particular Chapter 5, 'Are you a Shadean, a Kinbotean or a Botkinian?', in which the Botkinian interpretation is added.

12 The discovery of the manuscript is a recurring trope in pseudotranslations as it ascertains the presence of an original text in a foreign language (one can find a similar passage in *Don Quixote*, Part 1, Chapter 9; see in particular Cervantes 2000: 77). The *Slovo*, however, was never accused of being a translation without an original: the absence of an original was problematic only in a historic perspective, to prove its authenticity.

13 On the Scottish theme in *Pale Fire*, see Meyer 1988b: 70. Actually, the connection between Scotland and Ukraine is not so surprising if one is to believe Simon

Karlinsky: 'by the 1820s, the Ukraine was assuming the same function in the Russian popular imagination that, through Burns and Scott, Scotland had assumed in the English imagination' (Karlinsky, qtd in Hoisington 1981: 31).

14   About Nabokov's falling out with Roman Jakobson, see Boyd 1991: 136, 145, 215 and 311.

15   'I made a first attempt to translate *Slovo o Polku Igoreve* in 1952. My object was purely utilitarian – to provide my students with an English text. In that first version I followed uncritically Roman Jakobson's recension as published in *La Geste du Prince Igor*. Later, however, I grew dissatisfied not only with my own – much too "readable" – translation but also with Jakobson's views' (*The Song*: 82). About the differences between Nabokov's two translations, see Shvabrin 2019: 286–92.

16   According to Goldblatt, the Jakobson-Nabokov debate actually reflected a completely different vision of Russian literature and patriotism: 'In seeking to continue the work of early Russian scholarship, Jakobson emerged as the patriotic defender of the cultural heritage of medieval Russia. [...] From Nabokov's point of view, however, it would seem that what might be perceived as Jakobson's "patriotic stance" and his preoccupation with the issue of authenticity somehow took attention away from purely artistic concerns' (1995: 667).

17   I wish to thank Daria Sinichkina (Sorbonne Université) for informing me of Zaliznjak's clarification of the matter, which she also explains in her article.

18   Romantic literature was important for Nabokov, and it is interesting to note the prevalence of pseudotranslation during the Romantic era (Toremans 2017: 81–2).

19   The following remark, written about the *Slovo*, can apply to all texts stemming from an oral tradition, including Macpherson's *Ossian*: 'we might wonder whether notions such as "authentic text," "original text," "genuine text," "apocryphal work," "forgery," or "fabrication" should be applied to the history of a monument for which we cannot provide (1) precise information on the problems of dating and authorship, (2) tangible evidence that the Slovo, as it has come down to us, is the product of a single author (rather than co-authors and compilers), or (3) concrete proof that we are dealing with a "closed tradition" and a compact textus traditus (i.e., a process of faithful textual transmission)' (Goldblatt and Picchio 2006: 129).

20   Interestingly, Borges also wrote a short story on *Don Quixote*, which according to Gray presents parallels with FitzGerald's translation: 'The distinctive methods of the *Rubáiyát* are illuminated by another of Borges's stories [...] "Pierre Menard, Author of *Don Quixote*". [...] Menard's unusual project makes him a remarkably close fictional approximation of FitzGerald, as is evident from Borges's brief, beautifully perceptive sketch, "The Enigma of Edward FitzGerald"' (Gray 2011: 771).

21   See for example Shafiei 2012.

22   Though many critics quote this expression, no one indicates where FitzGerald used it. The first one to have made this claim is Michael Kearney in the biographical preface which is included in the fourth edition: 'he used to say that the suggested

addition of his name to the title would imply an assumption of importance which he considered that his "transmogrification" of the Persian poet did not possess' (Kearney 1888: 17).

23 Hesitation between translation ('traduction') and literary creation ('création littéraire') appears in the title of a French article by Nabokov specialist Christine Raguet and her two co-authors (Raguet, Mahdavi and Nakhaei 2015).

24 After quoting Toury on the innovative impact of pseudotranslations on literary systems, Adam Talib hastens to deny any link with FitzGerald's translation: 'This seems to describe rather exactly the literary evolution brought on by FitzGerald's *Rubáiyát*, which is not a pseudotranslation' (Talib 2011: 187).

25 Michael Nott only concedes doubts, which are shared by another critic he quotes: 'Arguably, FitzGerald's *Rubáiyát* also approaches the status of pseudotranslation. Rangarajan writes that FitzGerald's "radical narrativization pushes the poem in the direction of a pseudotranslated oriental tale; replacing both urtext and poet with the quasi-fictional 'Omar' is reminiscent of earlier orientalists' fictional negotiations of the mythic reality of a textual Orient'" (Nott 2016: 669).

26 An earlier sign of Nabokov's growing vexation with FitzGerald's 'translation' could be concealed in the last stanza of Nabokov's poem 'Pity the Elderly Translator', which Nabokov composed in 1952 to express 'his dissatisfaction with the artistic mode of translation' (Shvabrin 2019: 274). The reference to 'the poem from the Persian' could be an allusion to the original language of the *Rubáiyát*: 'Such books are irrelevant. Sooner or later / The gentle person, the mime sublime, / The incorruptible translator / Is betrayed by lady rime. / And the poem from the Persian / And the sonnet spun in Spain / Perish in the person's version, / And the person dies insane' (Nabokov 2008a: 13).

27 Many blogs written by poets and translators use the expression, but one can note the following scholarly article, entitled '"Better a Live Sparrow than a Stuffed Eagle": Towards a Translation of Guillaume de Machaut's "Dit de l'Alerion"' (Thaon 1978).

28 The origin of Kinbote's line was debated on Nabokv-L in 2009 and the members of the discussion seemed to agree on the fact that Jacques in *As you like it* was 'the predominant reference'. See http://www.thenabokovian.org/sites/default/files/2018-01/NABOKV-L-0016185___body.html

Chapter 3

1 I use this term largely in the way Bozovic does, with the idea of mingling literary and linguistic traditions from different countries; for example she describes 'interpenetrating European traditions' and uses the adjectives 'transnational and translinguistic, continental but also specifically Russo-Franco-American-centric' (Bozovic 2016: 4).

2   The play was published in Pushkin, Lermontov, Tyutchev (1944) and can be found
     in a bilingual edition in Nabokov 2008a: 144–51.

3   On *Pale Fire* as an intralingual translation of *Eugene Onegin*, see Trubikhina 2015:
     86–140.

4   For an analysis of these passages, see Johnson (n.d.); an excerpt can be found on
     The Nabokovian website: http://thenabokovian.org/node/21850.

5   On the various musical adaptations of *Les Chansons de Bilitis* by French composers
     and their relation to Debussy's creation, see Lazzaro 2014.

6   For an analysis of the difference in form and prosody between the original
     poems and Nabokov's translations, see Shvabrin 2019: 48–50 and Shvabrin 2007:
     31–43.

7   In my analysis, I use the translation by Richard Stokes because it is very literal and
     thus it is very useful to perceive the nuances of the French original ('The Tomb of
     the Naiads', available online: https://www.oxfordlieder.co.uk/song/2843). However,
     for the first line, I chose to use my own translation because Stokes's translation
     is less literal when it comes to 'couvert de givre' (he uses 'frost-bound'). All the
     translations from Nabokov's Russian version are mine.

8   This is something that Shvabrin (2007) also underlined.

9   See for example Nabokov [1966a] 1990: 259.

10   See Shvabrin 2019: 192–201.

11   The Russian title is sometimes translated as 'The Miserly Knight', but I will be using
     Nabokov's translation, 'The Covetous Knight'. Pushkin himself used this title, but he
     spelt it erroneously: 'When it first appeared in 1836 Pushkin's "small tragedy" *The
     Covetous Knight* bore on its title page the parenthetical words "Sceny iz čenstonovoj
     [*sic*] tragikomedii: The Cavetous [*sic*] Knigth [*sic*]"' (Gregg 1965: 109).

12   On top of space constraints, there are several reasons for this choice. First, the play
     is much longer than the poem and it is more complex, especially regarding the
     English intertext. Then, it was written in 1941, which is the same year as 'The Art
     of Translation'; on the other hand, 1947 – the year when Nabokov translated 'Iz
     Pindemonti' – does not really have any significance in his evolution of translation.
     And finally, Nabokov produced two translations of 'Iz Pindemonti'; the 1947 one
     is available (Nabokov 2008a: 207) but the second one is unpublished, so studying
     one which is 'based on a close lexical variant of the original' (Shvabrin 2019: 216)
     without the other would do a disservice to the analysis on Nabokov's practice and
     theory of translation. For an extensive analysis of 'Iz Pindemonti', see Dolinin
     (2007).

13   It is mentioned by Nabokov (Pushkin [1975] 1991, I: 183). Sandler writes that
     'Pushkin was fascinated by Chénier. He translated or adapted four of Chénier's
     poems into Russian' (1983: 187).

14   See Ober and Ober (2004) and Cadot (1995: 46).

15 The poem is also known as '*Ne dorogo tsenyu ya gromkie prava…*' ('I don't value highly the loud rights…').

16 In the entry 'Nabokov and Pushkin' in *The Garland Companion to Vladimir Nabokov*, Sergej Davydov uses the erroneous spelling 'Chenston' (1995: 485). Brian Boyd also used the Russian spelling and presented 'Chenston' as a mystification in his analysis of Calmbrood's 'The Night Journey' (Boyd 1990: 370). This claim is also made repeatedly by Alexey Sklyrenko in his annotations on *The Nabokovian*. One needs to note, however, that some Pushkinians willingly refer to Chenston, not Shenstone. Commenting on the choice between 'miserly knight' and 'covetous knight', translator Nancy Anderson argues that the typo was intentional on Pushkin's part: 'One possibility, of course, is that Pushkin simply made a mistake in his English. However, there is also a more interesting possibility: that after having created a non-existent English work to distance himself from imputations that his play was based on real life, he then wished to distance himself as well from the nonexistent English work. Hence the spelling of the author's name as Chenston (or Chenstone) – which suggests, but is not the same as, William Shenstone – and the description of this work as a "tragicomedy," whereas Pushkin's work is clearly a tragedy. Substituting "covetous" for "miserly" in the title of this nonexistent work would then be another way of producing this close-but-not-the-same effect' (Anderson in Pushkin 2000: 199–200).

17 In his Commentary to *Onegin*, Nabokov does not introduce *Skupoi Rytsar'* as a pseudotranslation willingly forged by Pushkin, but rather as a false attribution by someone else. However, as we will see in our next chapter, Nabokov presents Shenstone (which he spells 'Chenston' here) as a victim of pseudotranslation when he associates him with his own creation, Vivian Calmbrood, in his own pseudotranslation 'The Night Journey', written in 1931.

18 See also Hoisington (1981: 345).

19 Proffer made the same suggestion (1968: 353).

20 According to Shvabrin, this choice could be related to 'its treatment of the Jewish theme', more specifically 'the vacillation between the neutral ethnonym *evrei* and the pejorative *zhid*' (2019: 197–8).

21 See Bethea (2009), Struve (1933: 399–404) and Tilliette (2020).

22 See Hoisington (1981).

23 Musset's *L'Anglais mangeur d'opium* (1828) was presented as a translation of Thomas de Quincey's *The Confessions of an English-Opium Eater* (1821), but Musset inserted passages which were completely invented or largely autobiographical: see Ledda (2013) and Castagnès (2013). In a quite symptomatic way, the text is generally presented as a not very faithful translation of de Quincey's text (for example on Wikipedia), showing once again the blurred limit between free translation and pseudotranslation.

24 See Shvabrin 2019: 131–5, 168–77. A short quote from *Hamlet* ('words, words, words') is used in Pushkin's other pseudotranslation, 'Iz Pindemonti', and Nabokov preserved it in his translation into English, at least in his 1947 version (Nabokov 2008a: 207).

25 See also Schuman (1995: 513).

26 Respectively, 'which', 'number six', 'one', and an omission: 'Отпирает сундук' (opens the chest) is translated as 'unlocks'.

27 In linguistics, the limit between loanwords and foreign words is highly debated, but one of the easiest ways to distinguish them is to consider their assimilation into the language, English for example; one criterion that is rather common is the use of italics for foreign words; for loanwords, their presence in the dictionary as English words shows that they have been assimilated, and their recognizable foreign origins are indicated as such in the *OED*. For a very thorough analysis of loanwords with a diachronic perspective, see Durkin (2014); for a vulgarized presentation of the difference between foreign words and loanwords, see the introduction to Bliss (1966).

28 The word is usually spelled in one word in English, 'rendezvous', as attested in the *OED*, and its hyphen preserves the French quality of the expression more than the loanword 'rendezvous'.

29 'Meeting-place: *you know the rendezvous*, Hml. IV, 4, 4'. (Schmidt 1902; http://www.perseus.tufts.edu/hopper/text?doc=Perseus%3Atext%3A1999.03.0079%3Aentry%3DRendezvous). I want to thank Shakespeare specialist Mylène Lacroix for her help with Shakespearian prosody, motives and use of French words.

30 For a refutation of the postulation that this letter is a translation from French into Russian, see New 2020.

31 Bocquet (2019) mentions it as such.

32 For the moment, my focus is on the diegesis, not on the language, which is why I am quoting *Onegin* in English (in Nabokov's revised version of 1975).

33 'Intersemiotic translation or *transmutation* is an interpretation of verbal signs by means of signs of nonverbal sign systems' (Jakobson 1959: 114).

34 On a smaller scale, Tatyana's letter is suffused with traces from French translations of other European literatures like Byron and Goethe (see Pushkin [1975] 1991, II: 390–1).

35 See also Toury 1981: 20.

36 Preferring the translation over the original is reminiscent of the exasperation which Nabokov expressed about Conrad: 'He once wrote that he preferred Mrs. Garnett's translation of Anna Karenin to the original! This makes one dream – "ça fait rêver" as Flaubert used to say when faced with some abysmal stupidity' (Nabokov [1973] 1990: 57).

37 A diachronic perspective is interesting here: in his 2001 retranslation, Maurice Couturier is much more modern and has Charlotte and Humbert switch to '*tu*' after they are married. Very often, in the French translation of texts in English

(especially in audiovisual translation), the translators switch pronouns from '*vous*' to '*tu*' after the characters had sex or kissed for the first time.

Chapter 4

1   *Grani*, 2 (1923), 69–99. Reference found in Boyd (1990: 556).

2   Diment also exposed some elements of the plot: 'It is the story of two English brothers, a criminal and an upright citizen, who were separated early in childhood and accidentally meet each other in a London pub in 1768' (1995: 587).

3   Before *The Wanderers*, Nabokov wrote another play that was never published: 'On 28 January/10 February [...] Vladimir wrote his first "play," "Vesnoy" ("In Spring"), "a lyrical something in one act"' (Boyd 1990: 141); see also Diment 1995: 587.

4   The letter in which Nabokov expressed his desire to return to 'The Wanderers' has now been published in *Letters to Véra*. The letter, written in Russian from Prague and dated 8 January 1924, is thus translated into English: 'After Morn I will write a second – final – act to "The Wanderers." I suddenly feel like it' (Nabokov 2014: 18).

5   About this novel, see Nabokov (1957b: 13) and Pushkin ([1975] 1991, II: 352–4).

6   On the figure of the 'Wandering Jew', see Nabokov (1957c: 46–7) and Pushkin ([1975] 1991, II: 354–7). I want to thank Anoushka Alexander-Rose for the reference found in Pushkin's commentary.

7   These letters are kept in the Berg collection.

8   Here I use the new Russian orthography but Shvabrin, in his book, uses the old one, just as Nabokov did in his translation.

9   I want to thank my Russian teacher Natacha Montsarrat who pointed out to me the similarities between the two plays.

10 'Не царствует ли это божество / в глухих лесах от Глумиглэн до Гровсей / и по дороге в Старфилд?' (Nabokov [1923] 1999: 650–1).

11 See Willoughby (1921: 314).

12 See Mennie (1938).

13 The term '*разбойник*' is also present in a poem by Pushkin, 'The Robber Brothers' (*Братья Разбойники*), but the theme is very different: the brothers stay together and are only separated by death.

14 See Shvabrin (2019: 246–8).

15 In French, 'Robert' is actually pronounced with a silent 't', which makes it sound like the English word 'robber' or the German '*Räuber*' if those words were uttered with a French accent.

16 See Willoughby (1921).

17 For a detailed analysis of Nabokov's translation of Lermontov's poem, see Connolly (2021: 105).

18 The title is given in Connolly (2021: 105).

19 This death's head could also indicate that Ivanov belonged to the Masonic order. See
    Skonetchnaïa (2000: 386). Once again, thanks are due to Natacha Montsarrat for
    informing me of this symbolism.

20 This metaphor has already been underlined by Frank (2012) about Nabokov's works
    and autobiography: 'Unsteady, flighty and ephemeral, butterflies in Nabokov's work
    encapsulate the inherent instability of the self in fiction and life' (192).

21 See, in Chapter 2, the section on FitzGerald's *Rubáiyát*.

22 See my introduction to the concept of pseudotranslation.

23 These two lines (Chapter 6, XXI, l. 1–2), which precede Lensky's 'verse effusion,
    were VN favorites', as we can read on the website *AdaOnline*. The Russian original is:
    'Стихи на случай сохранились; / Я их имею; вот они' (Pushkin [1833] 2003: 189).

24 This theory has also been put forward by Anne-Laure Rigeade who, to the best of
    my knowledge, is the only one who has called Pnin's letter a pseudotranslation; she
    has also made the connection with Tatyana's letter (Rigeade 2007: 188).

25 In this novel, the transcription into Russian is not as clear as the system which
    Nabokov was to use in his later novels: the double vowels (in '*zasstrianoo*', '*eeboh*'
    and '*dokoochayou*' for example) are particularly surprising.

26 For the links between bilingualism and madness in Nabokov's novels in English, see
    Loison-Charles (2014: 317–26).

27 For the accusations that Nabokov's Russian was not Russian enough, see Loison-
    Charles (2020a: 155) and for the Russianized English he supposedly used in his
    translation *Eugene Onegin*, see the second part of the present book.

Chapter 5

1   For a psycholinguistic approach, see Pavlenko (2014); for a perspective on bilingual
    writing by the writers themselves, see de Courtivron (2003), and for writers who
    write in English as their second language, see Nien-Ming Ch'ien (2004).

2   'The world "translation" comes, etymologically, from the Latin for "bearing across."
    Having been borne across the world, we are translated men. It is normally supposed
    that something always gets lost in translation; I cling, obstinately, to the notion that
    something can also be gained' (Rushdie, qtd in Casanova 2004: 136).

3   On the debates about Nabokov's (un)Russianness, see Beaujour (1989: 81) and on
    his belonging or not to a literary nation, see Loison-Charles (2020a).

4   For a detailed analysis on the apparent contradictions between Comparative
    Literature and Translations Studies, in particular on the notion of World Literature,
    see Bassnett (2019). In this text, Lawrence Venuti's comments are rather telling
    on the misunderstandings that separate those disciplines, as the following quote
    shows: 'He accuses comparative and world literature as having latched on to the

ideas of "untranslatability" as a way of side-stepping investigation into the actual processes of translation and the ideological frames within which translations happen' (2019: 6).

Chapter 6

1   This is the edition I generally use to quote Nabokov's translation. Though the paperback edition of the 1975 text exists in two physical volumes, it retains the pagination and references to volumes. Therefore, this edition in two volumes can indicate 'II', 'III' or 'IV' as in volume 2, 3 or 4, even if the three of them are included in the 'physical' second volume.
2   See Lopoukhine (2018).
3   See Eells (2018).
4   For a short analysis of the debate around Nabokov's translation, see Boyd (1991: 492–9); for the relationship between Nabokov and Wilson, see their correspondence in Nabokov (1979a); and for a detailed analysis of their relationship, including their dispute around the translation, see Meyers (1994).
5   The retention of iamb was mentioned in the first of his Russian articles from 1957: '*Одно, что сохранил я, это ямб*' (Nabokov 1957b: 130) (the only thing I kept is the iamb, my translation).
6   In his review of Nabokov's translation, Conquest criticizes the contradiction of not having versification while keeping iambs (1965: 237).
7   Gerschenkron paid Nabokov the following compliment: 'Nabokov went to great pains to discover the precise meaning of every term, however trifling, so that meats, pies, and fruit juices, berries and flowers, trees and animals could all receive their proper gastronomical, botanical, and zoological equivalents' (1966: 337).

Chapter 7

1   'Translatese', 'translationese' or 'translatorese' are defined in the same way by the *Oxford English Dictionary*: 'The style of language perceived as characteristic of (bad) translations; language in a translation which appears awkward, unnatural, or unidiomatic, esp. as a result of the translator attempting to replicate closely the specific features of the source text'. However, their first recorded uses vary slightly: 'translatese', 1908; 'translationese', 1914; 'translatorese', 1915.
2   Arndt had already translated *Evgenij Onegin*, and his 1963 translation had been violently attacked by Nabokov in his review 'Pounding the Clavichord'. The 1972

translation is actually a double one, described in the following terms by Shaw: '*Pushkin Threefold: Narrative, Lyric, Polemic and Ribald Verse* offers a refutation – in performance as well as in argument – of the theory of translation argued for and exemplified in Vladimir Nabokov's translation of *Evgenij Onegin*. [...] Walter Arndt has accepted Nabokov's challenge: his "threefold" includes (1) the Russian texts of the poems, together with (2) a "linear" (that is, literal or almost literal, line by line) translation on facing pages, and in addition (3) a "metric" translation which attempts to reproduce Puškin's Russian poetry as English poetry in the same poetic forms (including meter, stanza forms, and even the alternation of masculine and feminine rhymes)' (Shaw 1974: 313).

3   On Nabokov's multilingual style in his novels in English, see Loison-Charles 2014 and 2016.

4   The following pages contain analyses that were presented in my PhD in French; however, those have never been published in English.

5   Nabokov is reported to have declared the following to Simon Karlinsky: 'to write "about Pushkin and also about me" one had to know French literature' (Boyd 1991: 571).

6   'Nabokov's translation can and indeed should be studied, but despite all the cleverness and occasional brilliance it cannot be read' (Gerschenkron 1966: 340).

7   The *OED* describes this word as 'now chiefly hist. [historical]'.

8   About Nabokov and machine translation, see DiLeonardi (2021).

9   See for example Dolinin (1995: 125).

10   On translating into the target language of one's time or into the language used at the time when the book was published, see Georges Mounin on 'the scent of the century' (my translation) (Mounin [1955] 1994: 74, 80).

11   Philip Durkin distinguishes three approaches, and the one I use, after Louis Deroy, is the stylistic one: 'The third, essentially stylistic approach, is rather different, being fundamentally based on the analysis of texts rather than of words across time, and requiring sensitivity to speakers's perceptions about words, as well as to the fact of their history (which are often entirely opaque to speakers, and are at best reflected indirectly through aspects of word structure and phonology)' (Durkin 2014: 12).

12   Some of the chapter mottos are in foreign languages (French, Italian, English), but in Pushkin's text, they are in Roman, probably due to their liminal localization (between chapters); Nabokov reproduces the same typography and does not translate them into English.

13   See Loison-Charles 2022 on dubbing French words in English-speaking TV shows into French.

14   About Nabokov translating differently (and better) than dictionaries, see the following remark on his practice of self-translation: 'Two Russian scholars

compiled an English-Russian dictionary of Nabokov's *Lolita*, listing only the words that Nabokov had translated in ways other than any of the existing English-Russian dictionaries – and that usually mean better, more accurately or more vividly. The dictionary was two hundred pages long, the novel itself, three hundred' (Boyd 2012: 8).

15 'Довольно скучен высший тон' (Pushkin [1833] 2003: 35).

16 It gives me particular pleasure to note that Nabokov's affirmation on '*ton*' finds an echo in the recent Netflix success *Bridgerton* which keeps using this word, thus prompting the online news platform *Elite Daily* to ask 'Here's the 1 question most "Bridgerton" fans are afraid to ask' in their article 'What is "The Ton" in "Bridgerton"? Here's a Regency vocabulary lesson': https://www. elitedaily.com/p/what-is-the-ton-in-bridgerton-heres-a-regency-vocabulary-lesson-59058146

17 On the use of French to speak about fashion in English, see Deroy (1956: 173) and Chadelat (1999: 104).

18 'в малиновом берете' (Pushkin [1833] 2003: 256).

19 See also Nabokov 2019: 284–5.

20 'швейцара' (Pushkin [1833] 2003: 28); 'hall porter' (Pushkin 1964, I: 109); 'concierge' (Pushkin [1975] 1991, I: 107).

21 'новы' (Pushkin [1833] 2003: 43); 'new' (Pushkin 1964, I, p. 122); 'novel' (Pushkin [1975] 1991, I: 119).

22 'хозяйки' (Pushkin [1833] 2003: 108); 'lady of the house' (Pushkin 1964, I, p. 174); 'chatelaine' (Pushkin [1975] 1991, I: 170).

23 '*Which of the languages you speak do you consider the most beautiful?* My head says English, my heart, Russian, my ear, French' (Nabokov [1973] 1990: 49).

24 'Похоронили' (Pushkin [1833] 2003: 43; Pushkin [1975] 1991, I: 121).

25 *OED*: 'Middle English < Old French *enterrer* (11th cent. in Littré)'.

26 On this word and its Gallic dimension, see Poulin (2005b).

27 'If in translating *toska lyubvi Tat'yanu-gonit* (Three: xvi: 1), "the ache of love chases Tatjana" […], I put "chases" instead of the "pursues" that Mr. Wilson has the temerity to propose, I do so not only because "pursues" is in Russian not *gonit* but *presleduet*, but also because, as Mr. Wilson has not noticed, it would be a misleading repetition of the "pursue" used in the preceding stanza (*tebya presleduyut mechty*, "daydreams pursue you"), and my method is to repeat a term at close range only when Pushkin repeats it' (Nabokov [1966a] 1990: 259).

28 'Mr. Arndt's most bizarre observation, however, comes on page vi, towards the end of his preface: "The present new translation… is not aimed primarily at the academic and literary expert, but at a public of English-speaking students and others interested in a central work of world literature in a compact and readable form." – which is tantamount to proclaiming: "I know this is an inferior product

but it is gaily colored and nicely packed, and is, anyway, just for students and such people"' (Nabokov [1964a] 1990: 240).

29 'A reviewer writing in the *Novyy Zhurnal* (No. 77), Mr. Moris Fridberg [...] confuses me with Professor Arndt whose preliminary remarks about his "writing not for experts but students" Mr. Fridberg ascribes to me' (Nabokov [1966a] 1990: 245).

Chapter 8

1   A digitalized version of a 1861 edition is available online: https://gallica.bnf.fr/ark:/12148/bpt6k5452523p.texteImage

2   See for example Cancogni (1983, 1995) and Poulin (2005a).

3   Even in the entry 'Nabokov and Chateaubriand' in *The Garland Companion to Vladimir Nabokov*, Chateaubriand's translation of Milton is not mentioned. In her book, Bozovic mentions Chateaubriand's role as a translator, but it is her only comment on the topic: 'Lest we miss the parallel to the humble translator, another political exile fond of racy themes, Nabokov's "Translator's Introduction" opens with an epigraph from Pushkin, on Chateaubriand. Clearly, Chateaubriand forms an important part of the heritage that Nabokov is claiming throughout his *Onegin* project' (Bozovic 2016: 61). There is, however, one article which draws parallels between Nabokov and Chateaubriand as translators, by someone who is not a Nabokov scholar, Clayton (1983).

4   For an extensive analysis of the concept of 'transparency' in its various meaning in translation studies, see Arber (2018).

5   For example, he often associates word-for-word translation with another type of translation as if they were the same: 'a literal, word-for-word translation', 'Obviously, in his effort to present Milton word-for-word Chateaubriand has failed to remain true to the meaning and the style of the original. Interlinear translation can never be true' (Pushkin 2013: 26).

6   George Steiner translates this sentence differently and does not keep the image of glass: 'Chateaubriand has made a tracing of the original' (Steiner [1976] 1998: 333). In this chapter, all translations from the French are mine, unless I quote from a translation of the French stated as such in the bibliography.

7   This is the original Russian: 'Переводчик поступил так, что его не видишь: он превратился в такое прозрачное стекло, что кажется, как бы нет стекла. Во II томе "Одиссеи" это еще более поразительно, чем в первом' (Letter from Gogol to Zhukovskii, 28 February 1850). I want to thank Stephen Blackwell for his help with this translation from the Russian.

8   Several articles in French study Chateaubriand's translation, and the most important one is Berman (1985). An extensive analysis has been recently published

in a bilingual edition with Milton's *Paradise Lost* and Chateaubriand's *Le Paradis Perdu* published *en regard*, and more than one hundred pages of commentary by Christophe Tournu (Milton 2021).

9   'It is hoped that my readers will be moved to learn Pushkin's language and go through EO again without this crib'. Nabokov [1964b] 1991: 8.

10   On Chateaubriand's Latinizing translation, see Berman (1985: 123–4).

11   According to Berman, 'literal translation is the expression of a certain rapport to the mother tongue, to which translation necessarily makes violence' (Berman 1985: 117).

12   The latest publication on the topic, Grant (2021), has the great advantage of balancing Nabokov's hubris with his use of humour in the commentary to *Onegin*.

13   '*je ne fais point mon apologie*'. The word '*apologie*' is particularly hard to translate because it means both 'apology' and 'apologia', so the segment could almost be translated in the following, contradictory ways: 'I am not saying how sorry I am' or 'I am not saying what an amazing job I did'.

14   Venuti uses 'minoritizing', while the translations of the French philosophers use 'minorizing'. Jean-Jacques Lecercle, who bases part of his theory on Deleuze and Guattari and who is quoted by Venuti, does not resort to a verb coming from 'minor': he just opposes the adjectives 'minor' and 'major'.

15   The stylistic dimension of Deleuze and Guattari's theory works very well for an analysis of Nabokov's style, as I have done in the penultimate chapter of my 2016 book. Its political dimension is harder to use, at least for Nabokov.

16   See my previous chapter for a detailed analysis.

17   'This translation ethics does not so much prevent the assimilation of the foreign text as aim to signify the autonomous existence of that text behind (yet by means of) the assimilative process of the translation' (Venuti 1998: 11).

18   On literature and politics in Nabokov's novels, see Edel-Roy (2018).

19   One should note that what Venuti calls 'foreignizing translation' is called 'ethic translation' by Berman, or more precisely he talks of the ethical aim of translation ('*la visée éthique de la traduction*' (Berman 1984: 16); this French expression is translated as 'ethical aim of translation' in Berman (2000: 285).

20   Edel-Roy explains that, before Nabokov and Wilson's fallout about Nabokov's translation, 'their major and essential disagreement was Russian political history, and mainly the figure of Lenin' (2018: 379; my translation). In Nabokov's literary works, she also analyses the 'L disaster' in *Ada* as the symbol of Lenin himself (746–7).

21   See for example a letter dated 13 December 1956, in which Nabokov chided Wilson for his vision of Russian history (Nabokov 1979a: 304)

22   On the translations of Pushkin in connection with the Cold War, see Gauthier 2017.

Chapter 9

1   I want to thank Emily Eells for drawing my attention to this possible contradiction
     in my understanding of Deleuze and Guattari's, but also Venuti's, theories.
2   See for example Venuti 1998: 65.

Chapter 10

1   On Nabokov's practice of self-translation, the two reference works are Grayson
     1977 and Oustinoff 2001.
2   On this short story and its different translations, see Poulin 2021.
3   For studies on Dmitri Nabokov in connection with collaborative translation and
     genetic translation studies, see works by Chiara Montini, especially Montini 2020
     and 2021.
4   Nabokov, Vladimir Vladimirovich. [Bakhman. French] Bachmann. Typescript
     (carbon) of short story, translator unknown, unsigned and undated. 19 p. Berg
     collection.
5   I want to thank Agnès Edel-Roy for her help with the published translation.
     Durand, the translator of 'Bachmann', also produced the French translation entitled
     'Musique', but it was made from the English translation made from the Russian by
     Dmitri Nabokov in collaboration with the author.
6   Nabokov, Vladimir Vladimirovich. [Bakhman. French] Bachmann. Typescript draft
     of short story, translated by Vladimir Nabokov, with annotations in the hand of
     Véra Nabokov, unsigned and undated. 12 p. Berg collection.
7   In studies pertaining to collaborative translation, especially in literary translation,
     the liminal case of revision by an external person is sometimes included. See
     Hersant 2019 and Monti and Schnyder (2018: 261–94).
8   A typical example of the borderline cases which exist in collaborative translation
     is 'Mademoiselle O' in English. Indeed, this text was first written in French, and
     then an English version was produced. In the foreword to *Speak, Memory*, Nabokov
     wrote that '"Mademoiselle O" was translated by the late Hilda Ward into English,
     revised by me, and published by Edward Weeks in the January, 1943, issue of *The
     Atlantic Monthly*' (Nabokov [1966b] 1996: 361) but Grayson argued that Nabokov
     prepared the translation and was assisted by Ward (1977: 139).
9   It is noteworthy that both Hersant and Edel-Roy associate Nabokov and Milan
     Kundera. Edel-Roy mentions that, for both writers, 'the desire to control the
     meaning is [...] to be linked with the political context [...] because their oeuvre,
     even written in the West, can still be manipulated' (2018: 27; my translation);
     Edel-Roy links this fear with Nabokov's practice of self-translation from English

into Russian. As for Hersant, he makes a similar argument: 'In each case, the fear of betrayal is a powerful motivator, encouraging the author to monitor closely his translator, and then replace him' (2016: 101).

10   One notable exception should be noted: when he needs to ascertain the validity of certain theories on Nabokov's texts, Brian Boyd frequently refers to the French translations of *Lolita* and *Ada*, just as he does when he turns to the Russian *Lolita*, which suggests that he considers these as self-translations, or something close to it.

11   Institut Mémoires de l'édition contemporaine, in English: Institute for Contemporary Publishing Archives.

12   For novels written in Russian, see Anokhina 2014 and 2016.

Chapter 11

1   On the various meanings of Nabokov's expression ('dragonize' or 'subject to dracon scrutiny'), see Shrayer (1999: 557–9).

2   To have confirmation that gender does not have much to do with style, see the chapter entitled 'He Wrote, She Wrote' in Blatt (2017).

3   As late as the mid-1980, Véra Nabokov forbade any republication of the *Gogol* translation by Sibon, quoting the letters by her husband to make her point. (IMEC)

4   In a letter on November 1932, he highly praised Denis Roche: 'He is now busy checking every phrase of his translation minutely, conscientiously and rather talentedly. He has already corrected many of the things you and I found there. And our proofs have gone to Levinson. He (Roche) has got hold of a thick volume – chess and other games – and is drawing his information from there. To me, he's an ideal translator, in that sense' (Nabokov 2014: 201). I want to thank Chiara Montini for drawing my attention to this correspondence.

5   Denise Clairouin was a translator and a translation prize was created in her honour in 1945.

6   The coincidence with the main character from *Invitation to a Beheading* is very striking, but so far my research to confirm any direct link has led nowhere.

7   About the Pertzoff-Nabokov collaboration, see Anokhina 2014.

8   Nabokov made a similar remark to Wilson (Nabokov ([1966a] 1990: 251).

9   Incidentally, Nabokov wrote to Ergaz on 29 March 1960 (Cornell): '*If you have a chance to talk to Eric Kahane, please tell him that in an article entitled "Pour saluer Lolita", in Défense de l'Occident, January 1960, the critic writes: "The French translation by M. E. H. Kahane is a wonder of fidelity, ingeniosity and style, and it would really deserve a prize!"*'

10   Kahane became famous in the field of audiovisual translation, where he started in 1971: *The Panic in Needle Park* was his first experience with subtitling, and his

first dubbing into French was Kubrick's *A Clockwork Orange* (1971) after François Truffaut recommended him (despite some sources that say otherwise, Kahane did not take care of Kubrick's *Lolita*). See Grugeau 1993.

11   To find out more about Maurice-Edgar Coindreau, see Coindreau (1974), Chauvin (2018: 28–30) and Gresset (2002).

12   To find out more about this publisher, see Dosse (2014).

13   Once again, I want to thank Brian Boyd for showing me his notes on those letters which are now lost.

14   Véra did mention he would want to be paid in a letter to his literary agents on 9 July 1969, but he was then still with Gallimard and I did not find a mention of payment by Fayard in the existing archives.

15   Towards the end of 1973 (so before their collaboration on *Ada* started), Nabokov had been sent two sample translations for *Transparent Things*, and he had preferred that of Donald Harper to that of Blandenier: 'Donald Harper's version is incomparably better than Blandenier's which swarms with errors. So please let us have Harper' (letter from Nabokov to Schébéko, 7 January 1974, Cornell). However, Nabokov grew dissatisfied with Harper and, at some point, Blandenier came to help: the translation is credited to both Harper and Blandenier (Nabokov [1979b] 2020: 946).

16   See chapter 5 in my 2016 monograph.

17   'I shall be very grateful to you if you help me to weed out bad grammar but I do not think I would like my longish sentences clipped too close, or those drawbridges lowered which I have taken such pains to lift. In other words, I would like to discriminate between awkward construction (which is bad) and a certain special – how shall I put it – sinuosity, which is my own and which only at first glance may seem awkward or obscure' (letter to Katherine White, 10 November 1947, in Nabokov [1989] 1991: 77).

18   See my introduction to pseudotranslation.

Chapter 12

1   Nabokov evokes this translation in his autobiography: 'Then, in June again, when the fragrant *cheryomuha* (racemose old-world bird cherry or imply "racemosa" as I have baptized it in my work on "Onegin") was in foamy bloom, his private flag would be hoisted on his beautiful Rozhestveno house' (Nabokov [1966b] 1996: 416).

2   This strategy corresponds to what naturalists recommend: 'The translation from the Latin represents the most frequent method in botanic neology, even if the translation from another source language, for example English, also exists, especially in Northern America' (Grandtner and Beaulieu 2010: 561; my translation).

3   In this quote translated from the French (as explained in the previous chapter, such quotes are given in English and in italics), I added italics to the French words in order to clarify the discussion on translation choices. I do the same in other quotes to avoid too much ambiguity in these terminological explanations.

4   On Nabokov translating trees, see Boyd (2012: 17–19).

5   For the presence of French words in *Pnin* and their translation into French, see Stankovic (2013), and for a study of the translations into French and Serbian, see Stankovic (2014).

6   See Loison-Charles 2021 for an extensive study of the translation of multilingualism in *Ada* and Loison-Charles 2013 for an overview of the question in several novels.

7   On a few occasions, the right spelling was not respected in the final text. Thus, Nabokov had checked the following mistake in his corrections of 15 April 1975: he indicated that 's glazami' should be used instead of '5 glazami', but the published version reads 'sglazami' in one word.

8   On the translation of food, see Loison-Charles 2020b.

9   See https://www.cnrtl.fr/definition/couple. The *CNRTL* dictionary is comparable to the *OED* when French is concerned.

10   https://www.cnrtl.fr/definition/fashionable

11   About Nabokov and censorship, see Loison-Charles 2017.

Chapter 13

1   I want to thank my Master student Marie Bocquet for bringing this quote to my attention.

2   https://www.en-attendant-nadeau.fr/2021/11/10/dante-deuxieme-pleiade/ I want to thank Stanislas Gauthier for bringing this information to my attention.

Conclusion

1   See Bernard-Léger (2021) and Scheiner (2021) for studies on the figure of the translator (in *The Gift* and *Pale Fire* respectively), even if it is not in the framework of the 'fictional turn'.

2   I want to thank Isabelle Poulin for raising again this important question in a discussion we had with Marie Bouchet and Agnès Edel-Roy about a forthcoming Nabokov conference on the theme 'Education without borders'.

Bibliography

The Song of Igor's Campaign [1960], trans. V. Nabokov, New York: Vintage.

Alladaye, R. (2013), *The Darker Shades of Pale Fire: An Investigation into a Literary Mystery*, Paris: Michel Houdiard Editeur.

Allain-Roussel, M. (2021), 'Des ajouts dans les traductions françaises de *Lolita*', in J. Loison-Charles and S. Shvabrin (eds), *Vladimir Nabokov et la traduction*, 181–9, Arras: Artois Presses Université.

Ambrosiani, P. (2018), 'Translating Forms of Address in Nabokov's *Lolita*', in M. Mushchinina (ed.), *Formate der Translation*, 279–301, Berlin: Frank and Timme.

Anokhina, O. (2014), 'Traduction et réécriture chez Vladimir Nabokov: genèse d'une œuvre en trois langues', *Genesis*, 38: 111–27. Available online: http://journals. openedition.org/genesis/1306 (accessed 19 December 2021).

Anokhina, O. (2016), 'Vladimir Nabokov and His Translators: Collaboration or Translating under Duress?', in A. Cordingley and C. Frigau Manning (eds), *Collaborative Translation: from the Renaissance to the Digital Age*, 113–31, London: Bloomsbury.

Apter, E. (2006), 'Translation with No Original: Scandals of Textual Reproduction', in E. Apter, *The Translation Zone: A New Comparative Literature*, 210–25, Princeton: Princeton University Press.

Arber, S. (2018), 'Traduire "sous verre" ou "à la vitre": l'imaginaire de la transparence en traduction', *Itinéraires*, 2 and 3. Available online: http://journals.openedition.org/ itineraires/4625 (accessed 19 December 2021).

Babikov, A. (2006), 'On Germination of Nabokov's Main Theme in His Story "Natasha"', *Cycnos*, 24 (1). Available online: http://revel.unice.fr/cycnos/index.html?id=1062 (accessed 19 December 2021).

Bahous, A. (1990), 'The Novel and Moorish Culture: Cide Hamete "Author" of *Don Quixote*', PhD Dissertation, University of Essex, Essex.

Bahous, A. (2010), 'Don Quichotte: Cervantes et Cide Hamete', *Synergies Algérie*, 9: 239–46.

Barthes, R. (1968), 'L'effet de réel', *Communications*, 11: 84–9. Available online: https://www.persee.fr/doc/comm_0588-8018_1968_num_11_1_1158 (accessed 19 December 2021).

Bassnett, S. (2019), 'The Rocky Relationship between Translation Studies and World Literature', in S. Bassnett (ed.), *Translation and World Literature*, 1–14, London and New York: Routledge.

Beaujour, E. K. (1989), *Alien Tongues: Bilingual Russian Writers of the 'First' Emigration*, Ithaca: Cornell University Press.

Beaujour, E. K. (1995), 'Translation and Self-Translation', in V. E. Alexandrov (ed.), *The Garland Companion to Vladimir Nabokov*, 714–24, New York: Routledge.

Benjamin, W., ([1968] 2000]), 'The Task of the Translator', trans. H. Zohn, in L. Venuti (ed.), *The Translation Studies Reader*, 15–25, London and New York: Routledge.

Bensimon, P. (1990), 'Présentation', *Palimpsestes*, 4.

Berman, A. (1984), *L'Epreuve de l'étranger*, Paris: Gallimard.

Berman, A. (1985), 'Chateaubriand traducteur de Milton', in *Les tours de Babel: essais sur la traduction*, 109–25, Mauvezin: trans Europ Repress.

Berman, A. (1990), 'La retraduction comme espace de la traduction', *Palimpsestes*, 4.

Berman, A. (2000), 'Translation and the Trials of the Foreign', trans. L. Venuti, in L. Venuti (ed.), *The Translation Studies Reader*, 285–97, London and New York: Routledge.

Bernard-Léger, S. (2021), 'De Fiodor traducteur à traducteur traduit, ou les différents plans de traduction dans *The Gift*', in J. Loison-Charles and S. Shvabrin (eds), *Vladimir Nabokov et la traduction*, 243–53, Arras: Artois Presses Université.

Bethea, D. M. (2009), 'Of Pushkin and Pushkinists', in *The Superstitious Muse: Thinking Russian Literature Mythopoetically*, Boston: Academic Studies Press.

Blatt, B. (2017), *Nabokov's Favourite Word Is Mauve: The Literary Quirks and Oddities of our Most-Loved Authors*, London: Simon and Schuster.

Bliss, A. (1966), *A Dictionary of Foreign Words and Phrases in Current English*, London and New York: Routledge.

Bocquet, C. A. (2019), 'Les pseudo-traducteurs et leurs motivations', in L. D'hulst, M. Mariaule and C. Wecksteen-Quinio (eds), *Au Coeur de la Traductologie: Hommage à Michel Ballard*, 261–86, Arras: Artois Presses Université.

Boswell, J. ([1775] 1859), *Journal of a Tour to the Hebrides with Samuel Johnson, LL.D.*, London: Routledge, Warnes and Routledge.

Bourdin, P. (2011), 'Le brigand caché derrière les tréteaux de la révolution. Traductions et trahisons d'auteurs', *Annales historiques de la Révolution française*, 364: 51–84.

Boyd, B. (1990), *Vladimir Nabokov: The Russian Years*, Princeton: Princeton University Press.

Boyd, B. (1991), *Vladimir Nabokov: The American Years*, Princeton: Princeton University Press.

Boyd, B. (2012), 'Nabokov as Translator: Passion and Precision', *RUS (São Paulo)*, 1 (1): 5–24.

Bozovic, M. (2016), *Nabokov's Canon: From Onegin to Ada*, Illinois: Northwestern University Press.

Branch, A. (2013), 'La traduction fictive en tant qu'élément érotique dans le roman *Elles se rendent pas compte* de Boris Vian', in P. P. Boulanger (ed.), *Traduire le texte érotique*, 57–71, Montreal: UQAM. Available online: http://oic.uqam.ca/fr/publications/traduire-le-texte-erotique (accessed 19 December 2021).

Bristow, J. and R. N. Mitchell (2015), *Oscar Wilde's Chatterton: Literary History, Romanticism, and the Art of Forgery*, New Haven and London: Yale University Press.

Brown, E. J. (1965), 'Nabokov and Pushkin (with Comments on New Translations of Eugene Onegin), '*Slavic Review*, 24: 688–701.

Burgess, A. (1965), 'Pushkin & Kinbote', *Encounter*, 24 (5): 74–8.

Cadot, M. (1995), 'Pouchkine poéticien et comparatiste', in *Romantisme*, 89: 45–58. Available online: https://www.persee.fr/doc/roman_0048-8593_1995_num_25_89_3009 (accessed 19 December 2021).

Cancogni, A. (1983), '"My Sister, Do You Still Recall?": Chateaubriand/Nabokov', *Comparative Literature*, 35: 140–66.

Cancogni, A. (1995), 'Nabokov and Chateaubriand', in V. E. Alexandrov (ed.), *The Garland Companion to Vladimir Nabokov*, 382–8, New York: Routledge.

Casanova, P. (2004), *The World Republic of Letters*, trans. M. B. Debevoise, Cambridge (Mass.) and London: Harvard University Press.

Castagnès, G. (2013), '"L'Anglais mangeur d'opium. Traduit de l'anglais par A. D. M.": de la traduction à la création, l'acte de naissance d'Alfred de Musset', in S. Ledda, F. Lestringant and G. Séginger (eds), *Poétiques de Musset*, 81–91, Mont-Saint-Aignan: Presses universitaires de Rouen et du Havre.

Cervantes, M. de (1949), *The Ingenious Gentleman Don Quixote de La Mancha*, II, trans. S. Putnam, New York: The Modern Library.

Cervantes, M. de (2000), *The Ingenious Hidalgo Don Quixote de La Mancha*, trans. J. Rutherford, London: Penguin Classics.

Chadelat, J. M. (1999), *Valeurs et fonctions des emprunts français en anglais à l'époque contemporaine*, Villeneuve d'Ascq: Presses Universitaires du Septentrion.

Chateaubriand, F. R. de (1836a), 'Avertissement', in J. Milton, *Essai sur la littérature anglaise et considérations sur le génie des hommes, des temps et des révolutions*, trans. F. R. de Chateaubriand, 3–18, Paris: Furne et Charles Gosselin Editeurs. Available online: https://gallica.bnf.fr/ark:/12148/bpt6k65347479/f16.item.texteImage (accessed 19 December 2021).

Chateaubriand, F. R. de ([1836b] 1861), 'Remarques', in J. Milton, *Le Paradis Perdu de Milton*, trans. F. R. de Chateaubriand, i–xv, Paris: Renault et Cie, Libraires-éditeurs. Available online: https://gallica.bnf.fr/ark:/12148/bpt6k5452523p.texteImage (accessed 19 December 2021).

Chauvin, S. (2018), 'Le traducteur, auteur sans œuvre ou auteur sans style?', in C. Berthin, L. Sansonetti and E. Eells (eds), *Auteurs-Traducteurs: l'entre-deux de l'écriture*, 27–37, Nanterre: Presses Universitaires de Paris Nanterre.

Chovich, B. L. Chovich, N. Nesterova, S. Stankovic and M. Loncar Vujnovic (2014), *Двојезичност аутобиографске прозе В. Набокова: нови 'преводни жанр' и/или 'међујезичке игре' / Bilinguism of the Autobiographical Prose of V. Nabokov: A New 'Translation Genre' and/or 'Interlingual Plays'*, Mitrovica: Kovovska Mitrovitsa.

Chupin, Y. (2017), 'Review: Marijeta Bozovic, *Nabokov's Canon, from "Onegin" to "Ada"*', *Studies in Russian Literature and Theory*, 95 (4): 740–2.

Clayton, J. D. (1983), 'The Theory and Practice of Poetic Translation in Pushkin and Nabokov', *Canadian Slavonic Papers*, 25 (1): 90–100.

Coadou, B. (2018), 'Quand Cervantès se mesure à Héliodore: traduction(s), pseudo-traduction et création', in C. Berthin, L. Sansonetti and E. Eells (eds), *Auteurs-Traducteurs: l'entre-deux de l'écriture*, 237–52, Nanterre: Presses Universitaires de Paris Nanterre.

Coates, J. (1999), 'Changing Horses: Nabokov and Translation', in J. Boase-Beier and M. Holman (eds), *The Practices of Literary Translation*, 91–108, London and New York: Routledge.

Cobelo, S. (2007), 'Pseudotradução e Dom Quixote', *Fragmentos*, 33: 63–9.

Coindreau, M. E. ([1974] 2002), *Mémoires d'un traducteur: Entretiens avec Christian Giudicelli*, Paris: Gallimard.

Collombat, I. (2003), 'Pseudo-traduction: la mise en scène de l'altérité', *Le Langage et l'Homme*, 38 (1): 145–56.

Connolly, J. W. (2021), 'Nabokov's Translations of Lermontov's Poetry: "The Demon Tamed"', in J. Loison-Charles and S. Shvabrin (eds), *Vladimir Nabokov et la traduction*, 99–109, Arras: Artois Presses Université.

Conquest, R. (1965), 'Nabokov's *Eugene Onegin*', *Poetry*, 106 (3): 236–38.

Cordingley, A. and C. Montini (2015), 'Genetic Translation Studies: An Emerging Discipline', *Linguistica Antverpiensia, New Series: Themes in Translation Studies*, 14: 1–18.

Cordingley, A. and C. Frigau Manning (2016), 'What Is Collaborative Translation?' in A. Cordingley and C. Frigau Manning (eds), *Collaborative Translation: from the Renaissance to the Digital Age*, 1–30, London: Bloomsbury.

Courtivron, I. de ed. (2003), *Lives in Translation: Bilingual Writers on Identity and Creativity*, New York: Palgrave MacMillan.

Couturier, M. (2000), 'Traduire *Lolita*', *Revue des études slaves*, 72 (3–4): 521–9. Available online: http://www.persee.fr/doc/slave_0080-2557_2000_num_72_3_6683 (accessed 19 December 2021).

Curley, T. M. (2009), 'The Great Samuel Johnson and His Opposition to Literary Liars', *Bridgewater Review*, 28 (2): 7–10.

Davydov, S. (1995), 'Nabokov and Pushkin', in V. E. Alexandrov (ed.), *The Garland Companion to Vladimir Nabokov*, 482–96, New York: Routledge.

Davison, C. (2014), *Translation as Collaboration: Virginia Woolf, Katherine Mansfield and S. S. Koteliansky*, Edinburgh: Edinburgh University Press.

De la Durantaye, L. (2013), 'Review of Vladimir Nabokov and the Play of Art by Karshan, Thomas', *The Slavonic and East European Review*, 91 (3): 599–604.

Delabastita, D. and R. Grutman (2005), 'Introduction. Fictional Representations of Multilingualism and Translation', *Linguistica Antverpiensia, New Series: Themes in Translation Studies*, 4: 11–34.

Deleuze, G. and F. Guattari (1975), *Kafka: pour une littérature mineure*, Paris: Éditions de Minuit.

Deleuze G. and Guattari F. (1983), 'What Is a Minor Literature?', trans. R. Brinkley, *Mississippi Review*, 11 (3): 13–33.

Deleuze, G. (1997), *Essays Critical and Clinical*, trans. D. W. Smith and M. A. Greco, Minneapolis: University of Minnesota Press.

Deroy, L. (1956), *L'Emprunt linguistique*, Paris: Les Belles Lettres. Available online: https://books.openedition.org/pulg/665?lang=fr (accessed 19 December 2021).

DiLeonardi, S. (2021), 'Nabokov and the Mathematics of Language', in J. Loison-Charles and S. Shvabrin (eds), *Vladimir Nabokov et la traduction*, 265–74, Arras: Artois Presses Université.

Dolinin, A. (1995), '*Eugene Onegin*', in V. E. Alexandrov (ed.), *The Garland Companion to Vladimir Nabokov*, 117–30, New York and London: Routledge.

Dolinin, A. (2007), 'Об одном источнике стихотворения "Из Пиндемонти"' (Ob odnom istochnike stihotvorenia 'Iz Pindemonti'], in *Pushkin i Angliya: tsikl statey*, 226–36, Moscow: Novoe literaturnoie obozrenie.

Dosse, F. (2014), 'Charles Orengo. L'homme mystérieux', in F. Dosse (ed.), *Les hommes de l'ombre. Portraits d'éditeurs*, 305–24, Paris: Perrin.

Durkin, P. (2014), *Borrowed Words. A History of Loanwords in English*, Oxford: Oxford University Press.

Edel-Roy, A. (2017), 'Lolita, le livre "impossible"?', *Miranda*, 15. Available online: https://journals.openedition.org/miranda/11265?lang=fr (accessed 19 December 2021).

Edel-Roy, A. (2018), 'Une "démocratie magique": politique et littérature dans les romans de V. Nabokov', PhD Dissertation, Université de Paris Est Créteil, Paris.

Eells, E. (2018), 'Du côté de Lydia Davis: entre traduire et écrire', in C. Berthin, L. Sansonetti and E. Eells (eds), *Auteurs-Traducteurs: l'entre-deux de l'écriture*, 115–32, Nanterre: Presses Universitaires de Paris Nanterre.

Frank, S. (2012), *Nabokov's Theatrical Imagination*, Cambridge and New York: Cambridge University Press.

Frantz, P. (2008), 'Le crime devant le tribunal du théâtre: Les *Brigands* de Schiller et leur fortune sur la scène française', *Littératures classiques*, 67 (3): 219–30.

Diment, G. (1995), 'Plays', in V. E. Alexandrov (ed.), *The Garland Companion to Vladimir Nabokov*, 586–97, New York: Routledge.

Gaskill, H. (2013), 'Introduction: The Translator's Ossian', *Translation and Literature*, 22 (3): 293–301.

Gauthier, S. (2017), *Cosmopolitisme et guerre froide. Aragon, Landolfi, Nabokov, traducteurs de Pouchkine*, Paris: Hermann.

Gerschenkron, A. (1966), 'A Manufactured Monument?', *Modern Philology*, 63: 336–47.

Gogol, N. (2013), 'On *the Odyssey* as translated by Zhukovskii', trans. B. J. Baer, in B. J. Baer and N. Olshanskaya (eds), *Russian Writers on Translation: An Anthology*, 29–30, London and New York: Routledge.

Goldblatt, H. (1995), 'The Song of Igor's Campaign', in V. E. Alexandrov (ed.), *The Garland Companion to Vladimir Nabokov*, 661–72, New York: Routledge.

Goldblatt, H. and R. Picchio (2006), 'Old Approaches and New Perspectives: Once Again on the Religious Significance of the "Slovo o polku Igoreve"', *Harvard Ukrainian Studes*, 28 (¼): 129–54.

Grandtner, M. M. and M. A. Beaulieu (2010), 'Quelques principes de normalisation des noms botaniques français: les arbres d'Amérique du Nord', *Meta*, 55 (3): 558–68.

Grant, P. B. (2021), 'Howlers, Humour, Hubris: Translation and Truth in Nabokov's Onegin', in J. Loison-Charles and S. Shvabrin (eds), *Vladimir Nabokov et la traduction*, 59–71, Arras: Artois Presses Université.

Gray, E. (2001), 'Forgetting FitzGerald's *Rubáiyát*', *Studies in English Literature, 1500–1900*, 41 (4): 765–83.

Grayson, J. (1977), *Nabokov Translated: a Comparison of Nabokov's Russian and English Prose*, Oxford: Oxford University Press.

Gregg, R. A. (1965), 'Pushkin and Shenstone: The Case Reopened', *Comparative Literature*, 17 (2): 109–16.

Gresset, M. (2002), 'Maurice Edgar Coindreau, traducteur ou "passeur"?', in P. Carmignani (ed.), *Figures du passeur*, 385–92, Perpignan: Presses universitaires de Perpignan. Available online: http://books.openedition.org/pupvd/129 (accessed 19 December 2021).

Grugeau, G. (1993), 'Entretien avec Éric Kahane – Profession: adaptateur', *24 images*, 65: 26–30. Available online: https://www.erudit.org/fr/revues/images/1993-n65-images1078494/22674ac.pdf (accessed 19 December 2021).

Haugen, K. L. (1998), 'Ossian and the Invention of Textual History', *Journal of the History of Idea*, 59 (2): 309–27.

Hersant, P. (2016), 'Author-Translator Collaborations: A Typological Survey', trans. N. Manning, in A. Cordingley and C. Frigau Manning (eds), *Collaborative Translation: From the Renaissance to the Digital Age*, 91–110, London: Bloomsbury.

Hersant, P. (2019), 'La troisième main: réviser la traduction littéraire', in E. Hartmann and P. Hersant (eds), *Au miroir de la traduction*, 45–70, Paris: Archives contemporaines.

Hoisington, S. S. (1981), 'Pushkin's Belkin and the Mystifications of Walter Scott', *Comparative Literature*, 33 (4): 342–57.

Jakobson, R. ([1959] 2000), 'On Linguistic Aspects of Translation', in L. Venuti (ed.), *The Translation Studies Reader*, 113–18, London and New York: Routledge.

Jenn, R. (2013), *La Pseudo-traduction, de Cervantès à Mark Twain*, Louvain-la-Neuve: Peeters.

Johnson, D. B. (n.d.), 'Nabokov's *Ada* and Pierre Louÿs' *Chansons de Bilitis*: The Tree of Knowledge' (electronically circulated manuscript quoted in Shvabrin 2019: 350).

Kearney, M. (1888), 'Biographical Preface', in O. Khayyam, *Rubáiyát of Omar Khayyám in English Verse*, trans. E. FitzGerald, 7–24, New York and Boston: Houghton, Mifflin and Company. Available online: https://archive.org/details/rubiytomarkhayy00keargoog/page/n22/mode/2up (accessed 19 December 2021).

Koçak, M. I. (2015), 'Pseudotranslations of Pseudo-Scientific Sex Manuals in Turkey', in Ş. T. Gürçağlar, S. Paker and J. Milton (eds), *Tradition, Tension and Translation in Turkey*, 199–218, Amsterdam and Philadelphia: John Benjamins.

Krabbenhoft, K. (2016), '*Don Quixote* and *Lolita*', *Atlantis*, 18 (1–2): 213–27.

La Martelière, Jean-Henri-Ferdinand ([1792] 1793), *Robert Chef de brigands, Drame en cinq actes, en prose, imité de l'allemand*, Paris: Maradan. Available online: https://gallica.bnf.fr/ark:/12148/bpt6k48292r.image (accessed 19 December 2021).

Lazzaro, F. (2014), 'Bilitis après Debussy. Hommage, influence, prise de distance ?', *Revue musicale OICRM*, 2 (1): 159–90. Available online: https://doi.org/10.7202/1055851ar (accessed 19 December 2021).

Lecercle, J. J. (1990), *The Violence of Language*, London: Routledge.

Ledda, S. (2013), 'Stratégies de la pseudo-traduction: Mérimée et Musset', *Les Lettres Romanes*, 67 (3–4): 417–30.

Lejeune, Ph. ([1975] 1996), *Le pacte autobiographique*, Paris: Éditions du Seuil.

Lermontov, M. (1958), *A Hero of Our Time: A Novel*, trans. V. Nabokov and D. Nabokov, New York: Doubleday Anchor Books.

Lievois, K. (2014), 'Suppositions de Traducteurs: les Pseudo-Traductions d'Andreï Makine', *TTR*, 27 (2): 149–70.

Loison-Charles, J. (2013), 'Traduire le multilinguisme de Nabokov', in E. Eells, C. Berthin and J. M. Déprats (eds), *L'étranger dans la langue*, 251–67, Nanterre: Presses Universitaires de Paris Nanterre.

Loison-Charles, J. (2014), 'Les Mots étrangers de Vladimir Nabokov', PhD Dissertation, Université Paris Ouest Nanterre, Nanterre. Available online: https://bdr.parisnanterre.fr/theses/internet/2014PA100051.pdf (accessed 19 December 2021).

Loison-Charles, J. (2016), *Vladimir Nabokov ou l'écriture du multilinguisme: mots étrangers et jeux de mots*, Nanterre: Presses Universitaires de Paris Nanterre.

Loison-Charles, J. (2017), 'Nabokov et la censure', *Miranda*, 15. Available online: https://journals.openedition.org/miranda/11223 (accessed 19 December 2021).

Loison-Charles, J. (2020a), 'Multilinguisme, psycholinguistique et écriture chez l'écrivain Vladimir Nabokov', *Silène*: 155–69.

Loison-Charles, J. (2020b), 'Translating Taste and Switching Tongues', in M. Bouchet, J. Loison-Charles and I. Poulin (eds), *The Five Senses in Nabokov's Works*, 139–56, New York: Palgrave.

Loison-Charles, J. (2021), 'Traduire les mots étrangers dans *Ada*: un cas d'étude sur le chapitre 38', in J. Loison-Charles and S. Shvabrin (eds), *Vladimir Nabokov et la traduction*, 125–38, Arras: Artois Presses Université.

Loison-Charles, J. (2022), *Traduction audiovisuelle et multilinguisme: le français dans les séries anglophones*, Arras: Artois Presses Université.

Loison-Charles, J. and S. Shvabrin, eds (2021), *Vladimir Nabokov et la traduction*, Arras: Artois Presses Université.

Lokrantz, J. (1973), 'The Underside of the Weave: Some Stylistic Devices Used by V. Nabokov', PhD Dissertation, Uppsala University, Uppsala.

Lopoukhine, J. (2018), 'Jean Rhys traductrice: positions ex-centriques', in C. Berthin, L. Sansonetti and E. Eells (eds), *Auteurs-Traducteurs: l'entre-deux de l'écriture*, 149–64, Nanterre: Presses Universitaires de Paris Nanterre.

Louÿs, P. ([1894] 1898), *Les Chansons de Bilitis: Roman lyrique*, Paris: Mercure de France.

Maher, B. (2013), 'A Crook's Tour: Translation, Pseudotranslation and Foreignness in Anglo-Italian Crime Fiction', in B. Nelson and B. Maher (eds), *Perspectives on Literature and Translation: Creation, Circulation, Reception*, 157–70, New York and London: Routledge.

Maine, G. ([1953] 1995), 'Edward FitzGerald', in G. Maine (ed.), *Rubáiyát of Omar Khayyám Rendered into English Verse by Edward FitzGerald*, 5–26, Tehran: Nahid Publishing House.

Mennie, D. M. (1938), 'Sir Walter Scott's Unpublished Translations of German Plays', *The Modern Language Review*, 33 (2): 234–9.

Meyer, P. (1988a), *Find What the Sailor Has Hidden: Vladimir Nabokov's Pale Fire*, Middletown, Conn.: Wesleyan University Press.

Meyer, P. (1988b), 'Igor, Ossian and Kinbote: Nabokov's Non-Fiction as Library', *Slavic Review*, 47 (1): 68–75.

Meyers, J. (1994), 'The Bulldog and the Butterfly: The Friendship of Edmund Wilson and Vladimir Nabokov', *The American Scholar*, 63 (3): 379–99.

Milton, J. (2021), *Paradise Lost (1674) / Le Paradis perdu (1836)*, trans. F. R. de Chateaubriand, bilingual edition, introduction and notes by Christophe Tournu, 2 vols, Paris: Honoré Champion.

Mingant, N. (2010), 'Tarantino's *Inglourious Basterds*: A Blueprint for Dubbing Translators?', *Meta*, 55 (4): 712–31. Available online: https://www.erudit.org/en/journals/meta/2010-v55-n4-meta4003/045687ar/ (accessed 19 December 2021).

Monti, E. and P. Schnyder eds (2018), *Traduire à plusieurs: Collaborative Translation*, Paris: Orizons.

Montini, C. (2020), 'The Strange Case of the Nabokovs' The Enchanter', *Palimpsestes*, 34 (1): 15–28.

Montini C. (2021), '"Mon livre": Dmitri Nabokov, *The Enchanter* et L'Incantatore', in J. Loison-Charles and S. Shvabrin (eds), *Vladimir Nabokov et la traduction*, 139–51, Arras: Artois Presses Université.

Mounin, G. ([1955] 1994), *Les Belles infidèles*, Villeneuve d'Ascq: Presses universitaires du Septentrion.

Nabokoff-Sirine, V. (1936), 'Mademoiselle O', *Mesures*, 2: 147–72.

Nabokov, V. ([1923] 1999), Скитальцы [*Skital'tsy*], in *Sobranie sochineniy*, 10 vols, I, 647–73, St Petersburg: Simpozium.

Nabokov, V. (1931), 'Из Калмбрудовой поэмы "Ночное путешествие"' [Iz Kalmbrudovoi poemy 'Nochnoe puteshestvie'], *Rul'*, 3223: 2.

Nabokov, V. ([1934] 1990), Отчаяние [*Otchayanie*], in V. Nabokov, *Sobranie sochineniy v chetyrex tomax*, ed. V. Erofeev, 4 vols, III, 331–462, Moscow: Pravda.

Nabokov, V. ([1938] 1990), Приглашение на казнь [*Priglashenie na kazn'*], in V. Nabokov, *Sobranie sochineniy v chetyrex tomax*, ed. V. Erofeev, 4 vols, IV, 3–130, Moscow: Pravda.

Nabokov, V. ([1937–1938] 1990), *Дар* [*Dar*], in V. Nabokov, *Sobranie sochineniy v chetyrex tomax*, ed. V. Erofeev, 4 vols, III, 3–330, Moscow: Pravda.

Nabokov, V. ([1941a] 2008), 'The Art of Translation', in V. Nabokov, *Verses and Versions: Three Centuries of Russian Poetry*, eds B. Boyd and S. Shvabrin, 2–11; 14–15, Orlando: Harcourt.

Nabokov, V. ([1941b] 1996), '*The Real Life of Sebastian Knight*', in V. Nabokov, *Novels and Memoirs, 1941–1951*, ed. B. Boyd, 1–160, New York: Library of America.

Nabokov, V. ([1947] 1996), '*Bend Sinister*', in V. Nabokov, *Novels and Memoirs, 1941–1951*, ed. B. Boyd, 161–358, New York: Library of America.

Nabokov, V. ([1955a] 1996), *Lolita*, in V. Nabokov, *Novels, 1955–1962*, ed. B. Boyd, 1–298, New York: Library of America.

Nabokov, V. ([1955b] 2000), 'Problems of Translation: "Onegin" in English', in L. Venuti (ed.), *The Translation Studies Reader*, 71–83, London and New York: Routledge.

Nabokov, V. ([1957a] 1996), '*Pnin*', in V. Nabokov, *Novels, 1955–1962*, ed. B. Boyd, 299–435, New York: Library of America.

Nabokov, V. (1957b), 'Заметки переводчика' [Zametki perevodchika], *Новый Журнал*, XLIX, 130–44.

Nabokov, V. (1957c), 'Заметки переводчика II' [Zametki perevodchika II], *Опыты*, 8, 36–49.

Nabokov, V. (1959a), *Lolita*, trans. E. H. Kahane, Paris: Gallimard.

Nabokov, V. (1959b), 'The Servile Path', in R. Brower (ed.) *On Translation*, 97–110, Cambridge: Harvard University Press.

Nabokov, V. ([1960] 2010), *Invitation to a Beheading*, trans. (from the Russian) D. Nabokov in collaboration with V. Nabokov, London: Penguin Classics.

Nabokov, V. ([1962] 1996), '*Pale Fire*', in V. Nabokov, *Novels, 1955–1962*, ed. B. Boyd, 437–667, New York: Library of America.

Nabokov, V. ([1963a] 1991), 'Foreword', in A. Pushkin, *Eugene Onegin: A Novel in Verse*, vii–xii.

Nabokov, V. ([1963b] 2001), *The Gift*, trans. (from the Russian) M. Scammell and D. Nabokov in collaboration with V. Nabokov, London: Penguin Classics.

Nabokov, V. ([1964a] 1990), 'Pounding the Clavichord', in V. Nabokov, *Strong Opinions*, 231–40, New York: Vintage.

Nabokov, V. ([1964b] 1991), 'Translator's Introduction', in A. Pushkin, *Eugene Onegin: A Novel in Verse*, trans. V. Nabokov, 2 vols, 1–88, Princeton: Princeton University Press.

Nabokov, V. ([1965a] 2010), *Despair*, trans. (from the Russian) V. Nabokov, London: Penguin Classics.

Nabokov, V. ([1965b] 2020), '*Feu pâle*', trans. M. E. Coindreau and R. Girard, in V. Nabokov, *Œuvres romanesques complètes*, 3 vols, III, 153–401, Paris: Gallimard.

Nabokov, V. ([1966a] 1990), 'A Reply to My Critics', in V. Nabokov, *Strong Opinions*, 241–67, New York: Vintage.

Nabokov, V. ([1966b] 1996), '*Speak, Memory: An Autobiography Revisited*', in V. Nabokov, *Novels and Memoirs, 1941–1951*, ed. B. Boyd, 359–635, New York: Library of America.

Nabokov, V. ([1967] 2004), *Лолита* [*Lolita*], Moscow: Ast.

Nabokov, V. ([1969] 1996), *Ada or Ardor: A Family Chronicle*, in V. Nabokov, *Novels, 1969–1974*, ed. Brian Boyd, 1–485, New York: Library of America.

Nabokov, V. ([1971] 2006), '*Glory*', trans. (from the Russian) D. Nabokov in collaboration with V. Nabokov, London: Penguin Modern Classics.

Nabokov, V. ([1972] 1991), '"EO" Revisited', in A. Pushkin, *Eugene Onegin: A Novel in Verse*, trans. V. Nabokov, 2 vols, xiii–xiv, Princeton: Princeton University Press.

Nabokov, V. ([1973] 1990), *Strong Opinions*, New York: Vintage.

Nabokov, V. ([1974] 1996), '*Look at the Harlequins!*', in V. Nabokov, *Novels, 1969–1974*, ed. Brian Boyd, 563–747, New York: Library of America.

Nabokov, V. (1975), *Ada ou l'Ardeur*, trans. G. Chahine with the collaboration of J. B. Blandenier, revised by V. Nabokov, Paris: Fayard.

Nabokov, V. ([1977] 2000), 'Bachmann', trans. (from the English) G.H. Durand, in V. Nabokov, *Nouvelles Complètes*, 217–26, Paris: Gallimard.

Nabokov, V. (1979a), *The Nabokov-Wilson Letters: Correspondence between Vladimir Nabokov and Edmund Wilson, 1940–1971*, ed. S. Karlinsky, London: Weidenfeld and Nicolson.

Nabokov, V. ([1979b] 2020), '*La Transparence des choses*', trans. D. Harper and J. B. Blandenier, in V. Nabokov, *Œuvres romanesques complètes*, 3 vols, III, 945–1027, Paris: Gallimard.

Nabokov, V. (1983), *Lectures on Don Quixote*, ed. F. Bowers, San Diego, New York and London: Bruccoli Clark.

Nabokov, V. ([1989] 1991), *Selected Letters, 1940–1977*, ed. D. Nabokov and M. J. Bruccoli, Londres: Vintage.

Nabokov, V. (1990), *Sobranie sochineniy v chetyrex tomax*, ed. V. Erofeev, 4 vols, Moscow: Pravda.

Nabokov, V. (1996a), *Novels and Memoirs, 1941–1951*, ed. B. Boyd, New York: Library of America.

Nabokov, V. (1996b), *Novels, 1955–1962*, ed. B. Boyd, New York: Library of America.

Nabokov, V. (1996c), *Novels, 1969–1974*, ed. Brian Boyd, New York: Library of America.

Nabokov, V. (1999), *Œuvres romanesques complètes*, ed. M. Couturier, I, Paris: Gallimard.

Nabokov, V. (2001), *Lolita*, trans. M. Couturier, Paris: Gallimard.

Nabokov, V. (2008a), *Verses and Versions: Three Centuries of Russian Poetry*, ed. B. Boyd and S. Shvabrin, Orlando: Harcourt.

Nabokov, V. (2008b), *Трагедия господина Морна. Пьесы. Лекции о драме* [*Tragedija gospodina Morna. P'esy. Lektsii o drame*], Saint Petersburg: Azbuka-Klassika.

Nabokov, V. (2010), *Œuvres romanesques complètes*, ed. M. Couturier, II, Paris: Gallimard.

Nabokov, V. (2012), *The Tragedy of Mister Morn*, trans. A. Tolstoy and T. Karshan, London: Penguin Books.

Nabokov, V. (2014), *Letters to Véra*, ed. and trans. B. Boyd and O. Voronina, London: Penguin Classics.

Nabokov, V. (2019), *Think, Write, Speak. Uncollected Essays, Reviews, Interviews, and Letters to the Editor*, ed. and trans. B. Boyd and A. Tolstoy, New York: Vintage.

Nabokov, V. (2020), *Œuvres romanesques complètes*, ed. M. Couturier, III, Paris: Gallimard.

New, K. (2020), 'Pushkin's Mystification: Tatiana's Letter, a Translation from French?', *The New Collection*, 14: 39–60.

Nien-Ming Ch'ien, E. (2004), *Weird English*, Cambridge (Mass.) and London: Harvard University Press.

Nott, M. (2016), 'Photopoetry and the Problem of Translation in FitzGerald's *Rubáiyát*', *Victorian Studies*, 58 (4): 661–95.

Ober, K. H. and W. U. Ober (2004), 'Pushkin and Southey: Russia's Greatest Poet Translates England's Poet Laureate', *Russian Literature*, 55: 529–547.

O'Sullivan, C. (2005), 'Translation, Pseudotranslation and Paratext: The Presentation of Contemporary Crime Fiction Set in Italy', *EnterText*, 4 (3): 62–76.

O'Sullivan, C. (2011), 'Pseudotranslation', in Y. Gambier and L. van Doorslaer (eds), *Handbook of Translation Studies*, 2, 123–5, Amsterdam and Philadelphia: John Benjamins.

Olson, R. (2013), *Arras Hangings: The Textile That Determined Early Modern Literature and Drama*, Newark: University of Delaware Press.

Orsenna, E. (1997), *Deux étés*, Paris: Fayard.

Oustinoff, M. (2001), *Bilinguisme d'écriture et auto-traduction: Julien Green, Samuel Beckett, Vladimir Nabokov*, Paris: L'Harmattan.

Oustinoff, M. (2004), 'Les *Lolita* de Vladimir Nabokov: traductions ou adaptations?' *Palimpsestes*, 16: 117–35.

Pavlenko, A. (1998), 'Second Language Learning by Adults: Testimonies of Bilingual Writers', *Issues in Applied Linguistics*, 1: 3–19.

Pavlenko, A. (2014), *The Bilingual Mind, and What It Tells Us about Language and Thought*, Cambridge: Cambridge University Press.

Poulin, I. (2005a), 'Chateaubriand et le Nouveau Monde', in I. Poulin, *Vladimir Nabokov, lecteur de l'autre: incitations*, 93–110, Pessac: Presses universitaires de Bordeaux.

Poulin, I. (2005b), 'La *nega* gallique de Pouchkine', in I. Poulin, *Vladimir Nabokov, lecteur de l'autre: incitations*, 131–47, Pessac: Presses universitaires de Bordeaux.

Poulin, I. (2017), *Le Transport romanesque: Le roman comme espace de la traduction, de Nabokov à Rabelais*, Paris: Classiques Garnier.

Poulin, I. (2021), 'La ligne traductive de Vladimir Nabokov: Une pensée de la trace', in J. Loison-Charles and S. Shvabrin (eds), *Vladimir Nabokov et la traduction*, 45–6, Arras: Artois Presses Université.

Proffer, C. R. (1968), 'Pushkin and Parricide: "*The Miserly Knight*"', *American Imago*, 25 (4): 347–53.

Pushkin, A. ([1833] 2003), *Евгений Онегин* [*Evgenij Onegin*], Moscow: Eksmo.

Pushkin, A. ([1944] 2008), 'From *Скупой* Рыцарь / A Scene from *The Covetous Knight*', trans. V. Nabokov, in V. Nabokov, *Verses and Versions: Three Centuries of Russian Poetry*, eds B. Boyd and S. Shvabrin, 144–51, Orlando: Harcourt.

Pushkin, A. (1964), *Eugene Onegin: A Novel in Verse*, trans. V. Nabokov, 4 vols, New York: Bollingen.

Pushkin, A. ([1975] 1991), *Eugene Onegin: A Novel in Verse*, trans. V. Nabokov, 2 vols, Princeton: Princeton University Press.

Pushkin, A. (2000), *'The Little Tragedies'*, trans. N. Anderson, Yale: University Press.

Pushkin, A. (2013), 'On Milton and Chateaubriand's Translation of *Paradise Lost*', trans. N. Olshanskaya, in B. J. Baer and N. Olshanskaya (eds), *Russian Writers on Translation: An Anthology*, 26–7, London and New York: Routledge.

Pushkin, A., Lermontov, M. and Tyutchev F. (1944), *Three Russian Poets: Selections from Pushkin, Lermontov and Tyutchev*, trans. V. Nabokov, Norfolk, Conn.: New Directions.

Raguet, C., Mahdavi Z. and Nakhaei B. (2015), 'Le Rythme et la Rime dans les Robâïât de FitzGerald: Traduction ou Création Littéraire', *Revue des études de la langue française*, 7: 26–36. Available online: https://hal.archives-ouvertes.fr/halshs-01396025 (accessed 19 December 2021).

Rath, B. (2014), 'Pseudotranslation', *ACLA Report on the State of the Discipline*. Available online: https://stateofthediscipline.acla.org/entry/pseudotranslation (accessed 19 December 2021).

Rigeade, A. L. (2007), 'Vers une pensée du texte traduit: une lecture de *Pnine* et *Feu pâle* et d'un extrait des deux traductions françaises de *Ulysses*', *Palimpsestes*, 20: 177–200.

Robinson, D. (2000), 'Pseudotranslation', in M. Baker, G. Saldanha and K. Malmkjær (eds), *The Routledge Encyclopedia of Translation Studies*, London and New York: Routledge.

Sakhno, S. (2001), *Dictionnaire russe-français d'étymologie comparée: correspondances lexicales historiques*, Paris: L'Harmattan.

Sandler, E. M. (2010), 'Review: Thomas M. Curley, *Samuel Johnson, the Ossian Fraud, and the Celtic Revival in Great Britain and Ireland*', *Eighteenth-Century Studies*, 44 (1): 142–43.

Sandler, S. (1983), 'The Poetics of Authority in Pushkin's "André Chénier"', *Slavic Review*, 42 (2): 187–203.

Schmidt, A. (1902), *Shakespeare Lexicon and Quotation Dictionary*. Available online: http://www.perseus.tufts.edu/hopper/text?doc=Perseus%3Atext%3A1999.03.0079 (accessed 19 December 2021).

Schleiermacher, F. (2000), 'On the Different Methods of Translating', trans. S. Bernofsky, in L. Venuti (ed.), *The Translation Studies Reader*, 43–63, London and New York: Routledge.

Schuman, S. (1995), 'Nabokov and Shakespeare: The Russian Works', in V. E. Alexandrov (ed.), *The Garland Companion to Vladimir Nabokov*, 512–17, New York: Routledge.

Shafiei, S. (2012), 'FitzGerald or FitzOmar: Ideological Reconsideration of the English Translation of Khayyam's Rubaiyat', *English Language and Literature Studies*, 2 (1): 128–41.

Shakespeare, W. ([1623] 1988), '*As You Like It*', in S. Wells and G. Taylor (eds), W. Shakespeare, *The Complete Works*, 627–52, Oxford and New York: Oxford University Press.

Shaw, J. T. (1965), 'Translations of "Onegin"', *Russian Review*, 24 (2): 111–27.

Shaw, J. T. (1974), 'Review of "Pushkin Threefold: Narrative, Lyric, Polemic and Ribald Verse by Walter Arndt"', *The Slavic and East European Journal*, 18 (3): 313–14.

Scheiner, C. (2021), 'Brutal Betrayers and Their Evil Translations: The Willful Reshapings of Kinbote and Conmal', in J. Loison-Charles and S. Shvabrin (eds), *Vladimir Nabokov et la traduction*, 255–63, Arras: Artois Presses Université.

Shrayer, M. D. (1999), 'After Rapture and Recapture: Transformations in the Drafts of Nabokov's Stories', *The Russian Review*, 58: 548–64.

Shuttleworth, M. and Cowie M., eds (1997), *Dictionary of Translation Studies*, London and New York: Routledge.

Shvabrin, S. (2007), 'Vladimir Nabokov as Translator: The Multilingual Works of the Russian Period', PhD Dissertation, University of California, Los Angeles.

Shvabrin, S. (2013), 'Nabokov and Heine', *Russian Literature*, 74 (3–4): 363–416.

Shvabrin, S. (2019), *Between Rhyme and Reason: Vladimir Nabokov, Translation, and Dialogue*, Toronto: University of Toronto Press.

Simmons, R. W. (1966), 'Review of "Notes on Prosody. From the Commentary to His Translation of Pushkin's Eugene Onegin by Vladimir Nabokov"', *Books Abroad*, 40 (2): 212–13.

Sinichkina, D. (2020), 'Le Dit de l'ost d'Igor dans la poésie russe des années 1920: de la réactualisation des motifs à la réinvention du langage poétique', *Silène*: 100–21. Available online: http://www.revue-silene.com/f/index.php?sp=comm&comm_id=266 (accessed 19 December 2021).

Skonetchnaïa, O. (2000), 'Масонская тема в русской прозе Набокова', *Revue des études slaves*, 72 (3–4): 383–94.

Stankovic, S. (2013), 'Les éléments lexicaux français dans *Pnin* de V. Nabokov et leur voyage de l'anglais au français', in *Agapes francophones 2013*, R. Malita, M. Pitar and D. Ungureanu (eds), 341–52, Szeged: Jate Press. Available online: https://ciccre.uvt.ro/sites/default/files/af/agapes_francophones_2013.pdf (accessed 19 December 2021).

Stankovic, S. (2014), 'Француске лексичке јединице у роману *Pnin* в. Набокова: из енглеског у српски и француски језик / Les unités lexicales françaises dans le roman *Pnin* de V. Nabokov: de l'anglais au serbe et au français', in B. Chovich, L. Chovich, N. Nesterova, S. Stankovic and M. Loncar Vujnovic (eds), *Двојезичност аутобиографске прозе В. Набокова: нови 'преводни жанр' и/или 'међујезичке игре' / Bilinguism of the Autobiographical Prose of V. Nabokov: A New 'Translation Genre' and/or 'Interlingual Plays'*, 109–36, Mitrovica: Kovovska Mitrovitsa.

Steiner, G. ([1976] 1998), *After Babel*, Oxford and New York: Oxford University Press.

Sternberg, M. (1981), 'Polylingualism as Reality and Translation as Mimesis', *Poetics Today*, 2 (4): 221–39. Available online: https://www.jstor.org/stable/1772500 (accessed 19 December 2021).

Struve, P. (1933), 'Walter Scott and Russia', *The Slavonic and East European Review*, 11 (32): 397–410.

Taher-Kermani, R. (2020), *The Persian Presence in Victorian Poetry*, Edinburgh: Edinburgh University Press.

Talib, A. (2011), 'Le Gallienne's Paraphrase and the Limits of Translation', in A. Poole, C. van Ruymbeke, W. H. Martin and S. Mason (eds), *FitzGerald's Rubáiyát of Omar Khayyám: Popularity and Neglect*, 175–92, London and New York: Anthem Press.

Thaon, B. (1978), '"Better a Live Sparrow than a Stuffed Eagle": Towards a Translation of Guillaume de Machaut's 'Dit de l'Alerion', *Meta*, 23 (1): 37–46. Available online: https://id.erudit.org/iderudit/004469ar (accessed 19 December 2021).

Thomson, D. S. (1952), *The Gaelic Sources of Macpherson's 'Ossian'*, Edinburgh: Oliver and Boyd.

Tilliette, M.-A. (2020), 'Rob Roy et Pougatchev: le hors-la-loi dans l'Histoire nationale', *Silène*: 64–73. Available online: http://www.revue-silene.com/f/index.php?sp=comm&comm_id=263 (accessed 19 December 2021).

Toremans, T. (2017), 'Pseudotranslation from Blackwood's to Carlyle', in M. Woods (ed.), *Authorizing Translation*, 80–95, London and New York: Routledge.

Toury, G. (1980), *In Search of a Theory of Translation*, Tel Aviv: The Porter Institute for Poetics and Semiotics.

Toury, G. (1981), 'Translated Literature: System, Norm, Performance: Toward a TT-Oriented Approach to Literary Translation', *Poetics Today*, 2 (4): 9–27.

Toury, G. (1995), *Descriptive Translation Studies*, Amsterdam and Philadelphia: John Benjamins.

Toury, G. (2005), 'Enhancing Cultural Changes by Means of Fictitious Translations', in E. Hang (ed.), *Translation and Cultural Change*, Amsterdam and Philadelphia: John Benjamins.

Toury, G. (2012), 'Descriptive Translation Studies – and Beyond', Amsterdam and Philadelphia: John Benjamins.

Trubikhina, J. (2015), *The Translator's Doubts: Vladimir Nabokov and the Ambiguity of Translation*, Boston: Academic Studies Press.

Trzeciak Huss, J. (2018), 'Collaborative Translation', in K. Washbourne and B. Van Wyke (eds), *The Routledge Handbook of Literary Translation*, 389–406, London and New York: Routledge.

Venuti, L. (1995), *The Translator's Invisibility: A History of Translation*, London and New York: Routledge.

Venuti, L. (1998), *The Scandals of Translation. Towards an Ethics of Difference*, London and New York: Routledge.

Venuti, L. (2000), '1940s–1950s', in L. Venuti (ed.), *The Translation Studies Reader*, 67–70, London and New York: Routledge.

Vomero Santos, K. (2016), '"The Knots Within": Translations, Tapestries, and the Art of Reading Backwards', *Philological Quarterly*, 95 (3/4): 343–57.

Wheeler, M. (1972), *The Oxford Russian-English Dictionary*, ed. B. Unbegaun, Oxford: Clarendon Press.

Wickman, M. (2013), 'Review: Thomas M. Curley, *Samuel Johnson, the Ossian Fraud, and the Celtic Revival in Great Britain and Ireland*', *Modern Philology*, 110 (4): 277–81.

Willoughby, L. A. (1921), 'English Translations and Adaptations of Schiller's "Robbers"', *The Modern Language Review*, 16 (¾): 297–315.

Wilson, E. (1965), 'The Strange Case of Pushkin and Nabokov', *The New York Review of Books*: 3–6. Available online: http://www.nybooks.com/articles/archives/1965/jul/15/the-strange-case-of-pushkin-and-nabokov/ (accessed 19 December 2021).

Wood, M. (1994), *The Magician's Doubts: Nabokov and the Risks of Fiction*, Princeton: Princeton University Press.

Wood, M. (2019), 'Do You Mind Cutting out the French? Nabokov's Disinvention of Europe', in Y. Chupin, A. Edel-Roy, M. Manolescu and L. Delage-Toriel (eds), *Vladimir Nabokov et la France*, 27–8, Strasbourg: Presses Universitaires de Strasbourg.

Yohannan, J. D. (1977), *Persian Poetry in England and America: A Two-Hundred Year History*, Delmar N.Y.: Caravan Books.

Zabalbeascoa, P. and M. Corrius (2014), 'How Spanish in an American Film Is Rendered in Translation: Dubbing Butch Cassidy and the Sundance Kid in Spain', *Perspectives, Studies in Translatology*, 22 (2): 255–70.

Zaliznjak, A. (2004), *Slovo o polku Igoreve: vzgljad lingvista*, Moskva: Jazyki slavjanskoj kul'tury.

Dictionaries online

https://www.cnrtl.fr
https://oed.com

Publications by Nabokov

Nabokov wrote in three languages: Russian, English and French. In the alphabetical listing below, the heading is the title as written in the language the publication was first written in (for Russian, the title is given in the Latin alphabet, then in the Cyrillic alphabet); other titles may follow if its title in another language is given in the monograph. When titles are names (for example *Lolita*) and it implies the title is identical in different languages with the same alphabet, only one spelling is given.

For the texts which Nabokov translated, their original title is given in parentheses, after the title of Nabokov's translation.

Index Nominum

The following index includes mainly critics, researchers and writers, as well as Nabokov's translators, publishers and literary agents. For obvious reasons, Vladimir Nabokov's name is not mentioned, but I decided to include Véra in the index, even if her name is often present 'merely' because she acted as Nabokov's secretary: however, their voices often seem to mingle in this collaborative correspondence, so on top of not wanting to erase her presence, I did not wish to erase her voice. For Pushkin, due to the great number of occurrences, I decided to remove all those that were purely bibliographical (see the index of Nabokov's publications for these). Some Russian names have different transcriptions and transliterations, which explains some minor variations in my text or index, depending on the sources I quote. Likewise, I have not always been able to trace back the first names hiding behind the initials of some critics, especially for older documents.

Names of fictional characters are not included: one should look in the index of Nabokov's publications, at the heading of the corresponding novel.

Adamovich, Georgy 76–7, 78
Alladaye, René 227n11
Allain-Roussel, Morgane 198
Ambrosiani, Per 56, 58
Anderson, Nancy 49, 231n16
Anokhina, Olga 163, 180–1, 241n12, 241n7
Apter, Emily 35–6, 227n6
Arber, Solange 238n4
Aragon, Louis 2
Arndt, Walter 99, 104, 126, 136, 235–6n2, 237–8n29, 238n30

Babikov, Andrey 63–4, 66
Bahous, Abbes 18, 227n3
Bailly, Edmond 36
Balmont, Constantin 39
Barabtarlo, Gennady 79–80, 226n12
Barthes, Roland 81, 83
Bassnett, Susan 234n4
Baudelaire, Charles 69, 93, 95
Beaujour, Elizabeth Klosty 3, 89, 165, 234n3
Beaulieu, Marc-Alexandre 242n2
Beckett, Samuel 2
Benjamin, Walter 218–19
Berman, Antoine 110–11, 139, 217, 238n8, 239n10, 239n11, 239n19

Bernard-Léger, Sophie 243n1
Bethea, David M. 231n21
Blandenier, Jean-Bernard 187–8, 242n15
Blatt, Ben 241n2
Bliss, Alan 232n27
Blackwell, Stephen 238n7
Blok, Aleksandr 63, 73
Bocquet, Catherine Anaïs 226n2, 232n31
Borges, Jorge Luis 29, 228n20
Boswell, James 22
Bouchet, Marie 223, 243
Bourdin, Philippe 70–1
Bowers, Fredson 17
Boyd, Brian 3, 13, 18, 20, 32, 62, 73, 76, 77, 78, 88, 131, 158, 161, 165, 186, 187, 216, 223, 227n1, 228n14, 231n16, 233n1, 233n3, 235n4, 236n5, 237n15, 241n10, 242n13, 243n4
Bozovic, Marijeta 35, 129, 148, 149–50, 229n1, 238n3
Branch, Andrew 226n6
Briod, Blaise 168, 169, 174
Bristow, Joseph 227n7
Brontë (sisters) 14
Brown, Clarence 3
Brown, Edward J. 104